This Is *Our* Song

SAMANTHA CHASE

D0188264

sourcebooks
casablanca

Published by Sourcebooks Casablanca, an imprint of Sourcebooks, Inc.
P.O. Box 4410, Naperville, Illinois 60567-4410
(630) 961-3900
Fax: (630) 961-2168
www.sourcebooks.com

Printed and bound in Canada.
MBP 10 9 8 7 6 5 4 3 2 1

Prologue

Eighteen years ago...

Silence.

Riley Shaughnessy let the last notes of the song fade until he couldn't breathe. Looking down from where he stood at the front of the church, he stared at his mother's casket and prayed he'd wake up from what he was certain was a bad dream.

When the priest thanked him, Riley realized it wasn't a dream. This was truly happening. His mother was gone. His father and his brothers were all sitting in the front pew, tears streaming down their faces. He went to rejoin them but refused to cry.

His twin brother, Owen, reached over and held his hand. They were ten and well beyond the age where they should do it, but right now it was comforting. He squeezed Owen's hand and felt his brother's head rest on his shoulder. There was no need to ask if he was all right; Riley already knew the answer. None of them were.

But Riley wanted to be strong for his mom. It was one of the reasons he was holding on to Owen right now and why he had chosen to sing "Over the Rainbow" at her funeral.

It was their song.

She had helped him choose it when he'd wanted to

perform in his kindergarten talent show, and ever since then, hearing him sing it had always made her smile.

He hoped she was smiling in heaven right now.

The priest was reading scripture, but Riley didn't hear it. For a few minutes, he allowed himself to think about a time when everything was perfect.

Lillian Shaughnessy stood and clapped louder than anyone in the room. She looked around and nodded to Ian and her four sons—Aidan, Hugh, Quinn, and Owen—to join her. On the stage, five-year-old Riley Shaughnessy took his first bow and straightened and smiled. It was exciting. All these people were clapping for him. Him!

Looking around, he felt a sense of pride. He'd done this. He'd practiced and practiced and practiced until his throat hurt because he didn't want to mess up, but he'd never expected to like it this much!

When Mrs. Maddox—his teacher—came and took the microphone, she thanked everyone for coming and encouraged them to stay for cookies and punch. Riley walked off the stage with her. "You were fantastic!" she said to him when they were backstage. "I know you were nervous about going out there by yourself, but you did a great job, Riley."

"Thank you, Mrs. Maddox." He smiled.

"There you are!"

Riley turned and saw his family coming toward him. His mom was practically running, and when she reached him, she scooped him up in her arms and swung him around.

"That was so beautiful," she cooed as she put him

back on his feet. "Look at my face! I'm crying! Your voice was so magical, it made me cry!"

Behind her, his older brothers snickered. "Yeah, you're adorable, Riley," Quinn said with a roll of his eyes.

Lillian shot him a warning glance and turned back to Riley. "Do you want to stay for the cookies and punch or would you like to go home and have the super-secret dessert surprise I made for you?"

His mom made the best super-secret desserts and Riley was kind of torn. Looking up at her, he said, "Could we maybe stay for a little while? Mrs. Maddox said we should all stay and thank the parents for coming."

"Aren't you the sweetest," Mrs. Maddox said as she ruffled his hair.

"Yes he is," Lillian readily agreed. Then she took Riley by the hand and let him walk her around the room to meet his friends and their parents.

When it was time to leave, Riley asked his mom to wait by the classroom door. His dad and brothers had already started to head out to the car. He ran over and whispered something in Mrs. Maddox's ear and when she smiled and nodded, Riley thanked her. Quickly, he went over to the table that was decorated and loaded with food and took a giant sunflower from the centerpiece. Then he skipped over and handed it to his mother.

Lillian smiled down at him. "What's this for?"

"'Cause you helped me pick my song, Mom, and everyone loved it. So I wanted to give you something to say thanks."

Her eyes shone with unshed tears as she lovingly cupped his cheek. "That's very kind of you."

"It sounded good, right?" he asked eagerly as she took his hand and led him down the hall toward the exit.

"Riley, it was better than good. It was the greatest song ever."

He smiled and looked up at her and began to sing it again. This time Lillian joined him and together they slowed their pace and made their way out to the car.

Yeah, it was their song.

Riley looked around and noticed everyone was standing. He and Owen joined them and that's when he saw it. They were wheeling the casket out of the church. His chest tightened, his throat hurt. He wasn't ready. He wasn't ready to say good-bye. Not yet. It was too soon.

Ian Shaughnessy stood back and let his sons walk ahead of him and then began the long walk up the aisle. Riley turned around and looked at him and saw how his dad looked older all of a sudden. Sadder. Lost. He knew the feeling. Beside him, Owen openly sobbed and Riley squeezed his hand again. It wasn't going to change anything or make anything better, but he needed to do something.

At the door to the church, Riley could see through to the outside. It had been cold and cloudy when they went into the church, and now it looked as if the sun was trying to come out. Not that it would matter. The gray sky matched his mood.

They stood as a family, holding on to one another as the white casket was gently placed in the hearse. Once the door was closed, Ian stepped forward. "Come on, boys," he said softly and led the way to the limousine that would take them to the cemetery.

Beside him, Owen gasped and elbowed him. "What?" Riley whispered. Owen pointed up to the sky, and Riley couldn't help but smile.

A rainbow.

Yeah, it was their song, and she had heard it and was smiling.

And he knew right then and there, he would never sing it for anyone but her ever again.

Chapter 1

THE SOUNDS COMING FROM HIS GUITAR SEEMED rough even to his own ears. Disgusted, Riley Shaughnessy put the instrument aside and raked his hands through his hair. Head lowered, he stared at the ground in defeat.

"Something's got to give, Ry."

Riley didn't need to look up to know his manager, Mick, was standing in the corner of the room. The man was like some sort of ninja—you never seemed to see or hear him coming or going, and yet there he was.

"Yeah, I know," Riley said quietly.

Stepping farther into the room, Mick stopped and sat down on the sofa opposite Riley's. "We've all been patient. We've given you time. This album has been at the halfway point for far too long. You need to finish it."

Riley's head snapped up and his eyes narrowed. "You think I'm not trying, Mick? For crying out loud, I've spent every minute of every day trying to come up with something—anything—to make it happen! I…I can't seem to get what I want from here"—he pointed to his head—"to there." He pointed to the guitar.

"Maybe it's time for us to bring in someone to write the music for you and you just…you know, sing it."

For a minute, Riley felt like he was going to be sick. It wasn't an unusual suggestion and in the past, when he was still playing with his band, they had done it. But this was his solo project—his chance to prove to the world that he had the talent to stand on his own. The rest of the guys were doing well with their solo work; Riley didn't want to be the lone failure.

"No," he said firmly.

Mick relaxed against the sofa and looked at him with what could only be described as pity. "Dude, you need to know when to call it a day. No one's saying this is a bad thing. We're just trying to speed up the process a bit. You wanted some time off, we gave you some time off. You wanted to do this solo crap, we were happy to let you do it. But now? Riley, come on. You're asking too much. The label is getting antsy and you're not giving them anything to work with. Take the gift. Take the damn songs, record them, and let's wrap this thing up. Maybe once you get on the road and tour a little bit, you'll get your muse back."

If only it were that easy.

The look on his face must have conveyed that because Mick sighed and leaned forward, his tone a little gentler.

"Look, Riley, I get it. I do. I know what you're trying to do here and I think it's great. And no one was cheering louder for you than me. But it's not happening the way we thought. No one's going to think less of you because you're using some songs written by other people on this project."

"I think you're wrong," Riley said a bit defensively. "Just like the people from the documentary—"

"Man, you have got to let it go!" Mick snapped. "It wasn't even that big a deal! Quit harping on it and move on!"

"I can't!" he shouted and jumped to his feet. "I was on top and everything was going freaking great, and then this documentary comes along, and the next thing I know, rumors are starting to swirl that I'm not relevant enough or talented enough or…whatever the hell else people were saying! It's not so easy to pick up and dust that shit off!"

Slowly, Mick stood and walked over to Riley. "Okay, you're right. I'm sorry." He paused. "The thing is, the label is going to cut you loose if this project isn't wrapped up in the next three months."

"What?"

Mick nodded solemnly. "I did everything I could, Ry. I really did. They're tired of waiting."

"There's got to be something…something I can do to show them I'm trying—I'm really working hard at this because I want the album to be a success." Damn, he was almost begging and he hated it. "Mick, there has to be some sort of goodwill gesture to show them I'm good for this."

"Well…there was the other songwriter…"

Riley shook his head vehemently. "No. Something else. There's got to be another option on this one."

"Dude, you're killing me."

Riley was about to say the same thing when Mick's phone rang and he stepped away to take the call. This whole thing was a nightmare. His whole life, he'd never had a problem writing songs. Whether it was rock music, ballads—he'd even written a couple of country music songs—but nothing was coming to him for this particular album.

For so long he imagined how he wanted this project to go and once he'd gotten the green light, the first few songs flew out of him and then…nothing. And Mick could say whatever he wanted; the documentary was a big deal and the rumors about him that went around afterward—like how he was the least talented of his own band—had seriously affected Riley's self-esteem.

He sighed and walked over to the window looking out on the city. His house on the hill had become his prison. Even though it had a great view, it still felt as if the walls were closing in on him. He was afraid to go out—didn't want to risk hearing people talk about him. Hell, he'd even taken a break from seeing his family because for some reason, his insecurities seemed to be right at the surface whenever he was around them and they were all starting to call him out on it.

It sucked.

Out of the corner of his eye, he saw Mick heading for the door. He put whoever he was talking to on hold and looked at Riley. "I'll be back at three. We'll finish up then." And then he was gone.

Shit. Now what? He basically had a few hours to either come up with six songs to complete the album or admit defeat and take on someone else's music. No, that wasn't an option. He needed to get his head straight and figure out what to do. He needed…

His phone rang and when he saw his twin brother's face on the screen, Riley nearly sagged with relief. Before he could say hello, Owen was talking.

"As a scientist, it's hard for me to accept this twin telepathy, and yet I found myself driven to call you because I felt you were really sad. Are you okay?"

Riley smiled and sat on the couch and relaxed. "Come on…you mean to tell me after all these years you doubt the telepathy thing? I would have thought you'd be anxious to run experiments on us."

"I don't know if it would really prove much. We know each other so well there's hardly any science involved. We're siblings, we grew up together, why shouldn't I know what you're thinking? Besides, the whole twin telepathy thing is less common in cases like ours."

"Wow, did you just oversimplify something, Owen?" Riley asked with a chuckle.

"I am capable of doing it from time to time."

Even as fraternal twins, they were as different as night and day. Where Riley had always been an extrovert, Owen was an introvert. Riley was a singer and a performer, Owen was an astrophysicist. He was scary smart and it tended to make him socially awkward, but there wasn't another human being alive who understood Riley like his brother.

"So you felt compelled to call me, huh?"

"I did," Owen said simply. "I was in the middle of teaching a class and you were just there so strongly—it was almost as if you were standing right there."

"Sorry about that. How did the rest of your class go?"

"Oh, they're still in there. I gave them some work to do and stepped out into the hall to call you."

"Owen Shaughnessy!" Riley mocked. "Now you're telling me you ignored your job because of this telepathy? That tells me you really are beginning to believe it's a thing! Come on. Admit it!"

Owen groaned. "Are you going to tell me why your negative thoughts and feelings are interfering with my life or am I supposed to guess?"

"You tell me. Can't you read my mind?" Riley couldn't help but tease.

"So they're still giving you a hard time about the album."

Damn. "Okay, now you're freaking me out."

"It really wasn't that hard a conclusion to draw, Riley. This is hardly new information. Why are you still struggling with this? Music comes as easily to you as breathing."

"It used to. I don't know, Owen. It's like I can hear the music off in the distance and I just can't reach it. Like it's behind a closed door and no one will let me open it."

"Have you thought about talking to a therapist?"

"Hell no. The press would have a field day with that."

"So? Seems to me if it helped unlock the music, it shouldn't matter if the press finds out. It's all for the greater good."

Riley stopped and considered his brother's words. "What's going on with you? What… Why… You're not talking like yourself."

"I don't know what you mean," Owen said.

"Bro, normally you would have quoted all kinds of statistics about mental blocks and therapists and named a couple of renowned doctors and scientists to back up what you're saying. But you're not. What gives?"

Owen sighed loudly. "You know, sometimes there is no pleasing everyone. I get criticized when I talk like a scientist and then I get criticized when I don't. Honestly, Riley, I didn't expect it from you!"

Uh-oh. Something was definitely up with his brother. "Okay, okay, you're right. Sorry. And for the record, I wasn't criticizing. I was merely making an observation."

"Whatever."

Riley burst out laughing.

"What? What's so funny now?" Owen demanded.

"Nothing," Riley said, instantly sobering. "Nothing at all. Look, go back to your class. I'm just trying to work this stuff out. Mick came to me and suggested using someone else's songs to finish the album. The label's getting pissy and basically everyone's losing faith in me. They gave me three months to finish things up."

"Okay. So do it."

"Seriously?" Riley asked with a bit of frustration. "You—who knows me better than anyone—think I need to quit?"

"I don't see it as quitting. I see as moving on from a project that has proven not to work. We do it all the time in the labs. You test a theory and when it doesn't work, you move on. You wanted to try this solo project and you did. It's not working for you so stop forcing it."

Now Riley growled. "You know, I think I liked it better when you said stuff I couldn't understand. This getting right to the point is kind of hurtful."

"I'm sorry!" Owen said quickly. "All I meant is—"

"Don't. It's okay. You're saying what everyone else has. And coming from you? Well, that tells me what I needed to know. It just doesn't make me feel like any less of a failure."

"You're not a failure, Ry. You're a gifted musician. No one says you can't try again in the future. You just need to let this project go."

Emotion clogged Riley's throat and he nodded silently. And just as he suspected, his brother knew it.

"You're going to be okay, Riley," Owen said softly.

Normally Riley would agree simply because his brother was rarely wrong.

Only right now, he was having a hard time keeping the faith.

———

As promised, Mick was back at three o'clock sharp. The man was a stickler for keeping a schedule. Well, he normally was. He'd been a little more than frustrated with Riley's lack of one lately.

As soon as Riley got a glimpse of his manager, he knew something was up. It was written all over his face. "Okay," Riley began as soon as they sat down. "Out with it."

Luckily Mick wasn't the type to play dumb. "I spoke to Rich Baskin earlier—that's who called when I was here."

Rich was the head of Riley's record label, and it was all Riley could do just to nod.

"I told him you really weren't on board with using outside writers to finish the album."

"And what did he say?"

"What do you think he said? He's pissed."

"Great."

"However," Mick began, "he is willing to give a little."

Riley's head shot up and for the first time in what seemed like forever, he felt hopeful. "Okay. How?"

"Do you know Tommy Vaughn?"

Riley's eyes went wide. "Of course I do! Who doesn't? The man is right up with Jagger, Mercury, Lennon, Bowie... I mean, the guy is a rock god. Why? Is...is he one of the song writers? Does he want back in on the music side rather than writing about it?"

"Okay, so you're aware of his magazine."

Reaching over the side of his sofa, Riley pulled a copy of *Rock the World* magazine. "Aware of it? I subscribe to it!"

"That's good," Mick said. "Because you're going to be in it."

Riley pulled back and frowned. "What do you mean?"

"Look, I don't play dumb with you, don't do it to me." Mick paused. "Tommy wants to do a huge piece on you—possibly multi-issue. He doesn't do it very often. He's got someone lined up to work with you. Rich wants this. So if you're hoping to get back in anyone's favor, you're going to do this."

"Mick, you know how I feel about interviews. Especially right now!"

"Then you're going to have to get over it. Fast. Because if this deal doesn't happen, they'll pull the plug on the album even sooner, and think of the lousy publicity that is going to cause. 'Riley Shaughnessy cut loose because he didn't want to talk and couldn't write any songs.'"

"That was pretty low," Riley sneered. "Even for you."

"I'm not here to candy coat it for you. I've been doing it for too long and now look where we are." He shifted in his seat. "You never asked for much and you were never complicated to work with—you were certainly never a diva—so when you started to struggle, I let it slide. Well, I'm done with it now. It's time for some tough love. You need to stop with the pity party and get your ass back in the game." His phone beeped and Mick looked at it and stood. "I've got another appointment to get to. You're gonna get a call from the magazine. Take it and be thankful." And he headed for the door.

"Mick—"

"I'm not kidding, Riley," Mick interrupted. "Everyone's done playing around. We want an album from you, and we wanted it six months ago. Don't turn into a diva on me now. Do the interview. Hell, who knows, maybe talking to someone—even a magazine reporter—can be…what do you call it? Cathartic. Yeah, I think that's the word. Maybe you'll finally get out of your head and get the music down like you need to." With a pat on Riley's back, Mick walked to the door. "I'll talk to you in a couple of days. Think about it—but don't screw this up."

Riley stood and stared at the closed door for a solid five minutes before he could force himself to move. When he did, it was to go back to the couch and collapse.

He'd sworn he wouldn't do any interviews until the album was done and he knew it was perfect. Now what was he supposed to talk about? How he couldn't write? Couldn't play? Couldn't sing?

Yeah, the fans would love that.

Unfortunately, he knew he was screwed and there was no way out. So he'd give the interview—a superficial one. No one said it had to be deep and meaningful. And it wasn't written anywhere that he had to be sincere or enjoy it. The label wanted this? Fine. He'd do it. But Riley would do it on his own terms, not theirs.

Jumping to his feet, he almost felt like some sort of evil genius. He'd say all the right things and smile at all the right times. They could take their pictures and think they were getting a glimpse into the real life of Riley Shaughnessy.

But they wouldn't.

They never would.

There was a time when Riley loved this part of his celebrity—the interviews, the press tours. But lately these things felt like a chore—just one more thing to piss him off and make him resentful toward the talent that had deserted him.

He walked back over to the window and looked down at the city. Somewhere out there was some reporter thinking they'd struck gold by getting the chance to sit down with him. He had a reputation for being a great subject. Well, news flash, that guy was gone and no one had seen him in about a year.

God, he was sounding morbid.

Maybe it would work for him. Maybe—rather than being a phony during the interview he would be just…difficult. Morbid, depressing, angsty. Or maybe just indifferent.

Well shit. Now he was more confused than he was a minute ago.

There was only one thing for certain right now: he honestly felt sorry for whoever Tommy Vaughn was giving this interview to.

—⁘—

"Change of plans."

Savannah Daly looked up from her laptop to see her boss standing next to her desk. Before she could inquire about what plans specifically, Tommy continued.

"You are interviewing Riley Shaughnessy."

Normally Savannah enjoyed a good challenge, but this was not one she was willing to take on. "You promised me the story on Coldplay. I've been researching and planning the whole thing for a month. I've talked to their people and I'm scheduled to go on the first three California stops of their upcoming tour with them— which starts in two weeks! I don't have the time to deal with Riley Shaughnessy."

"Like I said, doll…change of plans. Blake's taking the Coldplay story. I need you on Riley's." Tommy Vaughn was a rock and roll legend back in his time, and now at the age of sixty-two, he ran one of the biggest music magazines in the business. At six-foot-four, he wasn't someone you would say no to.

Or at least you *shouldn't* say no to.

Savannah chose to ignore the memo. "No," she said firmly. "You promised me Coldplay. This was going to be my big piece. The cover!"

"Riley's story will be even bigger, I guarantee it. You'll still get your cover…it will just be after Blake's Coldplay one."

She let out a very unladylike whine. "Come on, Tommy," she pleaded. "What's the point in giving me your word if you're just going to take it back?"

He leaned in close. "Sweetheart, I didn't give you my word. I offered you the story, you accepted. There's nothing written in stone and you know it. Now, you can sit here and whine and complain and do the damn piece, or…" He paused and straightened. "You can pack your stuff and go back to cutting hair at the local salon for all those soccer moms who seem to be everywhere. Your choice."

She couldn't believe it. He was threatening her? Seriously threatening to fire her if she didn't take this stupid story? Unable to simply accept it, Savannah took a different approach. "Can I ask you something?"

"Sure."

"Why me? Why do you think it has to be *me*—specifically—who writes this story? You have dozens of reporters on staff, some who are real fans of the guy. Why would you think I'm the right fit?"

Tommy studied her for a long minute before sitting down on the edge of her desk, crossing his arms over his chest. "Savannah, when you and I first met, you were a journalism graduate who was paying her bills cutting hair, do you remember?"

Seeing as how it was only a little over a year ago, she did. Rather than give him a snarky comeback, she simply nodded.

"That day we were doing a story on some local band who had recently hit it big, and you happened to be one of the stylists on the set of the photoshoot. You weren't even supposed to be there, but their usual stylist got the flu and you were called in. I remember watching you. You weren't starstruck and you didn't get overly chatty with the band, you just did your job."

"Tommy… I don't…"

He held up a hand to stop her. "When the guys walked away for the shoot, you and I stayed back and talked. It didn't take long for me to realize you had a good head on your shoulders. You weren't some naive chick and you weren't easily impressed. I was the guy there to write the story, but you were the one who essentially gave me the interview."

She looked at him quizzically. "What do you mean? You never said—"

"I was there—just like you—because someone had called in sick. Another reporter was supposed to do the interview so I was there with very little prep time and wasn't sure what exactly I wanted this piece to say. But you," he said with a smile, "you seemed to hone in on these guys and figure out their personalities pretty quick. And you were spot-on. Had I not talked to you, I would have looked at them as four morons who happened to get lucky. What I had by the end of the interview was a pretty deep piece showing a side of a band no one had explored before." He shrugged. *"That's* why I hired you."

"Riley Shaughnessy has done dozens of interviews over the years, Tommy. Believe me, you're not going to find anything deep about the guy. He's a pretty-boy rock star. That's it. You ask me? *He* got lucky."

"You don't think he's talented?"

Now it was her turn to shrug. "It really doesn't matter what I think. Obviously millions of people think he is."

"But you don't," Tommy concluded. "This is why I want you on this story."

"Because I don't like the guy?"

"Because you won't be easily swayed." He looked around the newsroom and lowered his voice when he focused on her again. "Riley Shaughnessy is one of those stories you have to be careful about who you send in there to do it. Some of the girls on staff? They're going to go and flirt and write some bubblegum piece more suited for a teen magazine. Some of the guys on staff? They'll go in there and make it a pissing contest and then I've got a story that is off-balance." Then he smiled. "But you? You'll go in there and try to figure him out because it's what you do. You want to write a story that makes people think and will show off your skills. And you know you're not going to get that if you write fluff."

"So basically you're saying I'm the only writer on staff who can be trusted to write a story on this guy?" She shook her head. "Uh-uh. I'm not buying it. You can try and stroke my ego all you want, Tommy, but I don't believe you."

With a huff, he stood and motioned for Savannah to follow him. When they reached his office, she stepped inside and watched him as he shut the door. "A year ago, Riley got turned down for some legends of rock documentary. Word around town is it messed with him. He can't finish his album, he's in a funk."

"So he's pouting," Savannah stated.

But Tommy shook his head. "I think there's more to it. I think it's something deeper. The guy's been spewing out hits for years. Technically, he's too young to be considered a legend and he didn't really belong in the documentary—you know it. I know it. Hell, even his record label and agent know it. So what's his deal? Why the retreat?"

"Like I said, he's pouting. It's ego. He wanted something and he didn't get it. End of story."

"No, Riley Shaughnessy was a publicity machine. The guy knows how to work the paparazzi, reporters, the late-night talk show hosts…everybody loves him. Then a year ago, he just clams up? I'm telling you, there's a bigger story here and I want you to get it. Call it ego stroking or whatever you want, but you and I both know you're the only one on this staff who is going to give this piece the kind of in-depth attention it needs."

"But…but…Coldplay. Chris Martin…"

Tommy patted her on the shoulder. "I'll still get you backstage for one of the shows, but Blake's doing the piece, Savannah. That's final."

She crossed her arms and frowned.

"Now who's pouting?"

"I can't believe you're doing this to me," she grumbled.

"Hey, it's not like I'm sending you on tour with some boy band or something."

Just the thought of it made her stomach clench. She'd been there, done that, and had the heartache to prove it. Not that she'd ever share that bit of information with Tommy.

Or anyone.

"You might as well be." She sighed and sat down in the chair closest to him. She took a minute to get her thoughts together. "Okay, say I decide to take this on."

Tommy's bark of laughter almost shook the walls. "Seriously? Did you just make it sound like there's a possibility you won't?"

Savannah shrugged. "Maybe I miss cutting hair."

"Yeah, okay. And I miss eating ramen noodles ten times a week. Cut the crap, Savannah. You and I both know you're going to do it."

She acted as if he hadn't spoken. "If I agree to this piece, how do you propose I get Riley to agree to an interview? He's been turning down people left and right for a year. I heard he turned down Ellen! And you really think I'm going to be the one to convince him to sit down for a conversation? You're crazy!"

Tommy smirked as he slowly walked around his office and sat down behind his desk. Then he took his time getting comfortable and folding his hands in front of him. "Sometimes it amazes me how little you think of me."

She rolled her eyes.

He held up a hand dramatically. "No…no. It's all right. Let me enlighten you on how I make things happen. For starters, I know *everyone* in this business. Everyone. Secondly, Riley's people are just as anxious to get him back out in the spotlight as his fans are. So much so they're guaranteeing he'll agree to this interview."

"You mean…"

Tommy grinned. "They're probably breaking the news to him as we speak."

"He'll never agree to this," Savannah said hopefully.

Tommy shook his head at her. "We nailed the exclusive. You've got an all-access, monthlong pass to work with Riley Shaughnessy."

"*A month*? Tommy, I'm writing a piece for the magazine, not his autobiography."

"Yeah, well…from the way I understood it, Riley may be a little gun-shy so this isn't something you're going to accomplish in a couple of sit-downs. Hell, for all I know, you may get enough information to make it a multi-edition story, and I'm okay with it. But we've got a basic timeline. All you have to do is reach out to him." He handed her Riley's number.

Stuffing the paper in her pocket as she stood, she glared down at him. "You know, you can be a real jackass sometimes, Tommy."

He stood and chuckled. "Only sometimes? I'll take that as a compliment."

Dread filled Savannah as she walked to the door.

Turning around, she pleaded one last time. "Come on, Tommy. Seriously. Someone—anyone—else would do a better job on this story. Please reconsider."

He leveled her with a hard stare. "I hear there's a sale on hair dye at Walmart this week. You won't even need a coupon. You interested?"

Heat crept up her cheeks at his implication. She was screwed. There was no way out of this nightmare of a story no matter what she tried to do. Without another word, she walked out of Tommy's office. She wouldn't give him the satisfaction of seeing the defeat in her eyes.

Back at her desk, she sank down in her chair and sighed. In the past year, she'd done more than her share of lackluster interviews. It was supposed to build character, Tommy had told her. Only she had hoped by building her character, she'd start getting the assignments she really wanted. Better yet, she'd get first choice of incoming assignments.

No such luck.

While she knew she owed a lot to Tommy Vaughn—hell, she probably *would* still be cutting hair if it weren't for him—it didn't mean she had to like him.

And right now, she didn't.

The decision to stay and work or leave and vent warred in her head. Tapping her keyboard, she watched her computer come back to life and immediately began a Google search on Riley. Instantly there were dozens, if not hundreds, of pictures, links, and blurbs about him. Not that it was surprising, but Savannah wasn't one who subscribed to the motto of more is better. Her first hit went to Wikipedia.

Riley Shaughnessy is an American singer-songwriter, record producer, philanthropist, and actor, best known as the founder and front man of the rock band Shaughnessy. During his career, he released four studio albums with his band, which to date have sold over fifty million albums worldwide, making them one of the world's bestselling music artists. Currently Riley is embarking on a solo career.

"Bor-ing." Savannah sighed and then clicked through photos of Riley throughout his career. Tall, lanky, dark hair...all things she normally found very yummy in a man. So why did it make her almost want to sneer when it was this particular man? He had the look—the sexy grin, the earring, and probably had a tattoo. She snorted. "Typical rock star."

She skimmed the rest—four brothers, one sister. Mother dead, father alive. Grew up in North Carolina. No marriages. Just the basics.

Savannah did a quick search to see what the rest of the boys in the band were doing while Riley was doing his solo thing. "Hmmm," she began, unconsciously reading out loud, "Matt 'Matty' Reed is writing the music for a Broadway musical and starring in it. Not bad."

Scrolling down a bit, she continued. "Dylan Anders, the partier of the group, has been popping up onstage with various other artists...drunk. Lovely." *Scroll, scroll, scroll.* "And last but not least...Julian Grayson." She sat back and almost smiled. "Just got married and has a baby on the way. He's taken up photography in his downtime and has no musical plans at the present." She nodded with approval. "Good for him."

Okay, maybe this assignment wouldn't be the worst thing…

"Hey, Van," Blake Jordan said as he sauntered by her desk—using the nickname he knew she hated. "Tough break about the Coldplay story. I promise I'll give Chris and the boys your regards."

Once he was out of sight, she flipped him the bird. "Bite me."

Now she was even more ticked off than she had been five minutes ago. Knowing she wasn't going to accomplish anything here, she closed her laptop and packed it up—along with a few other items—and made her way out to the parking lot. The sun was shining as she fished around in her oversized purse for her sunglasses. Sliding them on, she hastily combed her long black hair out of the way and trudged to her car, cursing Tommy, Blake, and Riley Shaughnessy the entire time.

Once she climbed into her Jeep, Savannah secured her computer bag and purse and then pulled a clip out of the glove compartment and clipped up her hair. Driving such an open vehicle had become a love-hate relationship. Deep down, she loved her Jeep. It was her to a T. It just wasn't conducive to her long hair. Luckily hers was pin-straight and it didn't matter if the wind blew it or she clipped it up or threw a baseball cap over it, it was still going to look the same. And really, doing all those things was for her own safety—she'd learned relatively quickly that long hair, wind, and open sides on a vehicle were not a good combination.

Never let it be said Savannah Daly needed a ton of bricks to fall on her.

Pulling out onto the main strip, she began to drive aimlessly. It seemed too early to go home, but there wasn't any place in particular she wanted to go. With a muttered curse, she forced herself to just drive for a while—to enjoy the sights and sounds of the city. Not that downtown L.A. was anything spectacular, but it had the potential to be a good distraction.

An hour later, traffic was becoming more of an issue and Savannah decided she'd cooled off enough. She could go home and think about this new assignment without feeling an immediate urge to strangle someone. The next right turn would lead her to the freeway, which would take her home. Her stomach growled loudly and she cursed again. "Yeah, yeah, yeah…I was supposed to food shop yesterday," she said.

Knowing that shopping for groceries was even less appealing than doing research on Riley Shaughnessy, she stayed on the road and opted to find someplace to grab takeout.

"All the usual suspects," she murmured as she flew by restaurants and cafés. Did she really want to go home and eat? Shaking her head, Savannah knew at this rate with traffic, any food she purchased would be cold by the time she arrived at her home. That left a sandwich or salad to go or dining alone at the restaurant of her choice.

Suddenly, the thought of a sandwich became really appealing. No need to go for anything fancy. She could grab a sandwich and maybe hit the beach. She'd driven far enough that she was minutes away from Hermosa

Beach. "Okay, for once, my aimless driving has paid off." Slowly, she drove through town and found a place to park. Grabbing her bags, Savannah felt at peace. The sun, the sand, the surf…and a sandwich. Not a bad way to spend the early evening hours. She was thankful for the currently cool California weather.

With so many places to choose from and her stomach getting more and more vocal, she found a small bar and grille with outdoor seating facing the beach and opted to go there. A burger was just like a sandwich, wasn't it? And sitting at a table was a bit more civilized than the sand. The hostess led her to a table for one, and Savannah smiled and got herself situated. It was tempting to take out her laptop and do some work, but she opted to go with just taking out her phone and checking email.

She ordered her dinner and a drink and was happily scrolling through her inbox when someone slammed into the back of her chair, nearly causing her to drop her phone. There was no apology and Savannah turned around and glared at the culprit. The guy had his back to her and essentially had his chair right up against hers. Seriously? Was this guy for real?

Unable to help herself, she nudged her chair back with a little more force than was probably necessary and waited to see if he'd acknowledge her now.

He didn't.

He wore a baseball cap pulled low over his eyes and a newspaper opened to the point where it was practically a wall; Savannah decided the guy was clearly a jerk. Rather than getting into a fight with him, she moved her chair around to another side of the table—and found herself still looking out at the beach. Smiling, she went back to her phone, pulled up the camera, and took a couple shots of the sun on the water. Yeah, it was beautiful and peaceful. There was a light breeze that felt glorious and…

There was a newspaper in her face.

"You have got to be kidding me!" she snapped as she peeled the paper from her face, crumpling it up. It didn't matter if the wind blew and it was an accident, this guy was seriously messing with her peaceful evening and she was done playing nice. "Hey!" she said as she tapped the guy on the shoulder.

He looked up at her, but between the sun and the cap basically shielding his face, Savannah had no idea what the guy looked like.

"Seriously, you bang into my chair, your newspaper blows in my face, and you can't be bothered with an apology?" she demanded, hands on her hips.

"Um…sorry," he mumbled and took the crumpled paper from her hands and turned back to his table.

"That's it? That's all you have to say?"

Without turning around, he said, "You asked for an apology and I gave you one."

Well damn. He had her there. "Oh yeah… Well… fine. Just…keep your crap on your table, okay? I'm trying to relax over here." When he made no further comment, Savannah went back to her seat. Within minutes, her meal was in front of her and she felt all the tension leaving her body—a good burger could do that for a girl.

And the fries were damn near orgasmic.

She let out a little moan of pleasure and noticed

Mr. Personality was staring at her. She saw he hadn't ordered any food yet. The waitress had inquired several times, but he continued to send her away.

His loss.

When she looked over and saw he was still staring, she put her burger down and stared back. "Problem?"

He shook his head. "I was just wondering what you ordered that had you sounding like that."

"Like what?"

"Really?" he said with what sounded suspiciously like sarcasm.

Rolling her eyes, she motioned to her plate. "Bacon cheeseburger—pepper jack cheese, avocado…the works. And fries." She picked one up. "These are the culprits. They're so good they should be illegal."

He chuckled. "I don't think I've ever heard someone describe french fries that way."

"Trust me."

"I guess I'll have to," he said and for a minute, he just sat back and smiled at her.

"Look…um… Can you turn around? You know, go back to your reading? You're starting to freak me out. And besides, didn't your parents ever tell you it's rude to stare?"

He laughed again. "As a matter of fact they have. But I wasn't a very good listener."

"So it's a lifelong problem?"

"Tell you what, you let me have one of your moan-inducing fries and I'll go back to reading my paper and leave you alone."

"Is that a promise?"

He nodded. "Scout's honor."

Somehow she couldn't envision this guy ever having been a Boy Scout, but whatever. Watching him warily, she picked up a fry and held it out for him. "One fry and then you turn back around so I can eat without an audience, right?"

He nodded again when suddenly the wind picked up, and in the blink of an eye, Savannah's napkin blew off her lap. She bent over to reach it at the same time he bent over to help her. Their heads bumped and with a startled "*ow*" coming from both of them, Savannah reached up to touch her head. On the ground was his baseball cap. Out of the corner of her eye, she saw him reach for it. After she had her napkin safely back in place, she realized she was still holding the french fry.

"Hey, aren't you gonna…" She looked up and gasped.

Staring back at her was none other than Riley Shaughnessy.

Chapter 2

RILEY KNEW THE INSTANT SHE RECOGNIZED HIM. Sure, she tried to cover it up quickly, but he saw the flash of recognition and now scrambled to put his hat back on, cursing himself for indulging in this silly bantering. He couldn't say why he had wanted to eat out, but after his afternoon with Mick, he had needed to get out and get some air.

Should have just driven around with the windows down.

With his hat pulled back down, he mumbled his thanks and took the fry before turning around. If he was lucky, this would be the end of their conversation, and she wouldn't feel the need to point out who he was or whether she was a fan.

The nonfans were the hardest to deal with. No one really needed to hear how much someone disliked them, but on more than one occasion people had stopped him specifically to tell him how much they hated his music. Keeping a smile in place was always his go-to response even when he felt like lashing out. He'd seen too many celebrities respond badly only to have the entire incident on the front page of some newspaper or magazine the next day. Riley's motto was to only let them see him smile.

He settled back in his seat, and when the waitress returned, he gave her his order—a bacon cheeseburger and fries—and thanked her. For some reason, he was sure the woman sitting behind him was smirking.

Burgers weren't his usual choice when he dined out—it could get messy and, again, didn't make for good photo ops—but when she had described her meal, his mouth had watered.

Or maybe just looking at her had done it to him.

Her eyes were such an odd shade of blue that they almost looked violet. Added to a beautiful face, jet black hair, and lips that…well…he'd be wise not to let his thoughts go there while out in public. Yeah, it was safer just to say she was attractive.

Okay, very attractive.

And in different circumstances he'd probably flirt with her a bit before asking to join her at her table. But his mood was just off, and he knew he wouldn't be good company for anyone. Hell, he could barely stand himself anymore.

Behind him, he heard her thank the waitress and ask for the check. The urge to turn around again and talk to her was pretty strong. It had been a while since he'd been interested in a woman—probably because he just wasn't feeling particularly good about himself. But this woman? The one with all the attitude? Riley thought he wouldn't mind getting to know more about her.

The waitress returned with his dinner, and Riley thought it might be cute if he turned around and offered one of his fries to the woman. But when he went to do it, she was already gone. Damn. He hadn't heard her get up and leave.

He looked at his dinner and sighed. It did look good. Too good to waste because he was feeling sorry for himself. Again. Pulling it back toward him, he picked up the burger and took a bite.

And moaned.

She was right. It was a good choice for a meal.

And then he cursed himself again for not taking a chance in getting to know her better. Or at least finding out her name.

———

Savannah overtipped the waitress in her haste to leave. The service was good, but the waitress certainly didn't deserve a seventy-five percent tip!

"Dammit," she cursed as she quickly walked along the sidewalk, anxious to put as much distance as she could between her and Riley Shaughnessy.

Okay, maybe she was being a little dramatic. He had no idea who she was, and she hadn't given him any obvious indication she'd recognized him so they were cool. Hopefully by the time she was forced to sit down with him, he wouldn't remember they'd met before. Not that they'd *met,* but...

So maybe getting up and walking away wasn't the best way to handle the situation. And if she was being honest with herself, she did it more for him than for her. The guy deserved to have a meal in peace without the press pouncing on him—especially after everything she'd learned from Tommy today. It was better this way. She'd noticed the flash of panic on his face when his hat had come off, and she was pretty sure he'd been wondering if she was a fan or someone who was going to bug him. So she'd clammed up and left. They'd have a clean start when the interview was officially scheduled.

"Ugh. Enough," she muttered to herself as she approached the beach. She was far enough away from the restaurant where she felt good about kicking off her shoes and walking in the sand. True, lugging her giant purse and laptop wasn't much fun but to be able to sit and watch the sunset seemed like a great way to end the day.

Trudging out so she was midway between the sidewalk and the surf, Savannah pulled a sweatshirt out of her bag and put it down on the sand. Once she got comfortable, she pulled her laptop out, took a deep breath—taking in the amazing scent of the ocean—and let it out slowly. It took all of thirty seconds for her to realize that the wind, sand, and her laptop did not make a good combination. With a sigh, she stuffed the computer back in the bag and decided to just relax.

"Yeah," she purred. The beach was her happy place. Someday she'd have a place of her own where she could have a view of the ocean whenever she wanted it. Or the mountains. Savannah had to admit they had some good qualities she enjoyed too. If only there was a beach with mountains nearby, she'd be set.

For about thirty minutes, Savannah was content to sit and listen to the waves crashing. One minute everything was peaceful, the next all hell had broken loose. A rumble of thunder and a flash of lightning had Savannah springing into action. She pulled her sweatshirt on, put the hood up, and began to jog back to her Jeep. With any luck she could get there before the rain came down too hard.

Unfortunately, she wasn't the only one going in that direction, and there was a brief moment of panic when she almost got caught up in the mob and knocked off her feet. Quickly dodging to the right when everyone went to the left, she picked up her pace and made it to her Jeep just as the sky seemed to open up.

"Thank God for small favors," she said with relief as she climbed in and closed the sides. She was slightly sweaty and out of breath, but she was glad to have cover now that the rain was really coming down. It didn't make any sense to try to pull out of the parking spot just yet—it seemed like dozens of people were doing the same thing—so she waited.

The windshield wipers were swishing back and forth, and Savannah simply sat back and people watched for a few minutes. And then she found herself looking at one person.

Riley.

He was standing at the front of her Jeep, looking a little lost. He hadn't noticed her—or at least he hadn't acknowledged her sitting there. A small part of her wanted to hit the horn and make him jump, but she couldn't do it. The image, however, made her giggle.

For another minute, she just watched him curiously. Why wasn't he going to his car? Was he looking for someone? His driver? And then, as if it were happening in slow motion, she noticed there was suddenly a crowd around him. Girls were screaming his name, and in the quick glimpse she got of him before he was surrounded, she noticed a look of pure panic on his face.

She should have pulled away sooner.

She should have taken her chances with the traffic jam.

The crowd seemed to be a little overzealous, and Savannah felt an uncharacteristic, overwhelming need to help him. The Jeep was running, and most of the cars that had been around her a few minutes ago were gone.

She opened her door, stood on the side step, and called his name.

"Riley!" Unable to believe he heard her over the crowd, she was shocked when he looked up and caught her eye. "Get in!" she cried.

He broke through the crowd and grabbed the passenger side door like a lifeline. He swung inside at the same time she did, and she threw the car in reverse and took off across the lot. He was breathing hard, his head thrown back, his eyes closed. "Thanks," he said after a minute.

"Don't mention it. That looked a little brutal."

"I wasn't expecting it. I didn't think anyone recognized me." He turned his head and looked at her. "Except for you during dinner."

"I didn't—I mean, I had no idea…"

He grinned at her. "Yeah, you did. I saw it in your eyes and then you immediately covered it up. It's not a big deal. I kind of appreciate it. As you can see, most people don't react the same way."

She chuckled. "It was a little amusing at first, but then it seemed to turn into a bit of a frenzy."

He nodded.

"What were you looking for? I mean, you were standing there in front of the Jeep for a few solid minutes. Why didn't you just get in your car and go?"

"Promise you won't laugh?"

She gave him a bit of a wicked grin. "I make no promises."

He laughed. "I can respect that, I suppose. Honesty." He paused. "I just sort of ended up out here tonight. I hadn't planned on it. I parked down by Manhattan

Beach and walked and I… I couldn't remember which way to go."

Savannah looked at him funny for a minute before she started laughing. "So you're lost? Seriously?"

"Hey, it's raining, I'm not familiar with this part of town and I was trying to see if I could grab a cab or something…"

That just had her laughing harder.

"I'm not really sure what's so funny about this…" Riley said, perplexed.

"It's just…" She stopped and laughed some more. "When I picture a celebrity out and about, I picture them with a driver or a bodyguard or something, and I guess you should really consider doing that because if your sense of geography is this bad—"

"Okay, okay," he cut her off. "Ha-ha. Yes, the lost rock star is hysterical." He threw his head back and tried to look offended, but he ended up laughing with her.

It took Savannah a few minutes to realize he had a really great laugh and she could appreciate his ability to laugh at himself. Taking a few steadying breaths, she finally managed to stop laughing. She had pulled out of the parking lot and was heading toward Manhattan Beach.

"All kidding aside," she began, "do you kind of remember where you parked?"

Riley sat forward and looked around, shaking his head. "Honestly, I haven't been out this way in ages. Today I just drove until I didn't feel like driving anymore and then I stopped." He shrugged. "Then I walked on the beach until I was hungry."

"Sounds a lot like my night," she said. "Were you

by the beach when you parked, or in a bigger public lot where you had to cross the street to get to the beach?"

"By the beach," he said.

"And what kind of car are we looking for?"

"It's a black Ford pickup."

She looked over at him, eyes wide.

"What? What's wrong?"

Savannah shook her head. "Um…nothing. It's just… I figured you more of the sports car kind of guy."

He shrugged. "I'm not going to lie. I do have a sports car, but I enjoy driving the truck. I blend in a little bit easier." He stopped and looked around. "Oh, there it is!" He pointed to the far corner of the parking lot Savannah had turned into. She slammed the brakes hard, and Riley had to brace himself against the dash. "What the hell?"

"That's your truck?" she cried.

"Um…maybe…"

"You made it sound like you drive a run-of-the-mill pickup truck. *That* is not a vehicle that blends, Riley." She almost sounded offended, betrayed.

"All I said was I drive a black Ford pickup. *That*'s a black Ford pickup. I don't see what the problem is."

With a snort of disgust, she put the Jeep in gear, drove over to his truck, and then threw the Jeep into park. "Okay, end of the line. Next time pay attention to where you're going."

Riley turned in his seat and stared at her incredulously. "So that's it? You're just throwing me out?"

"Uh…yeah. Why? What were you expecting?" she asked and then held up her hand. "On second thought, don't answer that. Knowing the type of people you usually hang out with, I'm sure you would expect all kinds of things."

"You know, you're pretty big on making assumptions," he said, losing his humor.

Savannah's eyes went wide. "Me?"

"Yeah, you. First there was the fact that I didn't have a driver, then it was the kind of car I drive, and now it's about the people I know and hang out with. What's your deal?"

She shrugged and just wished he'd get out of the damn car. She'd hung out with enough celebrities—primarily musicians—who were the very reason she made the assumptions she had. "I don't have a deal. I'm just basing these observations on what I've witnessed—firsthand, mind you—from people who work in the entertainment industry."

"So you're in the entertainment industry?" he asked, seeming genuinely interested.

This was not the conversation Savannah wanted to be having. She knew she was going to have to tell him who she was eventually; she had simply hoped it wouldn't be tonight. She wasn't mentally prepared for it and was seriously regretting giving him a ride. "Yes," she finally said. "I work in the entertainment industry."

"Interesting. And all the people you know drive expensive sports cars or have chauffeurs drive them around and expect sex in return for favors, do I have that right?"

For a minute, Savannah felt the blush creeping up her cheeks. It was exactly how she'd made herself sound. "Okay…no. And I'm sorry. I…I shouldn't have judged." She expected him to get smug and cocky. She certainly didn't expect understanding.

"It's all right. I get it. It is how a lot of the industry behaves but…it's just not my thing. Any of it."

"I really am sorry. I…I usually give people more of a chance, and I didn't do that with you." She sighed. "Anyway, I'm glad I was at least able to get you back to your truck. Do you know how to get home from here?"

He smiled. A genuine smile—not the sexy grin he normally wore for photos. He relaxed against the door and studied her for a moment. "What is it you do for a living?"

And here it was. Time to come clean. A small nervous chuckle escaped before she could stop it. "I'm a writer," she said slowly and then watched him for his reaction.

"Like an author? What have you written? I'm an avid reader."

"Someday I hope to have a novel of my own out there, but currently I'm a reporter. I write for *Rock the World* magazine." It took a minute, but she knew the exact moment it all came together in his mind. "You may not believe this, but your phone number is in my pocket. I was planning on reaching out to you tomorrow. It seems I'm going to be doing a piece on you."

Riley's smile slowly faded and his relaxed manner seemed to go tense. He straightened. "Was tonight an honest-to-goodness coincidence or did you orchestrate it?"

Savannah wanted to take offense to his question, but she realized how bad it looked for her right now. Riley was well within his rights to come to this conclusion. "It really was a coincidence. Maybe I should have said something sooner, but…" She shrugged. "There didn't really seem a way to throw it into the conversation."

He sighed loudly and raked a hand through his hair.

"I don't even… Wow. I just have no idea what I'm supposed to say to all of this."

"I know it's been a weird night and all, but maybe we can meet up tomorrow—under normal circumstances—and just sort of pretend tonight didn't happen." Her expression was hopeful and if Riley's reputation was anything to go by, she felt pretty certain he would go along with her suggestion.

"I don't know," he said warily. "I'm sure you're aware of my hesitance in doing this interview."

Nodding, Savannah reached out and placed her hand on his arm and realized there was a lot of muscle there. *Focus!* "I'll be equally honest with you, Riley. I'm not so keen on doing the interview myself."

Now his eyes went wide. "Excuse me?"

"It's a long story," she said, hoping he'd let it go at that.

"I've got nothing but time, sweetheart." It wasn't an endearment.

Savannah rolled her eyes and pulled her hand back. She shared with him how she had gotten the assignment and the one she'd lost. "I'm a damn good writer," she said when Riley stayed silent. "I'll admit something about you makes me jump to the wrong conclusions, but I'm hoping after tonight to get a better grip on it."

Riley simply continued to glare at her.

Apparently he was Mr. Nice Guy to other people, but he certainly wasn't ready to maintain that persona here. "Look, I can keep apologizing all night long, but I can't change the way we met. Rather than being all pissy with me, how about remembering that I got you out of that mob a little while ago? Or maybe look at your truck-on-steroids over there and remember that you would still be walking in the rain looking for it if it weren't for me!" She was breathing raggedly after her little outburst, but she wasn't quite done. "Now I'll admit I'm not thrilled with writing this story on you, or even on anyone like you, but that doesn't mean I'm not going to do a kick-ass job on it. I was honest with you, Riley. You should appreciate that. If you were looking for someone to come in and kiss your ass and stroke your ego, then you're out of luck. It's not who I am, and I don't plan on changing for you. But if you want to get the word out there on who you really are and you're interested in being taken seriously, then I'm the perfect person for you."

She gasped when she realized what she said and quickly tried to correct it. "I mean for the story! I'm the perfect person to write the story!"

Riley still didn't look convinced.

"Fine," she huffed. "I'm not going to grovel. Do the story. Don't do the story. It's not a big deal to me. If *you* back out, there're no consequences for me. Now, maybe you have nothing but time, but I don't. It's been a long day and I have a long drive home." She hoped Riley would take the hint and get out, but he stayed firmly in his seat.

Damn him.

"Were there going to be consequences if you refused to write the story?" he asked quietly, his eyes never leaving hers.

Unable to stand his intense scrutiny, Savannah looked away. "I'll lose my job." Her voice was equally quiet as she studied her hands.

"I see."

Savannah was just about to plead with him one last time when the interior light came on. She looked up to see Riley getting ready to climb out of the Jeep. "You're…you're going?"

He nodded. "I think it's for the best."

"But…um…" She paused and cleared her throat. "Do you—I mean, would you like to get together tomorrow?"

"It depends," he said, his voice a little softer than before.

"On?"

"I feel at a bit of a disadvantage here. You know who I am and I'm sure you know a lot about me. I, on the other hand, know nothing about you. Not even your name."

Oh. That. Holding out her hand, Savannah did her best to at least try to be professional. "Savannah Daly." When Riley took her hand in his, she almost sighed. It was big and warm and his skin felt rougher than she imagined.

"It's nice to meet you, Savannah Daly," he said, a slow smile crossing his face. Riley continued to hold her hand. "So about tomorrow—"

"It's up to you," she said quickly. "My only job for the next month is to interview you and write the story. I'm prepared to work around your schedule." The truth was she wasn't really prepared for that, but the words were out before she could stop them.

Riley's smile grew.

"I'll tell you what. You give me your phone number, and I'll call you tomorrow to set up a time."

Savannah tried to pull her hand back—which she was surprised to find he was still holding—as she frowned. "Why can't we just decide on it now? Why wait?"

He shrugged. "I'm still coming to grips with this whole thing," he replied. "I'd like to have a little time to think things over." His thumb lightly stroked her wrist. "And I would imagine you're feeling the same way too."

She couldn't speak so she nodded.

"Okay then," he said, his voice a little lower. Slowly, his hand released hers. It was a slow glide of skin on skin, and Savannah almost moaned at the sensation. Riley shifted a bit, pulled out his cell phone, and entered Savannah's number as she dictated it to him. "Well, Savannah, it's been an interesting night."

"Yes," she said and cleared her throat again. "Yes it has."

"I'll talk to you tomorrow." He climbed down from the Jeep and faced her one last time. "Be careful driving home."

"You too." She almost wanted to kick herself for how breathy her voice suddenly was.

Riley gave her one last smile before closing the door. Savannah watched and waited while he climbed into his truck and got it started. She really hoped he knew how to get home but figured a truck like that had a GPS system in place to help him.

With a sigh, she pulled away and began to wonder how she was going to survive spending the next month with Riley Shaughnessy if just one touch of his hand and one lingering smile practically stole her breath away.

Finally a perk to being forced to do this damn interview!

Driving home, Riley was damn near euphoric. Savannah Daly. He smiled. The name fit. Never could he have imagined the intriguing woman he met at dinner was going to come back into his life in such a spectacular way.

Her initial dislike was apparent and he appreciated her honesty. He wasn't intimidated by it. If anything, it was going to make the entire process a lot more interesting. Riley had never had a problem with winning people over—even those haters who insisted on how much they disliked his music eventually gave him a smile and a compliment after they talked for a few minutes.

And so had Savannah by the time he climbed out of the Jeep.

As he drove down the freeway, images of her played in his mind. It wasn't the best time for it to be happening but he couldn't seem to stop them. Her long hair intrigued him—he wondered how long it really was and how it would feel when she took the clip out. And those eyes. Were they blue? Were they violet?

She dressed like a bit of a badass—black skinny jeans, black T-shirt, and silver jewelry. Nothing frilly or overly feminine, and yet he could equally imagine her in silk and lace. He'd bet she looked spectacular in leather too.

He groaned.

And then it hit him—he hadn't seen her fully. Both times—in the restaurant and the Jeep—she'd been sitting down. He couldn't wait to see her figure standing in front of him in the light of day. But for now, a guy could use his imagination, right?

By the time he arrived back at his place, his mind had created quite a vivid picture. He both prayed it was accurate and prayed it wasn't. If it was accurate, he was in deep trouble. He'd probably spend the majority of their time together with his tongue hanging out.

Probably not the best way to win the girl over—by drooling.

This whole project was wreaking havoc on his life. First he was against it and now he was all for it. Hell, if he'd thought for a minute that Savannah would have gone for it, he would have invited her to get started tonight. But she had a long drive home.

They had a month. Could he stretch an interview out that long? After all, he still had the problem with getting the album finished. Now was definitely not the time to be messing around with a reporter or a woman.

And now he had both those things rolled into one glorious package.

He just hoped he survived them both.

It was still raining the next morning when Riley got up. The sound of it the previous night had lulled him to sleep, but by now he was ready to see the sun again.

With his morning cup of coffee, he sat down on the sofa, pulled out his phone, and looked at Savannah's number. He wanted to call her and talk to her—and it had nothing to do with the damn interview.

The interview.

He groaned. There were a million reasons why he didn't want to do it and only one reason he did. Everything had seemed fairly cut-and-dried yesterday. He'd come to grips with doing the piece as long as he did it on his terms. But meeting Savannah had changed everything. Now he was torn. If he did the interview, would he be able to do it without making it about getting Savannah to like him? Would he be able to keep himself detached?

And would he be able to keep his hands to himself?

Yeah, that was going to be a tough one.

Cursing, he began scrolling through his contacts. He needed to talk to someone. Not Mick. His manager would tell him to do the interview and stop overthinking it. That wasn't what he was looking for right now. He needed advice. Normally—where women were concerned—Riley didn't seek out anyone's help. He'd never had a problem there. But for some reason his initial reaction to Savannah scared him.

Should he call Aidan? Maybe. Aidan and Zoe's relationship had pretty much scared the crap out of his oldest brother. Riley chuckled. It had been kind of amusing to hear that his normally staid brother was so thrown for a loop by the woman who was now his wife.

Or maybe he should call Hugh. He'd spent a lot of time with Hugh right after he'd met Aubrey. That was another interesting relationship he had watched develop. Aubrey had managed to make his overcautious brother lose some of his inhibitions, and for that Riley was glad. But they'd just had a baby, and he was sure his brother had better things to do than give him relationship advice.

There was always Quinn. Then Riley shook his head. It had taken Quinn over twenty years to realize Anna Hannigan was in love with him. Probably not the best guy to ask about how to proceed with a woman. Although it was nice that Quinn and Anna were now engaged and planning their wedding.

He shook his head again. No. He had a feeling talking to Quinn right now would only lead to mocking and then wedding talk. No thank you.

So that left his twin. Riley loved talking to Owen, he really did. But Owen wasn't exactly a ladies' man. Hell, there were times Riley had to wonder if his brother even dated. With a sigh, he scrolled to Owen's number. "No time like the present to find out."

"Two phone calls in two days," Owen said as he answered the phone. "What's wrong?"

Riley chuckled. "Why does something have to be wrong for me to call you? We talk all the time."

"We normally talk two to three times a week with a minimum of two days between calls. It's barely been twenty-four hours. So again, what's wrong?"

If Riley wasn't mistaken, his normally mild-mannered twin had a bit of attitude this morning. "Maybe I should be asking you the same question."

"What do you mean?"

"I mean, little brother…"

"By two minutes! You are older by two minutes!"

Yeah, Owen was in a snit over something. "As I was saying, it seems to me you're a little out of sorts this morning. Everything okay in the lab?"

Owen sighed loudly. "I don't only work in a lab, Riley. I'm here at the university and I spend a lot of time in the observatory and—"

"Yeah, yeah, yeah…you've got options. I get it. But you sound tense and before you tell me you're not, I'm calling bullshit. What's going on?"

"Now you're going to play the twin telepathy thing?"

"Owen, save us both a lot of time and just tell me what's wrong," Riley said lightly, knowing he normally had to prod his brother to get him to talk about anything personal.

"The administrators here are on me to be a little more…personable."

"Personable? What the hell does that mean?"

"It means they think I'm like a...a...robot! Like I don't interact with my students or other members of the faculty. They want me to work on my people skills!"

"Did you tell them it makes you break out in a rash?" And the thing was, Riley was being completely serious.

"I did," Owen said dejectedly. "They suggested Benadryl."

"Well, damn. So what are you gonna do?"

"There's some faculty dinner next month I have to attend. I had already declined the invitation and was told that wasn't acceptable. Now I have to show up. And after that, there are some activities on campus I have to go to." He sighed again. "Why can't I just teach? What does going to a bonfire have to do with astronomy?"

"I'm sorry, Owen. I really am. But...it could be a good thing."

"I don't see how."

"You might enjoy yourself. You know, make some friends!" Riley was going for optimistic, but he knew his brother too well: being social wasn't something Owen was interested in.

"Somehow, I doubt it." He paused. "So what about you? What has you calling?"

Riley told him about Savannah and the interview. "It's a game changer. Now I'm not sure what my motivation is for doing the damn thing."

"Hmm. I know this may seem like an odd question, considering how well I know you, but can't you just, you know, *not* be attracted to her during the time of the interview?"

"I'm afraid it doesn't work that way," Riley said.

"And this also just stands to enforce why you need to be around people a little more often."

"I don't see how—"

"Haven't you ever felt an instant pull of attraction to a woman, Owen? I mean, I know you don't date a lot, but you can't tell me you haven't been attracted to a woman before."

Owen was silent for a solid minute before he answered. "It doesn't matter. Most women don't even see me. And can we not talk about this right now? Can we just focus on you?"

As much as Riley wanted to argue with him, he really needed the help. "Fine. But we're going to come back to this at some point."

"Fine. Consider me warned," Owen said. "So you're attracted to this woman and you think she's going to be a distraction to the interview."

"Exactly."

"It seems to me you really don't have a choice here. You know you have to do this interview. It's not negotiable. And you know Savannah's going to be the one doing it. I think you're going to have to wait and take your cues from her. This may all be a moot point. She may not feel the same way about you."

"I kind of think she does—"

"Of course you do. In your line of work, most of the women you meet want to sleep with you," Owen said, sounding bored.

"Did you just use sarcasm on me?" Riley asked with a chuckle.

"Focus, Riley," Owen snapped. "If you're looking for permission to hit on her, it's not my place to give it.

If you're looking for someone to smack your hand and tell you to back away? That's not for me either. You're going to have to wait and see for yourself how it goes. There is no way to plan this one out."

And this was why he'd called Owen. He had a way of putting it out there bluntly. "I know you're right."

"Are you going to be okay?"

Walking over to the bank of windows, Riley noticed the rain had finally stopped and the sun was starting to come out. "I don't know yet. I'm kind of nervous."

"That's good," Owen said. "I think you—specifically—need that once in a while."

It was pointless to ask what he meant because Riley already knew. "Yeah, fine. Whatever," he grumbled but with a smile. "I'm going to call her now. Thanks, bro."

"For what? I didn't do anything."

"Sometimes just talking to you makes me feel better. So…thanks."

"You do the same for me, Ry," Owen said.

They hung up and Riley reached for his coffee, finishing it in one big gulp. With a fortifying breath, he looked at his phone and scrolled to Savannah's number, his finger paused over the send button. His heart was racing and his throat suddenly went dry.

Can I really do this? he asked himself. There wasn't a clear answer. He was going to have to wait and see and keep his fingers crossed that everything was going to be all right. Lifting his head, he looked outside and smiled.

A rainbow.

"Yeah. I got this," he said and immediately hit Send.

Chapter 3

IN THE LAST YEAR, SAVANNAH HAD INTERVIEWED some of the biggest names in the music business along with some who were on their way up. She'd gone into each of those meetings filled with confidence and an attitude that basically said, "They're no different than me."

Yeah, that wasn't the case today.

Riley had called her three hours ago and suggested they meet at his place for lunch. At first she was apprehensive, but then she remembered how things had gotten out of hand last night with the crowds and figured he was doing it more for the sake of privacy than anything else. Savannah could respect that—it wasn't uncommon to meet one of her subjects at their home or the hotel they were staying at while on tour. It wasn't the norm to meet someplace public.

And yet it was sort of what she had been hoping for with this first official meeting with Riley.

The thought of being alone with him was a bit... overwhelming. Considering that twenty-four hours ago she'd wanted nothing to do with the guy and now she was suddenly nervous and fluttering around like a schoolgirl, was it any wonder she would have preferred the safety of a public space?

Looking at her reflection one last time, she cursed. This was her fourth outfit, and no matter what she put on, none of it felt right.

And that just pissed her off.

While not a slave to fashion, Savannah did enjoy clothes and had the closet to prove it. Why then couldn't she seem to put together one simple outfit so she could leave and get to Riley's on time?

Because you want to impress him.

"No, I don't," she said out loud to her reflection. "I don't have to impress him. This is who I am and I have nothing to prove. He needs to impress me—not the other way around."

Turning, she growled and peeled off her jeans. As she tossed them in the corner with a little more force than necessary, she went with the "they made my butt look big" excuse for not wearing them.

"Okay! That's it!" she cried. Whipping her shirt off, she stood there in her underwear and stalked back into her closet. "Whatever goes on isn't coming off. This is ridiculous!"

Three more outfits later, she climbed into her Jeep.

She drove the thirty miles to Riley's place with a nervous stomach and a running dialogue in her head. Looking down at herself briefly, she still questioned her clothing choice—long black maxi skirt, white tank, black sandals, and tons of clunky, multicolored jewelry. It wasn't anything original but at least she was comfortable and looked a tiny bit professional.

She yawned. There'd been very little sleeping the previous night. After spending time with Riley, Savannah had been inspired to start planning out the article. Online research had given her the basics she'd needed to get started, but she wasn't so much interested in Riley's past and how he got started. She wanted this piece to really flesh out who he was at this moment in time.

Why had he decided to go solo?

Why was he taking a hiatus from public life?

And why was this new album taking so long to finish?

And those questions were just the tip of the iceberg, she was sure. Her usual method was to have a loose outline of the things she wanted to know but then let her subject take the lead. Sometimes she ended up with fascinating information no one had ever written about before, and other times she ended up with a whole lot of nothing because the celebrities in question only wanted to brag about themselves.

That was the category she had pegged Riley for.

Why? Mainly because for so long he was just… everywhere. Every magazine, tabloid, late night talk show, radio station…there was no escaping Riley and his band. Primarily Riley. He knew how to schmooze and work the crowds, and it had always seemed to rub Savannah the wrong way because no one was that nice, that friendly, that damn personable! It had to be an act!

She was hoping she was wrong.

Pulling in to Riley's neighborhood, she was met with security gates and a guard. Savannah gave her name, showed her ID, and waited to be let through. She was used to the routine, and two minutes later, she was stopping in front of his house. For a moment, Savannah could only stare—she'd almost driven right by. With the exception of a wide front walkway, the entire front of the house was covered with a wall of greenery. Looking around, she didn't see any other cars parked on the street so she pulled forward until she found the driveway.

When she climbed out and grabbed her bags, she found herself to be a little surprised.

This wasn't a mansion. And it wasn't some ultra-modern monstrosity. It was just a cool-looking bunga-low high in the hills. She almost couldn't wait to get inside and look out the back to see the view. With a shaky breath, she walked to the front door and before she could knock, Riley pulled it open.

His smile almost had her in a puddle at his feet.

"Hey," he said softly, stepping aside for Savannah to enter.

As she did, her arm grazed his and she had to stifle a groan—painfully aware she might not survive the story.

He knew immediately she was nervous.

Riley wasn't normally a people watcher or even a decent judge of character, but something about Savannah just resonated with him. It was as if he already knew her, which was weird since twenty-four hours ago, he didn't.

While she looked around, he took advantage of her distraction to really look at her. She was taller than he thought. With a pair of heels on, she'd almost be his height. Her skirt swished around her ankles, and he caught a glimpse of red on her toes. But the snug-fitting white tank top almost had him swallowing his tongue. He hadn't quite noticed her curvy figure last night. Between their crazy conversation at the restaurant and then in the Jeep, she'd been sitting most of the time. But now? *Ho-ly...*

He swallowed hard. She wasn't slim—not by today's standards. No, Savannah had the body of a 1950s pinup girl—all lush curves. Damn. Dressed as she was right now, she looked a lot softer than she had the previous night. If he could just get the clip out of her hair, he'd be one hell of a happy man.

But he needed to focus and get them back on track. "That's a lot of bags you have with you," he said, motioning to the multiple bags hanging over Savannah's shoulder.

"Oh," she said and chuckled. "One's my purse, one holds my laptop, one has my notepads, pens, tape recorder, and whatnot, and the last one has snacks."

He looked at her oddly. "I'm sorry, did you say… snacks?"

Blushing, Savannah nodded. "I've learned that not everyone thinks about these things, and I tend to nosh while I work."

"Nosh?"

She nodded again.

Riley chuckled. "Okay, I've got to know… What kinds of things do you…um…nosh on?" He nodded toward the bag.

Rather than answer right away, Savannah walked farther into the house and put her things down on what she assumed was the dining room table. Taking her snack bag out of the pile, she looked at Riley and grinned. "Fine. But no judging."

He held up his hands as if to say, "Who me?"

There was only a moment's hesitation before she opened the bag and began pulling things out. "I have pretzels, crackers, Twizzlers, M&Ms, cookies." She paused and dug around a little. "Um…Pop-Tarts, Funyuns." She looked up and shrugged. "I tend to use

those at the end so no one has to deal with onion breath."
Back into the bag. "Starburst, a couple bottles of water,
and…microwave popcorn."

Riley stepped closer, inspected the pile, and whistled.
"Wow…that's impressive." He looked at her. "Do most
of your subjects starve you?"

She laughed at his question. "Not intentionally, but
I have gone on several interviews where the person I
was talking with had their staff bring them full-on meals
while I had to sit there and watch them eat. After the
third time it happened, I started packing my own food."

"This looks like a little bit of everything you'd find
at a rest-stop gas station."

"It pretty much is. Like I said, it just makes it easier
for me to have it with me. This way I don't interrupt
the interview and I can snack when the mood strikes."

"Do you share?" he asked, grinning.

"That depends," she replied, unable to stop her
own smile.

"On…?"

Savannah picked up the microwave popcorn package. "Will I be allowed to use your microwave should
the urge strike?"

Right then and there he wanted to tell her that
whatever he had was hers. Her face was glowing with
humor, and for a minute all he could do was stare.

"Riley?"

"Oh, right…of course. And just for the record, I
planned on feeding you." He motioned toward the
kitchen and then led the way. "I'm no gourmet, but I
can put a meal together when I need to."

"You really didn't have to go to any trouble."

"I invited you to lunch," he said over his shoulder, still smiling. "Although after seeing your stash of junk food, I may suggest skipping lunch and just going for the snacks."

Savannah laughed. "Tell you what," she began. "You feed me lunch, and I promise if at any point during the interview you want a snack, I'll share."

"You're on." They walked through the kitchen, which was done in dark wood and granite with stainless steel appliances, and out onto the deck. Savannah stopped in her tracks and gasped.

Riley didn't pretend not to know what she was reacting to. "I know. The view is amazing, right?"

"I would never leave here," she said softly, walking to the edge of the deck.

"On a clear day, you can see straight through to the Pacific Ocean. That's what sold me on this house. I hadn't planned on buying anything at the time. I was looking to rent. But my realtor took a chance and showed me this place. It was a clear day and I was sold."

"I'll bet," she said in wonder. "You must spend a lot of time out here."

"Believe it or not, the view is just as spectacular at night. The entire city is lit up and yet it's peaceful up here." He stood beside her and simply enjoyed looking at the city with her. A soft breeze blew and Riley knew if he didn't get them seated, lunch would be ruined. "Come on and have a seat. I'll grab the food."

"Can I help with anything?" she asked.

"I'm good," he assured her. "Sit down and enjoy the view and I'll be out in a minute."

Once he was back in the kitchen, Riley wondered

if he'd gone a little overboard. Cooking really wasn't his thing but he knew how to. And once he'd called Savannah and she'd agreed to come over, he had wanted to do something to prove he wasn't lazy or pampered. He didn't have a staff on hand, and he'd prepared their meal himself. "Too late to change that now," he muttered, putting oven mitts on and reaching into the oven to pull out their covered plates. Walking out to the deck, he was once again taken in by Savannah's beauty. Her hair was up in a clip—no doubt because she drove with the Jeep open—but her head was thrown back, her eyes closed as she sat, obviously enjoying the sunshine.

Clearing his throat, he walked over to her. "I really hope I made the right choice here. I knew you aren't vegan or anything like that because of your burger last night. But this is one of my favorites." Carefully placing their dishes on the table, he lifted the lid off hers first. "Beef shish kebobs, rice, pita wedges, and hummus."

"Riley!" she cried. "Oh my goodness! You didn't have to—" Stopping, Savannah looked past him back into the kitchen.

"I assure you I made this myself. No one cooks in my kitchen except me."

She smiled as he took the seat opposite hers at the table. "I am thoroughly impressed. Seriously. I was expecting pizza or maybe some sandwiches." Picking up her fork, she moved her rice around a bit. "Now I feel bad I don't have more snacks to share with you!"

He laughed along with her. "Well, we do have a month together. I can't guarantee a meal like this every day, but once in a while, it's nice."

"You really didn't have to," she said sincerely. "I would have been fine with anything."

"Yeah but then I might have ended up lumped into a category with some of your less hospitable subjects. I couldn't have that," he teased.

"No doubt of that happening now," she said as they both began to eat.

The conversation over the meal covered a wide range of topics—the weather, real estate, sports, and current events—everything except anything of a personal nature. Riley thought it was interesting how Savannah managed to keep them talking without making it feel like they were on the clock.

Sitting back in her chair, Savannah put a hand on her belly. "My God, Riley. That was amazing. If you tell me you do your own laundry and clean up after yourself, I may ask you to marry me." She laughed at the statement and then seemed to realize what she'd said. "I mean… Crap. I just meant…"

It would have been fun to tease her a little but he decided to put her out of her misery. "It's okay, Savannah. I'm not going to hold you to it." He stood and collected their plates before giving her a sexy grin. "Although— for the record—I do my own laundry, I clean up after myself, I love to vacuum, and I can bake brownies that are so good they'll make you weep." With a wink, he turned and walked back into the house, fighting the urge to look back and see her reaction.

—⁓—

The urge to fan herself was nearly overwhelming. On shaky legs, Savannah got up, walked back into the house, and got her gear. Riley was cleaning up the kitchen and she called out to him, "Where would you like me to set up?" Then she groaned because her mind instantly went to the gutter and she easily imagined them sitting in bed talking.

Right. Talking.

"The living room is fine," he replied. "Give me five minutes and I'll be done."

"Okay."

Walking into the living room, Savannah couldn't help but react as she had to everything she'd seen so far with this house. The entire back wall was glass—custom sliding doors if she wasn't mistaken—and offered another way out onto the deck as well as the view of the city. "Damn." She sighed and forced herself to get set up.

There were two massive black leather sofas and she chose the one with its back to the view because she didn't want to be distracted. She set up her laptop, immediately noting the proximity of the nearest outlet should she need it, and then got all her writing paraphernalia set up. A quick test showed that her digital recorder was ready to go, and Savannah sat back and waited.

Riley walked into the room carrying two large glasses of water with lemon wedges on them. Savannah instantly reached for the coasters and set them out before thanking him for bringing the drinks in. For a minute, she expected him to sit beside her, but was a little surprised when he took a seat on the other sofa.

O-kay.

In faded blue jeans, a black T-shirt, and bare feet, Riley Shaughnessy still managed to look good enough to eat. That in itself annoyed her. Guys like him were used to women drooling over them, and she'd basically been doing exactly that since she arrived. He looked relaxed and at ease, and Savannah figured he was feeling pretty confident that she was wrapped around his finger.

And she almost was.

But Savannah was nobody's pushover. This story was going to give the world a look at the Riley they'd never been privy to before. She wasn't going to coddle him and she wasn't going to do him any favors. Sure, the lunch was good and he was easy to talk to, but it didn't mean she wasn't going to go for the jugular in order to get a legit answer out of him.

"Ready when you are," he said with an easy grin.

I'll bet, she thought. "Do you mind if I record?" she asked, holding up the small digital recorder.

"Not at all." Another easy grin as he put his feet up on the coffee table and seemed to get even more comfortable.

With everything in place, Savannah straightened, smiled, and hit record.

"Rumor has it the new album is in trouble. You can't write, you can't sing, and you're essentially blocked and refusing any help. That suggests a huge ego issue. How do you respond to that?"

―⁓―

White-hot rage filled Riley instantly at Savannah's opening question, but to his credit, he kept his smile in place. He had thought they had started to develop a good rapport—that maybe they would ease into the tougher questions. Clearly he was mistaken.

Rather than bring that up or dispute what Savannah was asking—which no doubt she was expecting of him—Riley reached out, picked up his glass of water, and took a sip. It was a stalling tactic and he was certain Savannah was aware of it, but she seemed to be content to wait him out.

"Everybody has an ego, Miss Daly," he began. "Artists and musicians are no different. The issue with the new album, however, has nothing to do with ego. I made a commitment to my fans to put out a quality product. If I were just to throw some filler songs on the album, I would not only be letting my fans down, but letting myself down." He shifted in his seat. "Tell me, out of your music collection, how many albums would you say you enjoy listening to from start to finish?"

"When I put music on, I have a playlist and I let it play."

He shook his head. "That wasn't what I asked. I'm not talking about putting a playlist together of your favorite songs. I'm talking about a specific album by one group or artist. Do you normally put one on and enjoy every song on it?"

"I don't think anyone can really say yes to that. Some songs resonate with some people, while others don't. And just because I may or may not like a specific song on an album doesn't mean it's not a quality song."

"Touché," he said with a nod. "However, you still haven't answered the question."

"I don't believe that's how this works," she challenged. "I'm here to interview *you*. This story is about you, not me."

"And I can appreciate that, but I think it's only fair I be able to defend myself. Especially if you're going to argue my responses."

"I didn't think I was arguing," Savannah said simply.

"Then answer the question," he said with a grin that now felt forced.

She huffed loudly. "Okay, fine. In my mind, I honestly can't think of one album I own that I listen to from start to finish. I'd say half of the music is good and the rest just feels…" She shrugged.

"Exactly!" he cried with a clap of his hands. Leaning forward, Riley put his feet on the floor and rested his elbows on his knees. "Now I'm not going to lie to you, the first six songs were ones I had been playing around with for a while before I hit the studio. And then I hit a wall."

Her eyes went wide as if she wasn't expecting honesty.

"In my head, I know what I want. I…I can almost hear it," he said with frustration. "But for some reason, I can't seem to get it to come through that way when I play it."

"What is it you're trying to do? Is this new music different from what you were doing with the band?"

"A little," he replied. "I wanted something softer, a little less edgy. I love the heavy sound the guys and I do together, and I know the fans do too. But if I want this to be a solo project, I can't simply play the same music. There has to be a difference."

"And I'm sure fans will appreciate that, but how long are they supposed to wait for this music? At what point do you say it's just not going to happen and move on?"

"I'm not sure. I haven't hit that point yet."

Savannah studied him for a moment, and Riley knew she was gearing up to hit him where it hurt. "Rumor has it your label is almost at that point."

Ouch.

"Rumors rarely resemble the truth, Miss Daly."

"Are we going for formality, Mr. Shaughnessy?" she challenged with a hint of amusement.

"I hadn't thought we were, but as soon as we sat down and you started recording, all traces of my charming lunch companion disappeared. I figured I'd just go with the flow."

He knew his snarky comment hit its mark because Savannah physically winced. Part of him felt guilty, but he certainly wasn't planning on sitting here in his own home and letting her simply attack him until they called it a day.

Then, in an act that surprised him, Savannah leaned forward and shut off the recorder.

"Can I ask you something?" she asked.

"I thought that's what you were doing all along," he said mildly.

She rolled her eyes. "Okay, let me rephrase that. Can I ask you something off the record?"

For a second, fear and panic threatened to overwhelm him. He had no idea what she was going to ask, but it didn't bode well that she shut the recorder off before she did. Looking over at her, he noticed the anxious look on her face. All he could do was nod.

"Can I hear the new music? I mean, the stuff that's finished already."

Wow. Riley had thought this might come up over the course of their time together, but he'd hoped they'd be further along in the interview before it did.

"Look," she said softly, "you don't know me and I get it. Most people in your position wouldn't want just anyone hearing their new stuff—especially if it wasn't polished and ready to hit the shelves. But…this is something that's going to keep coming up throughout the whole interview process. The new music. You don't have to play it all for me. Maybe just one song. I'm trying to get an understanding of where you're at right now musically."

He still couldn't speak. This whole process with the album had been a very personal one. No one except his management team and the people he trusted at the label—and of course his family—had heard any of the new music. Could he possibly let Savannah hear it?

"Tell you what," she finally said. "Why don't you just think about it? I love all genres of music. I have very eclectic taste, and I promise to keep an open mind."

"I…I just don't know, Savannah."

"Just…just promise me you'll think about it."

The thought of it made Riley's stomach clench, but he wasn't going to let her know that. So he nodded and let her believe he'd think on it. He smiled when she seemed to relax. And then he had an idea.

"Listen…I know you're anxious to get started on everything but I'm not… I'm not a hundred percent comfortable with the whole jumping-right-in approach. Would you mind if we sort of just…hung out today?"

"Seriously?" she asked, perplexed.

"Yeah. If this was just a fluff piece, it probably wouldn't matter to me. But you laid it all out on the line for me what you were expecting out of this, and I can't quite…relax. I feel like you're on the attack and I'm getting defensive, and I think this will be beneficial to both of us if we just took a step back and maybe spent a little time getting to know one another."

She looked at him with apprehension.

"I don't know, Riley. I don't think it's a good idea for us to try to, you know, become friends. It would totally affect the tone of my article and make it biased."

"Savannah, like it or not, if we're going to spend a month together, there's a pretty good chance of us becoming friends."

Or more, he inwardly added.

"I guess," she said, but didn't sound convinced.

"How about this—just for today. Today we put all the recorders and notebooks, pens and computers away and just hang out. Tomorrow we'll start up, and you can ask questions all the livelong day, and even if I'm not comfortable, I'll cooperate. What do you say?"

She still looked at him with a hint of confusion. "And…what would we do? I mean, it's only like two in the afternoon."

Riley jumped to his feet, excited to have the chance to convince her to give his reasoning a chance. "Well, clearly you haven't seen the whole house. It's not huge, but I do have a small studio and a game room. Do you like video games?"

Her apprehension slowly faded as a smile crossed her face. "I do."

"Do you like movies?" he asked.

"Depends on the type." And before he could comment she quickly added, "And I'm a girl so of course I like a good romantic comedy, but it's not the only kind of movie I'll watch."

He was impressed. Stepping closer to her as Savannah rose to her feet, he asked, "Tell me what other kinds you're interested in."

"I don't mind action movies but they're not my favorite. I enjoy a lot of classics—I keep Turner Classic Movies on in the background normally when I'm writing. Cary Grant and Jimmy Stewart are personal favorites. Musicals can be fun if I'm in the mood. But if I had to narrow it down, I would say almost anything from the sixties. I don't know why but I can pretty much sit down and watch any movie from that decade and be happy."

"Okay. Good to know." He paused and thought of a few other options. "How do you feel about Ping-Pong?"

Savannah burst out laughing. "You're kidding, right? We're going to skip an entire day of interviewing so we can play Ping-Pong?"

He stepped a little closer. "I'll let you in on a little secret. I take my Ping-Pong game very seriously. You could probably get more secrets out of me while I'm in the zone during a game than you'd get in a full day of recordings. Trust me."

"Hmm…interesting." She tapped a finger to her lip and looked to be considering her options.

"Honestly, I don't think we'll need a month to get you the information you want for this story, but I agreed to it. Shouldn't we at least make an attempt to like each other?"

"Okay, I know I said some things last night—"

Riley held up a hand to stop her. "It's okay, Savannah. You're entitled to your opinions, but you have to give me a chance to at least try to change your mind." His voice softened. "And it has nothing to do with the article. I just… I want you to see I'm not such a bad guy."

He was minutes away from begging and crying, and

if he didn't convince her soon, Riley was certain he'd lose the battle.

"Just for today though, right?" she finally said, and Riley almost sagged to the floor with relief.

"Absolutely! You're not going to regret this." Looking around the room, he took a minute to come up with a plan. "Okay, put all your stuff away and let's get started!"

"Hey! I have to give up work and my snacks?" she said with a smirk. "That hardly seems fair."

Riley stopped in his tracks. "You know what? You're right. But we'll deal with it when we get hungry. I have quite the snack stash too." Without thinking, he grabbed Savannah by the hand and gently tugged her with him.

He showed her the rest of the house—the bedrooms, the bathrooms, his office, his studio, and the game room. By the time he realized he was holding her hand, he felt a little pleased Savannah hadn't corrected him on it or pulled away.

Baby steps.

"So…where do you want to start?" he asked.

Savannah's expression was one of pure wonder. She was looking everywhere at once it seemed. "You have… There's a lot of… Wow."

Yeah, that's pretty much exactly what Riley was thinking—about her. "Come on. You can have the first pick of what we do."

"Really?" she asked excitedly.

"Really. Go ahead. Anything at all. Video games? Movie? Ping-Pong?"

"Is that a pinball machine in the corner?" she asked,

her voice filled with wonder as she finally took her hand from his.

"It is." He followed her across the room. "Guns N' Roses. It was hard to find but I had played this when I was younger and loved it. When I designed the game room, I was determined to find one and put it in here."

"And you have Pac-Man!" Savannah jumped up and down and then stopped and looked at Riley sheepishly. "Sorry. I haven't played that in years."

"Don't often get to an arcade, huh?" he teased.

"Strange, right?" She touched the pinball machine and the Pac-Man machine before walking around the perimeter of the room.

Riley stood back and watched, curious to see where she stopped and what they were going to do first. He wasn't lying earlier—he took all of his game playing seriously and tended to say things he wouldn't normally say just to get his opponent to stop talking. Not that he was mean or nasty. In his case he was brutally honest and couldn't seem to lie to save his life.

It was a curse, really.

On the surface it might look like he was conning Savannah or that he was simply trying to delay the inevitable. But as he stood there now watching her, Riley knew the truth. He couldn't keep his distance or—as Owen had put it—not be attracted to her while the interview was going on. It simply wasn't possible.

His fate was sealed.

Savannah Daly was someone he was going to be spending a lot of time with for the next month. The key was to make the most of their time and have her look at him not only as the subject of her magazine article, but as a person.

As a man.

And not a rock star.

He rolled his eyes at his own logic. There was no denying the rock star angle—it was the only reason she was here. But he needed her to see beyond that. He just wasn't sure exactly how yet.

"Is…is this like a real ice cream bar?" she asked, carefully circling the two-seat counter at the far end of the room.

Smiling, Riley slowly strolled over. "It is. If you walk around to the other side, you'll see it has three cooler slots. It may not be exciting, but I keep the basics in there—vanilla, chocolate, and strawberry." He saw her checking it all out.

"And the refrigerator underneath?" She stopped and opened it before straightening and looking at him. "Can we seriously make milk shakes in here?"

Riley nodded. "Sure can. There are cones down there too if you'd prefer one."

"Oh no," she said quickly. "Milk shakes are my favorite." Savannah looked around the room again. "Okay, I think I've got it."

No doubt she had worked out what she wanted to do and in what order. "Let's make milk shakes and then play some pinball. I haven't done that in years."

"Works for me."

"And then, maybe after we're done with our dessert, we can play Ping-Pong?"

"Care to make it interesting?"

If Riley didn't know any better, he'd swear she was instantly intrigued. "Go on," she said.

"I'm all for starting out like you said. But when

we get to the Ping-Pong table, we do maybe a best of three."

She shrugged. "What does the winner get?"

Now *that* was a loaded question, he thought. Saying "whatever they want" was too obvious so he had to give it a minute's thought. "After the third game, if you win…"

"Then no questions are off limits!" she quickly said, sounding excited.

It wasn't ideal but Riley knew he could work with it. "Only for that day," he countered. "And if I win?" He waited to see if Savannah had any suggestions, when she simply shrugged he said, "I'll need to think on that one. Is that all right?"

"It's fine," she said confidently. "You're not going to need anything because I am going to kick your butt. I am so good at Ping-Pong!"

He didn't agree or disagree. No need to get her riled up about it. For now, he'd let her think she had a chance to win. Afterward, when he was the winner, he'd share with her how he grew up with four brothers and how they used to spend hours out in the garage playing the game. Poor girl. He almost felt sorry for her.

"I already know the question I'm going to ask!" she taunted.

"Okay, good. You hold that thought while we make these milk shakes," he said mildly.

Within minutes they each had frosty mugs in their hands and were laughing over the music playing on the pinball machine.

When it was Savannah's turn, he stood back and realized he was having fun. Honest-to-goodness fun.

When the hell was the last time he had just relaxed with someone and did something like this? Normally he only did that with his family. Savannah might be the first new person in years Riley had let his guard down with.

He had friends. Tons of them. But he had a feeling some of them were only hanging around because of who—or what—he was. It happened all the time. It wasn't just him. It was one of the pitfalls of fame. People aren't necessarily honest about why they're with you or why they want to hang out with you. Most of the time it didn't matter—a good time was a good time and the more the merrier. But after driving around with Savannah last night and now hanging out with her today? Riley was going to have a hard time dealing with the fakers and the hangers.

Hard to believe that so much was already changing in the short time he'd known her.

Beside him, she screeched happily and jumped up and down. "Yes! I just tripled my score! You just try to beat that, Shaughnessy!" Then she twirled by him and picked up her mug and took a long sip from her straw. She was flushed and beautiful and…and he stepped up to the pinball machine before he did something stupid.

By the time they finished one game on the machine, they were each done with their drinks, and Riley could see Savannah was anxious to get over to the Ping-Pong table. He collected their glasses and put them in the sink by the ice cream bar and then made his way over to the table. She was practically bouncing on her toes as he approached.

"You sure you're not too full for this?" Riley asked, grinning.

Savannah was tossing her paddle from hand to hand as she chuckled. "I am more than ready to play. Sounds to me like you're a little nervous about it. Could it be you're not as strong of a player as you claim to be?"

Oh…she was going to taunt him, was she?

"Sweetheart, I think you should be careful what you say right now," he teased.

"Oh, really? And why is that?"

"Because I would hate for you to be embarrassed later." Reaching for a ball, he tossed it over to her. "Ladies first."

"I hope you're ready to pour your heart out, *sweetheart*," she said, bouncing the ball several times, "because the question I have planned for you may require one of those couches you find in a therapist's office."

She was adorable, he thought.

"Bring it."

"Game on!"

He didn't just beat her in the best of three.

Oh, no. That would have been too easy.

No, Savannah—who realized too late that she was a very sore loser—kept egging him on until he finally put the paddle down after beating her in twelve games. Twelve! Why did she have to keep taunting him? Even while they were playing she couldn't make herself ask him anything important. They talked about useless stuff—favorite bands, favorite foods—hell, at one point she'd even asked him his favorite color.

She hung her head low in defeat and put her paddle on the table. Riley had excused himself and went to get them each a drink. She prayed it was vodka. Something to make her forget this humiliation.

His prize at the end of the first three games was that she'd stay and have dinner with him.

After the next three she'd stay for a movie.

She really thought she was going to beat him in the third round. Unfortunately, it had been her biggest loss, and he'd simply chuckled and said he'd have to think about his reward. And he'd repeated that after the fourth and final win.

Riley cleared his throat when he walked back into the room and handed her a glass of ice water. They drank in silence for a few minutes. "That was fun," he finally said, and Savannah realized he wasn't being obnoxious and he wasn't gloating. He genuinely looked like he'd had a good time.

And despite all the losing, Savannah would have to agree. It was fun.

"How do you feel about salmon for dinner?"

"It's one of my favorites," she said and was relieved he wasn't gloating.

"It's kind of early yet. Maybe we can watch a movie first?"

That was a reasonable request, and she agreed. Together they picked out a classic Neil Simon movie from 1967, *Barefoot in the Park*. "Ooo...Robert Redford." She sighed. "Another favorite."

Tucked away in a corner was one of the biggest flat-screen TVs Savannah had ever seen. Riley noticed her stunned look. "It's one hundred ten inches. They don't come any bigger than this right now. The picture's great too."

Two oversized recliners were centered in front of the screen and they each sat down. Riley started the movie and within minutes Savannah was more relaxed and they were both laughing along with the story.

She kicked her sandals off and tucked her feet up on the chair beside her. Next she pulled the clip out of her hair so she could relax her head against the back of the comfortable chair. Looking to her right, she saw Riley was watching her. His expression was intense and for the life of her, she couldn't figure out what was wrong. "Is everything okay?"

He didn't answer right away.

"Riley?"

"I still have to decide what I get for winning those last two rounds," he said, his voice low and gravelly.

Savannah nodded, hypnotized by the way his eyes had gone so dark.

"I'm going to combine them into one request," he said, and it sounded more like a warning than a statement.

"Okay." Her own voice was almost a breathy whisper.

Leaning closer, Riley's eyes zeroed in on her lips before meeting her eyes. "Savannah?"

"Hmm?"

"I'm going to kiss you. Twice."

"Oh."

His hand snaked out and around her nape and slowly drew her closer to him. And then his lips touched hers and Savannah's brain simply stopped functioning.

Chapter 4

CHERISHED.

There was no other way Savannah could possibly describe how she felt right now. Even though Riley had told her what he was going to do, she wasn't prepared for the reality of it. And really, there was no way to prepare for something like this.

It wasn't rushed.

It wasn't heated and frantic.

She sighed.

Riley's hands slowly came up and skimmed across her cheeks before combing into her hair. His lips were softer than she would have imagined, and he seemed in no hurry to do more than lazily explore her lips.

It was a heady feeling.

Before she knew it, her hands were inching their way up his arms and stopped when they got to his wrists. He was hard and muscled and if it were up to her, Savannah would gladly stay locked like this forever. They sipped at one another—gently teasing and tasting. It was something she'd never done before—never bothered to take the time to merely enjoy the act of kissing.

With this one kiss it was possible Riley Shaughnessy had ruined her for any other man. She'd dated plenty in her life, but no one had ever kissed her like this. And she had a feeling no one else ever would.

Should she argue? Tell him this was more than two kisses? This wasn't part of the plan. Kissing Riley had never been part of any plan. Ever. How was she supposed to ever look him in the eye and ask him any questions when from this point forward, all she'd want is for him to kiss her again?

Riley must have sensed her sudden anxiety because he took one last taste and lifted his head. Not far, just enough to rest his forehead against hers. Savannah swallowed hard and had to fight the urge to pull his lips back to hers.

"Wow." He sighed.

Yeah…that was pretty much the only thing she could think of to describe what they'd just done.

It couldn't happen again. She had a job to do. An important job that was going to give her a cover story, and no kissing—no matter how damn spectacular it was—was going to get in the way of that. Although once she opened her eyes and forced herself to look at Riley, she could barely remember why the article was so important.

Focus!

Savannah forced the lust-fog to lift and cleared her throat. "Um…I think I should go."

Riley's hands were still in her hair and he gently massaged her scalp before letting his hands slowly move away. "You promised me dinner and a movie. Actually, you *owe* me dinner and a movie." His voice was soft and teasing and as much as she hated to admit it, it made her relax.

"I can't stay if you're going to do that again," she said honestly.

"What? Kiss you?"

She nodded.

Pulling back, Riley got himself resituated in his seat and sighed. "That's fine. I can do that." He looked at the TV screen. "Oh good. We haven't missed the telephone scene." Then he reached for his water and took a sip.

Savannah could only stare. That was it? No arguing? No persuading her that it wasn't a big deal or that it might or might not happen again? She wasn't sure if she was relieved or really pissed off. Beside her, Riley laughed at something happening on the screen.

Pissed. She was definitely pissed.

Shifting away from him, Savannah did her best to get comfortable and focus on the movie, but it took longer than she cared to admit.

Why would he kiss her?

And why didn't he seem fazed about it not happening again?

Oh crap! Was she a bad kisser? No doubt a man like him had probably kissed hundreds, if not thousands, of women. Was she so bad at it that he was fine—if not relieved—if it never happened again?

And really, why was she obsessing about this? She'd gotten her way without any argument. So fine, maybe she might not have minded another chance to kiss him again. And maybe it wouldn't be that big a deal or have any influence on her ability to be professional and write an unbiased story about him.

Glancing over at Riley, she saw he was engrossed in the movie. Inwardly, she sighed. This was for the best.

And maybe if she said it enough, she just might believe it.

—⁓—

It was after ten when Savannah left. Riley had watched her drive away before going back into the house and then right out to the back deck.

The city was almost hypnotic to him at this time of day. With a bottle of water, he sat on one of the chaise lounges and thought about the day. When he'd called Savannah that morning and invited her over, he'd never imagined things going quite like they had. He'd figured they'd eat, they'd talk, and Savannah would lay out how she expected this interview to go. Riley knew he would have argued a point or two just on principle, but eventually they would have a schedule ironed out.

Once business was out of the way, he had figured on them simply spending some time getting to know one another. Playing games, sharing two meals, watching a movie, and kissing her were never part of the plan.

Well, in his fantasy, kissing her was always a plan, but he hadn't planned on acting on the impulse any time soon.

Especially not this soon.

Cursing himself, Riley slouched down. Self-control was never an issue. He was the king of it. While he would never claim to be a saint, in the world of rock and roll, he almost was. He'd slept with his share of women, but he'd never understood the allure of one-night stands and sex with strangers. Personally, he preferred a relationship. He enjoyed sharing a bed with a woman who was interested in who he was and not what he did for a living.

Yeah, sometimes being a rock star sucked.

Not that he'd openly admit it. And really, he was surprised that no one in the media had caught on to the fact he wasn't a serial dater or partier. If anyone really knew that he preferred being at home reading a good book or hanging out with a couple of friends over going to bars and sleeping with a string of groupies, no doubt he'd be the laughingstock of the music world.

Of course with Savannah hanging around for the next month, she'd probably catch on to that fact about him. "One bridge at a time," he murmured.

Right now Riley had to cross that first bridge—facing Savannah tomorrow as if she hadn't blown his mind tonight with a kiss. They'd gone on to finish the movie and dinner. She'd managed to convince him not to cook and instead order a pizza. He was fine with it and they'd opted to eat in the game room while watching another movie.

For the most part, Riley felt he'd pulled off a casual, blasé attitude—acting as if it wasn't a big deal that he'd kissed her and that she'd asked him not to do it again. The reality was that his mind was screaming at him to do it again.

He chuckled. And for as cool as Savannah tried to play it, he knew she was just as affected as he was by the whole thing, and telling him not to kiss her again wasn't what she really wanted. He wondered if she realized how her eyes gave her away. One look at them after he'd raised his head and Riley knew she was panicking—no doubt worrying about the nature of their professional relationship now that he'd crossed the line.

Well, maybe not crossed but he was certainly teetering on the edge of it.

Honestly, he wasn't trying to sabotage the interview. He'd simply been fighting the urge to touch her, kiss her since they'd met. So he'd acted on it. It wasn't a crime and as far as kisses went, it was relatively chaste.

And it just made him wonder how she'd react if he had kissed her the way he had really wanted to. Hell, if it were up to him, he'd still be kissing her now.

No dinner.

No movies.

And no sending her home.

He groaned. How the hell was he supposed to survive a month of this if he was already this hot and bothered on the first day? How was he supposed to maintain control over what was put into this article when he wanted to give Savannah everything she wanted? Anything she asked for?

It was too late to call anyone, and really, if he called Owen once more in such a short period of time, he'd probably send Owen into some kind of panic attack and then he'd feel guilty and have to go see him.

He sat up straight as an idea hit him.

It wasn't ideal but it would serve a purpose. It was quite possibly the only way Riley could guarantee he and Savannah would get the interview done in a manner that would work for them both. Because if today was any indication, having the two of them locked in his house alone was a recipe for disaster. Okay, maybe not disaster, but it was certainly a recipe for sexual frustration.

Standing up, he stretched. Decision made. Tomorrow he'd make the calls and make sure everyone would be on board. And then he'd present it to Savannah.

He sighed and prayed she'd go for it. Looking out

over the city, he said, "Brace yourself, Savannah Daly. I'm taking you home to meet the family."

—⁘—

"Wait…what?" Savannah slowly sat down on the sofa in Riley's living room the next day, certain she had misunderstood pretty much everything he'd just said. "I don't think I understand."

Not that it was anything new—ever since she'd shown up here thirty minutes earlier, her brain had refused to focus on anything except for Riley's mouth. She'd asked him to repeat himself several times already but this was the first time she had genuinely heard what he said but was confused by it.

"I'd like for you to travel with me back to North Carolina for a few weeks," he said, grinning as he sat on the opposite sofa. "I figured you'd want to incorporate some interviews with my family into the article and this way you'd be able to do that with relative ease. With the exception of my sister Darcy, almost everyone is local. My dad is already organizing a family dinner for Saturday night…"

"But…it's…it's Thursday. You don't mean *this* Saturday, do you?"

Riley nodded. "Absolutely. Why wait? I think it could be a good way to get you started—by getting to talk to my family and hearing about how I grew up and then take it from there."

She shook her head. "No," she said firmly and then took a minute to regroup. "That really isn't how I had planned on doing things. I'm not writing your biography, Riley. I'm writing an article on you and where you're at right now. I mean…I had planned on talking to maybe one or two members of your family, but I certainly don't need to hang out with them for a couple of weeks. If you had a family trip planned already, then you should have told me. We can reschedule things for when you get back."

It was his turn to shake his head. "I want this to be part of the interview."

"But it's not necessary," she argued. "It's common knowledge you're from a big family and you have a fraternal twin who is an astrophysicist. I really don't think spending time with them is going to add anything new that would be beneficial to the story."

Leaning forward, Riley's expression turned serious. "All of that information is public knowledge. You're right. But no one—and I mean no one—has ever sat down with my entire family and had the chance to observe the dynamics. As a matter of fact, none of my siblings ever granted an interview or talked to the press about me. You'd have the exclusive here, Savannah. You've talked about the possibility of this being a multi-issue piece; why not use one of those segments to focus on my family? I'm not saying you have to look at it as learning solely about my past." He stopped and shrugged. "My family is everything to me and they play a huge part in who I am and what I do every day."

"I don't know, Riley—"

He held out a hand to stop her. "Did you know I almost had to deliver my nephew in the back of my brother's SUV?"

"What? You did? When?" Savannah asked, suddenly interested. She reached into her bag to grab her recorder or a pad and pen when Riley went on.

"I'll let Hugh and Aubrey tell you the story when you meet them," he said, grinning. "Aubrey still gets a kick out of it. Apparently my older brother and I share the same expression of terror." He chuckled.

"That's amazing," she said, unable to stop herself from chuckling at the image in her head. "You travel a lot, Riley. How much do you really see them?"

"You'd be surprised. I go home and visit every chance I get. And if I can't get there, I've met up with Hugh at one of his resorts. When Quinn was still on the racing circuit, I'd catch up with him at one of the races, and I've even gone and visited my sister at college." He shuddered at the memory. "That's not one I'll do willingly ever again. It was a little like Beatlemania at one point."

Savannah laughed. "Don't you have a bodyguard with you for things like that?"

"Sometimes. When my brother Aidan got married, I had announced I was going on hiatus and the press was hounding me."

"I remember that."

"I didn't want any issues to arise that would disrupt the wedding or the weekend with my family so I had someone with me for the weekend. We took a private plane and flew into a small airport. I don't normally do things like that, but sometimes it's necessary. I don't think I'm so important I need a security detail with me or an entourage. I just want to be able to go where I want to go and do the things I want to do."

"Seriously? Riley, no offense, but that's just delusional."

He shrugged. "Maybe. Don't get me wrong, I know it's not always practical, and sometimes things happen like they did the other night at the beach. I like having a connection with my fans where I can sit and talk with them or stop and take a picture. But every once in a while, things get out of hand. You never know when it's going to happen and it seems crazy to live every day as if it will."

"But you could really get hurt by not having some-one with you," she said, concern lacing her voice. "Not everyone is looking to get a picture or to have a short conversation with you. There are some crazed fans out there who'd like nothing better than to get a piece of you—clothing, hair—surely you've seen or heard of those things happening?"

"I have," he said with a nod. "But I've been fortunate and they haven't happened to me." He studied her for a long moment. "Will you be able to leave tomorrow?"

Savannah's eyes went wide. "I… This really isn't a good idea, Riley. I can't. I just can't do it."

He frowned. "Why not? You told me your only responsibility for the next month is this story. Do you have pets you need to take care of?"

"Well…no."

"Family members?"

"No."

As much as he hated to do it, he asked, "A boyfriend or husband?"

She gave him a wry look. "Seriously? No."

"Then why? I've told you why I think this is impor-tant to the interview. We can fly out tomorrow morning and we'd get in to my dad's tomorrow night. It's almost twelve hours of travel time with the time difference, but it's not so bad."

"Riley, really, I…I can't."

He jumped to his feet, clearly frustrated. "Look, I'm doing this interview under duress as it is! No one said I had to do it in L.A. and only in L.A.," he snapped. "I don't think I'm asking for too much! All your travel expenses will be paid for—the trip won't cost you a thing. I had planned on us both staying with family but if you'd prefer, I'll make reservations for you at a hotel and I'll cover those expenses too." He stopped and sighed. "Come on, Savannah. Just…trust me on this. It's going to be a good thing."

She looked up at him and was embarrassed by the tears she felt forming. "This has nothing to do with the interview and whether I think talking with your family will be a good thing or a bad thing." Savannah tightly clasped her hands in her lap as she looked down. "The truth is, I'm…I'm terrified of flying."

"What?" he asked and came to sit beside her.

Savannah looked at him and was mortified to have to admit it. "I'm terrified of flying. The last time I got on a plane, I had to be escorted off because I was having a panic attack. Luckily we hadn't left the gate yet, but it was humiliating to have so many people witness my freaking out."

Riley reached out and took one of her hands in his and squeezed it. "Okay, okay," he said soothingly. "Okay. What is it about flying that upsets you? Were you always afraid to fly?"

She shook her head. "I used to travel all the time. My family moved around a lot and we'd always fly to visit relatives. A couple of years ago I was on a flight that got delayed but we were already boarded. They wouldn't let us off the plane and we couldn't get up and...and... I just started to feel claustrophobic and panicked. We sat on the tarmac for hours and I just remember feeling like I was trapped. It was a full flight and no room to move around and..." She stopped and took a couple of steadying breaths. "Ever since then, I just can't do it. I tried and, like I said, I ended up being taken off the plane." She looked up at him pleadingly. "I can't do it again, Riley."

"How do you handle it with your other assignments? I'm assuming you travel for other interviews?"

She shrugged. "I've been fortunate where I've been able to meet up with people. I tend to do whatever I can to schedule our interviews here in California. I don't mind driving up and down the west coast."

"It's a hell of a drive across the country," he said with a nervous chuckle. "But if that's what it would take to help you, I'd do it."

"I can't ask you to do that," she said quietly. "Can we...can we just let this go for right now? You've thrown me for a loop here and I wasn't expecting any of this. Please understand, I'm not deliberately being difficult. If there was a way for me to fly without needing someone to shoot me with a tranquilizer dart, I'd do it. But I can't see myself boarding a commercial flight and being packed in like that again."

Riley nodded and gave her hand one more squeeze before he stood up. "What about a private plane?"

"What?"

Pacing the room, he seemed to be talking a little more to himself than Savannah. "A private plane. We'd be the only passengers—plus a crew—but essentially we'd have the space to ourselves. You'd be able to move around as you need to, the seats are much more comfortable, and really, the overall trip will go faster because it will be a direct flight rather than one that has to make stops like the commercial flights do. What do you say?"

"Oh, I don't know, Riley. Aren't those things normally pretty small? I think that might freak me out just as much!"

"Sweetheart, these are no ordinary private planes. The one we'd use, which belongs to my record label, is a little on the small side but you'll hardly notice." When she still didn't look convinced, he walked out of the room, grabbed his tablet, and did a Google search. When he found what he was looking for, he passed the tablet to her to read. "Go ahead, read it out loud."

"With seating for ten and four berthable beds, the Gulfstream G550 is an ultra-long-range jet especially designed for business efficiency. It includes the most advanced flight deck in business aviation, with an enhanced vision system and Gulfstream's best-in-class avionics achievements. Features a full-service galley and three temperature zones." Savannah looked up at him questioningly. "Is this for real? This plane really exists?"

Riley nodded. "It certainly does, and I've flown in it multiple times. Say the word, Savannah, and I'll make the arrangements. If it's not available for us tomorrow, I'll wait until it is so you can fly without any fear."

"We don't know that will happen, Riley. You can't know for certain I'm going to get on the plane and not flip out."

"Trust me. I firmly believe you are going to be just fine."

She made a face at him. "You can't guarantee it, Riley."

He sat back down and once again picked up her hand. "I'll make you a deal. I'm going to make the call and see if the plane is available and reserve it. If it is, you'll agree to go. And if we get on the plane and you find you aren't comfortable, we'll cancel the trip and do the rest of the interview here. Alone in my house. Just the two of us. For a month."

And that's when it hit her—he was just as nervous being alone with her as she was to be alone with him. She almost sagged with relief knowing she wasn't the only one affected by what had happened yesterday.

"Can we do that? Reserve the plane and then not use it? Won't you get in trouble or something?"

Riley shrugged. "I'll deal with it. The guys at the label aren't particularly thrilled with me right now. What's one more offense added to the list?"

Now she felt bad. "Riley, I don't want to cause any problems for you."

"You're not," he assured her. "This was my idea, and I really thought it would be a good thing for both of us. I had no idea about your aversion to flying so I probably should have talked to you first before getting my family involved and excited about meeting you."

"They're…they're excited about meeting me? Why?" she asked nervously.

"Let's just say they've probably been waiting for the opportunity to share embarrassing stories and let the world see what a dork I really am." He laughed. "You'll have five siblings, their wives, my dad, and who knows who else to share stories that no one's heard before. Trust me, if nothing else you'll be wildly entertained."

Savannah didn't doubt that. She also didn't doubt having people around them was a smart move. Right now she was tempted to crawl into Riley's lap and ask him to kiss her again. He was still holding her hand, his thumb gently caressing her knuckles, and it felt more intimate than it should.

Looking over at him, she noted the hopeful expression on his face. Maybe he was right. Maybe flying his way would help ease her anxiety. And really, how could she possibly pass up the opportunity to fly in such an extravagant aircraft?

"Okay," she finally said.

Riley's eyes went wide along with his smile. "Really?"

Savannah nodded. "I'm willing to try if you are." He pulled her in and hugged her, and she simply let herself enjoy the moment before pulling back. "Just remember—if I freak out and need to get off the plane, you're not allowed to make fun of me."

His expression turned serious as one hand came up and cupped her cheek. "Sweetheart, I would never make fun of you."

The silly thing was, she was starting to get used to that endearment, and between his words and the intensity of his gaze, she knew he was telling her the truth. With a nod, Savannah watched Riley stand and go in search of his phone.

With nothing to do, she sat back on the sofa and took a steadying breath. This was not the way she had planned on this interview process going. They were supposed to spend time in some nondescript place—at least in her mind she saw it that way—and she'd ask questions and he'd answer.

Now she was flying across the country. With Riley.

She was spending time with the Shaughnessy family. With Riley.

And she knew it was entirely possible she was falling a little bit in love. With Riley.

No! She admonished herself. It had been…what? Three days? It wasn't possible! Savannah wouldn't let it be possible. She was a practical woman. A responsible woman. She'd been alone with some of the hottest musicians in the world and had never felt like this with any of them. When she thought about how many times she had been propositioned and crudely groped by some of those guys, she wasn't sure if she should laugh or cringe.

She thought she was immune to it.

And never in her wildest dreams did she imagine she'd be softening toward the likes of Riley Shaughnessy. He was everything she thought she despised—the pretty-boy rock star who had more looks than talent. Unfortunately, she was finding she had misjudged him.

Completely.

She'd never admit it to him, but last night she had sat down and listened to the last album he'd released with his band. And listened to it in its entirety.

And she loved it.

Every. Damn. Song.

She cursed. She wasn't comfortable with this situation: being a fan while trying to write a piece that was raw and gritty and shattered the illusion of how the world saw him. Out of the corner of her eye, Savannah saw him come back into the room. He was smiling and talking on the phone, and from the sound of it, the plane was available for the next day. Without asking, he reached for her notepad and pen and began writing information down—departure and arrival times, airports and car service.

"No, I'll take care of arrangements on the other end," Riley was saying. "I'm sure one of my brothers or my father can pick us up, and we'll make arrangements for a car to use once we get there." He paused. "I'll be staying with family and Miss Daly will…" He put a hand over the phone and looked at Savannah. "Would you like us to make arrangements for a hotel or will you be okay staying with my family?"

The reality of it all was overwhelming. Staying with Riley's family? She looked at him and saw that easy expression and knew which option he'd like her to take. "I'll be fine staying with your family," she said softly.

They were going to travel to North Carolina together whether she was ready for it or not.

Another night staring out at the city. It was becoming a habit—one Riley knew he was going to miss over the next few weeks. This was his peaceful time—how he found his solitude and was able just to unwind after a frustrating day.

And frustrating it was.

Once the reservations for the plane had been made, they'd spent the next several hours talking about what Savannah should pack and bring with her and how they would be spending their time once they arrived in North Carolina. Unfortunately, Riley hadn't planned that far in advance. The packing part was a breeze—he told her the basic weather conditions and the kind of places they might go to. As for how they were going to spend their time and with who and when? Hell, he had no idea.

Clearly Savannah was a planner because his inability to present an agenda seemed to irk her.

She was going to get along perfectly with Aidan and Hugh.

Over lunch he explained to her the basics of his family and how—as of right now—they were going to stay at his father's house. He had the spare rooms and he would be the least intrusive out of everyone. Plus, it was the central hub where everyone met up. Although, if Riley'd had more time to plan, he might have chosen to stay with either Aidan or Quinn. And then if he thought about it even longer, he'd choose to stay at Quinn's. His and Anna's new place was amazing and had a lot of extra space plus a lot of the same amenities Riley's own house did—a game room, a pool.

Maybe they'd just house hop for part of the trip.

Or maybe he should have just reserved a room at a hotel for Savannah so she had someplace to escape to when his family got to be too overwhelming. They weren't even there yet and already Riley was beginning to feel that way. He knew he loved his family and enjoyed the times they spent together, but it didn't necessarily guarantee Savannah was going to feel the same way. Maybe he'd call Zoe or Anna and see if they'd make some time to include her in a girls' night or something. He'd ask Aubrey but she was busy with the new baby.

He thought of his nephew Connor and couldn't wait to see him now that he was a little bit bigger. The whole day of his arrival had been like something out of a bad comedy. Between Aubrey's water breaking while they were moving Quinn and Anna into their new home and Hugh almost passing out in the car while Bobby Hannigan drove like a lunatic and Riley seeing things no guy should ever see on his sister-in-law... He shuddered. By the time they arrived at the hospital, Aubrey was ready to strangle all three of them, and Riley had been more than happy to wait in the waiting room for the rest of the family to arrive.

They had celebrated that night like they never had before. A new member of the family. And not one who had married into it, but one who was born into it. That hadn't happened since Darcy. They cried and laughed together as a family, and at the core of it all was the celebration of a new life.

Riley sighed as he remembered the look of pure joy on his brother's face when he came out of the delivery room with Connor in his arms. And in that moment—and maybe for the first time ever—Riley was jealous of Hugh. Of anyone. All the fame and money he had from his music career didn't give him that look or what Hugh was feeling at that moment.

Clearly he'd hit the age where you realized there's more to life than being a celebrity. He didn't want to party and he didn't want to be alone. The thought of coming home at the end of the day to a wife and kids was suddenly way more appealing than it used to be. Before, he'd thought he was too young or that he wanted to accomplish more with his career, but as he sat here alone again, Riley knew everything he accomplished would mean so much more if someone were here to share it with him.

Savannah's face instantly came to mind.

Not that it was a surprise. He was drawn to her the first time he saw her, and no matter how much he tried to tell himself they'd only just met or maybe it was just a serious case of lust, Riley knew differently. He enjoyed talking to her. Sharing a meal with her. Playing a game with her. Looking around, he could still see her in every room of his house and she simply…fit. Before Savannah, he never invited women into his home. If it was for business—like this interview was supposed to be—he would have normally made arrangements to meet someplace neutral like the studio or at a restaurant. Pretty much anyplace but his home. Even when he was involved with a woman, they tended to meet either at her place or a hotel.

This was his private space.

His haven.

Until now.

Now he just felt lonely. Alone. With a growl of disgust, he stood and walked back into the house. He needed to pack and get things together for the trip. He'd already talked to Mick and made sure someone would come and check on the house while he was away. His housekeeper came in twice a month, but Riley knew Mick would make sure nothing out of the ordinary went on while he was away and ensure that security monitored the place.

Mick had been equal parts happy to help and annoyed with him. He was glad that the interview was moving forward, but the fact that it was happening back east seemed to hit a nerve. "What about work, Riley?" he'd snapped. "You've got music to work on and the studio is here! And what about public appearances? I thought we were going to start working on getting you seen out and about more?"

Ugh. Shit like this annoyed him, but in the end they had come to a compromise. Riley promised to keep working on writing the music while he was away—even without the use of a studio—and he'd keep in daily contact with his publicist so they'd be able to get occasional photo ops for the tabloids should they need them.

It was the lack of privacy that he hated the most—especially when he was back home with his family. It was one thing for him to be inconvenienced or followed. It was another when the press bothered his family. Unfortunately, this was probably the first time it was going to be a major issue. The local press left him alone for the most part. But with the current state of his career, he was having to play the games that he despised.

It wasn't as if Riley hadn't taken vacations and breaks before. He wasn't an idiot. He knew the drills to keep his voice in good shape and how important it was to do vocal exercises daily. Hell, sometimes he just ran through them in the shower or when he was bored. So why Mick was treating him like this was his first time away from the nest, Riley had no idea.

"Like a freaking mother hen watching over me," he murmured as he walked through the house.

In his bedroom, Riley walked through his closet and packed the essentials—he could almost do this in his sleep. When he had to be on tour, the amount of stuff he usually packed on his own was minimal because the rest was somewhat dictated by his team. And for a family trip? He kept some stuff back at his father's house so all he really needed was one suitcase.

"Well, that took all of five minutes," he said as he looked around his room. The clock read nine-thirty and Riley had no idea what to do with himself. The town car was coming to pick him up at seven in the morning and then on to pick up Savannah. Their flight was at ten.

He worried about it—the flight and how Savannah was going to handle it. As he relaxed on the bed, he pulled out his phone and decided to check on her. It was a legit reason should she question why he was calling, but the truth of the matter was he just wanted to hear her voice.

"Hey," he said when she answered the phone. "How are you doing?"

"Oh, hi," she said, sounding a little flustered. "I'm good. Just trying to sort through everything I think I'll need."

"You don't have to go crazy, Savannah," he said, smiling at the image of her surrounded by piles of discarded clothing choices. "If there's anything you need that you've forgotten, we can buy it there. It's coastal North Carolina and believe me, there are plenty of places to shop. And if I know my sisters-in-law, they'll want to take you out shopping at some point. It's their thing."

She chuckled. "It's a girl thing, although I'm sure there are some guys out there who enjoy a good shopping spree too."

"I'm not one of them."

"Good to know," she teased. "I've never been away from home for this long so I'm just not sure how much to pack."

"We're going to be staying with family so we'll be able to do laundry. Really, you don't need to go crazy.

Pack for a week to ten days and maybe a nice outfit or two in case we go out anywhere, and call it a day. Seriously, I don't want you to make yourself crazy over this."

"I know you're right. I think… I think I'm still freaking out about the flight. I know you said it's going to be fine and all but… I can't help but be nervous."

"I'm sorry I didn't know about how you felt about flying, Savannah—"

"You don't have to keep apologizing, Riley. We just met. How could you possibly know?"

She was right, but it didn't stop him from feeling bad. "What can I possibly do to help you relax tomorrow? I'll make sure the entire plane is stocked with whatever you want. Food? Snacks? Books? Movies? Music? You name it and I'll have it on board."

She was laughing. "I've got my Kindle. I can't imagine wanting to eat on board. Just thinking about it now makes me a little sick."

"Oh, come on," he said. "It will be like hanging out in my living room—only more comfortable."

"I find that hard to believe. Your couch is incredibly comfortable."

He chuckled. "Believe me, I know. That's why I bought it. But let's just say we take off and you're feeling all right. What would be something you'd like to snack on?"

"I really don't think—"

"Yeah, yeah, yeah…I get it. You can't imagine eating, you'll be sick, blah, blah, blah," he teased. "Just humor me, Savannah. If you could have anything you want on the plane to eat, what would you want?"

She sighed loudly and if Riley wasn't mistaken,

she was slightly annoyed. He could almost picture the frown on her face and those violet eyes glaring at him. "Fine. You want snack choices? I'll tell you: Double Stuf Oreos but only if there is ice-cold milk to go with them. Brownies—no nuts—and they have to have icing on them. You already know my love of chocolate milk shakes so I wouldn't say no to one of those either."

"I'm noticing a trend here…"

"You asked," she reminded him.

"What about normal food? You do eat regular meals, I know this. I've eaten some with you," he teased. "What do you like for, say, breakfast?"

"I rarely eat it."

"The most important meal of the day? I'm shocked!"

Savannah laughed out loud. "You're crazy, you know that, right?"

He laughed with her, amazed that he even enjoyed the sound of her laughter. What in the world was happening to him? It was as if she cast a spell over him. He shook his head and quickly reminded himself how ridiculous he was being. She was a reporter and he was being forced to do this interview. He needed to keep his mind on why she was in his life. This wasn't a… relationship. Not a real one.

"Okay, so not a big fan of breakfast," he said, forcing himself back into the conversation. "I happen to enjoy a good bagel and cream cheese—you know, in case you were wondering."

"Ooo…that can be good. With bacon! Extra crispy bacon on a bagel and cream cheese is amazing."

"So health food isn't your thing? Whew! You'll fit right in with my family."

"Oh yeah, I guess I have mainly been picking junk food here. But...bacon. Everyone loves bacon, right?"

"Absolutely. I would never argue that point. What about lunch?"

"Well, now you've made me want to ask for a salad."

"Considering you would have eaten about six pounds of chocolate and some bacon by that time, it might not be a bad thing."

"Riley!" she said, and he knew she was trying to yell at him, but it came out as laughter.

"With the time difference, it will be around dinner time when we land. Rather than eat on the plane, I just figured we'd eat with my dad. Is that all right with you?"

"That's fine. Really. I think it's the perfect plan. By that time I'm going to just want to get off the plane and have my feet on the ground."

"Believe me, I will too. I don't mind flying, but I much prefer to be on the ground. If it wasn't so far, I would drive it myself. But it's a lot of time confined in a car, and that has the potential to make me crazy."

"I don't know, I think a road trip could be fun. I did one the summer I graduated college with a couple of friends. We drove from Kansas to Nevada and went to Vegas for a week, but the drive was a blast," she said, and Riley could hear the smile in her voice.

"The first few years the band was together, we traveled by bus. And not one of those tricked-out ones you see nowadays. It was your basic charter bus. The seats were okay but it was pretty hard to sleep in them."

"Oh, yikes. You didn't stop at hotels for the night?"

"Uh-uh. We were really poor in those days so it just made sense to live on the bus and then shower and get ready at the venue. You have no idea how glad I am those days are over. I'm not much of a diva compared to some guys out there, but I definitely put my foot down and demand a hotel room to myself every night we're on tour."

"That's a fairly mild request," she said. "I've heard a lot of rock stars can make some outlandish ones."

"Oh, I know. I've heard them all. Personally, I don't see the point in being difficult. I'd rather pay someone to make sure we put on a kick-ass show rather than sorting out M&M's or placing white rose petals around the dressing room. As long as the space is clean, I'm happy."

"You're in the minority."

"And I'm okay with it."

Riley closed his eyes and smiled. Yeah, he really liked talking to her and right now, even with nothing to say, he liked knowing she was on the other end of the phone.

He was screwed.

The idea that being around his family was going to help him keep his hands to himself was quickly becoming a joke. Because right now, he was tempted to get in his car and go to her, and he knew spending time alone on the flight tomorrow was only going to heighten his awareness of her. Sleeping in the room next to her at his father's was going to be torture.

Yeah, he was screwed.

"Riley?" Savannah asked quietly.

"Hmm?"

"You're sure everything's going to be okay tomorrow?"

If he could, he'd wrap her in his arms right now and promise her anything. But for now, he only had his words.

"Savannah, I promise I will do everything in my power to make sure you feel safe, secure, and relaxed for the entire flight tomorrow."

She hummed sleepily. "Mmm…okay."

"We'll be to you around seven-thirty to pick you up, okay?"

"Okay."

"I'll see you in the morning."

"Okay." He heard her yawn.

"Savannah?"

"Hmm?"

"Good night," he said softly.

"Good night, Riley."

Chapter 5

"THIS ISN'T A REAL PLANE. THIS IS LIKE A MOVIE PROP."

"Why would I take you on a movie prop?"

"I have no idea but I'm telling you, this isn't real. I don't even think it can fly."

"I can pretty much guarantee you it can."

Looking over her shoulder at him, she gave him a look of disbelief. "And it's small. A lot smaller than I thought it would be. I'm not sure if—"

"Sit in one of these seats," Riley quickly interrupted. "I'm telling you, they're beyond comfortable. And I know it's smaller than a commercial jet, but you're not even going to notice it once we get in the air. You'll be too comfortable," he added with a grin.

Savannah wasn't so sure.

A flight attendant came out to welcome them and asked if they'd be interested in coffee or juice.

"I'll take some coffee, Lisa," Riley said and then turned to Savannah. "How about you?"

"Um…"

"Lisa, do we have any hot chocolate on board?" Riley asked.

"Yes, sir. I'll get those for you right away." And then she swiftly disappeared into the galley.

"Where would you like to sit?" Riley asked softly. "Every seat has a lap belt for takeoff and landing so wherever you think you'll be the most comfortable, that's where we'll sit."

Looking around, Savannah weighed her options. So far, the normal nerves she had about flying were the only ones she was feeling. The space was open, and with just the two of them, she couldn't imagine freaking out too much. Even if the flight was delayed and they had to stay on the plane, it wouldn't be a hardship.

"I think this sofa back here looks good. Plus it's close to the TV. Maybe we can watch something to distract me?"

"Whatever you want, that's what we'll do."

Wordlessly, Lisa placed a tray down on the coffee table with their drinks as well as some fresh fruit and muffins.

"Wow, she's good," Savannah said, taking a seat and shifting around until she found her seat belt. Riley sat down beside her and helped her. "Thanks. I think I'm all thumbs this morning."

"You're doing great," he said and reached over and picked up their mugs, handing Savannah hers.

"Why hot chocolate?" she asked. "I mean, I love it but why did you ask her to make it for me?"

"After our conversation last night it seemed like a safe choice. I knew you were probably wrestling with whether you could eat anything, but your love of chocolate came through loud and clear during our talk so I figured you would probably enjoy it." He took a sip of his coffee. "If you would prefer something else, don't hesitate to ask."

"Oh, I don't want to bother her. And besides, this really is fine." She tasted the hot chocolate and sighed with pleasure. "Oh yeah. This is better than fine."

"There's a chocolate chip muffin in the basket too—you know, if you're interested."

"I have a feeling if I keep hanging out with you, I'm going to need a whole new wardrobe because I won't fit into anything I currently own."

"And you'd still be beautiful," he said, and Savannah could only turn and stare at him. "It's true."

She swallowed hard, unsure of what to say.

"If you'll both fasten your seat belts," Lisa said softly as she came back to check on them. "We're preparing for takeoff. I'll be up in the galley area. If you need anything or when you're ready for breakfast—or lunch—let me know." Then she smiled and walked away as both Savannah and Riley thanked her.

This was it, Savannah thought to herself. She was on the plane and so far, no meltdowns. All around her she could hear what was going on—the main door was closing, the engines were running, and everything seemed to be all right.

Without her asking, Riley stood and closed all the window shades around them. It was a little unnerving how well he seemed to anticipate her needs and concerns. Some people enjoyed looking out the windows as their plane took off, but Savannah wasn't one of those people. She thanked him for being so considerate as he sat back down and buckled his seat belt.

The plane started to move, and Savannah instinctively dug her fingers into the soft leather of the sofa. There weren't any armrests near her—not like she would have on a standard airplane seat—so she just grabbed as much as she could, closed her eyes, and held on tight.

"We're just moving away from the terminal," Riley said quietly.

She could feel his breath on her ear, but she couldn't bring herself to open her eyes and look at him. It was safer to keep them firmly shut.

They were silent for several minutes when the plane came to a stop. "We're waiting for our turn to take off," he said, his tone soothing. "You need to breathe, sweetheart. I can tell you're holding your breath."

"I...I just hate this part. I know it's coming and I can't—" She paused and took a few breaths. "I can't relax."

"Okay," he said.

The next thing she knew, Riley pried one of her hands off the sofa and held it in his. It felt good. Warm. Comforting. Then his other hand came around and cupped her cheek, and she felt him rest his head against hers. It felt good, and Savannah felt as if she was drawing strength from him. For a few minutes, touching was all they did, but as soon as the plane started to move again, she immediately tensed up.

"Look at me," he whispered. "Open your eyes and look at me. Focus on my face and nothing else."

She opened her eyes, but the rest was impossible. How could she focus on his face and not think of how handsome he was? Or how kind and understanding his eyes were?

The plane began to pick up speed, and Savannah knew she was seconds away from a full-on panic attack. There was no way she wanted to do that in front of Riley—or anyone for that matter—so she did the only thing she could.

"Kiss me," she said.

To give him credit, Riley didn't question it. He simply closed the distance between them and captured her lips with his. It wasn't the sweet and gentle kiss of the other night. No. This one was all-consuming and deep and wonderful, and Savannah sighed into it as she pulled her hand free of his and let it rake up into his hair.

So many things were going through Savannah's mind as she touched him, but the most prevalent was *more*. She wanted to be free to touch more of him and for him to do the same in return. While Riley's lips and tongue were doing things to hers she never imagined possible, his hand had stayed in fairly chaste positions—her cheek, her nape. His fingers felt rough against her skin and she could only dream of how they'd feel on other parts of her body.

She cursed the seat belts, the couch, their clothes. Crowding closer to him, she tried to mentally tell him what she wanted. Somewhere in the back of her mind she knew it was crazy—this wasn't the kind of person she normally was. Wasn't the kind of woman who threw herself at a man—any man—even a rock star! But there was something about Riley that made her feel differently, act differently, and want differently.

The plane kept moving, time kept moving, and yet Savannah had no recollection of any of it. It was as if everything around them had ceased to exist and it was only the two of them.

And it was absolutely perfect.

There was a sound off in the distance that finally seemed to break through their haze and had Savannah hesitantly removing her lips from his. "What…what was that?" she asked dazedly.

Riley seemed just as disoriented as she was. Lifting his head, he looked around and then smiled. "The seat belt sign is off. It means we can get up and move around."

She looked around in confusion. "But…how…? We just…?" Then she focused on Riley. "Didn't we just take off?"

His hand stroked her cheek as he chuckled. "That was about ten minutes ago."

Her eyes went wide. "Really? I didn't even… I mean… I had no idea…"

His smile widened. "Yeah. Me too." He leaned in and gave her another quick kiss before releasing his seat belt and standing. "I don't know about you, but I'm starving. How about I get Lisa?"

"We still have this fruit and muffin tray," she reminded him.

"Yeah, but it's not what I'm in the mood for. What do you say?"

Honestly, she didn't know what to say. She was still baffled by the fact they were in the air and she hadn't even been aware of it. And besides that, she couldn't believe she had just had one of the longest make-out sessions ever—at least for her—with one of the biggest rock stars in the world. And now he wanted to talk about breakfast!

Who was she and what had happened to her uncomplicated life?

Unbuckling her own seat belt, Savannah slowly rose to her feet and was surprised how…normal everything felt. She wasn't nervous. She wasn't panicking. And, if she thought about it, she was hungry. Interesting. She wondered if Tommy would agree to budgeting private jets to get her to all her future assignments. She chuckled at the look of shock that would undoubtedly be his response to her request.

Riley came up behind her, put his hands on her hips, and gently squeezed. "Food will be out in about five minutes. You doing okay?"

Nodding, she said, "I am. I was just sort of standing here marveling at the whole thing." Turning in his arms, she smiled up at him—not realizing until just now how tall he was. At five foot seven, Savannah knew most guys were at least a little taller than she was, but she was always wearing some sort of footwear with heels. Today she had gone for flats, and next to Riley's six-foot frame, she felt a little small. And the way he was looking at her made her want to curl around him and dive back in for another taste.

"It's not hard to relax when you're in this kind of an environment," he said easily, his eyes scanning her face.

"It's not only the environment, Riley. You…you really helped me."

He rested his forehead against hers. "Anytime you need help like that, Savannah, don't hesitate to ask. Ever. I'm serious."

She was ready to ask for it right now, but Lisa discreetly cleared her throat as she walked over and placed another tray of food on the coffee table along with new hot beverages. "I wasn't sure if you wanted another hot chocolate, Miss Daly, so I also put a cup of coffee on the tray for you."

Savannah smiled. "Thank you, Lisa."

"I'll be back in the galley if either of you need anything," she said and then walked away.

Looking over at the new tray of food, Savannah groaned playfully. "What did you do?"

He grinned like the Cheshire cat. "What? What's wrong with this?"

Sitting down, Savannah examined her plate. "Is that bacon on there?"

"Extra crispy," Riley confirmed as he sat down and reached for his own plate. When she looked over at him, he shrugged. "You said you enjoyed bagels and cream cheese with crispy bacon. I merely relayed the information to the crew when they were stocking the kitchen." He nodded toward her plate. "Now eat up. It's late, and I'm sure you didn't eat before we picked you up."

He was right, but she wasn't going to tell him that. Instead she picked up her bagel, took a bite, and groaned. "Oh, that's good."

"I must admit, I never tried this combination before, but it really is good. It may become my new breakfast of choice."

"What do you normally eat?"

He shrugged. "I like all kinds of breakfast food, from pancakes to Pop-Tarts. If you looked in my pantry at home, you'd see a huge variety of cereals—although I'm partial to Frosted Flakes. When I'm on the road, I take full advantage of room service and order all the things I'm too lazy to make myself at home."

"Like eggs Benedict and omelets?"

"More like Belgian waffles. I'm a sucker for those if they're on the menu."

Savannah chuckled. "I think I could write an article about you and your food choices alone. We seem to talk about it a lot."

"Food's important," he said simply.

"What about when you were growing up? What was your favorite food then?"

"Ooo…good one," he said, sitting back and relaxing, balancing his plate on his leg. "I come from a big Irish family, and my mom used to cook a lot of traditional Irish meals. But as much as I loved those, she was an incredible baker. She used to bake all kinds of cakes and cookies, and we all used to go crazy when we'd come home from school and find a batch of warm cookies waiting in the kitchen."

Savannah smiled. "That sounds like a great memory."

He nodded, his smile a little sad. "It is. She used those same treats as a weapon." Then he chuckled. "If you were bad or misbehaved? Then you couldn't have any. You'd have to sit there and watch everyone else eat them while you didn't."

"I'm sure that was torture."

"You have no idea!" He started to laugh harder as the memories came to him. "I didn't get punished often, but when I did, Owen would always sneak one to me so I didn't miss out."

"He's your twin, right?"

Riley nodded. "We always looked out for each other. Still do." He chuckled. "My brother Quinn, however, was the worst. When one of us was grounded and couldn't eat any, he was the one who would just taunt the hell out of the poor guy. He'd dance around waving the cookie. But on the flip side, he was the one who was normally in trouble and missed out."

"I hope you teased him right back!" Savannah cried, chuckling with him.

"We rarely got the chance to. He would disappear when it was time for our snack or dessert. It wasn't until years later that we found out our next-door neighbor Anna—who is now engaged to Quinn—used to sneak some of her mom's homemade cookies to him whenever he was grounded."

"Aww…that's kind of sweet! And they're getting married?"

Riley nodded. "She's been in love with him since she was little, and my brother was oblivious."

"Most men are," Savannah muttered and took a bite of her bagel.

"Hey!" he said with a mock pout. "I'm a man and I take offense to that."

"It's true and you know it. I'm sure you're no different."

"I don't know about that—"

"Tell me more about your brother and Anna. How did he finally find out?"

"I'd have to take credit for that one. It was priceless seeing the look on his face when I finally said what we all knew—that Anna was in love with him. We were at my brother Aidan's wedding and Quinn was hitting on all the married bridesmaids—"

"That's horrible!"

Riley held up a hand. "In his defense, he didn't know they were married. But even while he was busy making the biggest faux pas of the wedding, his eyes never left Anna. It had been like that for a while. She'd watch him and he didn't notice, but he watched her just as much."

She sighed. "Okay, and now we're back to sweet."

"Yeah, well, I was making fun of him for striking out with the bridal party when I noticed how pretty Anna looked. I commented on it and said I was going over to chat with her, and he nearly bit my head off. Now that I think about it, it was the rehearsal dinner, not the wedding." He took another bite of his breakfast. "Like I said, the rest of the family? We all knew the score and we were just waiting for him to open his eyes and see what was right in front of him. I merely poked the bear."

"So they hooked up?"

He shook his head. "Not right away, but that weekend definitely set things in motion. They got engaged not too long ago and bought a house, and in three months they're getting married."

"Wow, that's fast."

"They've known each other for about twenty-five years," he said, frowning. "So really, it's not as fast as you would think."

She nodded and together they finished their meals and sat back with a sigh. "That was so good," she said, her hand on her belly.

"Agreed." He paused. "Do you want to watch a movie or maybe do some work on the interview?"

Savannah knew they really needed to get to work on the interview. After almost four days she didn't have anything beyond the basics on him. Although with this trip, they were going to have more time together than she ever imagined—essentially 24-7. Maybe that was why she wasn't overly anxious to get started right now. She was enjoying this easy camaraderie. And really, a lot of what they had talked about was helping her get a better picture of who Riley Shaughnessy was.

It was also serving to reshape how she saw this article going.

She just needed to remind herself to stay professional; otherwise, she had a feeling she'd end up with a piece that belonged in a teen magazine with her name and Riley's in a big giant heart.

Ugh.

Realizing he was still watching her, she cleared her throat. "Um…a movie would be great. Another way to pass the time."

"And by the time it's over, it will be lunch time."

"Are you always hungry?" she asked with a laugh, but it quickly died when she saw his expression had turned serious and his gaze had gone dark and heated.

Riley nodded. "Lately? It seems like I am."

Oh my…

Forcing herself to look away, Savannah put a little distance between them. "So, a movie. What are our options?"

At least Riley didn't call her out on being a coward and changing the subject. He rattled off a list of movies they had on board, most of which were ones he and Savannah had talked about the other day at his house. She discovered he was a man who paid attention to the little things and remembered them.

It was a damn fine and admirable quality.

Like she really needed another reason to like him!

"What do you think?" he asked, standing next to the media cabinet. "Any of them sound better than the others?"

"I think since we both had so much fun with our Neil Simon movie the other day, we should try another one. How about *Murder by Death*?"

Riley grinned.

"What? What's that smile about?" She couldn't understand why he was smiling like that.

"You are clearly a woman after my own heart because *that* is a personal favorite of mine and I never seem to remember it. Whenever I get together with friends and we pick a movie, we end up with more recent titles. You're letting me indulge in some classics I haven't seen in a while."

That made her smile. "They don't make movies like they used to. After this movie, we may have to move on to a couple of Mel Brooks films. Those are amazing!"

"I hope you're talking about *Young Frankenstein* and *Blazing Saddles*."

"Um…what Mel Brooks marathon would be complete without those as a starting point?" she teased.

Riley put in the movie and sat back down beside her. Before she knew what he was doing, he grabbed her hand and kissed it. "If you can quote lines from either of those two movies, I may ask you to marry me."

His eyes twinkled as Savannah laughed at his play on the similar statement she'd made to him days ago. It was so tempting to quote multiple lines from each movie just to see his reaction, but she refrained. Instead she gave him a sweet smile, kicked off her shoes, and made herself comfortable as the opening credits began.

"We should be on the ground in thirty minutes," Lisa said as she took away the last of their lunch—gourmet deli sandwiches and salads followed by iced fudge brownies. She smiled at them both as she walked away.

"I may need assistance getting off the plane," Savannah said, slouching down in her seat.

Riley chuckled and studied her. He loved how she

wasn't afraid to enjoy her food—other than Darcy and his brother's wives, most of the women he spent time with tended to always be dieting and would pick at their food. Of course, he lived in California, and most of the women there dreamed of becoming a star of some kind.

"I will gladly help in any way I can," he said as he stood and stretched. "I'm not going to lie to you. As comfortable as this plane is, I'm still anxious to be on the ground and smell some fresh air."

"That would be nice," she agreed. "Is your father picking us up at the airport?"

"That's the plan. I can't wait for you to meet him. He's an amazing man."

They hadn't talked about it yet, but Savannah had done enough research on him to know his mother had passed away when he was ten. Knowing there were six Shaughnessy children who all seemed to be very successful, she understood Riley wasn't throwing out a blanket compliment about his father. It was the truth and she couldn't wait to meet him.

"We should probably sit back down," he said, motioning to the seats they'd vacated just moments ago. The chairs were large and covered in soft leather and served as recliners as well. Taking Savannah by the hand, he led her back over and waited for her to take a seat.

Savannah sat down and found her seat belt and Riley took his seat across from her. It was farther away than he wanted to be.

"Could we… Could we maybe go sit in the back again?" she asked nervously.

Riley nodded and they moved the few feet back to

the sofa they had used during takeoff. "How come back here?" he asked softly.

"I'm not much better at landings than I am at take-offs," she said, her head hanging down, her long hair shielding her face. She shrugged. "I feel a little bit safer in the back of the plane."

Reaching out, Riley tucked her hair behind her ear and whispered her name. When she looked up at him, he saw the fear and anxiety of earlier was back. "It's going to be okay. Have I been wrong about this trip yet?"

She shook her head. "I know, I know. Everything has been wonderful, but I'm afraid to let my guard down."

It didn't matter what her reasoning was, she needed him and he was here for her. Wrapping an arm around her shoulders, he pulled her in close. "Whatever you need, Savannah. I told you. Whatever you need from me, I'll do."

Then he watched the play of emotion on her face. God, was it really so easy? Was she *that* trusting of him? It was humbling, and the look of sheer gratitude on her face was almost enough to bring him to his knees. She'd done this for him. Had faced her fears for him. How could she think there wasn't anything he wouldn't do for her in return?

"What do you want, Savannah?" he murmured against her ear. "What do you need?"

Just as she was about to answer, the plane shook a little and she gasped, pulling him closer by clutching his T-shirt.

"It's just a little turbulence. It's normal when we're descending."

She shook her head. "It always sounds like the plane

is going to come apart. I hate it!" She buried her face in the crook of his neck, and he could feel her shaking.

Last time he didn't act until she asked.

Last time he let the decision be hers.

This time he wouldn't.

Without a word, Riley tucked a finger under Savannah's chin, lifted her head, and immediately captured her lips with his. He plundered, he explored, he took. His hand wandered from her chin to the back of her head—anchoring her to him.

She didn't hesitate, just began to kiss him back as hungrily as he was kissing her.

If it were any other time, or any other place, he'd have her naked and beneath him. There was no point in pretending otherwise. Physically, they were beyond attracted to one another. And personally? He really liked her and he knew—as much as she might hate to admit it—she liked him.

She was making him crazy. She challenged him, argued with him, and made him laugh. And right now all he wanted was to take away all her fears and make her happy, make her smile. God, he was getting sappy. And with the way Savannah's tongue was swirling in his mouth, he was getting aroused.

Who was he kidding? He'd been aroused since their first meeting. This kiss was simply adding gasoline to an already out-of-control fire. And even knowing it, he was unable to stop himself. So he let go of his own internal musings and concerns and put everything he had into kissing her and distracting her like she needed him to.

Not that it was a hardship.

She tasted like chocolate and sex—one of his favorite

combinations. He felt her relax beside him as she sighed and then he wrapped her in his arms and simply held her. In his mind, he wanted to let his lips and tongue linger on other parts of her, but for now he knew he had to settle for this—mainly because they'd proven this brand of distraction worked perfectly for her.

There would definitely come a time when he would try other ways to distract her, but it would have to wait until they weren't on an airplane with a crew of people around who could walk over and see them at any minute.

He let that thought settle in—not of the interruptions, but of the possibilities—and smiled to himself. Yeah, he couldn't wait to try them all.

They were on the ground but still on the plane. There was some congestion on the tarmac, and Lisa told them they were going to be delayed about twenty minutes. Savannah didn't mind. They were allowed to get up and move around, and that was really all she wanted—the freedom to move if she needed to.

Her head was on Riley's shoulder and she couldn't stop thinking about their kisses. She knew he was kind of doing it to distract her during the parts of the flight that terrified her, but she had a pretty good feeling he was enjoying himself.

God knew she was.

Then she thought about how he had kissed her at his house that day, and she realized a potential pattern was developing here that, if she wasn't careful, could make their working together very difficult—if not impossible.

What if, during the interview process, Riley used

this tactic to keep her from asking difficult questions? Would she be able to turn him down? Because really, she was only human and the man kissed like a dream. It wouldn't be the worst way to spend her time, but it also wasn't going to help her get her job done.

"You okay?" he asked, his hand lightly combing through her hair.

"Just thinking," she said honestly with a sigh.

"It doesn't sound like you're happy about it. What's going on? Is it because we're stuck on the tarmac?"

She shook her head. "No, this is definitely way different than being on a commercial flight, and it's been glorious."

He chuckled. "That sounds like a good thing."

"It has been. I'm just… I mean, I was thinking how…"

Riley pulled back and shifted them so she had no choice but to look at him. "What? Tell me."

Lord this was embarrassing. "I really…appreciate the way you, um…distracted me here on the plane."

He grinned. "It was my pleasure. Believe me."

Savannah couldn't help but smile at his tone. "But…I don't want it to become a…um…a habit. Do you know what I mean?"

The grin faded and apprehension replaced it. "No, I don't think I do."

"This has been like some sort of reprieve from my normal life for me. I don't travel in private jets or have my every whim catered to. But when we get off this plane, Riley, I need for us to be who we're supposed to be."

"And who is that?"

She sighed with a bit of frustration. "Business

associates of sorts. I'm a reporter, you're the subject. I'll admit it was nice having some time to ease into things and to get to know you a little bit on a personal level, but from this point on, we need to focus on why I'm here. I have a story to write and I can't have you…distracting me."

Slowly, Riley unbuckled his seat belt and put a little distance between them. "And you think I would use this particular distraction method to keep you from doing your job? Why?"

"It's no secret you're doing this interview under duress. I haven't forgotten that."

"So are you!" he snapped. "You told me from the start that you didn't want to do it and that you didn't even like me!"

With a roll of her eyes, Savannah took off her own seat belt and collected her thoughts. "I'll admit I was wrong about you. I'm fine with admitting it. I jumped to conclusions without knowing you, but that doesn't mean I'm not going to write this story the way I see fit. I can't let a few kisses cloud my judgment."

"First of all, they weren't just a few kisses," Riley corrected. "And second of all, I don't believe I asked you to write anything other than the truth! God, do you think so little of me that I would use…sex…to keep you from writing anything that wasn't flattering to me?"

She kind of felt a little bit ashamed that she had. "Riley—"

"No. You know what? This is good. I'm glad this came out now. For a minute there I almost thought we were connecting on some level, but maybe…maybe I was wrong about you."

"What do you mean?"

"I don't know anything about you or your credentials. For all I know, this is your…your thing. Maybe you have a thing for rock stars and celebrities and this is how you conduct your interviews. You know, get them to let down their guard, get them hot and bothered, and then pull back, saying how things can't go any further or it will disrupt the integrity of your precious story!"

"That's not what I do!"

He stood and was pacing now. "How do I know that? I only have your word for it! Maybe I need to make some calls and find out for certain. For all I know, Savannah, you've played this game a dozen times before and because no guy wants bad press, they go along with answering whatever you throw at them or they'd get hit with some kind of slander!"

She jumped to her feet, full of fury. "Is that really the kind of person you think I am?"

"I didn't until a few minutes ago! I really thought we were connecting, Savannah. I was really enjoying our time together. I never would have asked you to compromise on anything where this damn interview was concerned because of my attraction to you!" He spun away, raking a hand through his hair.

She was about to reply when the plane began to move. She immediately sat back down and clung to the armrest of the sofa. Riley didn't make any attempt to come near her. Instead he turned to move away.

He faced her one last time before he did. "You'll get your damn story. All of it. You'll have access to me and my family for as long as you need it. Don't make me regret that I trusted you with them because if I find out you've done anything to upset or betray them, I'll make sure this story never sees the light of day. Are we clear?"

All she could do was nod and watch as he stalked to the front of the plane, leaving her alone. Leaning forward, she dropped her head into her hands and fought the urge to cry. How could he think she did this sort of thing all the time? Didn't he realize how hard she was struggling with the fact it had happened between them? No other subject—famous or not—had ever turned her on so much.

Well, now she'd gone and put her foot in her mouth and had to live with the consequences. It was probably for the best. Riley Shaughnessy was nothing like she envisioned and was suddenly everything she wanted. But as he'd just pointed out, they were vastly different and clearly there were trust issues—on both their parts.

The rest of the month wasn't going to be easy—particularly while she was spending time here in North Carolina with his family. With any luck, she'd be able to get what she needed for the piece from them quickly and find an excuse to head back to L.A. where they could finish up either by phone or whenever Riley returned.

Thinking about returning to L.A. without him brought on a wave of anxiety that had nothing to do with the man and everything to do with her means of travel. She hated that. Hated how her fears were so strong that they almost obliterated the things she should be focused on.

The plane came to a stop, and a minute later Lisa appeared to tell her they were able to deplane and that her luggage would be waiting for her on the ground.

Savannah thanked her and stood. Slowly she moved across the plane and collected her purse and her computer bag—not that she'd needed either of them during the flight—and walked to the front of the plane. Looking out the door, she saw Riley was already on the ground talking and laughing with a member of the flight crew.

The sun was starting to go down—it was after seven North Carolina time—but the temperatures were mild. Slowly she made her way down the stairs and stood next to Riley while they waited for the rest of their bags. She smiled softly at the crew as they all came down the steps and thanked them all for a wonderful flight.

Someone stepped forward as soon as their luggage was out and immediately put it on a cart for them. Riley motioned for her to follow him into the small airport. "Is this a private airport?" she asked.

He shook his head. "No, but it's one of the closest to home, and even this will have us driving for an hour." His tone was pleasant but lacked any of the warmth he'd always shown with her. "If you're hungry, we can stop for something to eat on the way home."

Her appetite was pretty much gone.

Riley didn't push her for an answer, and soon they were inside the air-conditioned terminal. As she took a minute to get her bearings, she knew the instant he spotted his father. His pace picked up and his entire body seemed to relax.

"Dad!" he called out as he moved farther away from her toward the man who clearly meant the world to him.

"Hey! You made it! I heard you were a little detained out there." Ian Shaughnessy hugged his son fiercely for a minute before taking a step back and looking at him. "You're looking good, Riley. I hate how L.A. seems to agree with you so much. You know I'm always hoping you'll move back home."

Riley chuckled. "I'll have to retire sometime, right?"

Ian's eyes went wide for minute. "Don't toy with me." He chuckled. "I probably won't live to see the day you retire. You've got too much talent in you to do it any time soon."

"Oh, stop," Riley said before turning and facing Savannah, his expression going neutral. "Dad, this is Savannah Daly. She's a reporter and she'll be with us for a couple of weeks doing the article I told you about."

Ian looked at Savannah and then Riley and then back again. "It's a pleasure to meet you, Savannah."

"Thank you, Mr. Shaughnessy. I appreciate you being willing to have me around for a few weeks."

"Nonsense. And call me Ian," he said with an easy grin that reminded Savannah so much of Riley's.

Not that he was grinning right now. Far from it. If she had to choose a word for it, she'd say he was scowling. Fiercely.

Once again Ian looked between the two of them before clearing his throat. "Well, let's get your things and get moving." When Savannah went to grab her suitcase, Ian stopped her. "I've got it."

"Thank you," Savannah murmured, almost blushing.

"You don't have to do that, Dad," Riley said. "You're not here to wait on her."

Ian stopped in his tracks. "I believe you were raised with better manners than that, Riley," he said firmly. "Since when does a gentleman let a lady carry her own luggage?"

"It's on wheels," Riley pointed out and flinched

when Ian slapped him upside the head. "Ow! What was that for?"

"I should have done that more when all of you were kids," he grumbled. With Savannah's suitcase rolling behind him, he simply walked ahead of them toward the terminal exit.

Savannah couldn't help but chuckle, even when Riley turned to her and glared.

"You think that's funny?"

"As a matter of fact, I do," she said, unable to keep from grinning.

"Yeah, well...don't," he said and walked ahead of her.

She stood rooted to the spot for a minute, enjoying the view of Riley from the back. It was just as fine as the view of him from the front. There was an uphill battle coming and it had already begun on some levels. He was pissed at her and he was going to make sure his family was on their guard around her. Well, that was all fine and well. She'd win them over and then he'd see he was wrong.

About everything.

Riley stopped and spun around, looking at her with annoyance. "Are you coming or what?"

Nodding, Savannah put on her game face and caught up to him. He looked at her oddly before the two of them began to walk to catch up to Ian.

"I have food back at the house," Ian said when they got to his truck, "but I'd be more than happy to stop someplace for dinner on the way home."

"That's very sweet of you," Savannah said. "But it isn't necessary."

"Believe me, taking a beautiful woman to dinner is no trouble," Ian said with a smile. He had driven his pickup truck to come and get them. It wasn't particularly practical—or clean—but it was his only mode of transportation. "Sorry about the cramped space. I was going to borrow Zoe's car to pick you up but I got hung up at work and it was all I could do to get home and grab a shower before I had to get on the road to get here."

"It's not a big deal, Dad," Riley assured him.

Savannah readily agreed until she climbed in and found herself sandwiched between the two Shaughnessys. As much as she wiggled and shifted, she was thigh-to-thigh with them. Ian looked over with an apologetic smile.

"I promise to have a roomier car for the two of you to use while you're here," he said as he started the truck and pulled out of the parking spot.

"We're fine, Dad. Really," Riley said as his arm came around Savannah's shoulders and came to a rest along the back of the seat. "Whose car are we going to have?"

"Quinn's taking care of that. He said he had the perfect car for you. He and Anna were going to drop it off at the house tonight after he's done with work. If you want, you can call him and see if they'd like to meet us for dinner."

Riley shook his head. "No. That's okay. I'm not feeling overly social tonight. I think a nice dinner and a quiet night at home sounds like the perfect end to this day."

Yikes. Savannah had to fight the urge to elbow him in the ribs and ask him if maybe he wanted to take up acting! For all the ways he was being dramatic, he seemed to have missed his calling! She muttered, "Oh, brother," under her breath and could feel the heat of Riley's stare. She simply turned and glared back. If he wanted to act like a child, more power to him. She, on the other hand, was going to charm the hell out of his family.

"So tell me, Ian—" she began, but Riley instantly cut her off.

"We're all off the clock, Savannah. You can start your interview tomorrow. Can't you at least give the man a chance to get home before you start hammering him with questions?"

On the other side of her, she could tell Ian wanted to speak but she beat him to the punch.

"I was going to ask your father what the local food was like here. I'm primarily familiar with the Midwest and West Coast. I've never been east." She shrugged and smiled sweetly. "Just curious."

Riley's frown deepened as Savannah turned and put all her attention on the elder Shaughnessy.

For the remainder of the ride, Ian shared with her some of his favorite local foods and restaurants and even a few recipes. By the time they pulled up to one of the places he had mentioned, Savannah was starving.

Riley held out a hand to help her out of the truck, but she refused. As soon as her feet hit the pavement, she walked over and linked her arm through Ian's and happily walked inside. Riley followed a minute later—with a hat pulled low on his head—and it amazed Savannah he was able to walk into a place like this without anyone really noticing him. Even with the lame disguise.

By the time they were seated and having drinks, she was almost able to forget he was there. Ian was chatting her ear off about his business and the history of the seafood restaurant. If the rest of the family was as charming as Ian and Riley, there was no doubt she was going to be in love with them all by the time she was done with her story.

―᚜᚜᚜―

It was one thing for the locals to ignore Riley when he was in town. He was used to it. He appreciated it. Other than the waitress asking for his autograph, dinner had been fairly uneventful for him.

But having Savannah ignore him? That one was getting a little harder to deal with.

Granted, he had thrown the gauntlet down before they had gotten off the plane; he just hadn't expected her to take it to such an extreme. Looking over at her, he could only shake his head. He had to hand it to her, she was freaking delightful. She had his father eating out of the palm of her hand, and not once had any part of the conversation had to do with him, his celebrity status, or the interview.

And what was becoming more of an issue for him was how unbelievably chatty his father was! Ian Shaughnessy was a man of few words—normally—but for some reason, he hadn't stopped talking to Savannah since they got in the truck! When did this happen?

It wasn't as if Riley hadn't been around. With the way his brothers were all suddenly getting married or engaged, moving and having babies, he'd been home more in the past two years than he had in the last ten! And not once during that time had he noticed his father looking so…happy, relaxed, and just so… *Gah!* He had no idea how to describe it, but his father looked about twenty years younger and a part of Riley felt like the old guy was flirting with Savannah!

Unable to help himself, he murmured a quick "excuse me" and walked to the back of the restaurant where the restrooms were and out the back door, pulling out his phone and dialing Quinn's number.

"Hey! You've only been in the state for what—fifteen minutes?—and you're already calling me?" Quinn said with a laugh. "What's up?"

"Dad," Riley said. "What in the world has happened to Dad?"

"What are you talking about? We just saw him yesterday."

Great. Now Riley felt like an idiot because he was probably blowing things out of proportion. "I don't know. He's just…different."

"Ah…so you got Mr. Sociable out with you, huh?"

"Mister…what?" Riley asked with confusion.

"Yeah, it's gonna take you a couple of days to get used to it. Seems like dating Martha really got Dad to come out of his shell. It's kind of funny sometimes because it seems so out of character for him, but trust me, once you're done getting weirded out, you get used to it."

"I don't think that's possible."

"What's he doing? Singing karaoke? Flirting with the waitress?"

"How'd you know we're out to dinner?"

"Unless the freeway moved into Dad's living room, I'm guessing you're out to eat someplace. I can hear the traffic in the background. And the music."

"Oh."

"So come on. What's he doing?" Quinn asked with a chuckle. "It's a waitress, isn't it? That one was hard to watch the first few times, but they all seem to just eat it up. Anna says he's adorable but I'm not seeing it. No guy should watch his dad flirt. It's just wrong."

"He's flirting with Savannah," Riley said with disgust.

"Seriously? The reporter? Wow... Is she flirting back? How old is she?"

Riley raked a hand through his hair and paced behind the restaurant. "Maybe flirting isn't the right word. He just... He hasn't shut up since he picked us up! And she's all...giggly and hanging on his every word and then when she talks he just sits there grinning like a loon. It's weird!"

Quinn started to laugh.

"What's so freaking funny?"

"How old is this chick?"

"What does that have to do with anything?"

"Just humor me," Quinn said.

"My age," Riley mumbled.

"That's what I thought. Okay, for starters, stop pouting."

"I'm not—"

"Stop pouting," Quinn interrupted, "and relax. Dad's just trying to be charming. He's not flirting or hitting on...what was her name?"

"Savannah."

"Right. He's not hitting on Savannah. I think he's just finally at a point where he's comfortable talking to women again. Keep an eye on him. It will probably take Owen the same amount of time before he's comfortable doing it too."

"Shut up," Riley said, but he kind of chuckled. "Okay, so any other weird Dad things I should know?"

"Nothing too bad except he gets absolutely goofy

around Connor. Brace yourself. I'm telling you, the amount of baby talk he's willing to do to get that kid to smile is almost embarrassing."

"Connor's barely three months old. Do babies smile that young?"

"Dude, you're totally asking the wrong guy. Just… be prepared."

"Well, all right then." Riley sighed. "Am I going to see you tomorrow? Dad said everyone was coming for dinner."

"Yeah, that got changed to Sunday because of everyone's work schedule, and as far as I know, everyone will be there except Darcy. She's coming in next weekend for the christening."

"What christening?"

"Geez, do you even talk to anyone? Connor's christening! Hugh and Aubrey wanted to have him baptized here at St. Mary's since it's where we all were. Something about keeping with tradition. It's going to be on Saturday afternoon. "

"That's cool. I guess."

"A church is a church, but that's just me. Anyway, your reporter will get plenty of Shaughnessy family together time for her story at this rate."

"Great."

Quinn chuckled again. "I can tell you're not thrilled with the whole thing already, but Anna just walked in the door and I'd rather talk to her than listen to you whine. I'll see you Sunday, bro."

"Yeah. Fine." Riley put his phone away and groaned. So far, nothing was going according to plan, and he was no longer certain spending a couple of weeks here was a good idea. He was just about to walk back inside when he heard a familiar sound. Smiling, he spotted the three women who had just come outside to get to their car.

"Oh my God! Are you Riley Shaughnessy?" one of them asked. "Can I get your autograph?"

"Can I get a picture with you?" asked another.

He was willing to oblige.

At least someone was paying attention to him.

Chapter 6

BY THE TIME SATURDAY NIGHT ROLLED AROUND, Savannah wasn't sure if she was coming or going. Riley had remained distant, and when she tried to sit down with him earlier in the day to do some preliminary questions regarding his family so she could be better informed, he told her she'd be better off talking to his father.

Not that she minded. Ian reminded her a lot of her own dad and he was very easy to talk to. And rather than stay around the house, he had even taken Savannah out to show her around town and introduced her to what seemed like a hundred different people! Everywhere they went, Ian knew somebody, and from what Savannah could see, he and his family were well loved and respected in their community.

And the stories she'd heard about Riley had been great! It seemed that once Ian had explained who Savannah was and why she was in town, everyone had a story to share, from memories of hearing him sing for the first time to how popular he was in school and the plays and productions he starred in. She could tell that his community was definitely proud of their hometown celebrity.

Meanwhile, Riley had opted to stay home. No doubt he was pouting or thinking of ways to make her life difficult, but she refused to let him see how much it was bothering her. When she and Ian had arrived back at the house Saturday night with a pizza, Riley had claimed he'd already eaten and had gone up to his room. Luckily, Ian's lady friend Martha had driven over to join them so there was at least another new face to get to know.

"Savannah, you should have seen this house about a year ago. It was stuck in a bit of a time warp," Martha was saying as they were eating dinner. "Ian's daughter-in-law Zoe and I work together and she didn't feel right about being the one to work out the design and decorating and asked me. I'm telling you, I have had the most fun here!"

Ian was smiling and gazing at Martha with such affection that even if she didn't already know they were involved, she would be able to see it just by watching them.

"With four bedrooms and no one living here besides Ian—and Darcy when she's home on a break from school—we decided to turn the boys' old bedrooms into guest rooms. That's why you now have a queen-size bed to sleep in rather than a twin or a bunk bed!" Martha said, winking at Ian.

"The rooms are beautiful and I could tell they were newly done." Looking over at Ian, Savannah smiled. "I'm sure when everyone's home, it's still a little hard for them to get used to all the changes."

He nodded. "Hugh took it the worst, which is funny since he used to be the one who came home the least." He chuckled. "But now everyone's settling in closer to home and there's not as much of a need for everyone to be under one roof. But if we do, the married ones can sleep together at least."

"You're going to need a nursery soon for Connor,"

Martha said. "And soon you'll have Aidan and Zoe's baby, and you just know Quinn and Anna aren't going to be too far behind."

"I thought about it," Ian said with a serene smile. "I almost considered converting Darcy's room, but she still has two more years of school and she comes home on her breaks so I don't want to take that away from her just yet. Then I thought about converting one of the other bedrooms into a nursery, but then I'd lose a guest room."

"It's a good thing you have me, Ian Shaughnessy," Martha said with a grin, "because if you're feeling adventurous, I think I have a solution."

"Uh-oh." He chuckled as he reached for Martha's hand and squeezed it. "Go easy on me."

"You have two living spaces down here. We re-did the formal one and that's the one you primarily use when everyone's here. The one in the back of the house is a wonderful space. I was thinking we make it into a master suite for you—add a small extension out the back for a proper master bath—and then the master bedroom upstairs can be turned into a nursery. What do you think?" She looked at him with eyes full of warmth and hope.

"I think it sounds expensive and messy!" He laughed. "Although I think it would totally be worth it. I don't suppose you have any figures worked out for it already?" he teased.

"You know me so well," Martha replied.

Savannah sat back in awe as she watched the two of them. It would seem they were in sync with one another, and it amazed her that here was Martha essentially trying to reconfigure Ian's home and he was totally on board with it! She couldn't imagine going into Riley's home and telling him how to do it over. It would be awkward and she wouldn't feel like it was her place and…

She mentally kicked herself. Why did that have to be the example her mind immediately went to? There would never be a reason for her to do anything in Riley's house. It wasn't hers and it wasn't likely she'd ever be going there again.

That was a depressing thought.

Just thinking of the view from his back deck and the pool and the game room and… She sighed. That house didn't need any work. It was perfect.

It just needed a woman's touch. Maybe some colored pillows in the living room and some flower arrangements scattered about. And some artwork that wasn't related to Riley's music career and…

She was doing it again.

"What do you think, Savannah?" Martha asked. "What do you think of moving the master suite to the main floor?"

"Oh…um…I think it could be great. This way when you do have everyone home for an overnight visit, they'll primarily be upstairs with the kids and you get to still have your privacy down here. I think it's the best of both worlds."

Martha smiled and looked over at Ian. "I like her. I like her a lot!"

Riley thought he was surely going to see his brain soon because of all the eye rolling he was doing.

Traitorous family.

Each and every one of them was almost giddy to share embarrassing stories about him with Savannah, and she was clearly enjoying herself. Her recorder was going and she was laughing and writing things down, and he wanted nothing more than to tell everyone just to shut up and leave.

And then he'd kiss Savannah senseless until she couldn't think of another damn question to ask. All she'd be able to do would be to beg him to take her to bed.

Yeah, that need, that desire hadn't gone anywhere. *Dammit.*

But if he took a minute to be completely honest, Riley would have to admit that part of his annoyance with his family—particularly his brothers—was how they had something that he wanted. Stable relationships. Aidan and Zoe were solid—just one look at them and anyone could see it in the way Aidan lazily played with Zoe's long red hair or the way Zoe would reach out and fix a wayward lock of his brother's dark hair. It was enough to make Riley want to sigh like a damn schoolgirl.

And even more infuriating was watching Quinn and Anna. Always the gruffest and most unrefined of the family, his brother was now almost sappy in his attention to his soon-to-be wife. Anna—who had always been more of a tomboy when they were growing up—was now this beautiful woman, and Quinn took every opportunity to gush about it. And while Riley could admit that gone was the blond-haired, brown-eyed girl who used to kick all of their asses at almost any sport, to him she was still the same sweet girl.

Just with a kick-ass figure.

And Quinn had given him quite the glare the first time Riley had dared to linger on it.

Walking into the kitchen under the guise of getting a beer, he glared at Quinn, Anna, Aidan, and Zoe—all of whom were currently chatting with Savannah. Still. Weren't they done yet? Hadn't they shared enough? Maybe he should have set some parameters with them beforehand. Without a word he stalked back into the living room just as Owen was coming in the front door. Finally. An ally.

Owen put his small suitcase down next to the door before coming over to hug Riley. "How are things going so far? Are you surviving the interview?"

Riley pulled back and made a face. "Barely."

Taking a minute, Owen studied him. "Do you know where I'm sleeping tonight?"

"No idea. You're probably sharing a room with me, but it's only the one bed now, so no cuddling."

Owen made a face. "Why would I cuddle with you?"

"I'm just kidding," Riley huffed.

Without a word, Owen walked back over to the door and grabbed his suitcase and then headed for the stairs. He looked over at Riley and motioned for him to follow. Once they were in Riley's room, Owen shut the door and put his case down.

"Now I know something's really wrong. What happened?"

"What are you talking about?"

"You just snapped at me downstairs. You never snap at me." Owen sat on the bed and looked at his brother. "So what happened? Do you not like the reporter?"

Riley sighed and sat down beside him. "Yes. No."

He growled. "I kind of like her a little too much." He told Owen everything that had happened since meeting Savannah. "I know I overreacted and I didn't really mean the things I said. And now? Now I don't know how to get things back to the way they were before."

"Seems to me it would be pretty pointless to go back to that point."

"Why?"

"Because you're both a little wary of one another. Is that what you want to go back to?"

"Well…no. But I think we need to go back to the easy camaraderie so we can move forward."

"You're not going to accomplish that by avoiding her. It seems to me from what you just told me, you've essentially pushed her off on Dad. Now you're up here and she's down there with everyone, and the only one who seems bothered by the whole situation is you. If you keep this up, things are going to be even more awkward when you're finally alone tomorrow and officially start the interview."

"I thought you were going to be here for a few days. You have your suitcase with you."

Owen shook his head. "Only because the drive is so long. I wanted to be here today to support you, but I'm leaving in the morning after breakfast." He smiled. "So make sure you wake up before noon."

Riley chuckled at his brother's attempt at humor. "I'll have you know when I'm not on tour, I get up at a normal hour."

"Define normal."

"Very funny." Riley collapsed back on the bed and closed his eyes. "I have to go down there, don't I." It wasn't a question.

"You do."

"And I have to join the conversation and even laugh at myself."

"You do."

Riley opened his eyes and looked at Owen. "What if she, you know, isn't ready to forgive me for being a jerk?"

"She will eventually. Just don't push."

For the life of him Riley couldn't believe he was asking his brother for advice about a woman, but what choice did he have? Rising, he stood and stretched. "Come on. Let's get this over with. You're going to help me break the ice."

Sheer panic covered Owen's face. "Me? Why?"

"I'll bring you into the kitchen and introduce you to Savannah and when you sit down, I'll sit down. I'll be there like a buffer. I'll sit between you if you'd like."

"She's going to want to talk to me directly, isn't she," Owen said. It wasn't a question.

"She is."

"She's going to ask a lot of personal questions and want me to answer them."

Riley chuckled. "She is."

"This sucks," Owen said, coming to his feet.

A bark of laughter was Riley's only response. That was the closest Owen had ever come to cursing. But instead of pointing it out and making him feel awkward, Riley walked over and hugged him. "Come on. Let's get this over with."

"Or we can leave. No one knows I'm here yet. We can just get in my car and go someplace else for a while."

"Uh-uh…we're a team. You and me, bro. I know I

can get through this because you're there beside me."
And he meant it. They were different in so many ways,
but they were twins, and there wasn't another person
Riley wanted by his side when things were tough.

"Remind me to call you next time I have to interact
with a group of fifty students and want to run away. I'll
make you stand up there with me."

"I don't think it's quite the same. I enjoy talking to
groups of people and socializing, remember?"

"Oh…right."

"We can do this. And if we're lucky, Hugh and Aubrey
will be here soon with Connor and distract everyone for
a little while."

"Isn't it wrong to make an infant take the fall for us?"

"Don't be silly, Connor's not taking the fall. He probably loves all the attention. We're doing him a favor, really."

Owen didn't look like he understood or believed him,
but luckily he didn't argue. Together they left the room
and went to face the crowd.

Once in the kitchen, all conversation seemed to stop at
their appearance. Aidan and Quinn jumped up to say hello
to Owen, while the women sat and smiled. Riley looked
over at Savannah and knew she was trying to find any
similarities between him and his twin. Other than their
dark hair color, she wasn't going to find any.

"Owen," Riley said, stepping closer to the large table.
"This is Savannah Daly." His brother's blush was instantaneous and though he shook Savannah's hand, Owen
never met her gaze.

"It's a pleasure to meet you, Owen," Savannah
said. "Have a seat. We're all just getting to know one
another." She patted the chair beside her and looked

mildly miffed when Riley took it instead while Owen took the one next to him.

"I'm sure you're all having a lot of fun at my expense," Riley said, forcing himself to relax. "Don't stop talking on my account."

"Oh, we won't," Quinn said with an evil grin and then winced when Anna playfully smacked him in the back of the head.

Savannah interrupted. "I would love to get Owen's take on what we were just talking about."

"What were you just talking about?" Riley asked, blocking Savannah's view of his brother.

She frowned at him. "Aidan was just sharing about how you were always singing something—how you were rarely just sitting around quietly."

"Dude, you even sang when you were in the bathroom," Aidan said with a chuckle.

Now Riley frowned. "*That* you had to share?"

"She asked if you sang a lot as a kid. What was I supposed to say?"

"How about just yes?"

"Okay, boys," Zoe said, unable to hide her own amusement, "no fighting." She put her hand on Aidan's shoulder. "Be nice. I'm sure Riley could just as easily be sharing some of your more embarrassing life stories."

Aidan instantly pretended to zip his lip.

"So, Owen, you're the closest to Riley. Did you think he sang a lot when you were kids?" Savannah asked.

"I guess," he said quietly.

Savannah looked at Riley, who had a fairly smug smile on his face, before returning her attention to Owen. "What about you? Do you sing at all?"

He shook his head. "No. I...I don't sing at all."

"Not even in the car?" Quinn said lightly, as if sensing his brother's discomfort.

Owen chuckled and everyone seemed to relax. Riley was relieved when Savannah seemed to take the hint and went back to conversing with the rest of the family.

Anna stood and refreshed her drink, asking if anyone else needed anything. "I wonder when Hugh and Aubrey are going to get here," she said as she sat back down.

"It's nice how you pretend it's them you want to see," Quinn said as he pulled her close and kissed her. "You know you just want to hold Connor."

"Well, get in line," Zoe said with a big smile. "I call dibs."

Anna laughed. "You can't call dibs on a baby! That's just wrong!"

"You're just mad I did it first," Zoe countered. "I'll share, I promise. But I need the practice."

"Oh, stop. You're only three months or so along. You have plenty of time to practice. I just need my baby fix and then he's all yours."

"Which means you'll hold him until he poops and then hand him over to me," Zoe said with mock offense. "Nice try."

"Ladies, ladies, ladies," Hugh Shaughnessy said as he strode into the room with his son in his arms. "There is plenty of this baby—and his poop—to go around."

Everyone jumped up—including Riley and Savannah—and he found himself instinctively placing his hand on her lower back. She immediately stiffened, but Riley didn't remove it.

Aubrey joined them, introductions were made, and

soon they were all around the table including his father and Martha, who had also just arrived. It was a good thing the table could seat twelve, but it was still a bit tight. Riley moved his chair closer to Savannah's when they sat and even draped his arm along the back of her seat.

"So, Savannah," Aubrey said as she sat down, tossing her long blond hair over her shoulder, "has this group overwhelmed you yet?"

Savannah laughed. "No, not yet. Although I'm a little fascinated by it all."

"How so?" Aubrey asked.

"I'm an only child and even though most of my friends had siblings, I never experienced a large family like yours. I'm enjoying figuring out all the different personalities and quirks."

"I know exactly how you feel," Aubrey said before anyone else could chime in. "I'm an only child, too, but I was very sheltered growing up. I had no idea families even liked one another until I met Hugh."

Zoe raised her hand and smiled. "Only child as well. Unlike Aubrey, I knew families could be close, but these guys here? They're one in a million. I think I fell a little in love with each of them right from the start."

"Hey!" Aidan interrupted. "You're not allowed to be in love with anyone but me!"

She leaned over and kissed him. "You know what I mean!"

Aidan looked at Savannah and winked. "I do, but it's fun to tease her."

"You've heard all about us," Anna said. "Why don't you tell us something about yourself?"

Beside him, Riley saw Savannah squirm and knew

she wasn't normally on the receiving end of the questions. He smiled and waited to see how she'd handle it.

"Like I said, I'm an only child. My parents had me a little later in life and although I know I should have wished for a sibling, I was kind of okay by myself. My dad was in the military and we moved around a lot when I was little before finally settling down in Kansas."

Hmm…there was information Riley hadn't known about her.

"It's where my mom's family was and when we moved there when I was twelve, it was weird finally having one place to call home. We would still visit my dad's relatives, who lived all over the Midwest and California, but I think after a while, Mom just wanted to be able to sleep in her own bed for extended periods of time."

"I can relate to that," Hugh said and then looked offended when everyone started laughing at him. "What? What did I say?"

"You were the king of not even having your own bed," Aubrey said. "Up until a year ago, you didn't even have a place of your own. You kept apartments at your resorts."

"Yes, and those were my places," he corrected. "Not everyone has to have just one home, you know."

"Yeah," Quinn said, sounding as if he was defending his older brother. "But you took it to the point of being weird." He looked at Savannah. "He had a dozen apartments, but they were all decorated exactly the same. If you didn't look out the window, you wouldn't know which resort you were at."

Hugh frowned. "Screw you."

"Good comeback, buddy." Quinn laughed.

"Weren't we talking about Riley?" Hugh grumbled.

"No, we were talking about Savannah." Riley grinned and felt a sense of satisfaction when Savannah glared at him.

"I went to college for journalism but couldn't find work, so I went to night school and got my cosmetology license and found myself working in salons all over L.A."

"Seriously?" Zoe asked. "That's awesome!"

Savannah smiled. "It was a lot of fun and I met a ton of amazing people. It's how I got the job with the magazine."

Riley's head snapped toward hers. *What?* "How did that happen?" he asked.

She relayed the story about her cutting hair for the band Tommy was getting ready to interview. She shrugged. "He said I had some great insight and gave me his card and told me to come and see him when I wanted to write instead of cutting hair. I went to see him the next day."

"Wow!" Aubrey said. "Talk about the right place at the right time."

"Oh, I know," Savannah replied. "I am so thankful every day that he found me. Not that I wasn't loving my cosmetology stuff, but writing is my passion."

"So, who's the most famous person you ever interviewed?" Anna asked.

Riley tuned out at that point. It occurred to him just how much he didn't know about Savannah. Sure, they'd had a lot of fun in the few days since they'd met, but now he realized it was all superficial and on-the-surface stuff. She was going to learn a lot of intimate details about his life, and he was going to walk away not knowing anything more than he did right now.

Unless he changed the way things were going.

His hand landed on her shoulder. She was wearing a blue ribbed tank top that left her shoulders pretty much bare. Gently, his fingers began to stroke her soft skin and he was pleased when she didn't pull away.

He'd been a major jerk.

A colossal moron who put his foot in his mouth and now needed to take it out and eat some crow.

Looking over at her, he watched as she smiled and laughed with his family, and it gave him hope—hope that he hadn't messed things up too much. And if he had, he knew he had at least nine people who'd be willing to help him out.

Turning his head, he looked over at Owen, who wasn't smiling. Riley gave him a quizzical look but his brother simply turned away. He made a mental note to get him alone later and see what was bothering him.

———

Dinner had been like nothing Savannah had ever experienced before. It was loud and boisterous and delicious and it was amazing to her how she felt like she'd known this family her entire life. She loved it. And everyone was sure to include her in every topic of conversation.

Except Owen.

He was proving to be a tougher nut to crack than she'd thought. Riley and the rest of the family had warned her he was shy and he had a habit of talking in scientific facts and figures, but he wasn't even doing that.

Now as everyone chipped in to get the dishes done and the kitchen cleaned, Savannah looked around and noticed Riley had gone to take a call with his publicist and Owen was slipping out onto the back deck. With a quick check, she hoped no one would notice if she followed him.

The sun was going down and the temperature was pretty cool for a summer night, but she didn't mind. Stepping up beside him at the railing, she smiled. "I've always loved a cool breeze on a summer night."

Owen nodded.

"Dinner was amazing. Do you always have such massive meals?"

Again, he nodded.

She immediately realized if she wanted him to talk, she'd have to present him with a question he couldn't give a simple yes-or-no response to. "Why don't you like me?"

Owen's head snapped toward hers. "What?"

She shrugged. "I know when someone likes me and when they don't. I can tell you don't. I'm just curious as to why."

He looked around nervously. "I...I...don't really know you. How could I possibly form an opinion about whether I like you? Normally statistics say that every encounter presents an opportunity to meet people, network, and expand your professional contacts by making a positive first impression. You've got just seven seconds—but if you handle it well, seven seconds are all you need." He shrugged. "I don't necessarily believe that. Sometimes it takes much longer."

"So you're saying you need to have more time before you can decide whether you like me?" she asked hopefully.

Owen sighed. He straightened his glasses and faced her before taking a fortifying breath. "I want to like you, Miss Daly. I really do. But you've upset Riley. I take personal offense at that. My brother is one of the kindest people I've ever known, and I'm not just saying it because he's my twin. When we were growing up, he always defended me. I got made fun of a lot—I still do—and he has always been my champion. I never had the opportunity to do the same for him." If anything, he stood a little taller. "Well, I am now."

"Owen," she began softly, placing her hand on his arm and smiling when he stiffened, "I didn't mean to upset Riley. It was never my intention. I'll admit we got off on the wrong foot and then things were great and then…" She shrugged. "Believe me, I want things to go back to the way they were before…well, before things got out of hand and we both said a lot of stupid stuff."

She shook her head and pulled her hand away. "I didn't want to like Riley. And I told him so from the beginning. I formed an opinion of him that turned out to be untrue, and I've apologized to him for it."

"But you like him," Owen said firmly.

Unable to lie to him, she nodded. "I do. A lot. More than I should."

And then Owen seemed to transform right before her eyes. At first glance, Owen Shaughnessy was your typical scientist—his dark hair askew, the dark glasses and the nondescript outfit of khakis and a button-down shirt. But when he looked up at her this time? It was as if she was seeing him for the first time. His stance relaxed and he smiled shyly. "He used to sing in his sleep."

Savannah smiled back at him. "Really?"

He nodded. "I don't think he ever knew he did it, but I had the bottom bunk and would hear him."

"Did he have a favorite song he would sing, or was it random?"

Pausing, Owen looked back toward the house before facing Savannah again. "If I tell you, you can't use it anywhere in your story, and you can't tell Riley you know it."

She frowned. "Why not?" And then she stopped and held her hand up. "Maybe you shouldn't tell me then. I don't want you betraying your brother. That wouldn't be right."

If anything, Owen's smile broadened. "It's 'Over the Rainbow.' If he shares with you the importance of that song, then you'll know."

"Know what?" she asked, confused.

"Trust me, you'll just know." And with that cryptic little statement, Owen turned and walked back into the house, leaving Savannah alone outside and more confused than ever.

Riley happened to be standing by the back door when Owen came back inside. "What was that all about?" he asked.

Owen shrugged. "I needed to get out of the chaos in here for a few minutes, and Savannah followed me out."

Everything in him tensed. "What did she say to you? Did she upset you? Do I need to…?"

Owen chuckled and, in a very uncharacteristic move, leaned in and hugged Riley tightly. "Believe it or not, sometimes I can handle things on my own."

When he pulled back, Riley frowned. "I don't understand."

"She's really not so bad. If you think about it, it's not so unusual that you had a misunderstanding. You barely know one another. Don't try to move things along so quickly, Ry," Owen said, taking a step back. "Sometimes you can miss out on something amazing by being in a hurry."

And just like he had with Savannah, Owen walked away, leaving Riley confused. He didn't have much time to contemplate his brother's words because Savannah was coming through the doorway. "Hey," he said softly.

"Hi." She looked around nervously as if searching for an ally or an escape route.

Reaching out, Riley took one of Savannah's hands in his and gently pulled her right back out the door and onto the deck with him. When they were at the railing, he stopped and faced her.

"I'm sorry."

She looked relieved as her shoulders sagged and a smile began to cross her lips. "Me too. I...I never should have—"

"Shh..." He placed a finger over her lips and almost groaned at their softness. "There's no need for us to rehash it. I want us to get along and we need to be able to sit down with one another starting tomorrow and talk civilly."

"I hope we're being more than civil, Riley," she said softly. "I know we're business associates, but that doesn't mean we can't be friends."

Friends. It was like the kiss of death. So not the way he envisioned this conversation going. Not that he was expecting her to throw herself in his arms—although that would be awesome—but he had hoped she would maybe want a little more.

Sometimes you can miss out on something amazing by being in a hurry.

Great. Now he was again forced to take advice about a woman from his non-dating twin. How had he come to this?

"I'd like that a lot," he forced himself to say. It wasn't friendship he ultimately wanted from Savannah, but if it was what she was offering right now, then that's what he'd take.

That seemed to relax her even more. "I'm glad. I've been having such a wonderful time with your family, but I felt like there was so much…tension between us, and I hated it."

"Me too."

"Okay then," she said with a smile. "Does this mean we can go back inside and visit some more with your family and you won't be shooting daggers at me at every question I ask?"

He laughed. "I don't know. It depends."

"On what?"

"Are you just going to keep asking embarrassing questions?"

She laughed with him. "Maybe they seem embarrassing to you, but it's all helping me figure out how you became the man you are now."

Unable to help himself, he stepped in closer, his hands instantly going to her hips. "Or maybe you could just wait and ask me. I'd gladly tell you. Or show you."

The urge to kiss her was almost overwhelming, and if

he wasn't mistaken, Savannah just inched a little closer to him.

Violet eyes looked up at him—part wonder, part humor. "Somehow I don't think you'd share all the good stuff."

"Sweetheart, for you, I'd share whatever you asked."

Sighing, she leaned into him. "We're doing it again."

"Doing what?" he whispered, inhaling the scent of her—light and floral and capable of making him crazy.

"This. It's almost as if we can't get too close or we end up like this."

"I'm not complaining," he said and skimmed his fingers across her cheek.

"Riley… I—"

"Hey, you guys!" Hugh yelled out the door. "Dessert's on the table."

Riley was able to see just enough of his brother in the dim light to catch the knowing smirk on his face.

"Saved by the bell," Riley said, stepping away and linking his hand with hers once again.

———⁓⁓⁓———

The rest of the evening had a different tone—at least to Savannah. Maybe it was only she and Riley who had relaxed, but to her it seemed as though the entire Shaughnessy family had breathed a collective sigh of relief.

They continued to talk all through dessert and then everyone moved out to the living room, where Ian presented his children with his plan for more rehabs on the house.

"Not again," Hugh mumbled, raking a hand through his dark hair.

"My children all grew up in this house," Ian said, "and I'd like to see this be a place my grandchildren will grow up in too."

And when it was put like that, no one could really argue.

"It means things will be a little messy for a while so we may have to move our weekly dinners to someone else's house for a while," Ian began.

"We should rotate houses," Anna said, and everyone stopped and stared at her. "For dinners," she clarified. "I mean have dinners at everyone's house on a rotating basis. First Sunday of the month, it's at our house, the second one it's at Aidan and Zoe's, third at Hugh and Aubrey's, and so on. This way everyone gets to host—or you can look at it as no one is getting overburdened. Take your pick." She shrugged. "It can be fun and then once things are done here, we can just slip you back into the rotation."

Ian shook his head. "I think it's great how everyone wants a chance to host, but when this last bit of construction is done, there won't be any more rotations. This place will have been done over from top to bottom. It will practically be a brand-new house. Everyone's coming here. The nursery will be set up with multiple cribs and everything my grandbabies will need. You can all bring the food, but everyone's coming here. Your mother always said this house was the perfect home for her family, and she would love to know we're continuing on with the next generation of Shaughnessys here."

Savannah looked around and noticed everyone was smiling and there were a few unshed tears. Hell, she was a little misty-eyed herself and it wasn't surprising when she looked down and found Riley's hand covering hers.

She turned it over and grasped his, gently squeezing it for support. They were next to one another on the sofa, and his presence next to her was comforting.

As she hoped hers was for him right now.

"When are you looking to get started?" Aidan asked.

"We have to get permits and all first, but if you could maybe help me draw up some plans, I'd like to start as soon as possible. I know that's sort of putting you on the spot," Ian said apologetically, "but Connor's already growing too darn fast, and your baby will be here before you know it, and hopefully more won't be too far behind… I don't want to wait too long."

"I hate to think of you doing all this for the babies, Dad," Hugh said. "I understand why you want to and I'm not saying you shouldn't do it, but it's a big job to take on and it will be a little disruptive to you. You'll be living in a construction zone again. And so will Riley if you start it while he's here."

Beside her, Riley shrugged. "If it really gets to be too much, Savannah and I can work someplace else or head back to L.A."

"No," Ian said. "Absolutely not. You promised me you'd be home for most of the month, and even if the construction starts, you need to honor your word. You can stay at the apartment at Aidan and Zoe's or…or… Quinn and Anna have space. You have options. You don't have to leave and go to the other side of the country because I'm doing some minor renovations."

"You're adding a room on to the back of the house, Dad. It will pretty much entail opening the back wall of the house. Last I checked, something like that doesn't classify as a minor anything."

"Don't be a smart-ass," Ian warned. "We don't see you near enough. If I have to postpone the work until the end of the month, that's what I'll do, Riley. It's important to me that you stay."

Everyone was looking at Riley with a mix of pity and amusement.

"Fine," he finally said. "We won't head back to L.A. But if the work does become an issue, Savannah and I will find someplace else to stay because she has a schedule to keep with the magazine article and I've already put us behind."

"Well, like Dad said," Aidan smiled, "you have plenty of options. We've all got space for you."

"Thanks," Riley said. "I appreciate it."

"So what are the plans for next weekend?" Martha asked. "What do you need help with for the christening, Aubrey?"

Hugh and Aubrey smiled at one another. "Everything is set for the church. We have it reserved for Saturday at two o'clock and then we are going to have a dinner for everyone over at Aidan and Zoe's," Aubrey said. "Our place is so much farther away that it seemed silly to make everyone drive."

"Plus," Zoe interrupted, "since Aidan and I are godparents, we thought it was only right for us to host."

"That seems like it can be a lot of work," Martha said. "Surely there's something we can help with."

Hugh sat forward. "It's going to be a lot like today. We're going to grill and eat and visit and just celebrate being together—only with a few more people."

"Are both your parents coming, Aubrey?" Zoe asked. "You said you weren't sure last we talked about it."

"My mom is, but my dad said he couldn't make it."
She sounded sad but gave everyone a smile. "It's probably for the best. He and my mom still don't get along
very well, and I don't want to deal with that whole thing,
especially not on Connor's big day."

"Who's getting Darcy from the airport?" Zoe asked.
"Is she getting in on Friday?"

"She isn't getting in until Saturday morning. She
waited a little too long to book her flight," Ian said, shaking his head. "I knew I should have just taken care of it,
but she assured me she could handle it. I knew things
would get a little more complicated when she transferred
to a college out of state. And now she's making up extra
classes during a summer session. Lesson learned."

"Poor kid," Hugh said. "She's going to be exhausted."

"Yeah, but she's so excited to be coming home and
to finally see Connor in person that she'll be fine," Ian
assured him. "You're probably going to have to pry him
out of her arms at some point."

They all laughed.

"Speaking of which," Hugh said as he stood and
stretched, "we need to hit the road. We're trying really
hard to establish a routine with Connor, and part of it is
getting him to sleep in his own crib each night instead
of someone's arms." He gave Aubrey a subtle look. "If
we leave now, we'll have the timing right to get him fed
and bathed and changed just in time to put him to bed."

Aubrey stood. "And with any luck he'll sleep for at
least five hours. That's our goal."

Ian laughed heartily as he came to his feet. "You
two have read too many books and are too rigid. Babies
sleep when they want to and wake up when they want

to no matter how much you wish otherwise." He shook his head and took his grandson from Zoe, who was currently holding him, and kissed the baby on the forehead. "Let him simply be a baby. Don't let him get fussy like you, Hugh. He doesn't need a daily planner just yet."

"Hey!" Hugh grumbled but then couldn't help but laugh at himself. "Dad, sometimes having a schedule—especially with a new baby—is a good thing."

"Yeah, but you have a tendency to take things to the extreme, Son. Don't pass that trait on to this sweet, innocent boy."

Aubrey took the baby from Ian's arms and got him settled into his infant carrier. "Nobody's getting him a day planner," she chuckled softly. "We're just hoping for a good night's sleep. It's been a while."

"When the nursery is ready, Connor can spend the night with me," Ian said.

"Done!" Hugh and Aubrey said in unison while everyone laughed.

Within minutes, they were out the door and were soon followed by Aidan and Zoe and Quinn and Anna.

"Owen, you can sleep in Darcy's room tonight, if that's all right. I highly doubt you and Riley want to share a bed."

"Nah, he snores," Riley teased, and Owen shot him a look.

"It's fine," Owen said to his father. "I could just as easily sleep on the couch."

"Why? There's a perfectly good bed in your sister's room. And it's not like she still has Barbie sheets on the bed," Ian said. "They're purple but there's nothing particularly girly about them, and they're clean."

"Thanks, Dad."

Looking at his sons and Savannah, Ian smiled. "I'm going to take Martha home. I'm not sure if any of you will be up when I get back so I'll just say good night now. And Owen? I'll see you in the morning before you leave. We'll have breakfast together, deal?"

"Deal," Owen agreed.

When the door closed behind Ian and Martha, Riley shuddered.

"What? What's the matter?" Savannah asked.

"He's not sure if we'll be up because he's going to spend some extended time at Martha's. Ugh...that means... It means—"

"They're having sex," Owen finished. Riley let out a yell and stormed from the room. Savannah and Owen quickly followed. "I don't understand. Why is this so upsetting to you? I would think out of all of us, you'd be okay with it."

Riley's eyes went wide. "Me? Why?"

Owen shrugged. "You're just more open-minded than the rest of us. I guess I thought you'd be less freaked out."

Riley made a face and walked to the refrigerator to grab something to drink. He pulled out a bottle of water and handed one to Savannah before asking his brother if he wanted one. "It's not like I'm freaked out. But I just don't want to have to think about it. If he and Martha are—"

"Having sex?" Owen responded.

"Stop saying it like that!" Riley yelled. "It's even worse hearing *you* say the words!"

"Why? Why can't I say—"

"So help me if you say it again, Owen, I will punch you," Riley said seriously.

Owen instantly shut his mouth and took the beverage from Riley's hand. He walked back out to the living room and sat down on the sofa.

"That was a little harsh," Savannah said quietly. "Even I know he wasn't saying it to be obnoxious or to taunt you. To him it was simply stating a fact."

"Yeah well, he doesn't always have to state the facts," Riley said defensively, raking a hand through his hair as he sighed.

Savannah walked over and put her hands on his shoulders. "Riley, all day long I watched the way you and your brothers bantered with one another and teased each other, but not Owen. He's probably in there beating himself up. Please go tell him you're sorry."

"But—"

"Please? For me?"

"Why are you taking his side?" he asked with a pout.

"Because you're acting like a big bully and he's very sensitive," she said.

"You really have a spooky knack for figuring people out."

"It's a curse, really," she said with a grin. "Now go and make things right with your brother. He's leaving in the morning and you don't want to let this go. I'm going to go upstairs and read and go to bed."

"But…don't you want to talk to Owen some more? You might not have the opportunity to get this time alone with him again."

Reaching up, Savannah cupped his cheek and smiled. "It's very sweet of you to think of me and the interview, but I think Owen and I had a great talk outside earlier. Right now, it's the two of you who need some time together." Leaning in, she kissed him on the cheek. "Because you might not have the opportunity to apologize and make it up to him like you do right now. Now go," she said gently.

With her bottle of water in her hand, Savannah walked out to the living room and said good night to Owen. "It was a pleasure meeting you and I'm sure we'll see each other again soon."

"You're going to the christening next weekend, aren't you?" he asked as he stood up.

"It's a family thing," she said dismissively. "I don't want to intrude." Then before he could ask her anything else, Savannah leaned in and kissed him on the cheek too. "Don't go easy on him," she whispered in his ear. "Make him pay for being a bully."

Owen blushed and looked down at the floor. "Good night, Savannah," he said quietly and then looked up as she walked up the stairs and continued to watch until she was out of sight.

"If I didn't know any better," Riley said as he walked into the room with a smirk, "I'd say you were just checking out Savannah's ass."

"What?" Owen cried. "I wasn't… I didn't…"

Riley walked over and put his arm around his brother's shoulder. "It's all right, dude. But don't let it become a habit. Only one Shaughnessy is allowed to ogle Savannah, and that's me."

Pulling away, Owen opened his water and sat down. "I don't know, Ry. I think I kind of have a little crush on her."

Riley stared at his brother in shock. "You…you…
what?"

Owen grinned. "Have a seat and we'll talk about it."

Savannah slept in the next morning. It wasn't inten-
tional but she had hoped that by doing so, Ian, Riley,
and Owen would have had the chance to have breakfast
together—just the three of them—without her hovering.
She knew they didn't see her intrusion as a big deal, but
she also knew the importance of family time.

And she wasn't so sure she'd be as gracious as the
Shaughnessys if someone were going to be staying with
her for a month strictly for the sake of observing her.

Savannah knew this was all Riley's idea and everyone had agreed, but she couldn't help but feel a little bit
bad about it. No doubt there was going to be a discussion about her going to Connor's baptism next weekend
and it would turn into an argument. It was one thing to
be here to interview Riley and his family; it was quite
another to be there for an intimate family occasion.

She'd have to come up with a good reason why she
wasn't going to go—something that Riley wasn't going
to see through and figure out how to change. Maybe
she'd call her parents and see if they were up for a road
trip to come see her in North Carolina for the weekend.
It would be perfect. Surely Riley wouldn't deny her the
chance to go off and spend time with her own family?
And her parents certainly wouldn't want to impose on
the Shaughnessys so it was a win-win!

Picking up her phone, she immediately dialed her
parents' number. Her dad answered.

"Hey, Dad!"

"How's it going, Daily Scoop?"

She chuckled at the nickname. "It's going great." She told him about her trip to Riley's home and the private plane. "I'm telling you, I may be spoiled for life after that one."

"No doubt. That sounds amazing. How's the interview going?"

"We're off to a slow start. I spent the entire day yesterday with his family. They were all so gracious and friendly, and I got a really good feel for who Riley was and where he got his love of music. We're going to start sitting down together today and filling in the gaps."

"Okay, so you have a plan," Paul Daly said. "So this is just a checking-in call? Because I'm sensing there's something more."

Savannah chuckled. Her father knew her too well. "I was wondering if you and Mom were up for a little trip… for the weekend."

"You mean come to North Carolina?"

"Uh-huh. The Shaughnessys have a family event this coming weekend. Riley's nephew—the first baby in the family in over twenty years—is being baptized. I know they're going to insist I go, but I feel it should be a private, family thing. I don't want to feel like an intruder. They deserve to have a day without someone watching them."

"I'm sure they don't see you that way, sweetheart," he said sincerely. "But I know how strongly you feel about things, and if you're calling and asking, then I know it's important to you." He paused and Savannah could hear him typing away on his computer keyboard. "It's not exactly a short drive, you know."

"I know…I know." She sighed. "I'm sorry. I shouldn't have asked. I'll find something else to do. I just thought…well…it's been a while since I've seen you two and I missed you."

"You know we miss you too, and really, your mom and I have been talking about doing some traveling this summer. We just didn't know where."

"I don't want to pressure you on such short notice—"

"Nonsense. We've never really traveled east. This could be fun!"

"Really?" she cried. "You mean it?"

"You know I'm a man of my word, Savannah. Text me the address of where you're staying and I'll get the RV ready."

"Dad, you have no idea how much this means to me!"

"It means a lot to me that you called and invited us," he said sincerely. "Get me the address and I'll see you Friday."

She put her phone back down on her nightstand and smiled. She'd get to see her family, the Shaughnessys would get their privacy.

Everything was falling into place.

Chapter 7

FOR THREE DAYS, SHE AND RILEY HAD BEEN spending time doing nothing but working on the interview. They had eased into a routine where they met up for breakfast—after Riley did about thirty minutes of vocal exercises—and pretty much talked from morning until night. And what was most enjoyable to Savannah was that it didn't feel like an interview. They simply talked.

When Ian would come home at night, they'd have dinner together and he would chime in with funny stories about raising six kids. It was a nice break from simply talking about Riley and his career.

She had a lot of conversations on tape regarding his love of music and his life leading up to his big break, and Savannah knew at some point she was going to have to weed through it all and pick out points that would benefit the story the most. It was going to be hard because everything he'd shared with her, she found fascinating.

They didn't flirt with one another again—nothing even close since their time out on the deck Sunday night—and she found she missed it. Not that Riley didn't take every opportunity he could to touch her. Like when they were making breakfast and he'd walk by and his hand would skim her lower back. Or they'd be sitting next to one another and he'd touch her hair to get it out of her eyes.

They were little things—and ones neither openly

acknowledged—but they were slowly making Savannah…restless.

For the most part, she kept her hands to herself. Not because she didn't want to touch Riley, but because she had a feeling if she did, she wouldn't want to stop. And now that they'd started working on the interview, she didn't want to do anything to hinder their progress.

No matter how badly she wanted to.

Focus!

Thursday morning, she was up earlier than usual and met up with Ian and Riley in the kitchen. "Good morning," she said to them both. She had gotten up and showered and was ready to start her day.

"Good morning, Savannah," Ian said. "I wasn't expecting to see you up this early."

She shrugged. "Couldn't sleep and decided not to fight it anymore." She looked at the clock. "It's a little late for you, isn't it? I thought you were normally gone by eight."

He smiled at her and then looked over at Riley. "Change of plans for today. I took today and tomorrow off, and Martha and I are going into Raleigh to look at some furniture and fixtures and whatever else we may need to do this master bedroom makeover."

"And you have to go to Raleigh to do that?" Savannah asked and noticed Riley was frowning as he drank his coffee.

"There are a lot more businesses out that way for us to get what we'll need and at a lower price than what we'd find here at one of the big home improvement stores. I'm not looking to break the bank on this renovation." He took a sip of his own coffee. "She wants to go on to High Point too and look at furniture."

"How far is it?" Savannah asked.

"Raleigh's about three hours from here and High Point is an additional three hours west."

"Wow! That's a long day. You probably won't be back until after midnight. Lots of driving."

"We're going to make it a two-day event and stay overnight somewhere along the way. We're going to see where the day takes us and not rush."

"Oh," she said, trying not to sound surprised. Then she looked over at Riley and realized that was why he was frowning. He was still a little uncomfortable with this new aspect of his father and Martha's relationship. "I'm sure you're going to have a great time."

"There's plenty of food in the refrigerator for the two of you for dinner and—"

"You don't have to worry about us, Dad," Riley finally said. "We know how to fend for ourselves."

Ian frowned at his son. "I was merely stating some facts, Riley. I know you both know how to take care of yourselves." He put his mug in the sink before turning back to them. "I'll be back tomorrow night after dinner. What time are your parents getting in, Savannah?"

She had told them both of her plans for her parents' visit, and while Ian had seemed excited at the idea, Riley had seemed a little confused by it. "As far as I know, it will be around eight tomorrow night—if everything goes as planned."

"Great. I'll plan on bringing some dessert home with us and then we can all get to know each other while relaxing."

She waved him off. "Ian, I don't expect you to entertain them. They're coming here so you and your family can have a nice visit together without the pesky reporter hovering around. I gave them the address of one of the hotels close to the beach where they can park the RV and stay for the weekend. I already booked us two rooms."

"You did?" Riley asked, putting his coffee mug down with a little too much force. "When?"

Savannah shrugged. "I don't know. Tuesday, I guess. I took care of that when you had the conference call with Mick and your publicist. Or was that the call about artwork for the album cover? I can't remember. Why?"

He rolled his eyes. "We all told you that you were invited to the christening. I don't understand why you're not going."

"I already explained this to you, Riley. And besides, maybe I just want to have some time with my family. Have you thought about that?"

Ian walked over and picked up his overnight bag before coming back to the two of them. "I need to get going. But before I do, I'm going to add one more wrinkle."

"Uh-oh," Riley murmured.

Ian looked at Savannah. "I talked to both Hugh and Aubrey about your situation and how you felt and that your parents were coming to visit. So they invited your parents to join the party too." When Savannah made to protest, Ian held up a hand to stop her. "I have to go."

And then, in a move that surprised her, Ian leaned over and kissed her on the top of the head. "It's a day to celebrate, Savannah. And it would mean a lot to Hugh and Aubrey if you were there. But I'm leaving the choice up to you."

He leaned down and even kissed Riley good-bye before walking out of the kitchen and out of the house.

They both stood rooted to the spot, staring at the closed door. Although she couldn't speak for Riley, Savannah knew what was going on in her own head— they were going to have the house to themselves for two days.

Alone.

No disruptions.

No distractions.

Just then, Riley turned and looked at her, and she knew he was thinking the exact same thing. But rather than comment on it, Savannah decided the best plan of attack was just to act as if everything was the same— like it wasn't a big deal that Ian wasn't going to be home for lunch and then back for dinner.

Maybe she should suggest calling one of his brothers?

Or maybe she should call Anna or Zoe and see if they wanted to shop?

Or maybe…

In the blink of an eye, Riley was standing right in front of her—the sight of him making her gasp.

"We can go over to Quinn and Anna's if you'd prefer," he said, his voice low and gravelly.

She knew what he was asking, and Savannah wanted to think they had a little more self-control than this. They needed to. Eventually they were going to be back in L.A. and would have reasons to be alone again, and that shouldn't be a major issue.

Doing her best to sound calm and neutral, she said, "I don't think it's necessary." Walking past him, she went to the living room, picked her notepad up from the coffee table, and then went back to the kitchen. "I have an outline of things I'd like to cover today. With my parents coming this weekend, we really should make the most of the time we have."

Yeah, that could totally be taken a couple different ways, she chided herself.

Riley stared at her without speaking for several minutes before nodding curtly. He walked over to the cabinets and began scrounging around and mumbling.

"What are you looking for?" she asked.

"Tea," he said distractedly. "I know I normally keep some herbal teas here for when I'm home. They're… they're better for my throat than coffee."

"Is your throat bothering you?"

He shook his head but didn't turn around. "It's just something I tend to do when I'm home and I haven't since we got here. It just… It just seemed like a good time for a cup of tea."

Savannah sighed with relief that he wasn't arguing with her about her parents or about staying here to work on the interview.

They moved around the kitchen in silence, each doing their own thing. Savannah helped herself to one of the muffins Ian had brought home the previous day to go with her coffee. Riley opted for a bagel.

"We can start while we eat, if you don't mind," Savannah said as she sat down at the large table.

"Whatever," he replied, but his voice was fairly mild and calm. His spoon kept a slow rhythm as he stirred some honey into the steaming mug.

Flipping through her notes, Savannah took a bite of her muffin and got her head focused on what she wanted to begin with and how much she was hoping to get done by lunchtime.

"I think we've pretty much covered your life up until you moved to L.A.," she began. "I guess what I'd like to start looking at is how the sudden fame and fortune and notoriety made you feel." She paused. "After meeting your family and seeing how you grew up, I would imagine it was overwhelming."

Riley nodded. "It scared the hell out of me."

"Really?"

He nodded again. "I wasn't comfortable with it, and some of the guys in the band went a little wild—they bought mansions and cars and just started blowing through the money like it was water. I remember Matty going to one of those big rock auctions and spending almost a hundred grand on memorabilia—one of John Lennon's guitars, a jacket worn by Mick Jagger… It was crazy. Me? I called my dad and asked him what he thought I should do."

Savannah almost wanted to question it, but after spending so much time with his family, she was certain it was exactly something Riley would have done. "And what did he tell you?"

"He told me to invest and to invest wisely. It was okay to buy a house, but I didn't need to buy a mansion. I obviously would need a car, but I didn't need ten of them. My dad is very practical."

"I can see that. What was your first big splurge? Surely you had to have bought something that was impractical but you just had to have it."

Riley chuckled. "I don't know if I can tell you without having you laugh at me."

"Believe me when I tell you I've heard a lot of weird things during interviews. Nothing you say is going to shock me."

"Oh, I don't think it will shock you, but I think you'll laugh."

"Okay, I promise not to laugh."

He took a long drink of his tea and slowly put it down. "I flew home, rented a limo, and took the whole family to dinner and wouldn't let my dad pay the bill. Then I took Darcy to Disneyland." He smiled at the memory. "She'd never gone anywhere on a vacation. After my mom died, we stopped going. I asked my dad if he wanted to go with us and he said no—that it would be something special for me and Darcy. And it was. She was ten and I can still remember the way her eyes lit up the first time she saw Sleeping Beauty's castle. We watched the fireworks show that night, and when it was over, she looked at me and smiled and said it was the most magical day of her life."

Savannah reached out and placed her hand over his. "Why would I laugh at that?" she asked, her throat thick with emotion.

He shrugged. "Most guys would go out and blow the money on themselves and I took my sister to Disneyland. I'm like one of those cheesy Super Bowl ads."

She shook her head. "No. You are an incredible man with an incredible heart. I don't know very many people who would put not only their family, but their little sister first. You're amazing, Riley."

He looked up and their gazes locked. "It wasn't entirely selfless. I'd never gone to Disneyland either."

She smiled. "You wanted to do something for your family. I'm sure your father was very proud of you."

Riley nodded and his eyes welled up. "He cried. When we got home that night and everyone went to bed, we sat down on the living room sofa and he cried. He said he was proud of me—for following my dream and for proving that he and my mom raised me right." He sniffed and wiped at his eyes. "We said Mom was looking down on us and smiling with pride."

Savannah couldn't stop her own tears from falling. She squeezed his hand again because it was all she could do.

"Dad never expects us to do anything for him—only for each other. Sometimes I wish he'd let us do more. We all try—like the dinner or helping out when he was renovating the house—but he's always saying it's his job to take care of us. How it's what Mom wanted him to do." He swallowed hard. "I think she'd be happy to see us take care of him once in a while."

"You all do in your own way. And he knows it. And so does she. By coming home and supporting him in his endeavors, you're all taking care of him and giving him what he needs. He loves all of you so much—that much is obvious—and it's important to him to have a nursery here so you'll all stay close. I think it's wonderful. It's a lovely gesture and I know everyone feels the same way."

"Sometimes I feel guilty for living so far away, but it's where everything was happening for my career— the studio, management, the band—but I wouldn't be entirely opposed to having a second home here."

"It's beautiful here. When your dad showed me around town over the weekend, I was really impressed. Zoe was telling me about hers and Aidan's place and it sounds wonderful."

"Don't tell anyone I said it, but I like Quinn and Anna's place better."

She chuckled. "Only because they have a game room."

"Busted," he said and smiled at her and then looked at their hands. Their fingers were now twined together. He looked like there was something else he wanted to say, but he slowly disengaged their hands and sat back. "So…um…I have some pictures of my trip with Darcy that I think you could use in the article if you're interested. I mean…I don't know if you're going to use them, but if you wanted to…I have those available."

And she knew what he was trying to do—trying to keep them on track. Focused on business even though they were both like a moth to a flame with one another. It was bound to happen—they were going to hit a point when they wouldn't be able to deny it or ignore it. Savannah just hoped it wouldn't ruin everything. Sex had the ability to do that—ruin relationships, friendships, business agreements—yeah. Pretty much everything she had right now with Riley could be destroyed if sex got in the way.

Okay, so just don't have sex.

She wanted to tell her inner voice to shut up. Did her inner voice even *see* Riley Shaughnessy? It was easier said than done. He was a living, breathing fantasy. Her own rock and roll fantasy at that! And every minute of every day it was getting more and more difficult to ignore the attraction brewing between them.

Maybe she was just getting ahead of herself. Just because Riley touched her hand or her lower back or looked at her with those deep, dark, sexy eyes didn't mean he necessarily wanted to have sex with her, right? She'd been around enough musicians to know that, for some of them, that look came as easy to them as breathing.

Ugh…maybe she needed some fresh air.

Or a cold shower.

Or both.

Finishing the last of her muffin, she picked up her plate and rinsed it off before putting it in the dishwasher. Using cold water, she rinsed her hands to try to cool herself off—at least until she could get a cold shower. When she was done, she turned back to Riley as if she hadn't just been having all kinds of sexy thoughts of him.

"How about we go out to the living room and continue? Let's talk about the first real tour."

―――*―――

It was after one in the afternoon when they stopped to make some lunch. Savannah had offered to make them some sandwiches, and Riley decided he needed a few minutes to himself. She had been making him crazy all day. As soon as his father had announced he was going out of town for the day and night, Riley's mind had been racing with images of Savannah sprawled out in his bed.

Not that he'd done a damn thing to act on it.

Getting women to go to bed with him had never been a problem. But now Riley realized getting the *right* woman to go to bed with him wasn't an easy task at all. He didn't want to scare her off or have her reject him.

Which was another new thing—he suddenly had a lot less self-confidence than he'd ever had before in his life.

He followed Savannah into the kitchen and grabbed a bottle of water. "Um…if it's all right with you, I'm going to go up and grab a shower. I didn't get to do it earlier—we jumped into the interview and I…I'd just like to do that while you're getting lunch together."

She studied him for a minute. "Oh. Okay."

"If you need my help with lunch, I can stay and then just go up and shower afterward if you'd prefer."

"It's just sandwiches," she said evenly, although her expression was a little unreadable. "I'll be fine."

He nodded. "Okay then. Just give me about fifteen minutes to shower and—"

"I get it!" she snapped. "You're going to grab a shower. *Sheesh!* Do you have to keep saying it?" Then she turned away as if she was embarrassed by her outburst.

Riley reached out and put his hand on her shoulder, and she hissed and pulled away. "Savannah? What? What did I say?"

"It's…it's nothing. Just go do what you gotta do."

He wasn't a fool. Something was bothering her. This time he wasn't so gentle when he put his hand on her shoulder and spun her around. "Did I do something wrong?"

She shook her head furiously. "No. You're fine. Really. I…" She shook her head again. "It's nothing. Go. I'll have lunch ready by the time you're back down here."

For some reason, Riley didn't believe her. There was a slight tremor in her voice and she wouldn't meet his eyes. He reached up with one hand and cupped her face. "You don't have to wait on me. You're not here for that. I can put my own lunch together when I'm done if that's what's bothering you."

Now she did look up with him, her eyes dark with irritation as she shoved his hand away. "You think this is about a sandwich?" she snapped. "Geez, that just goes to show how clueless men are!"

"Now you've lost me," he said with a nervous chuckle. "Savannah, seriously, what's going on?"

She sighed loudly and moved away from him. "Nothing. Really. I'm sorry. Just ignore me."

"That's not likely to happen," Riley said darkly. "Not ever."

Her eyes widened as he stalked her from across the kitchen.

"There is no way I can ignore you—it's impossible. Just like it would be impossible to stop breathing." And then, because he figured they were already fighting, he might as well poke the bear a little more.

So he grabbed her and kissed her.

Hard. Wet. And wild.

Savannah's arms instantly went around him at the same time Riley's banded around her. Tongues dueled as they did everything they could to get even closer. One of Riley's hands came up and fisted in her long hair, gently pulling it. She gasped but her lips stayed with his.

Riley knew he was close to losing all control, and if he didn't release her soon, he'd end up taking her right there on his father's kitchen table.

And there was a bucket of cold water for you.

Pulling back, they both gasped for air. Savannah's lips were red from the force of his kisses and it only served to turn Riley on again. He wanted to touch her, soothe her, hold her. But right now, he knew what he needed most was to put some distance between them before they did something stupid.

On his father's kitchen table.

"I…" He cleared his throat. "I'm going to take that shower. I'll be back down in a few minutes."

Savannah nodded mutely and watched him go.

With each step Riley climbed, he cursed himself. How

could they keep ending up like that and not talk about it? Maybe he was beating himself up for nothing. Maybe he was pulling back when she really didn't want him to.

God knew he didn't want to.

Especially right now.

The shower would feel good, but Savannah in his arms would feel a hell of a lot better. They were alone and if she was worried about his father or anyone finding out, he could assure her that no one had to know.

With his mind made up, Riley decided that after lunch, they would finally address the elephant in the room. He wanted her, she wanted him, and he was tired of trying to pretend otherwise.

In his room, he stripped off his T-shirt and jeans before walking into the adjoining bathroom. Turning on the water, he gave it a minute to get the temperature right and wished he was home in his own spa bathroom. The shower was easily four times the size of this one and had about a dozen different jets. He sighed, knowing it would be at least another couple of weeks before he had that luxury again.

Pulling open the glass door, he stepped inside and let the hot water pound on his back.

It didn't feel as good as he'd hoped.

Not when all he wanted was Savannah's hands on him.

Leaning back, he stuck his head under the stream of water and raked his hands through his hair. They were shaking. He never should have kissed her again. Hell, he never should have kissed her that first day at his house— they didn't even know each other and yet he couldn't find the will to care. He quickly washed his hair and then his body as he tried to push the image of the two of them together out of his head.

THIS IS OUR SONG

THIS IS OUR SONG   181

It was impossible.

Granted, over the course of his career Riley had to admit he had slept with women he had known a lot less than Savannah, but he'd never wanted one this much. And somehow he doubted it was possible to want any other woman more than her ever again.

Shit.

He couldn't even argue it.

It wasn't so long ago he had given his brother Hugh a lengthy speech about going after what he wanted with Aubrey. And his brother—being the type of guy who planned everything—couldn't wrap his brain around falling for someone so fast. Riley had been the one to push him out the door that night—forcing him to face what he wanted and take it. So what the hell was he waiting for? If Hugh Shaughnessy—the man who planned his life down to the minute—could simply knock on the door of the woman he wanted and finally make her his, why was Riley agonizing over it?

He wanted Savannah.

He needed Savannah.

Shutting off the shower, he reached for a towel and immediately began drying himself off.

He was going to have Savannah.

———∿∿∿———

Lunch was the last thing on Savannah's mind. She stood in the kitchen and heard the shower turn on and all she could do was stand there and imagine Riley naked.

And she was certain her imagination wasn't doing him justice.

It took a minute for her to realize she was pretty

much mindlessly staring into the refrigerator. Slamming it shut, she cursed. Wandering around the kitchen, she knew she didn't want food. That wasn't what she was hungry for.

It was him.

As crazy as it was, it had been Riley since the moment they shook hands while sitting in her Jeep that night in the rain.

She could argue all she wanted to how getting romantically involved with Riley was going to be a distraction to the interview process, but it wasn't true. *Not* becoming romantically involved with him was proving to be the bigger distraction.

For most of her life, Savannah had played it safe—at least where relationships were concerned. Well, for once in her life, she was tired of taking the safe route. She wanted to be wild. She wanted to go after what she wanted with no regrets.

She wanted Riley.

Now.

Before she could change her mind, Savannah strode from the kitchen and marched up the stairs. The shower had been turned off and she knew Riley was probably drying off or already getting dressed. Not that it mattered. He wouldn't be that way for long.

Knocking loudly on his bedroom door, she tapped her foot impatiently.

"Just a minute!" he called out.

"Riley? I need to talk to you right now!"

"I just need a minute—"

"This can't wait!" she called back and gasped when the door immediately opened. There, before her, was

Riley. With nothing but a towel wrapped around his waist and droplets of water making their way down his chest, he was breathtaking.

"Are you all right?" he asked cautiously.

She stared at his chest, mesmerized by the sculpted muscles and the way the water was playing on them. "You have a tattoo," she said quietly, almost sounding surprised. It was a tribal tattoo of a cross with a blue diamond in the middle.

"Savannah? Is everything okay? What did you need? I…I just got out of the shower and…" He took a step back to partially hide himself behind the door.

She couldn't speak. Her mouth had gone dry at the sight of him. The urge to reach out and touch him was enough to make her tremble.

As if sensing her thoughts, Riley let go of the door and stood in front of her—his own body trembling. "What is it you want, Savannah?" His voice was so low it was almost a growl.

She looked up at his face finally as she licked her lips. He was going to make her say the words—to tell him why she was up here, knocking on his door and ogling him like the world's greatest treat.

"You," she said, her voice barely audible.

He closed the distance between them. "Tell me again."

She swallowed hard and seemed to stand a little taller. "You, Riley. I want you."

In the blink of an eye he took her hand and tugged her into the room and slammed the door behind them. "Thank God!" he groaned and hauled her into his arms.

She went willingly and it was a slow dance across the room as he tugged her tank top over her head before he started to kiss her. And then his hands were everywhere. For her part, Savannah kept her own hands anchored on his waist for a minute before she let them travel up his bare chest. He was wet and warm and so hard and muscular she couldn't help but moan at the feel of him.

"You have no idea how long I've wanted to feel your hands on me," Riley whispered as his lips traveled down her jaw and her throat before dipping his head to kiss the swell of her breasts over her lace bra.

"Yes, I do, because it's just as long as I've waited to feel your hands on me," she told him and chuckled as she moved her hands to help him get her bra off.

With the towel still wrapped around him, Riley took a step back and simply looked at her. Savannah felt hot under his gaze and while he stood there, she shimmied out of her jeans but left her panties on.

"Yeah," Riley hissed, reaching for her and pulling her flush against him until they were skin to skin. He cupped her cheek and studied her face. "I've been going out of my mind with wanting you, Savannah. Are you sure about this?"

"I can't focus on anything anymore," she said honestly. "Not on writing or the interview. Nothing. All I can think about is you. Just you and how much I need you."

Those words seemed to please him because a slow grin crossed his face. "I like that," he said. "I like the fact that you need me."

"I do, Riley. Let me show you how much."

His smile grew. "How about we show each other?"

Now she smiled. "I like that even more."

—∿∿—

"I feel bad."

"Not exactly the words a man wants to hear after making love to a woman."

Savannah chuckled. They were spooned together in Riley's bed—her back to his front—after a long afternoon in each other's arms. "We're supposed to be working."

"I think you learned more about me in the past two hours than you would have all day," Riley teased.

"Sure, but I can't put any of *that* into a magazine article. It would just be wrong."

He laughed and nuzzled her neck. "I wouldn't let you put any of this into any article. It's private."

"And fairly X-rated."

"Well…that too."

She turned in his arms and smiled up at him. "I wouldn't share this with anyone. I want you to know that. What happened here has nothing to do with a story I'm writing. It's about you and me."

Riley's expression turned serious too. "I know that, Savannah. And I know you have a job to do and we haven't been doing a very good job at doing it." Then he chuckled.

"What?" she asked suspiciously.

"Doing it…" He laughed harder. "Get it?"

Playfully, she smacked his shoulder as she laughed too. "Grow up!"

Pulling her tight against him, Riley kissed her deeply until she melted in his arms. When he lifted his head, his expression was just as blissful as hers. "Not that I'm complaining, but what made you change your mind and come up here today?"

Savannah placed a hand on his chest and gently traced the tattoo there. "I'm normally very reserved," she said quietly, "especially where sex and relationships are concerned. But from the moment we met, I felt out of my comfort zone. Everything about you just called to me." Her eyes met his. "That's never happened before."

His gaze scanned her face. "I feel the exact same way." His voice was rough as he spoke. "I've had plenty of women throw themselves at me in situations like ours and I never found it appealing. But being with you? You made me laugh and think and you challenged me. At first, I thought it was about getting you to like me," he admitted honestly. "But every time we were together, I realized it was so much more than that. You're smart and sexy and beautiful and on top of all that…I genuinely like you, Savannah. You wouldn't be here meeting my entire family if I didn't."

"I thought it was a diversion tactic to keep us from being alone," she said, blushing.

He kissed her again. "Yeah, it kind of was. But I wouldn't have thought to use it unless I wanted you here with them. If all I wanted from you was sex, I wouldn't have needed a diversion. I would have pounced that first day and gotten it out of my system without giving the interview a second thought."

"Can I tell you something?"

He nodded.

"I probably wouldn't have minded all that much if you'd pounced that day."

Riley burst out laughing. "Now you tell me! You mean we could have been naked for a week already?"

She struggled to get out of his arms as she laughed with him. "Maybe!"

Finally, he pinned her beneath him, both their breathing ragged. "I don't doubt for a minute it would have been amazing if you'd stayed with me that night, Savannah. But this? What happened here today? This was perfect. I'm glad we waited until now."

She frowned a little. "It's only been a week. It's not like we've been practicing abstinence for any extreme amount of time."

"Every moment I wasn't with you? Every time I couldn't touch you? It was torture."

Sighing, Savannah reached up and touched his cheek. "Tell me about the tattoo."

Rolling off her, Riley tucked her in close beside him. "It was one of those things I did when I first moved to L.A. I went to one of the most well-known places and had it done. It's a tribal cross. All the guys in the band were getting something and I had never really thought of getting one. It just wasn't on my radar. But after our first late-night talk show appearance, we decided to do it."

"It's very sexy," she said, her hand instantly going to touch it again.

"I can get another one if you really think so."

Savannah picked her head up off his shoulder and looked at him. "Tattoos should be about you and for you—not anyone else. And being as you only have one and the talk show was several years ago, I can tell it's not something you're really into."

He shrugged. "It wasn't so bad. Like I said, it's just

not something I think about. The guys all make fun of me because—as I'm sure you've seen—they're all heavily tatted. We keep threatening to do an intervention on Dylan because of his obsession. I'm okay with it, though. I wouldn't mind getting another one. I just haven't figured out what. Any ideas?"

She shook her head and relaxed against him again. "Not my call to make. It's your body, your decision."

He rolled his eyes and groaned. "Okay, spare me the politically correct answer. If you think this looks sexy, I would get another one right now." In a flash he rolled over and had her beneath him again. "I want you to think I'm sexy, Savannah. I want you to be so distracted by it that you're knocking on my door at all hours of the day and night because you need to touch me."

"That's already the case," she said softly.

His grin was slow and sweet. "Yeah?"

She nodded. "Yeah."

"Prove it," he whispered as he bent his head and began to kiss her cheek.

Wrapping her arms around him, Savannah pulled him down on top of her and showed him just how distracted he made her.

———

"So by the time the tour ended, I think I was just burned out. We had been on the road for almost eighteen months and I just couldn't stand the thought of another hotel room, another airport, or any of it. I just wanted to be home."

"What about the rest of the guys? Did they feel the same?"

"Yeah, we were all on the same page and really, it seemed like they all had other things lined up they wanted to do. I was the only one who just wanted to veg out and do nothing. At least that was the plan. Julian's the one who ends up vegging." He shook his head. "I still can't believe he's getting married."

Savannah scanned through some of her notes. "They all had some pretty big things planned—movies, Broadway, festivals, different music projects with other well-known musicians. Is that what made you decide to do a solo project, or was it something you had been thinking of?"

"No, it wasn't anything I thought I'd ever do. I'm in a band. I planned to continue playing in a band. We'd always been in sync and it kind of blew my mind when they told me all the things they'd each lined up. All I wanted to do was sleep for a week, and as soon as the plane touched down in L.A., they were hopping other flights to go on to their next big thing."

"Were you jealous? Angry? Did it bother you?"

"Honestly, I was just exhausted at the time and felt like I barely knew my own name. I thought we were working on new music, but it turns out they were all kind of going through the motions."

"So where is that music now? Is it going to be part of your solo project?"

He shook his head. "No. I have the recordings—which were essentially just jam sessions—and they're tucked away for us to think about at a later date."

"Has anyone heard them?"

"My family. I usually send them stuff when we're working on it to get some feedback. It's interesting getting their thoughts and ideas."

"What kind of reviews or advice have they given you in the past about the music you sent them? Anything that you took to heart and shared with the band?"

"Not really. Most of their comments are more about how my voice weakens in certain places or the drums are too strong…nothing major and most of the time it's not a finished product so I know those things would get corrected in the studio."

"What about the solo stuff you're working on? Have you shared it with them yet?"

Riley reached over and grabbed the glass of water from the bedside table. On the surface, this was a standard interview—Savannah had her recorder and all her pads and pens—the only difference was he was lying in bed wearing nothing but his boxers, and Savannah was sitting cross-legged on the bed, scantily clad in panties and a tank top.

And looking thoroughly mussed up after an afternoon spent making love.

Best. Interview. Ever.

"I sent the first few songs and then…I stopped."

"Why?"

He shrugged. "I don't know. I felt like everything I was writing and playing just wasn't how I wanted it to sound. In my head, I can hear it. I just…" He sighed with frustration. He knew they'd get to talking about this eventually, but the situation itself still angered him. Jumping up from the bed, he paced the room. "It's here," he said a little loudly, pointing at his head. "I hear it all the damn time, but I can't get it down on paper to write it or get it out on my guitar! Everyone's looking at me and telling me just to get it done and I can't! It's like I'm blocked—but not entirely. I'm slowly losing my mind and for the first time in almost fifteen years, I can't play!"

He expected sympathy and pity and some sort of comfort. He'd been getting those looks from just about everyone he encountered on the project. So when Riley stopped pacing, he prepared himself for it and prayed he wouldn't snap at her the way he'd been snapping at everyone else.

"Well, that sucks," she said and continued to scan her notes as if she was looking for something.

"That's it? That's all you have to say—'that sucks'?"

Savannah looked over her shoulder at him and shrugged. "What else am I supposed to say? I'm not a musician, I don't write music or even play. I have no idea what it's like to be blocked like that."

"So you've never had writer's block?" he asked sarcastically.

"Sure, but I don't think it's the same thing. I'm told what I have to write. Sometimes I'll get hung up on an opening paragraph or the closing one, but basically the story is done for me once I finish an interview. Your process is completely different."

Well…shit. That made sense. He collapsed back down on the bed and threw an arm over his eyes. "It's frustrating as hell," he muttered. "I feel like a complete freaking failure. And no matter what I do, I'm getting grief for it."

Savannah shut off the recorder, and put her stuff on the floor, and stretched out beside him. "In what way?"

"The album isn't getting done, so I'm getting grief from the record label. I said I needed to take a break from public life, so I'm getting grief from my manager and publicist. I mean, I can't seem to do anything right. And then I come home here—to the place that's like my second sanctuary—and everyone around me is thriving and being successful and I'm a damn failure."

Slowly, she pulled his arm away from his face and forced him to look at her. "First of all, you're not a failure. And I'm fairly certain no one in your family is looking at you like that."

"You don't know that," he grumbled.

"Riley, for the last week I've been watching you. You think you're not working, but you are. Every day I hear you singing and doing your whole repertoire of vocal exercises. You're on the phone several times a day with your manager, your agent, and whoever that guy is at the label that calls you at all hours of the day and night wanting to talk cover art and concept with you. Things are happening!"

"It's not the same—"

"Why? Because you're not seeing instantaneous results?"

Sighing, he began to count off the points of his argument. "Hugh and Aubrey just had a baby and Hugh's building this amazing beach resort here. Quinn and Anna just bought a house and his restoration business is featured monthly in a classic car magazine. Aidan and Zoe are expecting a baby and both of their businesses are booming. Darcy's acing her sophomore year of college. Owen's got this incredible teaching gig and Dad's happy as a freaking clam with his house renovation and his relationship with Martha. And what am I doing? Nothing. Everything I touch is failing."

"Wow…okay. Thanks," she said with a hint of snark.

He glared at her. "Seriously? You know what I'm saying, Savannah. Everyone's got their shit together and my life is just a damn mess."

"Let me ask you something," she said, scooting up to sit on her knees. "When you were touring the world in private jets and staying in five-star hotels, what was everyone else doing?"

He shrugged. "I don't know."

"Bullshit," she snapped. "You don't think each and every one of your siblings had a time in their lives where they felt unsure of themselves or like they were floundering? News flash, buddy, everyone goes through it. No one's business is a huge success from day one. No relationship is flawless from the first date. No one aces every class." She sighed. "Yeah, things kind of suck for you in your professional life right now, Riley, but it's temporary."

He sat up and studied her. "What if it's not?"

"What do you mean?"

"What if I can't finish this album? What if the guys in the band decide they like their other projects more and don't want to come back? What if I fade into obscurity and my legacy is how I couldn't finish one damn album on my own because I wasn't talented enough?"

They were at a standstill at the moment. Savannah stared at him and Riley could see she didn't know what to do or say. Not that he blamed her. Neither did he. When she shifted and began looking around the bedroom, he figured she was looking for a way to escape graciously. He wouldn't stop her. This certainly wasn't the way he envisioned them spending their time after the hours they'd spent exploring one another.

Finally, Savannah stood and walked over to the closet and opened the door.

"What are you doing?" he asked.

She stepped into the space and then back out holding his guitar. Walking over to the bed, she handed it to him. "You can say no, but I don't think you should," she began. "I'm not a music executive and I'm not family. I'm neutral on the entire thing. You can either try to play what's going through your head right now to me, or you can play something you've already finished and recorded for the solo project." She shrugged. "I don't care. Play 'Old MacDonald' if that's what you want. But you need to play. Something. Anything."

Reluctantly, Riley took the guitar from her hands and was only mildly annoyed by her high-handedness. Right now he'd rather be doing anything else other than holding a guitar and preparing to embarrass himself. He'd rather be holding her, kissing her, making love to her again, or taking her out to dinner—anything other than this. He was just about to voice it when she sat back down beside him.

"Play me one song—any song at all—and we'll call it a day," she said softly. "I'm starving and I tend to get cranky when I'm hungry. So I apologize if I'm coming off as being bitchy. But we've been here for a week and you haven't picked up your guitar once. That can't be a good thing, Riley. Even if you're struggling with the album and with the music, you should still be playing. I feel like I've kept you from doing something important."

He shook his head. "It's not you. I swear, Savannah. I just…even holding this right now? It gives me anxiety. I'm so into my own head on this that I'm sabotaging everything."

She leaned in and kissed him on the cheek, her hands on his strong shoulders. "Play something. For me. Please."

One look in her eyes and Riley knew he would deny her nothing. Taking a deep breath, he let it out and began to strum the guitar just to familiarize himself with the sound and get it somewhat in tune. After a few minutes, he put a little distance between the two of them and began to play one of the first ballads he'd ever recorded—"In the Stars." It didn't take long for the music to take over. Riley forgot he was in his childhood bedroom, sitting on the bed in his boxers, with no one but Savannah for an audience. He closed his eyes and sang, and it was as if he was onstage in front of thousands of people.

As the last note began to fade, his hands suddenly started to play again—only this time, it was something new. Something that had eluded him. As if sensing the change in him, Savannah carefully got up and grabbed her recorder and hit record.

Riley had no idea how long he played but when he finally stopped and opened his eyes, Savannah's were filled with tears. He flexed his fingers and gave her a lopsided grin. "Well?"

She wiped at her eyes and sat back beside him and wrapped her arms around him and held him tight. "That was so incredibly beautiful, Riley," she whispered and kissed him tenderly. "It was something new, right? Something you hadn't worked on yet?"

He nodded. "How did you know?"

"When you first started, I saw the look on your face—it was as if the wall was finally starting to come down and you were hearing it for the first time too. Thank you."

He looked at her quizzically. "For what?"

"For allowing me to be here and share this with you. It was…incredible."

Reaching up, he cupped her face in his hands. "No. You're incredible. Thank you for pushing me."

"I didn't mean to. I really didn't. I know everyone's been doing that to you, and I didn't want to get lumped in with them. I was hoping I was encouraging you."

"You did. You definitely did."

She smiled at him and visibly relaxed, her head on his shoulder. "I think this is cause for a celebration."

"I agree." He stood up and pulled Savannah to her feet and hugged her close. "I want you to get changed and we're going out to eat and celebrate."

"Really? We don't need to go out. We can make something here and…celebrate. Just the two of us."

"Oh, we'll hold another private celebration later. But right now I want to do what I've been dying to do since I met you."

"And what's that?" she asked coyly.

"I wanted to take you out. I want to wine and dine you and then bring you home and make love to you all night long."

"Ooo…I like the sound of that."

"I think you're going to like the feel of it, too," he said with a sexy grin. Then he kissed her soundly. "Go get ready."

She looked up at him and he could see the twinkle of excitement in her eyes. "Give me an hour—tops. Okay?"

"I'd wait forever for you, Savannah," he said

solemnly, stroking her cheek. Slowly she moved away and then scampered from the room—her curvy body enticing him with every step she took.

—✧—

It was well after midnight and they were lying in bed. "You're right. This was way better than dessert at the restaurant," Savannah said, still trying to catch her breath.

"I mean, don't get me wrong, their cheesecake and chocolate cream pies are great, but they're not nearly as satisfying as you are." Pulling her closer, Riley kissed the slender column of her neck and simply breathed her in.

"Mmm…" she purred. "I have to admit, Shaughnessy, you certainly know how to impress a girl."

He chuckled. "I do, huh?"

"Oh, absolutely," she replied, her voice going low and seductive. "Dark corners, hiding behind menus, and then practically getting thrown out of the booth so you could take pictures with the fans…very romantic."

He burst out laughing. "We were fine until that group of teenagers spotted us." Savannah elbowed him in the ribs and that simply had him laughing harder. "Uncle! Uncle!"

But she was laughing too. "It wasn't just the teenagers. How do you stand it? People were staring at you all night!"

He shrugged. "I'm used to it. And…for the most part…people keep their distance and respect my privacy. I don't mind them taking pictures across the room or anything like that. What happened at the end was really a bit out of the ordinary." His voice turned serious and he stroked her cheek. "I'm sorry about that. I didn't mean to ruin our night."

She sighed but smiled. "It didn't ruin anything. It was just a little…weird. Those girls were a little brazen. It was almost as if I wasn't even there!"

"Yeah." He grimaced. "Sorry."

"But on the flip side," she countered, "it meant that we got to bring our dessert home to share later."

"Do you want me to go downstairs and get it?"

Savannah shook her head. "Nope. I'm good."

"Yeah you are," he teased and kissed the top of her head.

"I'm going to miss this."

Riley instantly stiffened and sat up. "Miss this? What do you mean?"

Slowly she sat up beside him. "Riley, I'm not going to share a bed with you when your father gets home. It's not up for discussion. And my parents are going to be here tomorrow…well, later today…and I'm spending the weekend with them. So, yeah," she said, stroking his jaw, "I'm going to miss this."

He captured her hand, placed it on his chest, and held it there. "Then change plans," he said softly. "I know your parents are coming and you want to spend time with them, but—"

"But what?" she interrupted softly. "You're still going to be here, and I'm not comfortable sharing a room with you and everyone knowing about it. It's not right."

"It's not anyone's business but ours, Savannah," he said firmly. "What we do doesn't concern them."

She smiled at him patiently. "It's only for the weekend…kind of."

He frowned. "Then we'll stay someplace else after the weekend. With any luck, things will start getting done around here with the renovation and it will be too distracting to work here while construction is going on. We can go and stay at Quinn's or Aidan's and…"

Her other hand come up and stopped him. "Then it's still out there for everyone to know. I'm…I'm a private person, Riley. I don't need or want your whole family knowing we're sleeping together. They'll look at me like I'm some sort of groupie or something. I don't want that!"

"No one will look at you that way. I won't allow it," he said fiercely, leaning his forehead against hers.

She kissed him. "You can't control the way people look at me or what they think. That's just ridiculous."

He sighed. "We still have a lot of work to do on the interview and I don't want to have to say good-bye to you at the end of the day. Not after everything we shared today. Please. Tell me what we can do to make sure it doesn't happen. I'll deal with the weekend while your parents are here, but not for the next couple of weeks. I think I'd slowly go insane if I had to wait until we got back to L.A. to make love again."

Wow. Her heart rate picked up and she felt herself getting turned on all over again. If he had that kind of power over her with just his words, Savannah knew she'd never survive the next few weeks without him again.

"You mentioned Aidan having an apartment…"

He nodded. "It's a one-bedroom, Savannah. People are going to know we're sleeping together if we say we want to stay there."

"And it will be the same if we stay at a hotel," she said wearily.

"Afraid so, sweetheart. Face it, unless we pack up and head home—which would devastate my dad—people are going to know we're involved."

"Involved?" she chuckled. "That sounds so…cold."

In a move he was becoming famous for, he reached for her and rolled her beneath him as they both chuckled. "There's nothing cold about it. We are involved. We're dating. Seeing each other." He kissed her deeply before raising his head and saying, "You're mine."

Yeah.

And she loved the sound of it.

Chapter 8

"So by the time she started high school, she was pretty much destined to start up a school newspaper there!" Paul Daly was saying as he sat at Ian's kitchen table along with his wife Robyn, Ian, Martha, Savannah, and Riley. "That's where she got the nickname Daily Scoop!"

Savannah groaned and Riley chuckled along with everyone else.

"She pretty much got the whole thing off the ground. The high school still uses the template she created and follows all the guidelines she put in place. They even honored her last year for her contribution to the school and the community," Robyn Daly added. "We're so proud of her."

"And rightfully so!" Martha said with a huge smile. "That's quite an accomplishment!"

Beneath the table, Riley reached over and squeezed Savannah's hand in support. It was nice to see other parents who believed in bragging about their kids.

"So how was the drive?" Savannah asked, doing her best to change the subject. "See anything interesting?"

"Well, we got a bit of a late start so we didn't stop nearly as much as we would have liked," Paul began, "but we made a list of things we want to see on the way back when we have more time."

"How long are you going to stay in the area?" Ian asked.

"Just the weekend. Savannah told us about your

grandson's christening—congratulations, by the way. You must be very excited," Robyn added.

"We are," Ian said. "He's my first grandchild, but there's another on the way and I have a feeling there will be another not long behind."

"Wow! You are going to have your hands full!" Paul said with a huge grin.

"I wouldn't have it any other way," Ian said, smiling back at him. "Family is very important to me. It always has been. And I love how my kids are following in my footsteps." Everyone nodded. "So I know you're going with Savannah and staying out by the beach, but it would really mean a lot to me and to Hugh and Aubrey if you would join us tomorrow for the christening. It's going to be a small church ceremony and then we're going to my son Aidan's house for a barbecue—nothing fancy—but we'd love to have the three of you with us."

Savannah hung her head while her parents giddily accepted the invitation.

"We would be honored," Robyn said. "We traveled so much while Savannah was growing up and our family is scattered all over the country, but we understand and agree with you on the importance of it. Thank you for wanting to include us."

Ian smiled and looked over at Savannah before returning his attention to her parents. "We think the world of your daughter and even though we've only known her for a week, she's made quite an impression."

"Well, thank you," Paul said.

For the next hour, they all sat around enjoying the desserts Ian and Martha had brought home with them and talking about things to do in the area. Riley joined in as much as he could, but he couldn't help noticing how quiet Savannah had grown over the course of the night. He knew how she felt about not going to Connor's baptism but hadn't thought the whole situation would affect her quite like this.

There was no way for him to get into it with her right now with their parents around, but he vowed he was going to get to the bottom of it somehow.

When her parents stood and announced they were tired from their drive and wanted to get to the hotel, Savannah stood with them. Her suitcase was waiting by the front door and it pained Riley to see it there.

He, Ian, and Martha walked them all out and as the parents were all talking, Riley pulled Savannah to the side. "You okay?"

She nodded. "Yeah, why?" Her voice was soft but Riley could see the distraction in her eyes.

"You got really quiet in there, that's all. I just wanted to make sure you were all right."

She shrugged. "I knew your dad would extend the invitation, but I thought my parents would respect my request and decline. I thought they'd want to spend the weekend with me—and just me. I guess I was wrong."

"Hey," he said quietly, grasping her shoulders. "Don't take it like that. You know my dad can be charming and persuasive. Maybe they were just being nice. If you really don't want to go, talk to them. And I'll talk to my dad and get it straightened out. Okay?"

Savannah nodded and sighed. "I'm going to miss you tonight. I know we only got to sleep together last night but…I liked it."

He groaned. "You're killing me."

"It's what I do," she said saucily and looked over her shoulder toward her parents before turning back to him. "I really want to kiss you, but—"

"I know. I feel the same." He had to fight the urge to simply pull her into his arms. "Can I call you later? Maybe after everyone's asleep?"

"I'd like that. I have my own room and they're not adjoining or anything—the hotel was pretty booked. I was lucky to get two rooms. But if you give me a couple of hours, I should be back in mine and then we'll be free to talk."

"Okay."

She smiled sadly. "Okay."

When she moved out of his grasp, Riley dropped his hands and let her go. He slowly followed her over to the RV and stood next to his dad. "It was nice meeting you both," he said.

"Same here, Riley," Paul said, shaking his hand. "I'm sure we'll be seeing you again tomorrow."

Stepping back, Ian, Riley, and Martha let the Dalys climb into their vehicle and wished them a good night before watching them drive away. Ian squeezed his son's shoulder as if telling him he understood.

"I'm going to take Martha home," he finally said. "I'll see you in the morning."

And for the first time, it didn't bother him that his father was implying he might not be home until then.

If anything, it made him smile.

—∿∿—

The night sky was full of stars, and the breeze coming off the ocean was absolutely heavenly. Savannah relaxed in her seat by the pool and watched her father approach. He had two bottles of water in his hands and a smile on his face.

"Where's Mom?"

Paul Daly sat down and handed one of the beverages to his daughter. "She's soaking in the tub and giddy about sleeping in a real bed tonight. As much as we love the RV, there's no way to fit a king-size bed in there."

Savannah chuckled. "Definitely not." She took a drink and let her head fall back. "I never get tired of the sound of the ocean. If only I could afford it back home."

"As you can see, California isn't the only place you can find the beach, sweetheart. You're young. You can go wherever you want, and I can guarantee you, you're going to be able to find a surfside home in your budget once you leave L.A."

She shrugged. "Yeah, but...I like it there. My job is there."

"Your job makes it possible to work remotely. You know it and I know it. Tommy's lucky to have you and I think he'd be supportive if you wanted to move."

"I don't know about that."

When he looked at her quizzically, she told him all about the conversation she'd had with her boss on the day he gave her the news about interviewing Riley.

"Tommy can be a great guy, but when he doesn't get his way, he can be a real jackass. I'm never sure which version of him I'll be getting when I go into the office. I think one day he'd be fine with me working remotely and the next he'd insist I move back." She shook her head. "I don't know if I'm up for that kind of aggravation."

"All I'm saying, Savannah, is you have choices.

That's not the only magazine out there, and I didn't really think you wanted to be a music reporter for the rest of your life. What happened to writing your book?"

Ugh…why couldn't he want to go to bed too? "I work on it every now and then, but I haven't settled on any one story that I'm passionate about."

He nodded. "How's the interview going? Riley seems like a nice guy—definitely not the conceited rock star I was expecting."

"Yeah," she said, unable to hide her smile. "He wasn't what I was expecting either. I really had him pegged all wrong and I had to apologize to him for it."

He chuckled. "Sometimes you're too honest for your own good. Someone like Riley Shaughnessy doesn't need his ego stroked, I'm sure. You should have given him hell just for fun."

She laughed with him. "It did cross my mind, but—"

"But," Paul interrupted, "you found out you genuinely liked him."

There was no point in pretending otherwise. Her father was like an evil genius when it came to finding out her secrets. "I do."

"Nothing wrong with that. From what I observed tonight, he genuinely likes you too."

"What makes you say that?"

"For starters, he didn't take over the conversation. He let everyone talk about whatever we wanted to and never turned the conversation to himself."

"Dad, that hardly says—"

He shushed her. "Secondly, he wasn't openly groping you in front of me and your mother. It shows he has respect."

Savannah rolled her eyes. "Why would he be groping me at all? Sheesh!"

"Because under the table he was holding your hand," he said evenly. "I'm not blind, Savannah. And," he said with a smirk, "I was looking for any telltale signs."

"You're crazy," she said, but with humor. "I still don't understand why you would even think to look for anything. I'm here on assignment. I've traveled with rock stars before. Riley's hardly the first celebrity I've hung out with."

"Yeah, but he's the first one who brought you home to meet his family. And when you called and asked us to visit, I could hear it in your voice that you were nervous. You weren't your usual confident self. I knew right away something about this whole situation was different."

Well, damn.

Before Savannah could begin to explain, her father spoke. "You're a grown woman, Savannah. I'm not going to sit here and lecture you about getting involved with Riley. I think he's a very nice guy and his father is even nicer. Personally, I'm looking forward to meeting the rest of the family tomorrow."

"Um…yeah, about that…"

"Yeah, I know you invited your mother and me here because you didn't want to go to the party or encroach on their celebration, but now that I've met Ian and Riley? I think it will be a good thing to go."

"Dad…" she whined.

"You know, not everything is about you, sweetheart," he said. He was smiling but his voice was firm. "They were incredibly sweet to invite all of us and it's just rude to turn them down."

"But I wanted us to spend some time together. It's been a long time since we've done that."

"And whose fault is that?" he countered. "We invite you to come home to visit all the time but you're always busy. We drove all this way, we're spending time together now, and we'll still be spending time together tomorrow at the christening. You'll have to introduce us to everyone and I'm sure it's going to be a lot of fun."

Savannah really wasn't so sure. She frowned at him. "If I promise to come home more often, can we skip the party?"

Paul laughed out loud and finished his drink. "Why is this such a big deal?"

"Dad, it's a personal family event. We're not family. I would resent it if a bunch of strangers showed up for something like that. It's just not right."

He frowned at her. "In your line of work, you have gone to multiple events where the only reason you were there was because of a single person. You've shared stories about parties you've gone to, Savannah. You weren't related to anyone there. So why don't you just come out and tell me what's really going on."

She groaned. "All those other events weren't family parties, Dad. There's a difference."

"I don't see why. At least this one you were invited to—and according to Ian, the whole family wants you there. What does Riley say? Did he ask you not to go?"

"No!" she cried adamantly and then realized maybe she was overreacting. Taking a steadying breath, she shifted in her seat. "No. Riley wants me to go too," she said softly. "He was really upset I didn't want to go."

"I see."

Savannah looked over at him. "Do you?"

He nodded and smiled sadly. "Unfortunately, I do." Leaning forward, he took one of her hands in his. "I think the Shaughnessys scare you."

"What? You're crazy." There was no humor in her statement this time.

"Hear me out," he said. "We traveled a lot and moved around a lot when you were growing up, and you never really had the chance to observe what a normal, close-knit family was like. Whenever we visited relatives, it was a big, chaotic circus and because we lived so far away from everyone, you never had the chance to feel close to any of them. I'm sorry for that. But it doesn't mean you can't still experience it."

"Dad—"

"I'm serious. The only one looking at you as an outsider, Savannah, is you. From the little amount of time I spent with Ian and Riley, they don't strike me as the kind of men who extend invitations just to be polite. They genuinely want you there. And—if we're being completely honest—if you're involved with Riley, then you owe it to him to be there with him. By not going you're essentially saying you're ashamed to be seen with him or you're ashamed of the relationship."

Looking away, Savannah felt herself blush.

"Oh, come on! You're kidding me, right?" he asked, clearly frustrated.

"Riley isn't... He's not just a normal guy, Dad!" she cried. "He's one of the biggest rock stars in the world! And here I am…a reporter…and I'm supposed to be writing a story about him, and now I'm sleeping with him! How do you think it's going to look to everyone?"

"Okay, for starters, you didn't have to throw in how you were sleeping with him. TMI, Savannah," he said in an attempt to lighten up the situation. "And really, I don't think anyone's looking at you that way."

"But you don't know for sure!"

"And neither do you! I don't understand what it is that has my confident daughter suddenly doubting herself! It's not like you!"

Tears began to well in her eyes and she quickly wiped them away before they had a chance to fall. "I have never been someone to get involved with a subject," she said, hating the tremble in her voice. "Ever. I don't get starstruck. I don't fawn over people. And yet from the very first time I came face-to-face with Riley, I have felt completely… Everything's different. I don't even recognize myself some of the time."

Standing up, Paul grabbed her hands and pulled Savannah to her feet and hugged her. "It's going to be all right."

It was harder to stop the tears this time. "How do you know?" Her voice was muffled against his shoulder.

"Because I just do," he said. "Haven't you figured that out yet? Dads know everything."

She couldn't help the giggle that came out. "What if…what if I fall for him and…he doesn't fall back?"

Pulling back, Paul looked down at his daughter's face and gently wiped away her tears. "It's a risk we all take. You've dated plenty of guys, Savannah. Sometimes things don't work out. But the fact you're feeling this emotional tells me you may have met the one."

"Oh God…" she groaned and began to cry again.

"Shh…it's all right, sweetheart. Trust me."

And Savannah just let him hug her until she calmed down. It felt good to get it all out and share her fears with someone. And the fact that it was her dad was really just a perk. They'd always been close and there weren't any secrets between them—he wouldn't allow it. And right now there was comfort in simply standing there with him.

When she finally pulled herself together, she thought they'd sit back down, but he stopped her and kissed her on the forehead.

"It's getting late and I should go up and check on your mom. Are you going to be okay?"

She nodded. "Eventually. The whole thing basically terrifies me. I've never fallen so hard so fast. It's like being swept up in a tornado."

Paul chuckled. "That pretty much sums it up. But in the end, it can be amazing. Don't shy away from the tornado, kiddo. I think you'll find exactly what you're looking for when things calm down."

Sighing, she rested her head on his shoulder as they began to walk back toward the hotel. "Promise I can call you when I'm freaking out and you'll talk me down from the ledge?"

He chuckled. "Sweetheart, you can call me any time—day or night—and I promise I'll be there to listen and help you out."

"Thanks, Dad." She stopped and hugged him fiercely.

They walked inside and rode the elevator in silence. Paul and Robyn were on the tenth floor, Savannah on the twelfth. With a promise to see one another in the morning, she waved as her father stepped off the elevator and then hugged herself for the rest of the ride.

After a hot shower, Savannah slipped on her robe and wandered around the hotel room as she towel dried her hair. It was after eleven and she wondered if and when Riley was going to call. It was the first time in a week he was by himself and she was pretty sure he was enjoying the solitude.

She wasn't.

It was funny how in such a short amount of time her life was changing and the things she swore were a necessity to survive—like her peace and quiet and alone time—were suddenly not so important. She missed Riley—missed talking to him. Looking over at the king-size bed, she imagined how decadent it would be to share it with him.

Not happening.

Tossing the towel on the chair, she sat down on the bed and sighed. The christening party. Now that her parents were on board there was no way out of it. No doubt Riley would be thrilled when she told him, but it didn't make it any easier for Savannah to relax about it.

"I guess it won't be so bad," she muttered. It wasn't as if she didn't like Riley's family. She did. And now she'd get to meet his sister too and maybe get in some time talking with her for the article too.

"No! Dammit!" Jumping back to her feet, she wanted to kick herself. This was one of the main reasons she didn't want to go to the damn party. It was a family celebration, a party—and part of Savannah was sorely tempted to use it as a work opportunity. "What is wrong with me?"

Pacing back and forth, she thought of all the ways

she could avoid the temptation—unfortunately, not going was no longer an option and it was her number one excuse! Of course she'd leave her pad and pen and recorder at the hotel to eliminate the temptation. But how was she supposed to have normal conversation with everyone? Savannah figured they'd all be happy to share Riley stories with her again—particularly Darcy since she missed the first round of it—so how was she to stop them?

"For the love of it, it's not like I don't know how to carry on polite conversation with people I'm not interviewing," she muttered and grabbed the towel off the chair and went to hang it in the bathroom. And then realized she still didn't have anything to do.

Should she call Riley or wait for his call? Deciding that calling him after he said he'd call her made her needy, she shut off the bathroom light and walked back into the room. Grabbing a bottle of water from the mini-fridge, she sat on the bed and turned on the TV. Channel surfing seemed like a good way to pass the time.

Fifteen minutes later, she almost jumped out of her skin when her phone rang. She smiled when Riley's name and number came up on the screen. "Hey," she said softly and relaxed back against the pillows.

"Hey, yourself," he said. "How are you doing?"

"Good. Just relaxing."

"Did you get some time to visit with your folks?"

"Just my dad. Mom was tired and wanted to soak in a hot bath and crawl into bed. RV sleeping is not the greatest."

"I can relate to that. It doesn't matter how much they trick out those tour buses, the beds are never great."

"Exactly. So Dad and I hung out by the pool and chatted for a while and now I'm just flipping through the channels, hoping to find something to watch."

"I'm not a big fan of late-night talk shows," Riley said. "I've done almost all of them and they're all great guys, but I always feel bad for whoever they have on that night for the interview."

"Why?" she asked, curious.

"It can be really intimidating. The way you and I are doing the interview is laid-back and relaxing and no one is watching. But with a television interview, everyone's watching. Even though they tape it early in the day and air it later and some things get edited out, the studio audience is there for any blunder or stupid thing you do."

"I'm sure you haven't done anything stupid," she said sweetly.

"I threw up backstage at *The Tonight Show*—back when Leno was still hosting."

"No!"

"True story. I wasn't sick, we'd done the show before, but something about the whole thing had me twisted up in knots and when they came back to tell us it was time to go on, I just…hurled."

"Ew…gross!"

"Uh-huh."

"So what did they do? Did you still go on?"

"They moved some segments around and we went on and I was fine. But Jay didn't ask us back."

"Wow. That sucks."

"Yes, it did," he said. "So what are you watching? Anything good? I'll turn on the TV and it will be like we're watching it together."

Aww... "Um, I haven't really found anything good. The local news was just ending when I turned the TV on and I was just checking out some HGTV when the phone rang."

"Ooo...*House Hunters.* One of my favorites."

Savannah laughed. "Stop. It is not!"

"It's true! I watch a lot of HGTV. I get a kick out of watching other people figure out what kind of house they have to get because they can't afford what they really want."

"That's one way of looking at it," she chuckled and got more comfortable on the bed.

"Okay, hang on for a sec. Let me just grab something to drink..."

"Okay." She was about to reach for her own water when there was a knock at the door. Frowning, she approached it slowly. Was something wrong with her parents? Did they need something? Why didn't they just call? "Who is it?"

"Housekeeping!"

Housekeeping? She didn't call for anything. Peering through the peephole, she gasped and then unlocked the door. Pulling it open, she never got a word out as she jumped into Riley's arms and immediately met his lips in a searing kiss. Spinning them around, Riley slammed the door shut and backed her up against it.

When he finally lifted his head, he was smiling. "So you wanna watch some TV in bed with me?"

"With a king-size bed, I can think of a lot of other things I'd rather do with you," she said and then pulled him in for another kiss.

He carried her across the room and brought them both

down on the bed—where they spent the rest of the night exploring all the possibilities.

―∞―

The sun was coming up as Riley stood and stretched. The view from Savannah's hotel room was breathtaking. He'd stayed later than he had originally planned, but every time he tried to get out of the bed, Savannah would sigh or reach for him and he couldn't make himself leave.

Now, she was lying on her side watching him—a sleepy smile on her face.

"I'm going to see you later at the church, right?" Riley asked as he got dressed.

"Like I have a choice," she said with a grimace. "You and your nice family and their genuine invitations. How were my parents supposed to say no?"

He chuckled. "They weren't. And neither were you. Obviously I underestimated your stubborn streak."

"Well, now you've been warned, so be prepared." Rolling over onto her back, she sighed. "Do you really have to go?"

"Baby, I should have left hours ago. Not that I have a curfew or anything…"

Savannah laughed. "Yeah, but now you have to risk doing the walk of shame in front of your dad."

"As long as I do it before Darcy gets home, everything will be all right."

Sitting up, Savannah combed her hair away from her face. "Do I need to be worried about meeting her? Everyone seems just a little bit intimidated by your sister. And she's the baby of the family."

"Darcy is…" Riley shook his head. "She's definitely a force to be reckoned with. I think growing up with five older brothers has made her bold and we're all still getting used to it. She didn't start getting quite so vocal and argumentative until she was almost eighteen so it's still kind of new to us."

"I couldn't imagine what it was like for her. Seriously. You must have scared away every boy in town."

"And in the surrounding ones," he said with a grin, tucking in his shirt.

Slowly, Riley walked back over to the bed and kissed her thoroughly before reluctantly pulling away. "Try to get a couple more hours of sleep. I'll see you at two at the church."

"Stop reminding me," she sighed.

Riley was going to tease her but he could tell she was already half asleep. As quietly as he could, he walked to the door and left. Out in the hallway, he took a minute to catch his breath. He hated leaving her—even now he was arguing with himself about going back inside and staying with her until it was time for the christening. But Savannah needed her sleep and he needed to get home and face the music.

When the elevator doors opened, a young couple looked up as they were about to step off, their eyes going wide with recognition. "Morning," he murmured and smiled nervously as he stepped into the elevator and they stepped out. He pulled his cap down low and waved as the door closed.

And then breathed a sigh of relief.

On the ride home Riley hoped his father had chosen this morning to sleep in. He couldn't help but run through the scenario in his head—walking in the door and his father catching him. That hadn't happened since he was seventeen, and yet the fear was still there. He was a grown man and didn't owe anyone an explanation of where or how he spent his night, but the thought of his father finding out about him and Savannah made him uneasy. She wasn't ready for his family to know, and he wanted to respect her privacy.

For now.

Everyone was going to find out eventually—and sooner rather than later, he was predicting—because there was no way Riley could hide the way he felt about her. No matter who was watching. They were adults and as such, they were entitled to what they were feeling.

Damn interview. It was a pain in the ass no matter how he looked at it. But then again, if not for the interview, he would never have met Savannah.

"And there's your silver lining," he muttered as he pulled onto his father's block.

He was driving along and noticed a car coming in the opposite direction—which was odd for this time of the morning. And the closer he got, the wider his eyes got.

"Son of a…"

Ian Shaughnessy was just pulling into the driveway.

Riley had to laugh. What were the odds of him and his father sneaking in at the same time? Well, technically, Ian wasn't sneaking—it was his own house. But it still seemed incredibly comical. Parking behind his father's car, Riley climbed out. Together, father and son walked to the door without meeting one another's gaze.

Once inside, Ian went to the kitchen and put on a

pot of coffee. Riley sat at the table, staring at his hands. Within minutes, they each had a mug in their hands.

"I, um…" Ian began, "I would appreciate it if you didn't share this with your siblings."

"Right back at you," Riley murmured.

They drank their coffee in awkward silence before Ian put his mug down and finally met his son's eyes. "Can I just say that I hope it was Savannah who kept you out all night?"

Riley grinned.

And that, in turn, made Ian grin. "Good."

The church service was beautiful. Savannah couldn't help the tears that welled in her eyes as she sat in the pew next to her parents and Riley and watched as little Connor Rylan Shaughnessy was baptized in the arms of his godparents—Aidan and Zoe.

After the family took about a thousand pictures in the church, they stepped outside and waved to the few members of the paparazzi who were waiting outside. Everyone took it in stride, and for the most part, Savannah would say that Riley hid his annoyance well. From what she could remember from her research, there were hardly any photos of him at home with his family. So this was pretty much a first for them.

Afterward, they all drove over to the godparents' house for the party. Savannah still didn't feel one hundred percent comfortable, but it wasn't for anyone's lack of hospitality. From the minute she was spotted at the church, she had been hugged and welcomed and thanked by everyone. And so had her parents.

Well, by everyone except Darcy.

Savannah had been anxious to meet the lone Shaughnessy daughter, but she hadn't seemed to be around when initial introductions were made. Now that they were at the party, she almost felt like it was a mission to track her down.

The family was spread out between the massive yard and inside Aidan and Zoe's home. Savannah had managed to send Riley to get her something to drink while she went in search of his sister. Not that she told him her plan, but it was what it was. When she stepped outside and went to the edge of the deck, she spotted the girl off in the far corner of the yard sitting next to a large garden. With a steadying breath, Savannah began to head over.

Darcy Shaughnessy was beautiful. Not that Savannah expected anything less—the entire family seemed to have the beautiful gene. A gentle breeze was blowing and Darcy was combing her dark hair out of her face when she noticed Savannah's approach.

"Hey," Savannah said with a smile. "We didn't get to meet earlier. I'm Savannah Daly." She held out her hand to Darcy and frowned when she simply looked at it but didn't shake it. Trying not to take it personally, Savannah slowly lowered it. "Do you mind if I sit down?" There were two benches by the garden, and she opted to take the one Darcy wasn't sitting on when the girl merely shrugged.

"I hear you're only home for the weekend," Savannah said, trying to draw her into conversation. "That's got to be rough with all the flying."

Darcy shrugged again.

O-kay. Now what? Looking around the yard,

Savannah almost prayed for Riley to find her. "So…
what are you taking this semester at school?"

Finally Darcy acknowledged her.

With a roll of her eyes.

"Look, spare me the whole you-want-to-be-my-
friend thing," Darcy said. "You're a reporter. You're
here because you're doing a story on Riley. You're no
better than those photographers hanging around outside
the church." She paused and gave a look of disdain. "It's
not like you really care about me or who I am. You're
looking for dirt on my brother."

Wow. "And that bothers you?"

Darcy looked at her like she thought Savannah was a
moron. "Uh…yeah. It does. Why can't you people just
leave him alone? What gives you the right to come to
a private family party? I mean, it's a major invasion of
privacy! I don't think—"

"If it makes you feel any better," Savannah interrupted, "I didn't want to come. As a matter of fact, I
pretty much tried to make sure I wouldn't have to be
here. I convinced my parents to drive here from Kansas
so I'd have something to do."

"Then why are you all here?" Darcy asked sarcastically.

"Because your family is too damn charming and they
refuse to take no for an answer!"

A small twitch of Darcy's lips was the first sign that
maybe she was starting to relax.

"I had the whole weekend planned out—where we
were going to go, what we were going to do—museums,
aquariums, war ships! I had every tourist brochure for
the area highlighted and ready to go! But one hour with
your dad and all of a sudden they were like long-lost

friends who couldn't bear *not* to spend time together. It was pretty damn annoying."

This time Darcy did chuckle. "Tell me about it. Dad used to almost be antisocial; now he's like a friend to the friendless."

"It's not necessarily a bad trait."

"No, but…it's annoying. As you've clearly discovered." She sighed and studied Savannah. "So what were you going to do? Really. You know, if you weren't here."

"I wanted to show them the coast. Living in Kansas, they don't have any beaches. I thought it would be nice to spend the day out in the sun, maybe do a little swimming and fishing. Maybe grab some fresh seafood for dinner." She shrugged. "Turns out they wanted steak and a backyard. Who knew?"

"Wow. Bummer," Darcy said and then began to laugh.

Savannah nearly sagged to the ground with relief. She'd broken down the barrier. "I'll get over it. At least we're staying at a hotel on the beach. I can see and hear the ocean, and maybe before they leave I'll get to walk along the shore with them."

"When do they leave?"

"I think they're planning on hitting the road Monday morning. They've never been here on the East Coast so they've planned a bit of a road trip for themselves in their RV."

"Yikes. No offense, but RV living does not sound appealing."

"I'm with you on that. I'm glad they got into it after I moved out. We traveled a lot when I was growing up but luckily we flew. The thought of sleeping in a big box on wheels just…" Savannah shuddered. "Let's just say it's not my thing."

"It's a lot like the buses Riley uses on tour, I guess."

"I bet my parents wish it was more like one of those tour buses. Their RV is kind of small—really just for the two of them. Nothing glamorous about it."

"Well, that stinks," Darcy said and gave Savannah a small smile. "So now you're stuck here."

"It's not so bad," she replied honestly. "It's a beautiful day and the ceremony was very nice. I'd never been to a christening before so it was something new for me."

"You're lucky Connor was so good. I've been to ones where the baby screams the entire time. Those are not fun at all."

Savannah chuckled. "He seems like a really good baby. Hugh and Aubrey are very blessed."

Darcy shrugged. "I don't know about that."

"What do you mean?"

Looking around to make sure no one was listening, Darcy scooted closer to Savannah. "Aubrey had cancer when she was younger. They didn't think they'd ever have kids and there's always the possibility of the cancer coming back. I don't know if I could live like that."

"They told me about that last weekend and I felt the exact same way. But I think it's great that they don't let the fear rule their lives. They're so happy and now they have a beautiful baby." She sighed.

"I am happy for them," Darcy said, "and I hope when I'm home on my next break they'll let me stay with them for a bit and watch Connor."

"I'm sure they wouldn't turn down the offer."

"Here are my two favorite girls," Riley said as he strolled over, drinks in hand. "I see you finally met the princess."

Darcy groaned. "One trip to Disneyland and I can't shake that nickname!"

Riley sat down beside his sister and grinned. He handed Savannah her drink. "I hate to break it to you, but Disney has nothing to do with the nickname. That was all you way before then."

"Says you," she grumbled.

"So what are you two lovely ladies talking about?"

"RVs, buses, and babies," Darcy said and smirked at the confused look on Riley's face. "We started talking about Savannah's parents and their RV, which led to your tour buses, and then we moved on to Connor and how awesome he is."

"Ah," Riley said. "Got it." He sighed and smiled. "I'm glad we all got to be here for his big day."

"How long are you here for?" Darcy asked him.

"A couple of weeks. I wanted Savannah to get to meet everyone and see if she could interview them for the article."

"And that's going to take a couple of weeks? Seems to me you could be on a plane home Monday. I'm sure she's talked to everyone—God knows we've all been dying to share embarrassing stories about you with the press for years!" Then she looked at Savannah. "Let me tell you, it is no dream having a rock star for a brother!"

"What?" Riley cried. "It's not? Why am I just hearing about this?"

Darcy giggled. "You're such a dork." Then she

looked at Savannah again. "It was a nightmare at school once people found out I'm Riley Shaughnessy's sister. It makes it pretty hard to figure out who is really your friend and who is just mooching around in hopes of meeting him."

"Yeah, well, it wasn't such a dream for me either, you know, when I went to visit you at school. Those girls can be vicious!" Riley said defensively.

"Oh…poor you," Darcy cooed, patting his knee.

Savannah watched the two of them in wonder. They were ten years apart in age—which should be a huge deterrent to their relationship—and yet they were incredibly close to one another. It was very sweet to watch.

"Okay, so just to be clear," Darcy said, looking between the two of them, "you're okay with her interviewing me, and you didn't come here to interview me. Do I have that right?"

Both Savannah and Riley nodded.

"Believe me, the beach was calling my name today," Savannah said.

"And I pretty much insisted she be here," Riley said.

"That takes a lot of pressure off. Whew!" Darcy said with a smile as she stood. "If you will excuse me, I'm going to see who I have to steal Connor from so we can have some bonding time. Savannah, you and I will definitely talk later. Bye!"

It took a full minute after Darcy had walked away for Riley to move over to Savannah's bench and sit close beside her. "So that's my sister."

"She's…yeah. She's something all right."

"I did try to warn you."

"There is no middle ground with her," Savannah said. "She either likes you or she doesn't."

Riley nodded. "Yup."

Savannah looked at him and smiled. "I think she likes me."

He smiled back and rested his forehead against hers. "That's good. Because I do too. A lot."

"Yeah?" she whispered.

"Oh yeah. Definitely."

The happy sigh couldn't be contained.

"This is the part where you say you like me too," Riley said before adding, "a lot."

"I thought it was already implied."

"Well, it wasn't. So come on…" he teased, nudging her with his shoulder. "Just say it."

She giggled and playfully swatted him away.

"I'm not leaving until you admit it."

"Okay, fine," she huffed dramatically. "I like you too, Riley."

"And?" he encouraged.

"A lot," she purred and leaned in close to him.

"I'm trying to respect your wishes and all, but I really want to kiss you right now."

Looking around the yard, Savannah noticed that most of the group was back inside the house, and the few who were outside weren't paying any attention to them. "I think we're safe. Just be quick."

He chuckled and cupped her face in his hands, his thumbs stroking her cheek. "Sweetheart, I never want to be quick with you. Not in anything we do." Then he lowered his lips to hers and kissed her slowly—for a very long time.

And he didn't care who was watching.

It was after dark and it was down to the Shaughnessys and the Dalys sitting around Aidan and Zoe's living room. Riley couldn't help but hide his amusement at how animated his sister had become in sharing stories with Savannah and her family about life growing up as the only girl in an all-male household.

"Thankfully Anna was always around so I could ask her questions from time to time, because believe me, if ever you want to freak a man out, ask him to take you shopping for a bra or tampons."

Everyone laughed until Quinn cut in. "Tampons, yes and always. But bras? There is a definite difference between taking your sister shopping for a bra and taking your girlfriend shopping for one. Apples and oranges."

Darcy grinned and looked over at Savannah. "I traumatized them all. Sometimes I didn't need either of those things, but it was just fun to watch their reactions."

"I never took you shopping," Owen said, confusion lacing his voice.

"Be thankful, bro," Hugh said. "You got off easy."

"I freaked you out on a daily basis just by being a girl, Owen," Darcy said affectionately. "There was no challenge there and besides, you were too nice to do that to."

"Oh…well…thanks. I guess," he said and relaxed back in his chair.

"So what do you think, Savannah?" Darcy asked. "Did we give you enough ammunition to use in your article on Riley or do you need more?"

"I think she has more than enough," Riley answered before Savannah could. She was sitting on the floor in front of him and he was mindlessly playing with her hair. When he realized he was doing it, he slowly pulled his hand away.

"Nonsense," Aidan chuckled. "I'm sure we have more stories she would enjoy even if she doesn't use them in her article!"

For a few minutes it was barely controlled chaos as everyone vied for the best Riley story. He took it all in stride, but in his mind he was wondering when the hell they could all leave so he could sneak back over to Savannah's hotel room and be alone with her.

That wasn't entirely true. He was trying to figure out a way to get Aidan alone so he could ask about the possibility of staying in their apartment for the week. What Darcy had said earlier was true—now that Savannah had talked to his entire family, there wasn't really a point in staying any longer. And the thought of getting back to L.A. and not having prying eyes was even more appealing.

Rising to his feet, he made eye contact with Aidan as he walked toward the kitchen. Luckily his brother took the hint and followed.

"Don't tell me you want to get mad because I just incited a riot in there over stories about you," Aidan said with a laugh. He grabbed a couple of beers out of the refrigerator and handed one to Riley.

"No, dumbass. I needed to talk to you for a minute but it's been hard to get you alone all day."

"Hey, as godfather and host, I was busy." He took a pull of his beer. "What's up?"

"Dad's getting ready to start on the room renovation this week, and I was wondering if Savannah and I could stay at the apartment."

Aidan looked at him funny. "Sure...I mean...of course, but...you know it's only one bedroom, right?"

Riley chuckled. Leave it to his oldest brother to be the most clueless of the bunch. "Uh...yeah. We're aware of that."

Still looking a little confused, Aidan shrugged. "You could sleep here and Savannah can have the apartment. Or you can both just stay in here. Zoe won't mind but—" Then he stopped and Riley knew the instant the lightbulb went on. "Oh...okay. Now I get it."

"Took you long enough," Riley teased. "But listen, we're not saying anything to anyone about it so if you could, you know, keep it to yourself, I'd appreciate it."

"No problem. Although you're just lucky I don't pay attention to shit. How do you know no one else has caught on?"

"I don't. I'm just hoping."

"Why? What's the big deal?"

"Savannah feels weird about it. She doesn't want anyone looking at her like she's a groupie or just hanging out with me like that because of who I am or the story."

"Are you sure she's not?" Aidan asked seriously.

For the first time in his life, Riley was almost overwhelmed with the urge to punch his brother. "It's not like that," he said through clenched teeth.

"Okay, okay. Calm down," Aidan said, holding his hands up defensively. "Look, don't pay any attention to me, I didn't have a clue you were even into her. But if you say things are good, then they're good."

Riley sighed. "I think... I think they're more than good."

"Oh no..."

"What?"

"Why does everyone come to me with this stuff?"

"Right now I'm wondering the same thing," Riley muttered.

Aidan huffed and put his beer down and was just about to say something when Hugh walked in. "Hey, what's going on?"

Great. Now Hugh was going to figure it out too.

"It's nothing," Aidan said. "Riley was just whining because I wanted to tell more stories about him."

Hugh laughed and grabbed a beer for himself. "Oh. I thought he was in here drawing his and Savannah's names in hearts and telling you how dreamy she is."

"What?" Riley cried.

"Dude, you were playing with her hair and I saw you kissing her out in the yard," Hugh said, still laughing. "Relax. It's not a big deal."

"Well…" Aidan began.

"Shut up," Riley hissed at him.

"Oh…so there's more?" Hugh asked, his eyes getting big. "This is great. Come on, tell me. What's going on?"

"What's going on with what?" Quinn asked, walking in and frowning at his brothers all huddled together. "What are you guys talking about?"

Oh, for the love of it, Riley thought.

"It's nothing," Aidan repeated.

"Well, damn," Quinn sighed, taking the beer Hugh was handing him. "I thought we were talking about asking Riley to do all of our hair for my wedding. You know, since he seems to really be into that sort of thing now."

"Funny," Riley murmured while his brothers all laughed at him.

"Come on," Quinn said, slapping Riley on the back, "lighten up. It's adorable the way you were all mesmerized by Savannah's hair."

"Guys," Aidan said. "Knock it off."

"No, no...this is good," Hugh said. "Riley was the one who made fun of me when I was struggling with my attraction to Aubrey. I think it's only fair I get to have a little fun at his expense now."

"Hey, yeah," Quinn said. "Me too!" He looked at Riley. "Remember how you were ribbing me about Anna at Aidan's wedding? Turnabout's fair play, bro."

Owen walked in without a word, grabbed a bottle of water for himself, and walked right back out of the room.

"Seriously, we need to do something with him," Quinn said.

"Agreed." Hugh chuckled.

"Oh, so because he didn't want to jump on the pile, he's the bad guy?" Riley asked.

"Don't try changing the subject," Hugh said. "But nice try."

"Fine. But can we," Riley looked over his shoulder toward the living room, "can we at least go outside and talk?"

Quietly, the four of them stepped out onto the deck and Riley led them to the farthest corner away from the house.

"I kind of feel like we need the cone of silence," Hugh whispered.

"Shut up, jackass," Riley said and then huffed. "Okay, so...cat's out of the bag. I've got a thing for Savannah. I was asking Aidan if we could stay in the apartment this week since Dad's starting work on the house. There! Everyone happy now?"

His three brothers looked at one another and then back at him. "Well, that was a little anticlimactic," Hugh said. "Sheesh. Way to ruin it."

"Yeah," Quinn agreed. "You're supposed to deny it for a little bit so we can all make fun of you. Now it just seems mean."

"I told you all it was nothing," Aidan said, "but does anyone listen to me? No. I'm just the big brother who doesn't know anything."

They all groaned. "For the love of it," Quinn sighed. "Shut up."

As much as Riley was enjoying how there was now an opportunity to jump all over Aidan, he really did want some advice. "So no one thinks it's a big deal that we're seeing each other?"

"Not really," Hugh said, leaning against the railing. "You date a lot of women. Savannah's beautiful, and if she likes you too, why not?"

"Yeah." Quinn nodded. "What's the big deal?"

Riley and Aidan exchanged a look.

"The big deal," Aidan said before Riley could stop him, "is our little brother here is feeling serious toward the lovely Savannah. This isn't just a hookup."

Hugh and Quinn looked at him. "Oh…"

"Yeah, so…you see why I'm a little freaked out," Riley finally said.

"Oh, good! Now it's fun again!" Quinn said.

And though Riley groaned, he couldn't help but laugh. He'd take the ribbing and the poking fun—as long as it was only directed at him. There was no way he'd let anyone—not even his brothers—say anything derogatory about Savannah.

"Let me ask you something," Hugh said a few minutes later. "What the hell are you doing here with her then? Why would you bring home a woman you barely know and have her spend time with your family?"

"Didn't you do the same thing with Aubrey?" Riley reminded him.

"Yeah, but it was different. I brought her here because I had already planned on being here and didn't want to be without her. You clearly brought Savannah here before you got involved with her."

Quinn smacked Hugh in the chest. "I got it!" He looked at Riley. "You brought her here to use all of us as a distraction! I'm right, aren't I? You were freaking out because you had some serious feelings for her and you didn't want to be alone with her so you figured there'd be safety in numbers! Ha! Figured it out!" He raised his arms in the air in a victory move.

Riley shook his head. "I swear you are still the least mature out of all of us. And that's saying something because Darcy can still…"

"Darcy can still kick your butt."

They all turned at the sound of their sister's voice. Owen was beside her and closed the sliding door behind him.

"You cannot all sneak outside and have some secret family powwow and think no one's going to notice."

"Shit," Riley muttered.

"Yeah, we've all been bouncing theories around about what you're all talking about. Owen has Dad convinced you're all planning a surprise birthday party for him so…now you are."

They all groaned.

"I'm pretty sure that's not what you're all talking about," she said sassily as she came to stand in the middle of them all, "so you might as well fess up."

They all looked at one another as if trying to read each other's minds and figure out what they were going to say.

"Riley's falling in love with Savannah," Owen said as he stepped in closer. "And she's falling in love with him."

"Wait...what?" Darcy cried.

"Yeah...what?" Riley asked his twin.

Owen shrugged. "You're falling in love with her. It's fairly obvious. And for what it's worth, she seems to feel the same way about you."

"When did all this happen?" Darcy demanded. "Why am I always the last to know?"

"Because you have a big mouth," Quinn said and then pulled her in for a bear hug. He kissed the top of her head. "And besides, that's what happens when you move away. You miss out on all the good stuff. Aren't you glad you fought so hard not to be here?"

"Oh, shut up, you doofus," she teased and then looked over at Riley. "You and Savannah, huh?"

He gave her a small smile and nodded.

"Cool. I think she'd make an awesome addition to the family."

Chapter 9

"ARE YOU OKAY WITH YOUR FOLKS LEAVING TODAY?" Riley asked. It was three in the morning and they had yet to get to sleep.

"I am," Savannah said and yawned. "We had a nice day together Saturday with your family, and I got to have them all to myself yesterday. I never like saying good-bye to them, but it was a good visit."

"Are you upset that they made vacation plans with my dad and Martha?"

She chuckled. "I cannot believe how well the four of them hit it off. I think they're joining us for breakfast before my parents get on the road."

"I need to be home to let the contractors in, otherwise I'd be there too," he said softly, kissing the top of her head.

"That would have been nice. But once they leave, your father's going to bring me back to the house and we'll see how bad the noise is. Although…"

"Although what?"

She rolled over and propped herself up on one elbow to look at him. "I'm kind of done talking with your family. Darcy's on her way back to school, Owen's driving back to D.C., Hugh and Aubrey are back at home… I know you promised your dad you'd stay a little longer, but…" She shrugged.

"Yeah, I know," he said. "I was thinking about that

too. I kind of made arrangements for us to stay at the apartment Aidan has over his garage for the week and then I thought we'd talk about heading back. I can make the call and see if we can get the jet again."

Savannah sat up. "Or…" she began excitedly. "We can make it a road trip!"

Riley scratched his head and yawned before sitting up. "I think I may be delirious from lack of sleep because I thought you just said you basically wanted to drive across the country."

She nodded. "I do! Oh, Riley, it will be awesome! We can map it out and find some fun places to stop, and while we're driving we can do the interview!"

"Savannah, it's like…almost three thousand miles! It would take us—"

"Four or five days—depending on how much driving we get done each day and how many places we stop at." She looked at him, her eyes big and pleading. "Promise me you'll at least think about it before making a decision. Please?"

"I don't know… That's a lot of time in a car when we could be doing other things."

She swatted his arm. "Get your head out of the bedroom, Shaughnessy," she teased. "We have to work on the interview, and by doing it on the road, there wouldn't be any distractions. It would be neutral territory, and I don't mean to brag but I'm pretty awesome at the license plate game."

"Well…if you're awesome then…" he began and then grabbed her and rolled them around until she was straddling his lap. "I'm not making any promises except that I'll think about it."

Leaning down, she kissed him, letting her tongue trace his lips before tangling with his. When she heard him groan and felt his arms band around her, she let herself relax. A road trip across the country was something she'd always wanted to do, and the thought of doing it with Riley made it even more appealing.

Lifting her head, she smiled sleepily at him. "The alarm is set for seven. We need to get some sleep." Slowly, she crawled off him and snuggled up against his side, her head on his shoulder, her hand on his chest. When she was finally settled, she heard Riley sigh.

"This is the best part of the day," he said.

"Going to sleep?"

He shook his head. "No. Having you beside me like this. This is one of my favorite positions to be in with you."

Now it was her turn to sigh. "I like it a lot too."

"Mmm…good." He kissed the top of her head and within a minute, Savannah knew he was asleep.

She wasn't lying—she did like this position a lot. In truth, she loved it. The problem was, she was beginning to love a lot of things about their situation.

And Riley.

It would be foolish to tell him she was in love with him this soon. There wasn't any doubt in her mind that Riley had strong feelings for her, but she didn't think he was the kind to fall in love so quickly—or at all. It was a huge risk to have gotten involved with him, but there had been no way to stop it. Her biggest consolation was that it seemed to be the same way for him. She'd known from the first time their eyes met that he was going to be someone very important to her.

She just hadn't realized he was going to be her everything.

—m—

Riley closed the apartment door Monday night and let out a weary breath. "She's my sister-in-law and I love her, but she is exhausting."

Savannah smiled at him. "She was just being hospitable."

"Sweetheart, there is hospitable and then there's Zoe. Between the dinner, the tour of the apartment—which is only two rooms—the basket of muffins, the list of phone numbers, the stocked refrigerator…" He stepped away from the door and pulled at his dark hair. "I didn't think she was ever going to leave!"

"That was sort of how it was with my parents this morning. They just kept talking and talking and talking the entire time we walked to the RV and then they were inside and still kept talking to me and…ugh. By the time they pulled away, I was a little relieved to see them go!"

"And really, you got off easy. When your parents left? They truly left. Zoe's going to come back and want to refresh things and check on us, and then Aidan's going to stop over and want to make sure we're okay… It's never going to end."

Walking up to him, Savannah wrapped her arms around him and kissed him gently on the lips. "Poor baby. This is what happens when you come home. I'm an only child and even I know that. This is why my road trip idea is such a good one. Just us. No one else. No distractions. No prying eyes."

Riley kissed her before stepping back. "I think you're forgetting one key element here."

"What's that?"

"The press."

"I am the press," she joked. "What does that have to do with anything?"

He sat down on the sofa and patted the spot beside him for her to join him. "Savannah, I come home because no one bothers me here. I'm old news. It's a small town and most of the people have lived here their whole lives. They know me as just one of the Shaughnessy kids. But as soon as I leave here? I'm back under the microscope." He sighed loudly. "To be honest, this was the most disruptive trip I've had at home ever. I know some of it was orchestrated by my publicist but…" He shrugged wearily.

"Okay, I get that, but no one's going to be following us on the road, Riley. I know you're famous, but you're not so famous that we're going to have a swarm of paparazzi chasing us down the interstate."

He rolled his eyes. "I didn't say that. But when we stop someplace, there's that risk. Then people know where we are and they're going to figure out where we're going and at the next stop, more people will be waiting. It may be a handful of people, it may be a mob. I'm…I'm struggling enough right now with my career, and it's been kind of nice not having to deal with that one aspect of it."

"But they're your fans," she said simply. "Without them, you don't have a career, Riley. They're a necessary evil, so to speak. And once you finish this album and it's out there, you're going to have to deal with them again in full force."

"Yeah but…for now? I really need to…not deal with them. Can you understand that?"

Her head on his shoulder and a soft sigh came before she said, "I do."

Riley knew she was disappointed.

"But if we can't take a road trip, then I'm going to ask you to do something else for me," she said softly.

"Anything," he said, kissing the top of her head, and he meant it.

Savannah stood and walked into the bedroom. Riley watched her but once she was out of sight, he had no idea what she was doing. He was hoping it was going to be something sexy, something naughty and fun that she wanted them to do.

She walked out holding his guitar.

He began to sweat.

Savannah held it out to him. "I know I wasn't around all weekend, but you started to play last week and I have a feeling you haven't played much since. I want you to play for me while we're here."

"Savannah…"

But she held firm. "No. It's not negotiable. I gave up my plan of having a cross-country adventure, and you need to give up this plan you have of avoiding playing music."

"I sing every morning."

"Do-re-mi is not the kind of music you're going to put on the album, so knock it off. We can talk until we're blue in the face about your life and your career and your music. But if you don't ever play music, there's going to be no point in this article because you will no longer have a career."

He jumped up, ready to argue, but one look at her face and the fight left him. She was right. He was avoiding it.

It was too frustrating and painful to keep hearing music in his head when he couldn't seem to get it out.

"You started to make progress last week. I'm not saying you're going to complete the entire album while we're here, but I think while you're here and relaxed, it can't hurt to try to get at least one song done."

He collapsed back down on the sofa. "You have no idea how hard it is."

"You're right, I don't," she said, sitting back down beside him. "But I also know avoiding it isn't going to help. No one here is going to judge you, Riley. *I'm* not going to judge you."

"I don't think that." *Sort of*, he thought. "But at the end of the day, you're still here to do a story. We can pretend they're two separate things and be able to turn off the recorder and put the pad and pen away at the end of the day, but I don't know if it's really true. The whole point of this damn article is to get inside my head and figure out why I'm taking so damn long on this project!" He raked a hand through his hair and let out a growl of frustration.

"Riley…"

He grabbed the guitar and put some distance between the two of them and began to strum mindlessly. Over and over he went through the same chords—ones he'd learned over twenty years ago. Then he transitioned to some classic Led Zeppelin before going on to a medley of songs from the Black Crowes, Bon Jovi, the Eagles, and Nirvana.

And then, just as had happened the previous week, it was as if someone opened the door and Riley was allowed to hear what was on the other side of the wall.

Without looking up, he knew Savannah was getting her recorder and he began to play. This song was different from the one last week, but one that had been just out of his grasp for months. He played. He played until he thought his fingers would bleed. He played until his arms began to tremble. And all the while, right beside him, Savannah sat in silence.

Riley had no idea how long he played. It could have been minutes or hours or days. One song flowed into the next and when he couldn't do it any longer—couldn't hold the guitar, couldn't strum, could barely breathe—he stopped and gasped for air. Savannah rose and got him something to drink and never once uttered a word. She was good like that—she knew what he needed. Almost anticipated it. And then she would wait until the time was right to engage in any kind of conversation.

She clicked off the recorder.

She refilled his glass.

She took the guitar and placed it in the corner of the room.

And then, silently, she took him by the hands and gently pulled him to his feet and led him into the bedroom. In the darkness, she undressed him before undressing herself. Her kiss was chaste as her hands gently massaged his shoulders, his arms. When they finally walked over to the bed, she urged him to lie down first. Stretching out beside him, she caressed his face.

And without words, she showed him how much his music moved her. How his talent astounded her. And in her heart and mind, she silently prayed he knew just how much he meant to her.

—∿∿—

Everything changed after that.

They talked all day long—barely left the apartment—but during most of the interview, Riley had the guitar in his hands. The music was finally coming, and Savannah felt a sense of pride that she had helped it happen. She wasn't cocky or arrogant enough to believe it was all because of her, but she also knew that had it not been for her forcing the guitar into his hands, he would have let his fear and anxiety gnaw away at him indefinitely.

Mick had been so relieved when Riley had told him about having this musical breakthrough that he offered to send the studio musicians—and equipment—to North Carolina to start recording. Riley had turned him down but promised they'd be back in L.A. soon enough and to start getting ready.

They had dinner every night with his family. It wasn't at the same house every night, but whether they were at Aidan's home or Quinn's, it was always a room full of Shaughnessys. Savannah didn't mind—she was coming to love them all—but she started to wonder what their lives were going to be like when they returned to L.A. As much as she had encouraged their departure, it was slowly losing its appeal. They had a routine here. They were surrounded by people they loved. It was a very different life waiting for them back home.

It was Thursday night and she was working with Zoe to clean up the dinner dishes. Quinn and Anna had joined them, as had Ian, and Savannah had a feeling she was really going to miss this.

"So…we were thinking," Zoe said a little hesitantly.

"We?" Savannah asked.

Anna walked into the kitchen carrying the last of the dishes. "We being the two of us," she said with a smile.

"You've been here almost two weeks and you're probably heading home soon, but...we were wondering if you'd maybe want to have lunch and a little girl time with us tomorrow," Zoe asked hopefully.

"Girl time?" Savannah had no idea what exactly that meant.

"You know, lunch and then mani-pedis. It's sort of our thing," Anna said.

"Oh...well...yeah! What am I even thinking about it for?" Savannah joked. "I can't remember the last time I indulged in a little pampering."

Both Anna and Zoe looked relieved.

"We know you're busy with the interview and all, but we were hoping you would enjoy taking a little bit of a break," Zoe said. "I hope you don't mind, but I already mentioned it to Riley—just in case he didn't want to share you."

Savannah laughed. "Believe it or not, you may be doing us both a favor."

"Why?" Anna asked.

Savannah looked out toward the dining room to make sure the guys were all still busy talking before she looked at the two women. "He's finally started playing the guitar this week. It's as though his mental block with the music is finally starting to lift."

"That's great!" Zoe cried and then put her hand over her mouth as Anna slapped her arm and shushed her. "I mean, that's great," she whispered.

"Yeah, it is," Savannah said softly. "He doesn't mind

playing with me sitting there, but I think if he had some time alone, he could do more than just jam. He might really start writing lyrics and getting stuff down on paper. I kind of feel like I'm mucking up the process by being there."

"Hell no," Anna whispered. "If anything, you've helped him have this musical breakthrough. This is awesome."

"Okay, so we'll all meet here tomorrow," Zoe said softly, "around eleven and we'll head into town for lunch and then the spa. Will that work?"

"If it's okay with you, I was planning on the two of you just coming to the pub and having lunch," Anna said. "I've got some things I need to do there in the morning and it will just work better for me that way."

"The pub?" Savannah asked.

"It's Anna's business and she makes the best burgers in the world," Zoe said. "Trust me."

"Hard to trust a group of women huddled together whispering," Aidan said as he strode into the kitchen. "Here I thought you were hard at work cleaning up the dishes and getting dessert ready and you're all bunched up in a corner telling secrets."

"Says the man who was part of a rather large, secretive huddle not that long ago in our own backyard," Zoe said, breaking away from the women to go kiss her husband.

Aidan nervously looked at the three of them before slowly backing out of the room. "I...um...we're just going to hang out in the living room until dessert is ready." And then he quickly turned and walked out of the room.

"That was fun," Zoe said. "I'm telling you, some of the greatest moments of my day come when I get to freak my husband out." She rubbed her slightly rounded belly and smiled. "Sometimes I blame it on pregnancy hormones, other times it's just for my own amusement."

"Poor Aidan," Anna said. "It doesn't seem right."

"Trust me, he has things he does to me too so it's not entirely one-sided."

"I don't doubt it," Anna said. "I mentioned to Quinn the other day that Bobby—my brother," she added for Savannah's sake, "was going to move in with us because he wasn't happy in South Carolina."

"Seriously?" Zoe asked. "Oh my gosh! Is he all right? When did this happen?"

Anna grinned. "It didn't. Quinn was carrying on about how much easier his life has been since Bobby moved away, and I couldn't resist making him panic a little." She laughed out loud. "My brother is very happy and has no immediate plans to move back here."

Savannah looked between the two women and stood back with a very satisfied smile.

"What?" Zoe asked her. "What's that smile about?"

Savannah shook her head. "I think I'm really going to enjoy hanging out with the two of you. You're my kind of people."

Both Zoe and Anna smiled with her, and Savannah knew she'd made some friends for life right there.

When Savannah came home late Friday afternoon, Riley looked a little worse for wear. His dark hair was in complete disarray and there were dirty dishes and empty water bottles all around him along with dozens of crumpled up pieces of paper. She walked hesitantly into the apartment and was a little surprised when he didn't acknowledge her presence.

Rather than disturb him, she got herself something to drink and then went into the bedroom and took out her laptop and did some work on the rough draft of the article with what she had so far.

When the room darkened, she looked at the bedside clock and realized it was after eight and still they hadn't spoken to one another. Standing, Savannah stretched and quietly walked back out to the living room. This time Riley did look up—confusion written all over his face.

"When did you get home?"

"About four hours ago," she said lightly and walked over and kissed him. "You were very busy and I didn't want to disturb you."

"So what were you doing?"

"Writing. I started drafting the article and going over some of the notes I'd written down. It's not much but it's a start."

He stood and yawned and stretched before pulling her into his arms and kissing her properly. "Sorry. I was really deep in thought. I can't believe I didn't hear you come in."

"It's all right. It's a good thing. It must mean you're making progress too."

Riley looked around the room and grimaced at the mess. "Yeah," he said distractedly, picking things up and walking to the kitchen. "How was your day out with the girls?"

She smiled. "It was good. Really good. Better than I expected."

He put the dishes in the sink and washed his hands before turning back toward her. "What were you expecting?"

She shrugged. "I don't know. It's been a long time since I've had close friends who I would do the lunch and pampering thing with. I know it sounds weird, but I travel a lot for the magazine, and I found people who I thought were my friends really weren't after a while. They liked the perks of maybe getting in to free concerts or meeting celebrities. I don't know… I guess after a while I just stopped trusting people. It was easier that way."

"I can understand that."

Walking over toward him, she kissed him on the cheek. "I figured you might." Then she stepped back and tried to pick up some of the mess. "Anyway, it was a good day. Anna's pub is awesome. I totally never would have pegged her as someone who owns a bar, but she's done something really great there."

"Yeah, well…it was a long road for her," Riley said absently.

"She told me about it. It's a great story and she's the kind of person who really deserves it, you know? Some people get things handed to them and you think, 'Why them?' But with Anna? I totally get it."

"She's an incredible person," Riley said as he helped pick up the papers and put them in the trash. "I still can't believe she and Quinn are finally together. I mean, they've always been together because of their friendship, but it's different now and it's kind of cool seeing how it's softened both of them. But I can't believe she waited all that time for him."

"Some people are worth waiting for," Savannah said.

"She knew he was the one for her. Not everyone knows that. I think they're both very lucky."

"I know she's perfect for Quinn, but I just hope he appreciates her."

Savannah chuckled. "I'm sure he does. From what she was sharing at lunch, she's pretty much got him wrapped around her little finger. And I say good for her."

"I don't even want to know what she shared." He laughed. "I'm sure you could tell me more about my brothers than I would ever want to know right now. Zoe was probably chatty about Aidan too, right?"

"Oh yeah," she said with a grin.

"Okay then…just…just keep it to yourself. Some things a guy doesn't need to know about his family."

"Deal." Looking around, Savannah saw the room was almost back to normal and felt pretty pleased about it. "Looks good in here. Almost like the way I left it this morning," she teased. She glanced over at Riley and saw he wasn't smiling. If anything he looked…distracted. "Hey," she said softly. "Are you all right? I was just teasing, you know. I know you were busy here today and that's fine."

He didn't respond.

"Riley?" This time she felt a little uncertain as she said his name.

"Um…I need to talk to you about something."

For some reason, she was nervous. "Okay…"

"Things are really coming to me now and—for the first time in months—I feel motivated and confident about what I'm creating."

"That's great!"

"I called and made arrangements to have the plane

pick us up Sunday morning." He stepped closer to her. "I know I should have discussed it with you first, but…in the moment, all I could think of was how I needed more than my guitar here and if we were back in L.A.…."

Savannah closed the distance between them, her hands instantly grasping his and squeezing. "You don't owe me an explanation. I think it's great you're ready to do more than just jam here in the apartment. It's the best news you could have given me! I thought you were going to give me bad news!"

"But…once we get back… I…" He paused and cursed. "It's going to mess up our schedule with the interview. I want you to come to the studio with me and be there with me while I finish this up." He cupped her face. "If it wasn't for you, I don't know if I'd be able to do this."

"Riley—"

"No, I'm serious," he interrupted. "In the past couple of days, I've gotten three songs written. Three! They're all rough and nowhere near ready but… It's like everything that's been out of my reach is finally there and even though it's not enough to finish the album, I'm off to a great start. And when we get home, I want to keep seeing you. I want us to finish this damn interview and put it behind us so we can move forward." He kissed her soundly and pulled back. "I see us moving forward, Savannah. I've never seen that with any other woman, but when I look at you? I see my future."

Her heart simply melted at those words.

"I know we haven't talked about it much, but… there it is. The next month or so? It's going to be crazy.

I'm going to be crazy, and I need you to know that in advance because when I get in this zone, I'm kind of single-minded. We'll finish the interview, but the music has got to come first. Please tell me you understand."

Her head was spinning. "Of course I do and that's why…maybe…I shouldn't be there in the studio. Maybe I need to step away so you can do what you have to do."

His grip on her tightened as he shook her slightly. "I'm telling you I see a future with you and you're telling me you're walking away?"

She shook her head furiously and pulled out of his grasp. "That's not what I'm saying, Riley. Not really. I'm just trying to give you the space you need so you can focus!"

"*You* help me focus!" he shouted. "I wouldn't have this music to work on if it wasn't for you, don't you get it? I want you with me, Savannah! Hell, I need you with me!"

And then she was back in front of him, cupping his strong jaw. "Shh… Okay, okay. I'll be there. Of course I'll be there. I just didn't want you to…you know…ask me to be there if it was going to hinder you getting the album done. I'll be there for you. Always."

She expected an argument or, at the very least, another statement on why he needed her there. But what she got was Riley's hands raking back into her hair and tugging as his mouth crashed down on hers. It was wild and frantic and like nothing she'd ever experienced with him. Savannah had thought she'd seen and felt him lose control, but it was nothing compared to this. He backed her up until her she hit a wall and then he simply devoured her. His lips, his teeth, his tongue… She almost couldn't breathe.

But she also couldn't stop herself from clutching him closer and kissing him back with just as much wild abandon.

Savannah knew there was a lot of passion in Riley—she saw it in his music, in the way he did everything, and the way he treated people—but to be on the receiving end of something this intense was almost more than she could take.

But she did.

Mindlessly, clothes were stripped away.

Wordlessly, they moved together.

And breathlessly, they gave each other all they had.

Riley was strumming the guitar and watching Savannah type on her laptop. She had pretty much destroyed him earlier. Deep down he always felt he was in control of his emotions, but where she was concerned—particularly earlier—he found that he wasn't.

He'd been playing and messing around with the music all day, but as he was watching her, something new came to mind. Something…something that hadn't been there before. Without asking, he grabbed her recorder and got it going and then sat back and let the music lead him.

It started out slow—almost like a ballad. But he knew instantly that it wouldn't stay that way. At some point it was going to get a little heavier—not upbeat—but definitely heavier before going back to its easy beginning. The notes came to him, and somewhere in the back of his mind, lyrics began to appear. Quickly reaching over, he grabbed paper and pen and began writing the words down in between the chords he played.

If Savannah knew he was writing about her, she didn't let on. Not that she could know. For all she knew, he was just inspired. And he was. By her.

He couldn't wait to get them back to L.A. To have her back in his home where they could finally do all the things he'd fantasized about doing with her before they came here. Just the thought of it was enough to make his throat go dry and everything in him harden.

Savannah—oblivious to his sexy thoughts—quietly closed her laptop and sighed.

"What's the matter?" he asked, putting the guitar aside.

She looked over at him, her eyes a little wide. "Oh… sorry. I didn't mean to make you stop playing."

He chuckled. "You didn't. I think I'm onto something with this one, but I need to get to the studio and try it out on the piano and with some heavier guitars."

"It sounded wonderful."

Riley almost blushed. People praised his work and his music all the time, but coming from Savannah, he knew she genuinely meant it. "Thanks. I think it's going to be good."

"I'm sure it will." She stood and stretched. "We never ate dinner," she said with a sexy grin, "and now I'm hungry. What about you?"

He stood and followed her to the kitchen. "Zoe stocked the fridge so I'm sure there's something here we can heat up."

Within minutes, they had put together some chili and salads. "Would you mind if we watched a little

TV?" Savannah asked. "I know it sounds crazy, but it's what I do at home—I eat a lot of my meals in front of the television."

"Me too," Riley admitted, and together they got themselves situated on the sofa.

She turned on the TV and began flipping through the channels. "Oh my gosh!"

"What? What's wrong?" Riley asked, his mouth full of his first bite of food.

"*The Wizard of Oz*! Can we watch it? Please? Please?" she begged, her eyes huge and pleading with his.

Quickly swallowing and forcing his heart rate to slow down, he nodded. "Uh…sure. Yeah. No problem."

Her shoulders sagged. "You don't like it, do you? I know it's old and there's probably a lot of other things on. I'll keep scanning…"

"No," he said, placing his hand on her knee. "Really. It's fine. It's a favorite of mine, too."

She looked at him quizzically. "It is?"

He nodded.

"Because you sounded like…" She shrugged. "You seemed like you weren't interested."

How could he possibly explain to her the connection he had to this movie without either bursting into tears or forcing himself to be robotic?

Fortunately, Savannah put the remote down and began to eat her sandwich—a happy smile on her face as Dorothy's house spun in mid-air. They'd missed the very beginning of the movie, but neither commented on it. It wasn't as if they didn't know what happened first.

They ate in silence, each wrapped up in the movie.

It wasn't until the first commercial break that she turned to him and noticed a look of utter devastation on his face. Picking up the remote, she muted the TV. "Okay, out with it. Something's bothering you."

He sighed and put his plate down on the coffee table. "Do you remember the first night you met my family?"

She nodded.

"You asked what song I used to sing the most. Do you remember?"

Again, she nodded.

Shifting, he turned to face her. "When I was five, the very first song I sang in the school talent show was 'Over the Rainbow.'"

"Aww…" She sighed, her hand going over her heart.

Smiling, Riley shook his head. "I knew I wanted to sing in the talent show and my mom encouraged me to. She loved to sing and she used to do it all the time— especially when she was baking—but she sang a lot of traditional Irish songs. She would sing them to us as lullabies," he said wistfully.

Savannah reached over and held his hand.

"None of my brothers would sing with her." He looked at her and chuckled. "Because they couldn't. They all had horrible voices. But Mom and I would sing together in the kitchen. So when I told her I wanted to be in the talent show, she was so excited and we talked about what I should sing." In his mind, he could clearly see his mother as they spoke.

"Well, I think you could sing anything you want to, Riley," Lillian said, placing the oatmeal raisin cookie dough onto her baking sheets.

Riley stood beside her on one of their wooden stools so he could reach the counter. "But there are so many songs to choose from! I want it to be something great! Something no one else is gonna sing."

Lillian considered that for a moment. "If that's what you want, we have a whole song book of classic Irish songs. You can bet no one in your class is going to sing one of those."

Riley giggled. "Mom...those songs are crazy!" He almost fell off the stool in his fit of laughter.

"So you're telling me 'Paddy McGinty's Goat' is too crazy to sing?" she teased.

That made him laugh harder. "Come on, Mom!" he said between fits of laughter. "I don't know what to sing!"

And then Lillian gasped and looked at Riley with wide blue eyes. "I've got it!" She put her hands on her hips. "What did we just watch last night?"

"The Wizard of Oz," Riley said.

"And there you go! You've got your song!"

"Wait...which song?"

"Which song did we sing while we were watching it?" she prompted.

He shrugged. "We sang all of them, remember? Dad told us to hush because he couldn't hear the TV."

"You can sing 'Over the Rainbow,' Riley," she said with a smile. "You sing it so beautifully, and it's a very hard song to sing but you, my son, sing it better than anyone!"

He shook his head. "Uh-uh, not better than Dorothy."

Lillian nodded. "I think you do."

"Really?"

She nodded again. "I think it's your song. I bet if you sing it at the talent show, people will jump up and give you a standing ovation!"

Her excitement had him smiling. And then, on his little wooden stool, he faced the empty kitchen and began to sing. Lillian joined in and at the end, they each took a bow while holding hands. When Riley jumped down and released her hand, hers immediately went to her heart.

With a nod, she said, "That's your song, Riley."

He shook his head. "Uh-uh. It's our song, Mom."

Savannah squeezing his hand brought him back to the present.

He looked up at her and saw her eyes shining with unshed tears.

"From that point on, that's what it was. Our song." He gently skimmed his thumb across her knuckles and then her wrist. "I sang it at her funeral. It's the last time I ever sang it."

Gasping, Savannah, quickly put a hand over her mouth as her tears began to fall. "Oh, Riley…"

He pulled her in close.

But he wasn't sure if the embrace was for her benefit. Or his.

———ᨆᨆᨆ———

The flight back to L.A. was very different from the flight to North Carolina. Savannah was much more relaxed this time around, for starters, and that, coupled with the fact that Riley seduced her from the moment they took off to the moment they landed, pretty much ensured a pleasurable flight.

The town car driver took Savannah home first and at the door, Riley begged her to come home with him.

"I promise to see you tomorrow," she said, unlocking her door and stepping inside. "I've got to unpack and check my messages…" She playfully swatted him away when he reached for her. "And I'm sure you have to do the same. I can meet you at the studio or your house, whichever you prefer."

"I prefer you to come home with me now," he growled, hauling her into his arms and kissing her. "I've had far too many fantasies about making love to you in my bed for me to have to wait another day."

It did sound good, she thought. Lord knew she'd fantasized about it too. His bed. The game room. The deck in back of his house overlooking the city? Yeah, that one was one of her favorites. "Riley…"

"Please," he murmured against her ear. "Check your messages and I'll talk to the driver and we'll wait while you do what you have to do. Or I'll send him away and tell him to come back in an hour." He pulled back and pouted. "I won't go home without you."

Rolling her eyes, she pulled out of his arms. "Okay. Fine! Give me fifteen minutes and I'll be ready to go." She pushed him out the door and went to her home phone. She knew it was crazy to still have one—everyone used their cell phones—but she liked keeping her home number for her personal stuff and her cell for business.

She wrote down the handful of messages and made a mental note to make return calls when she was home next. Then she dragged her suitcase to her bedroom, dumped her dirty clothes in her hamper, and packed a smaller overnight bag with necessities to take with her to Riley's. Indulging him like this could become a bad habit, but the thought of sleeping without him tonight wasn't appealing at all.

Walking around, she checked to make sure nothing else needed her immediate attention before picking up her bag and locking back up. Riley stood beside the car with a very satisfied grin on his face.

"Don't get used to this," she playfully snapped at him.

"Used to what?"

"Getting your way. Sometimes it's not all going to go your way and you'll have to deal with it. I am going to have to come home eventually and there are going to be times when I can't be with you."

"I don't like the sound of that at all," he said, climbing into the car behind her.

"It's the way life is," she said. "Once our interview is done, Tommy's going to give me another assignment and…" She shrugged.

"How often do you travel?" he asked, frowning.

"Enough. Most of the time I get to meet up with people here in L.A., but sometimes I go along for several stops on a tour, or I have to meet the person on their terms. I never know."

"Now I really don't like the sound of that. Are you alone with these guys? These rock stars?"

She chuckled. "Please tell me you're not jealous!"

"I'm just saying… You're a beautiful woman and I know how these guys think. And act!"

With a patient smile, she patted him on the knee. "For the record, I'm flattered that you think other men find me attractive enough to hit on me. The reality is that when I'm doing an interview with someone, it's about the story. Most of the time they're busy and I'm a nuisance, so you don't have to worry."

He was still frowning.

She sighed loudly. "What?"

"So you've, like, never gotten involved with someone you've interviewed?"

It should have bothered her that he was asking—she thought they knew each other a little better than that—but the fact that he was insecure and willing to show it made her relax. Scooting closer to him, Savannah cupped his cheek and smiled. "Never. Only you."

His shoulders sagged as he leaned in and kissed her. "Okay then."

The rest of the drive to his home was made in relative silence, but Savannah's head was swirling with thoughts of what life was going to be like now that they were back home. There wasn't the distraction of his family—not that they had really been one—and now they had their homes and personal spaces to themselves with no one watching. It was definitely a perk.

As much as she was anxious to finish the interview, she realized she was at a point where she wasn't sure what to do with it. Her original intention to sort of put Riley out there—warts and all—no longer appealed. However, she couldn't possibly hand in a fluff piece that painted him in an angelic glow either.

The most important thing right now was to get him back into the studio. He was making such great strides with the songs he'd been working on, and Savannah had no doubt once he was surrounded by the instruments, equipment, and musicians, he would get them all done. She was curious to see him at work in that capacity and knew it would add to the story. So far his process had fascinated her, and she was really looking forward to seeing a song go from concept to completion.

They pulled up at his home and within minutes the town car pulled away and they were putting their luggage down inside. Riley immediately walked to the kitchen and grabbed them both something to drink.

"I may or may not have something here for us to eat. I probably should have thought of that on the way here." He gave her a lopsided grin as he handed her a bottle of water.

"It's all right. We ate on the plane and I'm not very hungry right now." The sun was still out and she immediately walked to the large sliding glass doors that led to the deck. Without asking, she unlocked the doors, pulled them open, and stepped outside. Turning her face up to the sun, she sighed. "This is what I was looking forward to." Straightening, she put her sunglasses back on and walked over to the pool and then looked out at the city below. "I missed this view."

Riley came up behind her, wrapped his arms around her waist, and kissed her throat, making her purr. "I wanted to do this with you that first day you were here," he murmured against her skin. "It was torture for me to have to stand back and watch you and not touch you."

She smiled as her head slowly fell back against his shoulder. "You're just spoiled. You're used to getting who or what you want whenever you want it."

Lifting his head, he carefully turned her in his arms until she was facing him. "I'm not going to lie to you, Savannah. I've been with a lot of women—more than any one person should be—and yes, I'm spoiled because

I never had to try. They were always there, ready and willing. But that lifestyle stopped being appealing a long time ago. It's been a while since I've been with anyone. And what we're doing here? I'm not messing around. This isn't because of proximity, it's because it's you."

Savannah wasn't stupid. She knew exactly how a lot of musicians lived—the partying, the women. She also knew it wasn't unheard of for those same guys to settle down and be faithful. Looking up at Riley and knowing what she did about him and how he was raised, she didn't doubt what he was saying or his fidelity to her.

"You're awful quiet," he observed.

"I hate thinking of you with all those other women."

"You may not believe this but I do too. I'm not proud of myself for it, Savannah, but I can't go back and change it either. None of them really meant anything to me. Just you. I love you."

She really loved hearing that. "It's a good thing, Riley, because I love you too." Then she pulled back and shook her head. "Are we crazy? It's so soon. Shouldn't we be cautious? Shouldn't we have waited longer to say it? To feel it? To know it's real?"

Taking her by the hand, Riley led her back into the house and gently tugged her down beside him on the sofa. "We're not kids," he said simply, "and I think when you meet someone and you know it's right, then what's the point in waiting to let them know how you feel? I would rather start planning our future now—even though it's only been a couple of weeks—than sit back and be scared or cautious and wait until…what? What are we waiting for? None of us is guaranteed a tomorrow. Losing my mother taught me that. You have to live every day to its fullest. Do the things you love. Be with the people you love. Don't wait because you may never get the chance again."

Savannah couldn't comprehend what it must have been like for him—for his entire family—to lose their mother so unexpectedly. It was no wonder he had the mentality he had, and he was right. What would be the point in waiting to say how they felt?

"You got quiet again."

She looked over at him and smiled. "I'm thinking you are a very wise man."

He chuckled. "No one—and I mean *no one*—has ever accused me of that."

"Then they're all not seeing the man I'm seeing."

"What are you seeing, Savannah?" he asked softly, his hands lightly touching her—skimming her arms, her shoulders, her cheeks.

"I see an incredibly talented man who has so much to give. I've watched you with your family and your fans and even with me, and you have a way of making everyone around you feel good. It's a gift you have."

"Is it wrong that I'm slightly obsessed with making you feel good right now?" he asked, giving her a sexy grin as he moved in and began to kiss her shoulder.

"Not at all," she said and then moaned when his lips moved to that sensitive spot below her ear. "I think… I think I wouldn't mind feeling good right now."

And then suddenly he was gone. Standing up. Savannah opened her eyes and saw him standing before her, his hand outstretched, waiting for her.

"Where are we going?" she asked coyly.

"I'm taking you to bed. And then later, when the sun

is down and there are a million stars in the sky? I'm taking you outside."

Oh my. On shaky legs, she stood and took his hand. Riley walked backward to his room, his eyes never leaving hers. Once inside his massive bedroom, he closed the double doors and smiled at her. Then, without a word, he stepped forward, closing the distance between the two of them, cupped her face and simply consumed her. His kiss was hot and sweet, sexy and wild and Savannah could barely stay upright.

Which worked out quite well because Riley simply scooped her up in his arms, and carried her to his bed—where he kept her for a very long time.

—⁓—

For the next three days, it was what Riley dubbed "sex, love, and rock and roll." Savannah stayed at his house and every morning they went to the studio together. She noted how positively ecstatic everyone was that Riley was finally back and had music to play. There was a constant flurry of activity coming and going—people needing approval on artwork, pictures for promos, and quotes from Riley to release to the press.

While he did his thing, she observed and worked on the story. Between her laptop and her phone, it was practically like having her own office. She checked in with Tommy and let him know the progress she was making and he sounded pleased. Especially since she had admitted that her initial observation of Riley as an artist and musician was wrong and that she planned to explore that in the article.

By the end of the third day, however, Savannah had

to put her foot down about going home. Riley's session musicians were working hard to capture what he wanted, and she knew it was going to be a late night. So she purposely waited until she knew he couldn't leave to tell him she was going. He put up a bit of a fight, but eventually she wore him down, and he was so distracted by the musical progress he was making that he finally kissed her and told her he'd talk to her in the morning.

It felt weird to be home and to be alone. She'd been on her own for at least six years and it was surprising to realize how quickly she had gotten used to Riley's presence.

"You're being ridiculous," she chided herself as she went about getting laundry started and unpacking all her things. Within an hour she was sitting in front of the TV in her jammies, eating some Chinese takeout, and felt like her old self. Not that there had been anything wrong with her new self, but it was good to feel like she wasn't becoming the type of clingy woman who wasn't comfortable enough to be on her own for a night.

Part of her felt a little twinge of guilt because she wasn't working on her article—or anything for that matter—but it had been such a nonstop process for several weeks that she needed some mindless time in front of the television where her most pressing thought was whether the couple on HGTV should love it or list it.

Around midnight, when her eyes were finally fighting to stay open, her phone rang. She didn't even need to look at the screen to know it was Riley. "Hey, you," she said softly.

"Mmm…why am I alone?" he said, and she could hear the weariness in his voice.

"Because you were on a roll and I was done working for the day."

"I thought you were going to be waiting for me in bed. I was very disappointed when I found out I was wrong."

"Don't pout," she teased. "I told you I was going home to do laundry and unpack and all the stuff you didn't let me do the other day when you pouted to get your way."

"I must be losing my touch," he chuckled and then yawned.

"Never," she assured him. "Get some sleep. It was a long day."

"I'm going to see you tomorrow, right?"

"Yes, but later on in the day."

"Why?" he asked, suddenly sounding fully awake.

"I still have things to do, Riley. You're working on the album and I've learned a lot about the process. I'm not needed there. I'm going to head into the magazine offices for a little bit, return some calls, do a little shopping, and then I'll stop by."

"Savannah—"

"You're not getting your way this time, Shaughnessy," she interrupted. "I know you like having me there and it's been fun to watch, but I do have a life and a career too. Once you're done with the album and I'm done with the article, I'm sure we'll settle more into a routine. But for right now, the album has to take precedence."

"So I need to hurry up and finish it if I want to have you all to myself again."

She couldn't help but laugh. "That's not what I said and you know it. We both work and right now you can't keep banker's hours. Trust me, everything will be fine."

"I miss you," he said softly, and her heart melted.

"I miss you too."

"I don't like sleeping by myself."

"I think you can handle it."

"But I don't want to." His words were a mere whisper and she knew he was almost asleep.

"Sleep, Riley. I'll see you tomorrow."

"Love you," he said right before the call disconnected.

Chapter 10

FOR WEEKS, RILEY WAS INVIGORATED. EVERYTHING was finally coming together with the music, and he and Savannah had found a balance so they were still able to have time together. He'd all but moved her into his house and all those things combined made him a very happy man.

"Everything's sounding great, Ry," Mick said as he came into the studio. "I just got done meeting with the guys upstairs and they are very pleased with the progress you've made." Putting his briefcase down on one of the stools, he opened it and pulled out a file. "We're already talking tour dates and media tour. Your first stop will be Friday night."

"Wait," Riley said, putting his guitar down. "This Friday night?"

Mick nodded.

"The album's not even done yet! What the hell could you possibly have planned for me already?"

Mick shook his head and gave Riley a condescending smile. "What are you, new at this? Now is the time to start schmoozing a little. You have to start paving the way with the press so they're anxious to get an interview with you when the album is out. You've done this dozens of times before, Riley. And honestly? This has been on the schedule for a while. You've just been too distracted to pay attention."

Raking a hand through his hair, Riley knew Mick was

right. It was just a part of the business that could be annoying. It almost felt as if he were begging people to like him. In the past, he at least had the rest of his band with him so they could divide and conquer. This would be the first time it was all on him. Which was exactly what he told Mick.

"Don't sweat it. You were always the most charismatic one in the group. People wanted to talk to you more than Matty, Dylan, or Julian. This will be a piece of cake for you."

He sighed. "Where and when?"

"Roger Gray is hosting a cocktail party to support the local ASPCA at his home in the Hills. You'll go, you'll mingle, you'll talk a lot about this project, and you'll give a hefty donation." He chuckled. "So all in all, everybody wins."

"I'll be bringing Savannah with me."

"Even better!" Mick beamed. "Seriously, she's a sweetheart. You really did well when you hooked up with her. It doesn't hurt having a member of the press in your pocket." Then he laughed heartily. "Or in your case, in your bed!"

Before Riley knew it, he had Mick against the wall, slamming his manager hard against the surface. "Don't you ever—*ever!*—say something like that again!" Then he shoved him away with disgust.

Mick stood wide-eyed for a long moment. He cleared his throat, straightened his tie, and moved away from the wall. "Riley…"

His head hanging, Riley took several deep breaths to calm himself before turning around. "Geez, Mick. I…I'm…"

Mick held out a hand to stop him. "We've known each other a long time, Riley. And in all that time I never… You never…" He paused. "I had no idea you were really serious about her. I'm sorry. I was out of line."

"Yeah, well, to be fair, how could you have known? I've brought more than my share of girls around here who didn't mean a damn thing to me."

"But never more than once," Mick said. "It should have been a huge tip-off to me that Savannah was different. Really…I'm sorry."

Riley looked at Mick and gave him a small smile. "We're good, man. Seriously." He pulled up a stool and sat down. "Let's forget about it, all right?"

Nodding, Mick picked up the file he'd pulled out. "I want you to go through this when you have a minute— sooner rather than later would be preferable—and see what you think of the plan so far."

"Where are you thinking of having the tour open?"

Mick smiled. "If I've played my cards right, the Hollywood Bowl."

Riley's eyes went wide. "Are you shitting me? *The Hollywood Bowl?* How? I mean…when did you start working on that?"

With a shrug, Mick scanned through the file. "It was my plan all along but because this album was taking a little longer and we didn't have a specific date…let's just say I have some connections there and called in a few favors. I thought it could be very cool to have you start the tour and do a couple of local dates to test the waters. We're already getting interest from all over the country, but I like the idea of starting here."

"I'd like to work in some dates back home in North Carolina if possible. I did a lot of writing there while I was home and it just...well...it's important to me to get some dates in there."

Mick pulled out his tablet and started typing. "I can't guarantee it will be one of the earlier dates. We're looking at here, Vegas, and then some dates across Texas. Nothing's written in stone yet, but..."

"I understand. I know how it works." He stood and paced the room. "I have to be honest with you, Mick, I didn't think it would ever happen."

"What? The tour?"

Riley laughed. "The album! Man, I didn't see myself being able to finish it. I was starting to lose my freaking mind!"

Mick laughed with him. "Yeah, well, you got a little spooked, that's all. That damn documentary messed with your head more than it should have." He shook his head. "You're a smart man, Riley. You know not everyone's going to love you or even like you. The fact that the producers decided to listen to some bullshit gossip and cut you from the project was their loss."

Although Riley knew Mick was right, it still stung. More than it should. He thought of how he felt when he first met Savannah and she told him she wasn't a fan of his either. You'd think by now his ego wouldn't be quite so fragile, and yet it was.

"Look, that project got a lot of airplay and publicity, but it was a bunch of hype. There was no substance to it. It was the same people telling the same stories. It wasn't worth your time. When this album is done and you're burning up the music charts, I can guarantee you the producers are going to be begging to do a project with you. And then you can tell them no!" He laughed. "Trust me, it will be very satisfying."

Riley shook his head and forced himself to laugh. While it would definitely be good to be the one to tell them no, he was desperate enough that he'd be willing to work with them just to prove he was talented and prove them wrong. Rather than share that with Mick, all he said was, "Yeah, we'll see."

"Okay, I can see you're not convinced yet. That's all right," Mick said, closing his briefcase. "Do what you gotta do here today and keep me posted on the progress with the tracks. I think you only need two more and we can call it a day."

Nodding, Riley said, "Two tracks. Got it."

"And don't stress about them. Everything you have on here is freaking amazing. It's okay to call a few in. Do a cover tune or two. Trust me, the fans are going to love it no matter what because they love you."

He hadn't considered doing any covers, but it was good to know there were some options. Honestly, he preferred to do all his own music—especially for his first solo project. Riley wanted people to know he was talented enough to carry it all on his own without any help. "I'll think about it," he said to Mick, "but I was hoping to use all original stuff."

"Believe me, we would all love that, but we can't wait another six months for you to come up with songs. If you have anything you haven't used yet, let's hear it and see what the guys can do to flesh it out with you. But if you're starting from scratch, you gotta know the pressure is on. This album needs to be done by the end of the month, Riley. They've already got songwriters on hand who are salivating at the idea of you recording one of their songs."

"Mick—"

"Yeah. I know. It's my job to let you know what's going to happen if you don't wrap this up. I told them you wouldn't be open to it and their response was…" He shook his head. "Let's just say you'd be doing us all a favor if you had a few more songs up your sleeve."

"I'm working on it."

With a nod, Mick grabbed his briefcase. "I'll see you and Savannah Friday night at Roger's place. Call me if you need anything."

As Mick walked out, his musicians walked in. They were a great bunch of musicians Riley had handpicked for the project. As everyone took their places and began fooling around with their instruments, Riley wondered if he was wrong. If he only needed two songs, why was he killing himself? He had bits and pieces of songs, but they hadn't gelled yet.

"Hey," he said, and everyone quieted. "So…Mick's telling me we only need two more songs and then we can call this one done."

"That's awesome!" his drummer Tyler said and everyone agreed.

"Here's the thing…I don't have two completed songs, and I don't know if what I do have is enough to work with. Mick tells me there are a couple of songwriters with songs ready to go for me."

"Dude, don't do it," Russ, his bass player, said. "Come on. Play what you have and tell us what you want. We can totally do this."

Riley smiled as everyone looked at him with excitement and determination written all over their faces. Picking up his guitar, he got himself comfortable and said, "Okay, here's what I'm thinking…"

———

Riley was home from the studio by three on Friday. Savannah was waiting for him at his house and had just gotten out of the shower when he walked into the bedroom.

"Damn," he said, seeing her wrapped in nothing but a towel. "I was hoping to get home before you did that."

"I wasn't sure what time you'd be back so I wanted to make sure I was done in the shower so you could get ready."

With a sexy grin, he stalked her. "I made sure I got home early enough so we could both get ready and shower together."

"Riley," she chuckled, walking backward and holding out a hand to ward him off.

In a flash, he had her hand in his and hauled her into his arms. "Join me in the shower," he said as his mouth began travel across her shoulders, licking up the moisture he found there. She sighed his name as his hand came up and tugged the towel away. She gasped and then he had them both in the bathroom.

"Join me in the shower," he repeated, his hands skimming up and down her back before resting on her bottom and pulling her snug against him.

"We really should…*oh*…we need to get ready," she panted as Riley placed open-mouth kisses everywhere he could reach.

"Plenty of time," he murmured. "Trust me."

"I do," she sighed.

Raising his head, he gave her a triumphant grin. With his eyes on hers, he turned the hot water on in the shower and stripped. And when he stepped into the huge, spa-like shower and tugged Savannah in with him, she didn't even pretend to put up a fight.

―᠁―

"So basically, I'm stumped."

Savannah was putting the finishing touches on her makeup when Riley made that statement. He was sitting on the bed in nothing but his boxer briefs, and she could see him in the giant mirror in the bathroom. "So all you need is one more song?"

He nodded. "It shouldn't be so damn hard, but nothing sounds right. Nothing is saying what I want it to say. Every song on this album is very personal to me." He looked up at her. "And you haven't even heard them all because you haven't been in the studio for over a week."

"You're pouting again," she reminded him and put her makeup away. Turning toward him, she rested against the vanity. "Besides, I'm just about done with your story, and the only reason I could finish it was because I didn't go to the studio. And now I get to be surprised along with everyone else when the album hits the stores."

He made a face. "I really wanted your input, Savannah. Your opinion is important to me."

She sighed. "Okay, look…this last song? Personally I think you're overthinking it."

"What do you mean?"

"You're looking for something new, something

fresh because it's what you think has to be done." She shrugged. "I don't think that's what it's all about. This album is about you—Riley Shaughnessy. And if you don't have something brand-spanking new, then I don't see a problem with doing a cover."

"I don't want—"

She held up her hand. "Not just any cover song, but a song that means something to you. *Really* means something to you. Think about the music you used to play in the garage when you were a teenager. Or songs you used to sing when you used a hairbrush as a microphone and watched your reflection in the mirror."

"I never did that," he grumbled.

"Everyone did that," she retorted. "Even those of us who cannot carry a tune to save our lives sang into a hairbrush and then accepted our Grammy award in the form of a can of hair spray. Deal with it."

He stood and walked over to her and placed a gentle kiss on her nose. "So you really sang into a hairbrush?" he teased.

She nodded with a grin. "Pat Benatar's 'Invincible' was a favorite."

"Nice."

With a quick kiss on the cheek, Savannah walked back out to the bedroom. "Everyone starts somewhere, and I think putting a song on the album that has a special meaning for you and your music career can be a great addition to the playlist." Looking over her shoulder at him, she smiled. "But that's just me. If you're that against it—"

"It's not that," he said quickly and then growled with frustration. "I feel like if I do that, then I'm giving up. Calling it in. Not…creative enough to finish the damn thing."

Savannah's shoulders sagged and she turned, went back to him, and hugged him close. "Riley, what is going on? Why is this such a big deal?"

"I want this album to be the best. I want all those critics who thought I was some sort of no-talent hack to see they were wrong."

Guilt swamped her because she knew not so long ago she had been one of those critics. "You have nothing to prove," she said quietly, pulling back to look him in the eye. "You are incredibly talented. Your talent astounds me. And anyone who can't see that and appreciate it isn't worth your time."

"Now you sound like Mick."

She smiled and kissed him. "That's good because he's a pretty smart guy."

"Yeah but—"

"No. No more negative talk. In the end you have to do what feels right to you. It's your name on the album and you need to have music on there that you're proud of. So take a little time to think about it. But not tonight. Tonight we get to go out on a real date!" She let out a little squeal of excitement. "No disguises. No hiding out. Tonight you get to be yourself. We get to dress up and go out and eat yummy food and have some champagne… I've been excited about this night all week!"

Riley looked at his reflection in the mirror and frowned. "I need a haircut. I should have done that before today."

Fishing through her makeup bag, Savannah pulled

out a pair of hair scissors and held them up for Riley to see.

"Seriously? You carry a pair of scissors around with you?"

"Tools of the trade," she said happily. "Come on. I'll give you a quick trim before we get dressed."

He grinned. "Will you do it naked?" He waggled his eyebrows at her.

"No, perv," she said but couldn't help the giggle that went with it. "But if you're good, I'll take my robe off and do it in my underwear."

Riley sprinted from the room and came back with one of the stools from the breakfast nook and then made a zipping motion over his lips. He sat down and looked at Savannah expectantly.

"Such a weirdo," she muttered and began finger combing his hair to get a feel for it. "I don't think we need to do a lot, but I'll clean it up a bit for you."

He smiled and nodded but didn't utter a word. Then he pointedly looked at her robe and then up to her eyes and back again.

"Oh, for crying out loud." She sighed and shrugged off her robe, letting it pool at her feet before kicking it aside. "There. Happy now?"

Another enthusiastic nod.

Savannah walked around him, trimming his hair and then combing through it to get the look she knew he favored. When she came back to stand in front of him, she stopped between his legs and was pleased with the results. Reaching past him, she put the scissors down and then used both hands to comb through his hair. "All done."

Riley's hands instantly went to her waist and squeezed as he stood up. "That was the hottest haircut ever."

She giggled. "Stop."

"I don't think I could ever let anyone else cut my hair again. Promise me you'll always do it for me and always be in your underwear." His hot gaze raked over her. "You look exceptional in purple silk and lace."

"You said the exact same thing about the red set I wore yesterday," she teased and tried to step out of his grasp, but he held firm.

"You look exceptional in everything you wear, Savannah," he said, his voice low and gravelly.

"You think so?" she asked, sighing as she leaned in and kissed his chest.

"I do."

"I think you look exceptional too, Riley. Particularly like this."

He groaned and hugged her tight. "If we didn't need to be at this party, I'd thank you properly for the compliment."

"How about a rain check? You can thank me properly *after* the party," she purred.

"You're on."

In her career as a writer, Savannah had found herself in many different social settings, but this party at Roger Gray's house was like nothing she'd ever experienced before. She'd been to parties and dinners with rock stars and, at the time, thought nothing could be more decadent.

She was wrong.

Gray's estate seemed to take up a city block and was

decorated like something out of a movie set. She was almost afraid to touch anything. Riley must have sensed it because he kept chuckling at her.

"It's okay you know," he whispered in her ear.

"What is?"

"You're allowed to touch things. You can't juggle with them, but it's okay to get close to them."

"One of those plates probably cost more than my car," Savannah whispered back to him. "I'd hate to get noticed because I broke something."

He kissed her cheek. "You wouldn't be the first."

"Not the way I like to make an impression."

He nuzzled her neck. "Sweetheart, this dress is a great impression. I'm the envy of every man in this room."

She blushed. "Somehow I doubt it. Isn't that Christina Jenkins over there? You know she was on the cover of *Cosmo* last month."

Riley shook his head. "I don't care. All I can see is you."

It was impossible to stop the girly sigh. The man certainly had a way with words. "If you keep talking like that we'll never get the opportunity for you to schmooze and make your donation." She playfully tugged at his shirt. "Because I'll drag you out of here and have my way with you."

He hummed against her. "I hate to break it to you, but all you're doing is encouraging me. Mick might get pissed because I didn't stay, but it would be totally worth it."

She laughed. "Okay, okay, I'll stop. Come on, let's mingle." Taking his hand in hers, Savannah did her best to put a little distance between them but she already missed the heat of his body.

They roamed the room, making small talk with the people they encountered. Savannah marveled at how Riley seemed to know the exact thing to say to everyone. He seemed to have something in common with everyone, and by the time they moved on, the people they had just spoken to were almost gushing over him.

To his credit, Riley never left her side. Whenever possible, his arm was banded around her waist or he was holding her hand, and he never missed an opportunity to introduce her to people and include her in the conversation. Truth be told, he was the most perfect and attentive date she'd ever had.

Mick walked over with a big smile on his face. "You've got everyone in this room eating out of the palm of your hand," he said so only they could hear. "I've been approached by about a dozen different people wanting to schedule interviews and appearances with you."

"That's great, Mick," Riley said.

"Savannah," Mick began, "do you know what the release date is going to be for the magazine?"

"Tommy and I talked about it being a multi-issue thing. He's waiting for me to finish editing before he'll commit to which date it's going to come out. The sooner the better as far as he's concerned."

"Perfect," Mick said with a huge smile. "If it's all right with you, I'm going to call him in the morning and get things moving. How soon until your edits are done?"

A wave of panic threatened to overwhelm her. She didn't like to be rushed, but she knew why Mick was anxious to get things moving. "Um…I…maybe by the end of next week?"

He nodded. "That sounds good. I'll talk to Tommy tomorrow." Reaching over, he patted Riley on the back. "Tonight is your night, my friend. Work the crowd a little more and in about twenty minutes we'll present your donation and then…" He winked. "You're free to go."

Riley pulled her a little tighter against him. "Thanks, Mick." After his manager walked away, Riley snagged them both a glass of champagne. "The way I see it, we can easily be out of here in about thirty minutes." His gaze met hers. "And then…there was talk of a rain check, I believe."

Blushing, Savannah looked around to make sure nobody could hear them. "I do believe we mentioned something about—"

"Riley Shaughnessy…the man of the hour."

They turned and saw Marshall Hall coming to stand beside them. He was a well-known television producer who specialized in working with MTV and VH1.

Riley held out his hand to shake Marshall's, and Savannah couldn't help but wonder where she'd met Marshall before. Everyone knew who he was, but she couldn't recall where it was they might have met.

"Good to see you, Marshall," Riley said easily, but Savannah could sense some tension in him.

"I'm hearing a lot of buzz about this upcoming album," Marshall replied. "Any chance we're going to hear any of it tonight?"

Riley shook his head. "Tonight's all about Roger and what he's doing for the ASPCA. I'm only here as a supporter."

Marshall chuckled. "Sure. That's why we're all here."

Savannah sensed the double meaning as well as the implied barb.

"Marshall, this is Savannah Daly," Riley said, clearly choosing to ignore the man's comment. "Savannah works for Tommy Vaughn."

Marshall's eyes went wide. "Wait…you're a reporter?"

Savannah nodded, but before she could speak, Marshall was talking again.

"You and I met a little over a year ago. I was doing a segment for VH1 Classics on Aerosmith and you were there to do a piece on Joe Perry. We talked over a cup of coffee while the crew was trying to get the lighting problems fixed."

She smiled. "Oh, yeah…now I remember. That turned out to be a fun piece. They're a great bunch of guys."

"Definitely," Marshall agreed. "But I must say, I'm surprised to see the two of you here together."

Riley frowned as he looked from Marshall to Savannah and back again and asked, "Why?"

Marshall chuckled nervously. "Well, at the time, Savannah was a little—shall we say—*vocal* about Shaughnessy and how you measured up to other bands who've stood the test of time. Like Aerosmith."

If Savannah thought Riley was tense a minute ago, he was like granite now.

"I don't recall ever trying to compare myself to guys like that. I mean, how could I? They've been around forty years longer than I have."

Marshall seemed to relax a little. "That's what I said, but we were talking about the documentary I was getting ready to do and we were going to do a segment on the next generation of rock stars—who were going to be the next Aerosmith or the Stones—and when your name came up…" He shrugged. "Let's just say she helped me narrow my choices down."

Everything in Savannah went hot and then instantly cold. *Son of a bitch!* It all came flooding back to her—the conversation, the interview, and how much of a condescending prick Marshall Hall was. It was one thing for them to have had the conversation, but there was no reason for him to bring it up now right in front of Riley.

So many retorts bounced around in her head, but Savannah knew now wasn't the time to make a scene. She glared at Marshall and caught his smarmy grin before he shrugged. "I guess I'll see the two of you later."

She waited until the crowd had swallowed Marshall up before she turned and tried to explain herself. "Riley, look… I—"

"Not here," he said, his voice low and deadly calm. "I think it's time we move toward the stage. I see Mick over there with Roger. Let's get through the presentation and we'll talk when there's no one around to eavesdrop."

Slowly, she nodded and noticed that for the first time all night, Riley moved away from her—his arm dropped from around her waist and he walked ahead of her toward the front of the room.

~~~

For the life of him, Riley had no idea how he had gotten through the rest of their time at Roger Gray's house. He had smiled for everyone, had even gotten up on stage and given his speech about the importance of the work of the ASPCA, and afterward, he had stood—with Savannah at his side—for a seemingly endless amount of photos. When they were finally able to break free, he arranged for their car to come and get them.

Through it all, Savannah had stood silently beside him. She smiled when prompted but didn't utter a single word. He thanked Roger for inviting them and quickly ushered Savannah out of the room and outside to wait for the car.

"Riley…" she finally said when they were alone, and he heard the tremor in her voice.

"Here's the car," was his only response. Once inside with the doors closed, he gave the driver Savannah's address. Out of the corner of his eye, he saw her head bow.

In a million years, he never would have thought she'd be the one behind the whole documentary nightmare. She was the reason he'd been cut. She was the reason for his depression and funk and inability to write or perform for almost a year! There was no way he could forget what Marshall Hall had said—no way he could look at her right now without feeling betrayed.

Maybe it wasn't rational—after all, he and Savannah hadn't even known one another back when she had the conversation with Hall. And, if he wanted to be fair, she had been honest with him from the very beginning about what she thought of him professionally.

Since then she had claimed to change her mind about him and his talent.

Or had she?

The silence was deafening but there was no way Riley was going to have this discussion with her with an audience—even an audience of one. So he waited until they pulled up to her house and asked the driver to wait for him. He walked Savannah to the door and when she stepped inside, he followed, shutting the door behind him.

"You're the reason I didn't get included in the documentary," he said as soon as she put her purse down. Calm was what he was hoping for, but what came out was an angry accusation.

"Riley, I had no idea! We were just talking that day! I had no idea what Marshall was planning or that he'd take something I said personally and use it against you. I mean, it was only a flippant conversation! It wasn't anything personal. You have to believe me!"

Pacing the length of the living room, he knew what she was saying made sense. A part of him knew it and was begging him to calm down before he did something stupid. Unfortunately, he had waited a year to have someone directly to blame for all the grief and aggravation the loss of the project had cost him.

It was unfortunate Savannah was that person.

"Do you have any freaking idea what that whole situation did to me? The way it messed with my head?"

She nodded. "At the time I didn't, but we've talked about this," she said quickly, her desperation coming through in her every word. "I never put the two together. I'm sorry! I…I don't know what else to say!"

"I think you've said more than enough," he snapped. "You know, people like you—the press—you think you've got everything all figured out. You look at musicians and celebrities and you form an opinion of us without knowing a damn thing. You see us out in public and if we make one wrong move, you create a story on what you *think* is going on and ninety-nine percent of the time you have it wrong."

"Riley—"

"I've read stories about myself where I have no idea how the reporter even came up with the information that was printed. Most of the time it's only nonsense and not worth my time to argue about, but you have got to realize how the things you do and say—as the press—affect people like me."

"I'm not like that, Riley! You know I'm not!"

He laughed but it wasn't filled with humor. "Do I? I thought I did, but apparently I was wrong."

"I made one stupid comment…and it was over a year ago!"

"And yet look at what it accomplished!" he yelled. "Sitting there on your pedestal, sitting in judgment on the people you interview. Did it make you feel good, Savannah? Did it make you feel good to put others down? Did it make you feel superior to the rest of us?"

"That wasn't what it was about! Dammit, Riley, he asked my opinion and I gave it. I didn't expect him to use it against anyone. And don't you dare stand there and act like you've never criticized anyone either. We've all done it. It's human nature!"

"I trusted you," he said, teeth clenched. "I shared everything about my life—everything that I am—and how am I supposed to know you're not going to twist it all around and make a damn fool out of me in this article?"

She looked at him as if he'd slapped her. "Wow. Just…" She shook her head in disgust. "From the moment we met, I was honest with you. Even when it wasn't flattering, I was honest. You can check my work, you can talk to every damn celebrity I've ever interviewed and find out for yourself that I'm true to my word!"

"It won't matter," he said and then sighed wearily. "I can't… I don't…" He looked at her sadly. "I look at you and all I see right now is the reason this last year has been hell."

He saw her eyes fill with tears. "I never meant…" she began.

"It doesn't matter. I can't be around you right now, Savannah."

She came up to him and grabbed his hand in both of hers. "It's okay. Take a few days to think about things. I'm so sorry. You have no idea how much."

Slowly he pulled his hand from hers. "It's not that easy. I don't know if this is something I can move on from."

Straightening, Savannah took a full step back. "I never lied to you, Riley. I didn't like you when I met you, but that changed the instant we started spending time together. Everything we shared—"

"Is now tarnished," he interrupted. "And I feel like a fool."

They stood there in silence, neither knowing what else there was to say. Finally, Riley walked toward the door and left without another word.

The entire weekend passed in a blur of tears for Savannah.

She'd started to cry after Riley had walked out, and it seemed she wasn't able to stop for more than a few minutes at a time. It wasn't as if she was an overly emotional person, but she knew what they had was over and it was the most painful thing she'd ever experienced.

By the time Monday rolled around, she started to feel a little like her old self. And as torturous as it was, she forced herself to sit down and do the final edits on Riley's story. The sooner she was done with it, the sooner she could move on to something new. For two days she hammered through everything she'd written and recorded. It was like a sweet form of torture to hear his voice on the recordings. But when she was done, she simply boxed up all her notes and tucked them away in her closet.

Tommy was thrilled when she emailed him on Wednesday, and when he called to congratulate her, she asked if he would meet her for dinner. He readily agreed and told her they would celebrate. She smiled at his enthusiasm and promised to meet him at seven at their favorite sushi place near the magazine's offices.

"Wait…you're not serious, are you?" he asked when they finally sat down to dinner.

Savannah nodded. "I am."

Tommy frowned and sat back, crossing his arms over his chest. "I don't understand. This is all coming out of nowhere. Last we talked, this was going to be a cover piece, multi-issue, and big things were going to start happening for you. I've got some sweet assignments lined up with your name on them."

"Give them to someone else. I'm done." There was little emotion in her voice as she said it but his intense scrutiny was making her squirm in her seat.

"What are you going to do now? Go back to doing hair and makeup? Come on, Savannah, we both know you're far too talented to walk away from your writing."

She shrugged. "I haven't figured it all out yet. But I wanted you to be the first to know. You're more than a boss to me, Tommy. You're a friend. A mentor. You can be a real pain in the ass sometimes, but that's just your style."

"You've got to give me something here, kid. I'm finding it hard to believe you're walking away from this on a whim. I talked to Shaughnessy's people on Monday and they're over the moon with you. We're meeting tomorrow to talk about distribution and how we can make this beneficial to all of us. You can't just walk away."

Willing herself not to start crying, she gave Tommy a weak smile. "I have to."

"Tell me what happened. Tell me what I can do to change your mind about this."

In her mind, when Savannah imagined this conversation with Tommy, he took her resignation in stride and they had a pleasant dinner and went their separate ways. She'd never imagined sharing with him everything that had happened between her and Riley. By the time she was done, she felt physically and emotionally drained.

"Well…shit," he murmured, running a hand over his face. "I freaking hate Marshall Hall. That guy's a major jackass with a God complex."

"Yeah, I still can't believe he said it all to Riley. I mean, what was the point?"

"He's mean like that. He's known all along how much that rejection bothered Riley, and he found the perfect way to rub it in even harder. Damn, Savannah. I'm sorry."

"I can't change what I said, Tommy. I've apologized and pretty much begged Riley, but he wouldn't listen."

"Maybe he just needs time to calm down."

She shook her head. "He had a box of my things delivered to me this morning. I don't think he wants time. He wants me gone."

With a curse, Tommy reached over and placed a hand over hers. "I get why you're upset and all, but quitting the magazine isn't going to change anything."

"Maybe not to you, but it will for me. Riley was right. I do pass judgment on the people I interview, and now that I've seen the way it can affect someone? Hurt someone? I can't do it anymore. I still want to write, Tommy, but not on this level. No more rock stars or celebrities. Maybe I'll apply to some women's magazine and do stories on hair and makeup. Put my cosmetology license to some good use."

Sitting back, he studied her. "Let me make some calls and see what I can do. I hate to see you reduced to doing stories on eye shadow after you flew in a hot air balloon with Sting. That's just wrong."

She chuckled.

And for the first time in days, she felt like maybe there was life after Riley Shaughnessy.

───※───

She was going to kill Tommy Vaughn.

Two weeks later, it was the only thing keeping Savannah sane—images of getting back to L.A. and wrapping her hands around his stupid neck! He had been good to his word and found her several lucrative freelancing gigs, most of which kept her busy and on the road—and that was helpful in keeping her mind off Riley. But right now? She would welcome being in a Riley Shaughnessy museum to this current assignment.

She was sitting in a barn in the backwoods of Washington State interviewing a young wood sculptor. Granted, the guy was brilliant. He did things with wood that, even though she saw him do it, didn't seem possible. Benjamin Tanner was twenty-six and had little to no interest in being interviewed. It was like pulling teeth to get him to speak more than a handful of words to her.

Unfortunately for him, he had made a bit of a name for himself and his agent had insisted on the article being done. So he was doing it, but he wasn't doing it graciously.

"So…um, Ben," she said, doing her best to get comfortable while sitting on a pile of hay, "how did you get started with your sculpting?"

He didn't even look up at her. Sandy blond hair was tucked under a knit cap and he looked like he hadn't shaved in days. Savannah thought he was cute in a scruffy kind of way, but his manners pretty much sucked. "My grandfather used to make furniture," he said stiffly. "He built the cabin he and my grandmother moved into when they first got married and then he started with the furniture. From the time I was five, he used to bring me out to his workshop and taught me about wood and tools and how to build things."

"So do you enjoy making furniture?" she asked and thought to herself how she really couldn't care less.

He shook his head. "I do it, but I don't enjoy it. I studied art in school and while my teachers were encouraging us to work with clay and stone, I decided to go with wood."

"How did your teachers feel about that?"

"I didn't care. We were told to do a project. I chose to do it in wood rather than their suggestions."

She smiled at his belligerent attitude. "What did you get as a grade on your first project?"

This time he did look up at her, and Savannah noticed that his eyes were an incredible shade of green and when he smiled, he had dimples. "It's still on display at the high school."

"Impressive."

He shrugged again. "I also did pieces for several teachers. They stopped making me draw things with chalk or whatever pointless medium they were trying to teach that week and pretty much let me do my own thing. It was the easiest grade I ever got."

Okay then, she thought. "So how did you get here?"

He looked at her quizzically. "I grew up here."

She chuckled and shook her head. "No, I mean here as in to the point where I'm here interviewing you."

"Oh."

For a minute Savannah was certain he was going to ignore her. He was currently working with a hammer and chisel and while she could appreciate his attention to detail, she'd also appreciate his attention to this interview.

"My parents were killed in a boating accident three years ago," he said quietly. "My grandparents are gone so it was up to me to provide for my younger brothers."

Brand. New. Information. She sighed and made a note of it. "How many are there?"

"Two. Jack is two years younger than I am and Henry is four years younger." He paused. "They were both in college when it happened and I didn't want them to have to quit. I had an art teacher in college who was always after me to show my work. I didn't see what the big deal was. I mean, I know my stuff is good, but I thought I was the only one who would appreciate it. After the funeral, I called him and asked him to help me set up an exhibit."

Savannah scanned through her preliminary research because that exhibit had made the national news. "He was very good at his job because you received a lot of attention for that show."

Ben nodded. "I still don't understand why. But I sold every piece I displayed for more money than I ever thought possible and then was commissioned to do a lot more."

"What's this piece you're working on now?"

"This is for a guy with too much time and money on his hands," Ben said sourly. "He's building a six-thousand-square-foot log home and wants custom pieces for several rooms. This one is a mini totem pole for his son's room. He told me what he wanted and I drew up the designs."

"That's pretty interesting."

"Not really. Essentially I'm ripping up my hands for a bunch of spoiled rich kids. Not exactly living the dream."

"So what would you be doing if it were up to you?"

Dropping his hands, Ben looked at her. "I'd be designing whatever the hell I wanted to and wouldn't have a reporter here watching me."

Yeah, she was going to strangle Tommy Vaughn.

"Hey, you've reached Savannah Daly. Please leave a message after the beep and I'll get back to you as soon as possible. Thanks, and have a great day."

It was the fifth time Riley had heard that message in the last week and he was getting pretty damn tired of it. The first three times, he'd left a message. Then he gave up. He was the one getting the message—Savannah didn't want to talk to him and really, who could blame her?

He'd spent a week holed up in his house after the whole Marshall Hall revelation. Mick had threatened to kick his front door down if he didn't come out, and there wasn't a doubt in Riley's mind that he'd do it. But even when he did, he wasn't worth shit to anyone.

"You have *got* to snap out of it," Mick said, helping himself to a beer. "I get that you were taken off guard and that you're upset, but to be fair you really can't hold this against Savannah."

Riley wanted to argue but Mick was right. It was the exact conclusion he had come to.

He just wasn't ready to fully accept it yet.

"Look, we're almost at the end of the month and you have one damn song left to do. You need to get off your ass and get it done."

"I don't have a damn thing," Riley said quietly. "I can't even think about a damn song."

"Then the label is going to pick one for you." Finishing his drink, Mick started to walk toward the front door. "I'll see you at eight tomorrow in the studio. Don't make me come and get you."

Once the door slammed shut, Riley walked over and collapsed on the sofa. All the blinds were closed; he hadn't been outside or seen the sun in days. With his head thrown back, he knew something had to give. Right now, he was every bit as mentally blocked as he had been before he'd met Savannah.

And she wasn't talking to him.

With a sigh, he called the only person he could think of who he really wanted to talk to.

His father.

"Riley!" Ian said as a greeting. "How are you? Any new music to send my way yet?"

"Almost, Dad."

"Good, good. I hope it's soon."

"How's the house coming?"

"It's done. I'm telling you it is amazing what can happen when you have the right people on the job."

Riley chuckled. "Aidan runs a tight ship, that's for sure."

"Yeah, but he wasn't here for a lot of it. All the subcontractors were quality guys. Everything fell into place, we didn't hit any snags, and now that it's done, I can't even remember what the house looked like before."

"You'll have to send me some pictures."

"You got it," Ian said. "Or you and Savannah could come back and see it in person. I know it's a lot to fly across country and all, but if you're almost done with the album, maybe you could take a long weekend and come for a visit. You tell me when and I'll make sure everyone's here for dinner."

The thought made Riley smile, but it quickly faded. "I…" He cleared his throat. "I'm not sure I can swing it any time soon. I'm under some pressure to finish the album. I've only got one song left to do and… I can't seem to do it."

"Why not? Seemed to me like you finally had a breakthrough and you had the music coming to you faster than you could write it down. Surely you've got enough material left over for one more song? What does Savannah think?"

"She thinks I'm a royal jackass and she's not speaking to me," Riley said honestly, and the pain that squeezed his heart at admitting it out loud almost brought tears to his eyes.

"I see," Ian said softly. "What happened?"

Riley told him the whole sordid story—including how he realized he was wrong but she wasn't taking his calls. "There's no music in me without her," he said quietly. "She took it all with her."

Ian was quiet for several long minutes. "You stopped singing for about a year after your mom died, do you remember that?"

"There wasn't any reason to sing."

"Nonsense, there are always reasons to sing, even if they're sad ones."

"Maybe for some people, but not me."

"Stop pouting, Riley," Ian snapped with a hint of humor. "I think you could as easily have been an actor as you were a singer."

"What exactly does *that* mean?"

"You're dramatic! For crying out loud, when you were little you would sing at the drop of a hat. It didn't matter what was going on—one time, you broke into a rendition of 'We Will Rock You' in church because the sermon was boring you and you thought the acoustics were good in the sanctuary! Another time we were out to dinner and you decided to stand on your chair and sing 'Don't Stop Believing' because you thought the waitress looked sad. And don't even get me started on all the times you sang in the grocery store because you knew it made Gladys the cashier smile. You're just telling yourself you can't sing."

"I can *sing*, Dad," Riley corrected. "I can't *write* a damn song. There's a difference."

"Why do you have to write a song? I'm sure Mick or

somebody can get you a song to sing or sing someone else's song. People do that all the time."

Did nobody get it? "I don't want to sing someone else's song! This is my damn solo album and I want to prove I can write the whole thing on my own!"

"Prove to whom?" Ian asked.

"Everyone!"

"Ah…see? Dramatic."

"What…? How…?"

"You want to do it so when it's done you can say 'See? Look at me, everyone, and love me because I wrote all my songs.' Goody for you."

Riley looked at the phone and wondered if someone had abducted his father because this person he was talking to was nothing like the father he grew up with. "Thanks for the sarcasm."

"Oh, I'm being completely honest," Ian said. "Riley, I've learned a lot of things in the past several years. And I'm honest enough to say it's taken me that long to start seeing things for how they really are." He paused. "I wasn't a very good father to you kids and I wasn't a very good husband to your mother."

"Dad, are you crazy?" Riley yelled. "What's gotten into you?"

"When you kids were little, I worked all the time. And when I was home, I wasn't really there."

"You're not making any sense. You were always there! Seriously, you're remembering things wrong."

"No, I'm not, Son. You are."

"Dad—"

"I worked long hours because I thought that's what I needed to do. Everyone told me your mother and I were crazy for having so many kids, that we were going to end up broke and living in a trailer somewhere. I was determined to prove them all wrong."

"You were providing for your family," Riley said. "There's nothing wrong with that."

"Riley, I worked sixty hours a week. I had a good job that provided for us even if I only worked forty. I took the extra hours because I was afraid someone would think less of me. That if something happened and we fell on hard times, I'd be the one to take the blame." He sighed. "I missed out on all that time with you kids and with your mom. She was the one who worked so hard to make everything good for all of you, and I was the guy who was too worried about what other people thought that I missed out on a life with my family."

Well, damn. "I don't know what to say to that," Riley admitted.

"Say you'll learn from your old man. If there's a song you want on the album, it shouldn't matter who wrote it. If there's a song in your heart that means something to you, you should sing it."

"That's what Savannah said."

"She's a smart girl," Ian said. "I knew I liked her."

"Yeah, she was smart enough to walk away from an idiot like me."

"Seems to me you pushed."

"In the moment? I couldn't think clearly. The damn documentary—"

"Wouldn't have done a damn thing for your career. The only one still talking about that thing is you. Do you still see it on TV?"

"Well…no."

"Anyone still bring it up in the papers or magazines?"

"No."

"Is Mick or anyone at your label pissed off because you weren't on it?"

"No."

"Then move on, Son. Everyone else has."

"I don't know if I can move on without Savannah. I miss her so much."

"Things have always come kind of easily to you. I see it in your brothers, too. But your career has been particularly easy for you. Most of us have to work at things." He chuckled. "Work a little, Son. It's good for the soul."

Riley wasn't so sure he agreed, but he did know that this version of his father was pretty damn cool to talk to.

Chapter 11

Robyn turned to Martha and asked, "Do you think we'll meet any celebrities?"

"I'm not sure, but I think we should be prepared just in case."

Paul Daly and Ian Shaughnessy stood back and looked at the women like they were crazy. "I don't know about you, Ian, but I feel like I'm in the middle of an *I Love Lucy* episode. I think we're going to have to watch those two."

"I'm exhausted already," Ian said, "and we just got here."

"Glad you guys finally made it," Riley said, walking across the hotel lobby toward the four of them. "How were your flights?"

"Good," Ian said. "Everyone else should be down in a little bit. They're all so excited to be here, and it was very nice of you to send the private plane. Zoe was particularly appreciative."

"Well, I know her doctor wasn't thrilled with her flying and Aidan mentioned how she's been uncomfortable lately so I thought this would help."

"Still, I know it's a big expense."

Riley waved him off. "The guys at the label are so giddy about the fast track things are on that I can pretty much ask for anything I want at the moment."

"Don't let it go to your head," Paul said, shaking Riley's hand. "But we certainly did appreciate the effort."

"Like I said, it was my pleasure." Riley looked around and spotted his family all stepping off the elevators. He looked at his father. "We're quite the large group nowadays."

Ian nodded. "And I love it." Turning, he took Connor from Hugh's arms. "There's my buddy!" He kissed the baby on the cheek as everyone stepped forward to say hello to Riley.

"You are officially my favorite Shaughnessy," Zoe said as she walked over and kissed him on the cheek.

"Hey!" Aidan cried.

"Oh, hush. Thanks to your brother I got to fly across the country while sitting in a recliner eating chocolate-covered popcorn." She looked at Riley again. "I love you."

"Chocolate-covered…?" Riley began.

"Don't ask," Aidan said and shook Riley's hand. "I've watched her eat stuff most people wouldn't eat on a dare."

Zoe smiled serenely and rubbed her swollen belly. "It's not my fault that your baby has some weird cravings."

"Let's hope they end when the pregnancy does."

"Do you know what you're having?" Riley asked. "Any chance of it being a boy who you want to name after your now-favorite Shaughnessy?"

"Nice try," Zoe said and patted his cheek. "But we want to be surprised."

"Damn, you're no fun."

"I think our table's ready," Martha called out to the bunch, and they all followed her into the hotel restaurant and took their seats.

"So our baby brother is singing at the Hollywood Bowl," Hugh said. "I'm seriously impressed."

All around him, everyone seemed to be talking at once. They were excited to be there with him and were talking about the things they wanted to see while they were in L.A. Riley was as happy as they were to be able to share this event with them, but he also couldn't help missing Savannah.

Eight weeks.

It had been eight long weeks since he'd seen her and every day it seemed to get worse. He'd finished the album and met all of his commitments, but he was still kicking himself for not going after her sooner. No doubt she'd decided he wasn't worth it and had moved on to someone else.

Mick told him she was no longer writing for Tommy Vaughn, but he didn't want to seem creepy and ask where she was working. He drew the line at being a stalker.

For now.

Beside him, Owen leaned closer. "You okay?" he asked.

Riley turned his head and gave a half smile. "I guess."

"You nervous about tomorrow night?"

"No. I'm more than ready for it. I know things are happening way faster than they normally do, but I don't think I could handle waiting any more. The band I've assembled are a bunch of great guys and they're as pumped as I am to get things going."

Owen nodded. "Do you miss her?"

"Always." Riley knew exactly who his twin was referring to.

"Did you invite her to the show?"

"Mick sent over a ticket and VIP pass to get her backstage, but she never responded."

"I'm sorry, Riley. I really thought the two of you were right for one another."

"Me too, bro. When I pictured this day? Like the whole finishing the album and concert thing? I always pictured Savannah being beside me. It feels wrong that she's not here."

"So go and talk to her," Owen said simply, like it was a no-brainer. "Why wait any longer?"

"Because I don't know what to say. I've tried calling and, as selfish as it sounds, I need to focus on getting ready for the show. I need my head to be in the game. I'll be in rehearsals tonight and most of the day tomorrow. There isn't time."

"I can go and talk to her for you."

And in that moment, Riley knew he was the luckiest man alive. Not only had his entire family flown in to be here to support him, but his socially awkward brother—who was prone to breaking out in hives when forced to speak to members of the opposite sex—was willing to break out of his comfort zone for his sake.

Yeah. He was definitely lucky.

"No. I want you and everyone to take some time today to do what you want."

"It's raining," Owen said. "So that leaves out some of the sightseeing everyone was talking about. Although I don't see what the big deal is about seeing where Bradley Cooper lives. It's not like he's going to invite us in."

"He's a pretty cool guy. I could probably arrange it."

Owen grimaced. "Please don't. I know Aubrey and Darcy would love it, but I don't think I could handle being around them after that."

Riley chuckled. "What about Zoe and Anna? Don't they want to know where he lives?"

Owen shook his head. "No, they were more interested in some guy with a lot of gray suits. I didn't understand why they'd want to meet someone so bland."

That made Riley laugh harder. "Bro, don't worry. I've got your back. No actors. No gray suits."

"Thanks."

The remainder of lunch was as chaotic as any family meal back home, and Riley loved every minute of it. By the time they were done and the check paid, he wasn't sure what everyone's plans for the rest of the day were. "I need to get over to the Bowl and rehearse. What's everyone doing?"

"What happens if it rains, Riley?" Anna asked.

"From what I understand, there's a long-standing Bowl tradition which says the 'show must go on,' so there are no rained-out concerts and no rain checks issued. Unless the weather is dangerous, I'm singing. I'd invest in some ponchos if I were you, just to play it safe."

"Well, that stinks," Anna pouted. "But I guess I can understand. We'll have to keep our fingers crossed that the weather clears up."

Riley nodded. "The forecast is clear for tomorrow so I'm not too worried. So what are you planning for the rest of today? Finding a map to the stars' homes?"

Everyone laughed. "Not if I can help it," Quinn said. "I don't mind doing some sightseeing, but I'm not stalking any celebrities."

"Thank goodness." Owen sighed.

"You know, you've got two drivers at your disposal.

If you want to drive around and see stuff, you can tell them. They're familiar with everything in this town. It's up to you."

"That's very generous of you, Riley," Ian said. "But don't worry about us. You go and get to your rehearsal, and we'll see you tomorrow."

He frowned. "I wish everyone could have stayed with me. I kind of feel bad that you're having to stay at a hotel."

"Oh, yeah," Darcy chimed in. "It's a real hardship staying at a five-star luxury hotel in Hollywood and having room service to cater to our every whim." She sighed. "Whereas if we stayed with you we'd be cooking and cleaning up after ourselves. Seriously, Riley, we're all very grateful to be here. Don't give it another thought."

"Such a brat," he teased and then gave her a loud smacking kiss on the cheek. "Okay, then. I guess you're all in good hands and I'll see you at the show tomorrow night. If you need anything, you have Mick's and my numbers."

"For crying out loud, go, Riley," Aidan said. "We're all fine."

He did a final round of good-byes before turning and walking out of the restaurant. It took him a minute to realize Owen was walking with him. When they hit the lobby, Riley stopped. "What's up?"

"I meant what I said back there before we ate. I'll go talk to Savannah if you'd like."

Emotion overwhelmed him and he grabbed his twin in a fierce embrace. "You are the best brother a guy could ever ask for," he whispered and then stepped back. "But the time's not right. Maybe after the media circus dies down I'll call her, but I don't think I should see her right now. I can't give her the kind of attention she deserves. Right now my life is full of chaos and it's only going to get worse after tomorrow night. It wouldn't be fair to her."

"You don't know that. For all you know, she might enjoy the chaos."

Riley smiled. "She might. But I'm barely holding on by a thread here. I need to do this with no distractions." He paused. "But thank you."

Owen frowned. "For what? You didn't let me do anything."

Riley reached out and squeezed Owen's shoulder. "Believe me, you did more than anyone else. I'll see you tomorrow night."

This time when he turned to walk away, no one followed. And when he stepped outside, Riley noticed the rain had stopped. It was going to make rehearsal a lot more pleasant. His driver pulled up, and as the valet stepped forward to open the door, Riley saw him pause and look up. Following the direction of his gaze, Riley looked up and smiled.

A rainbow.

And with a renewed sense of excitement, he climbed into the car and felt lighter than he had in a long time.

He knew his mom was smiling down on him and everything was going to be okay.

"Eating healthy is way too much effort," Savannah grumbled as she lined up the vegetables she'd just purchased and was getting ready to chop. "Burgers and fries come in a bag, ready to eat. So much easier."

With her knife in hand, she was about to start on the zucchini when her cell phone rang. A quick glance at the screen showed it was her dad. Smiling, she answered the phone. "Hey, Dad! How are you?"

"Good!" he said cheerily. "Really good."

"Is that right? Why? What's going on?"

"Your mother and I are here in California! Surprise!"

"Oh my goodness! Really?"

"Uh-huh. We're here with Ian Shaughnessy. And Martha," he added, "and the entire Shaughnessy clan. We're all here for Riley's concert tomorrow at the Hollywood Bowl."

Her heart sank. "Oh…wow. I…um…I didn't know you were thinking of doing that."

"Riley sent us the tickets and paid to fly us out here. We'd been planning to get together again with Ian and Martha, so this worked out perfectly! So…you're going to the concert, right?"

In that moment, Savannah did something she hadn't done since she was sixteen.

She lied to her father.

"Actually, I'm not."

"What? Why?"

"I'm…I'm still on assignment. This sculptor guy isn't big on talking so it's taking longer than I thought. So…yeah. I'm sorry I'm going to miss seeing you."

"Me too," Paul said and sighed. "Well, darn. After all the times we tried to coordinate a trip out here, your mom and I finally make it and you're not home. When do you think you'll be back?"

If she knew her parents, they were going to be in town for at least a couple of days. "I'm probably going to be here for another three or four days and then it's a two-day drive home. I really wish you would have told me you were coming."

"It's okay, sweetheart. It was all a little spur of the moment and we wanted to surprise you. And we understand. Work comes first."

"Believe me, if I could have finished up sooner, I would have." She loathed herself for lying, but she knew if her parents had any idea that she was in town, she'd get guilted into going with them to see Riley's concert and she wasn't ready for that.

"We'll have to try again at a later date," Paul said. "Look, I better let you get back to work. Your mom sends her love. Promise to give us a call when you're home so we know you made it back safely."

"I promise, Dad. And thanks."

"I love you, Savannah."

"Love you too, Dad."

When she put the phone back down, she felt terrible. At sixteen she had told her parents she was sleeping over at her friend Linda's house when the reality was they were going to a club in Wichita to see some band play. They had stayed out all night and, of course, her parents had found out and she'd been grounded. She'd sworn she'd never sneak out or lie again, and she'd had a pretty long run of keeping that promise.

It didn't make her feel any better about the lie she'd just told.

Picking up the knife, she chanted, "Just keep chopping. Just keep chopping." It was still a total drudgery to do, but it kept her from thinking any more about how her parents were staying so close by and she wasn't going to see them.

A knock at the front door startled Savannah enough that she nicked her finger with the knife. "Dammit," she cursed and immediately sucked on the wound. Tossing the knife down, she walked to the door and pulled it open. And froze.

"Dad? What are you doing here?"

Paul Daly stepped into his daughter's home and grinned at the stunned look on her face. "I had a suspicion you weren't really on an assignment. I mean, I know you were on an assignment a week ago, but I can't imagine the wood sculptor would have allowed you to hang around this long." He chuckled. "Or that you would want to stay that long."

Savannah sighed with defeat, closed the door, and wordlessly walked back to her kitchen. Picking up her discarded knife, she did her best to remain calm and continued to chop vegetables.

"I'm disappointed in you," he said, pulling up one of the stools and sitting before her.

She continued to chop.

"Aren't you going to ask why?"

Putting the knife down, she looked at him with a combination of annoyance and defeat. "I didn't think I'd have to. I figured you'd tell me no matter what."

He chuckled. "Okay, you got me there." He paused and looked at his only child. "For starters, we don't lie to each other. Ever. I hate to think we're at a point in this relationship where you're okay with lying to me."

"Dad, I really wasn't up to any more talk about Riley or the Shaughnessys, and that's what you were going to do. Hell, it's probably what you're going to do right now!"

With a nod, he reached out and snagged a strip of bell pepper and began to munch on it. "And on top of that, I never figured you to be a coward."

"Gee, Dad," Savannah began sarcastically, "I'm so glad you decided to stop by."

He gave her a wry look. "You've been hiding out long enough."

"I haven't been hiding out at all." *Liar. Liar. Liar*, her inner voice mocked.

"I thought we already covered the lying thing," he said wearily. "Look, I understand why you think you need to avoid this concert, but it's a big accomplishment, Savannah. One that you helped make happen."

"It had nothing to do with me. All that music was inside Riley. If anything, I'm the reason it took so long to come out!" She growled with frustration. "I'm the person who caused someone as crazy-talented as Riley Shaughnessy to spiral into a pit of depression and self-doubt! Because of me and my big mouth, spouting off crap I had no right—or reason—to talk about, that man lost a year of his life!"

Paul stood, came around the counter, and pulled his daughter into his arms. "Sweetheart," he began softly, "Riley didn't lose a year of his life. He learned something about his life. During that time when he couldn't write or play, he learned to look at himself and see what he really wanted with his life. He spent time with his family. It wasn't time lost. You have to know that."

She shook her head and burrowed her face against his chest. "I don't know that. What I do know is I'll never forget the look on his face when he realized I was the reason he didn't get a spot in the documentary.

The shock. The betrayal and finally…just disgust." She shook her head again. "I never want to see that look again. Ever."

Paul tucked a finger under her chin and forced her to look at him. "I hate to break it to you, sweet pea, but most people get that look more than once in their life. Hell, your mom gives it to me at least once a week." He was trying to make her smile but missed his mark. "You've changed magazines, you haven't done anything music-industry related, and you're back to cutting hair besides. I thought you were braver than this."

"Well, I hate to disappoint you even more, but I'm not. I'm human like everybody else," she said sadly.

Paul hugged her tight again. "I'm not really disappointed in you, Savannah. I know you're struggling and I know your heart's been broken. I always figured you'd fight a little harder."

"I can't, Dad. I can't argue about what I did and what I said. It was all true. I can't take it back, and I can't make Riley forget I said it. And even if he said he could forgive me, I can't forgive myself."

They stood like that for several long moments before Paul pulled away. "Then I guess I understand," he finally said. "I won't bring it up again. I support you, Savannah. I always have. And if this is what you feel like you have to do, then I'm here for you."

"Thanks, Dad," she said quietly. Picking up her knife, she went back to chopping vegetables. "How come Mom didn't come with you?"

He chuckled. "She and Martha and the rest of the girls are going to get pampered a little. They're all very excited about going to the Hollywood Bowl and the possibility of meeting celebrities. Your mom has several batteries already charged for her camera just in case."

"I hope she won't be too disappointed if she doesn't see any."

"She'll survive." Then he looked at his daughter. "We all will." He walked over and kissed her on the cheek. "I better get going. Ian and I are going to sit around and smoke cigars this afternoon." He chuckled. "You sure you don't want to come along?"

"To smoke cigars? No thanks." She couldn't help but grin. "I'm glad you came by, Dad."

"Are you sure? A few minutes ago you didn't feel that way."

"A few minutes ago I felt a little ambushed. We're good, right?"

He hugged her one more time. "We're always good, Savannah."

———

Her long hair was twisted up in a low bun and a cowboy hat was pulled low over her eyes. It was a hell of a way to travel, but desperate times called for desperate measures.

Parking around the Hollywood Bowl was a nightmare. She was mentally prepared for it, but the reality was far worse. After parking at a remote lot and taking the bus, Savannah knew she'd be lucky if she made it to her seat before Riley hit the stage. With her ticket grasped tightly in her hand, she was thankful for the connections she had made in the music business because the show had sold out in the first twenty minutes after tickets went on sale.

And using the ticket and VIP pass Mick had sent over was never an option.

Her seat was all the way in the back and had a fairly crappy view, but she was fine with it. She couldn't wait to see him. Hear him. It was the closest she'd allow herself. Keeping her head down, Savannah made her way to her seat and was thankful she didn't see anyone she knew and she hadn't missed Riley's introduction.

With her heart pounding in her chest, she couldn't help but look around. Somewhere in this sea of almost eighteen thousand were her parents and the Shaughnessys. No doubt they were down near the stage, and part of her was envious.

You could have been there too.

If she were honest with herself, she could have been on the damn stage—or backstage. Either way, she could have been close to Riley. Close enough to see the smile on his face when the audience sang along or when they cheered for him. She could have been close enough to see the tears in his eyes when he sang one of his ballads.

She could have been close enough to simply be close.

The lights started to dim and she sat up a little straighter in her seat, her heart rate now at a point where she was seriously considering going to the first aid station. But once the stage lights came on and the crowd began to scream and jump to its feet, Savannah was right there with them. She stood and cursed her stubbornness. Cursed the fact that he was so far away, barely visible to her naked eye. It didn't matter that there were giant screens showing her what he was doing. She wanted—needed—to see him.

His opening song wasn't one of his new ones—it was an upbeat rock song from his first album with the band. The crowd was going absolutely insane, and all around her Savannah heard cries of "I love you, Riley!"

Yeah, join the club.

As the song came to an end, Riley sauntered to center stage. Even at a distance she could see his swagger.

"Good evening!" he called out to the crowd. "And welcome to the Hollywood Bowl!"

The screaming of the crowd was almost painful to Savannah's ears, but she forced herself not to lose focus.

"It's been quite the journey to get here," he said. "In the past year, I had the pleasure of getting to know who I really was. I sat in the studio for hours when the music wouldn't come and then I'd go home and sit in my house—and again, the music wouldn't come. So when you're faced with times like that, you don't have much choice but to start examining your life."

"Marry me, Riley!"

"We love you!"

He smiled at the crowd. "I love you all, too!" he said and winked. A crew member appeared from off stage and brought out a stool and a guitar. He sat down and picked the instrument up and got himself comfortable. He strummed a few chords—nothing anyone would recognize—and waggled his eyebrows for a bit of comic relief.

"I spent a lot of time with my family and pretty much made them crazy with my presence." He chuckled. "I kind of put myself wherever I felt like being without really considering whether I was wanted there or not."

"You can live with me, Riley!"

He smiled. "And then the most amazing thing happened," he said dramatically. "I met someone who made me really look at my life. I thought it was what I'd been doing, but it didn't take long to realize I was only looking at what I wanted to see. I didn't see any of the bad stuff. I didn't see any of the selfish stuff. I was pretty good at looking at life as if I was the perpetual good person and everyone else was bad."

He strummed the guitar a little more to break up the speech. The crowd was still yelling nonsense, but all Savannah heard was Riley and his music.

"I was cocky. I was arrogant. And I figured everyone had to like me because…hey…I'm Riley Shaughnessy."

The crowd for some reason went even wilder at that statement and Savannah wanted to tell them all to shut up—to scream it. But she didn't. Her hands were plastered to her chest, trying desperately to keep her heart from beating out of it.

"It turns out I wasn't very likable. At least not all the time." He paused and looked out at the crowd as if searching for someone.

Searching for her.

"But this person—this incredibly amazing person—taught me to like myself again. And the thing is, she wasn't even there to see the transition or to know how much she did for me." A few more strums of the guitar. "Tomorrow, the new album hits the stores. Those of you here tonight will be the first ones able to purchase it on your way out."

The roar of the crowd was downright deafening at that news.

"But this is the first single being released—you

may grow tired of hearing it because I have a feeling it's going to get a lot of airtime." More strumming. "Anyway, here it is, the first song—'Always You.'"

It took about ten seconds for her to recognize the song—it was the one he had played back at Aidan and Zoe's apartment after their explosive lovemaking. Tears welled in her eyes. All around her, people continued to scream and it was hard for her to hear the lyrics, but she could feel the emotion and wanted nothing more than to run down the aisle toward him and beg for his forgiveness.

Instead, she stood—paralyzed—and forced herself to listen. She let the tears fall as he played every last note of every song off the new album. Savannah had no idea how long the concert lasted—she stopped paying attention to the time because all she could focus on was the sound of Riley's voice.

"I want to thank you all for coming," Riley said to the crowd. "This has been an amazing night and I'm incredibly blessed and humbled to have so many of you here to share it with me. Good night."

The stage lights went down, but Savannah knew he'd come back for an encore. In her heart and in her mind, she wasn't sure she could handle it. The sensible part of her told her to leave now. She'd beat the crowds and be out of here and home within an hour.

But the not-so-sensible side begged her to stay.

She owed it to him. Owed it to Riley to stay until the end. He'd accomplished what he wanted and even if she couldn't be with him, she'd still be able to witness his victory from the back row.

The crowd began to cheer and she looked up to see

Riley striding across the stage toward the lone stool in the center of the stage. One light came on—he was all anyone could see. Clearing his throat, Riley reached out and grasped the mic.

"Tonight was a very important night to me," he said seriously. Gone was the jovial performer of moments ago and in his place was simply a man with something important to say. "I've often heard people say that things come full circle, and for me, that happened tonight. Almost twenty-five years ago, I stood on a stage for the very first time. The crowd was much smaller," he said and gave a small smile, "but to me it felt just like this. And out in that crowd were all the people I loved."

Savannah was thankful no one shouted anything—it was as if they all realized he was speaking from the heart.

"Tonight, all those people are here—except one."

Her heart broke for him, and she heard the tremble in Riley's voice and was certain everyone else did too.

"So, for the first time in…oh…over twenty years, I'd like to share a song that is very near and dear to my heart. It's the final song on the album. It's for my mom and this was our song."

Gently, softly, Riley played a beautiful acoustic version of "Over the Rainbow." If there was a dry eye in the house, Savannah would be surprised. When the last note faded, it was so quiet you could almost hear a pin drop, and then everyone was on their feet—screaming, applauding, cheering. But Riley didn't speak. He took his bow. He waved to the audience. And he walked off stage.

Savannah could barely see through the tears, but she made her way out of her row and practically ran through the crowd—up the stairs, through the market-place area—until she was out in the parking lot. Her chest hurt, her breathing was ragged. Frantically, she looked from right to left trying to find the bus to take her back to her car. Lines were already forming and instead of waiting, she simply began to run again—out of the parking lot, out onto Highland Boulevard where she finally hailed a cab.

By the time she was back at her car, she was starting to feel normal—whatever that was anymore. The traffic was snarled and the drive home took longer than she wanted, but when she was finally walking through her own front door, she felt as if she'd lived a dozen lifetimes.

Riley had written a song about her.

And he'd sung for his mother.

Right now, he was no doubt celebrating with dozens of people—his family, his management, the record label—all of them thrilled for what he'd done tonight. Without a doubt, it was the best concert she'd ever been to. She only hoped Tommy had sent someone to cover it who could appreciate the emotionality of it all.

Tossing her cowboy hat aside, she pulled the clips from her hair holding it in place and shook it out. And sighed. It felt good to let it be loose. Shoes off, she roamed around as if searching for something or someone. There was nothing there. And no one. She was alone.

A glance at the clock showed it was almost midnight. Walking into the kitchen, she snagged a bottle of water before turning off the lights and heading to the bedroom. She'd done it. She went and faced her fears, faced Riley—sort of—and survived it. She did it on her own terms, and for that Savannah felt good.

There was no caving to pressure and no one there to witness her emotional breakdown or her sprint from the Hollywood Bowl.

Tiny victories.

Stripping down to her panties, she pulled a T-shirt from her drawer. The fact that it was one of Riley's was merely a coincidence. As she smoothed it down over her, another wave of sadness threatened to overwhelm her. It was the only item of his she'd kept—and he didn't even know she had it. Should she have gone with her parents and the Shaughnessys to the show? Should she have accepted the press pass Tommy offered? Or should she have at least answered one of Riley's phone calls?

The answer was yes to all of them. But it was too late now. The concert was over. Her parents would be leaving California tomorrow and no doubt the Shaughnessys would be too. And as for calling Riley, now that the album was out, his days were going to be filled with the press and media tour before he went on the road for an actual tour to promote the music.

She'd missed her chances.

All of them.

Not the greatest thought to end the day on, she thought as she climbed into bed and pulled the blankets up around her.

And in the dark, with only the sound of her own breathing, Savannah knew this would be the last pity party she'd allow herself. This chapter of her life was over, and as her father reminded her earlier, she was a fighter.

She needed to find something new to fight for.

—⁓—

Outside the room, there was a celebration going on. The thought of it made Riley smile. But right now he felt physically and emotionally drained. He'd done it. He'd finished the album. He'd performed the entire thing live. He'd made his family proud.

And yet all he wanted was to be alone.

There was a light knock on the door and he called out to whoever it was to come in. Relief swamped him when he saw it was his father. Ian closed the door behind him but didn't walk any farther into the room.

"Hey, Dad."

For the first time in recent memory, Riley thought his father looked ready to cry.

"What did you think?" he forced himself to ask, but was afraid to hear the answer.

"I had forgotten…" Ian said before his voice cracked. He sniffed before continuing. "I forgot that it was your song." He nodded and wiped at his eyes. "It didn't hit me until you started singing that you stopped singing it after…"

"After the funeral," Riley said quietly, coming to his feet and walking over to embrace the man who was the rock for his entire family.

"Do you have any idea how thrilled she would have been to see you up there like that tonight?" Ian asked, taking a step back. "She used to love to hear you sing. You know she's watching right now—probably bragging to St. Peter himself—and telling everyone in heaven how her boy sang for her at the Hollywood Bowl."

Tears streamed down both their cheeks. "I wanted to make her proud."

Ian nodded. "You did. You did that and more." He clapped a hand on his son's shoulder before walking farther into the room. "I had no idea what to expect tonight. You kept so much of the new music to yourself after you came back to L.A." He turned and looked at Riley. "That had me a little worried."

"All this music was very…personal. I hated to even have the guys in the studio hear it."

"You let Savannah hear it," Ian said thoughtfully.

"The only reason I had music to play was because of her," Riley said honestly. He took a steadying breath. "I really thought she'd be here tonight."

"Paul says she's on assignment."

Riley shook his head. "She's not."

"How do you know?"

"I just… Let's just say I had someone look into it. She's home. She's here in town. She didn't…" He sighed. "I hurt her, Dad. She's the most important thing in the world to me and I hurt her."

"You were hurting too, Riley. It was a crappy situation. I'm sure in time—"

"No," he said quietly. "No. I said some pretty horrible things to her that night. I've tried calling and texting and even going to her house, but she won't talk to me." He looked up sadly. "How could I have screwed it up so badly?"

"Seems to me you both screwed it up," Ian said. "Maybe this wasn't the relationship either of you thought it was. Maybe…maybe it's time to move on." He motioned toward the door. "You have about a hundred people out there waiting to congratulate you and tell you how in awe they are of your performance tonight. You should go out there and celebrate."

Riley looked at his father as if he'd lost his mind.

"Dad, I'm sitting here telling you I miss Savannah and you're telling me to go mingle?"

Ian nodded. "Oh, and have the champagne. It was incredible."

Frowning, he said, "Oh yeah? How much of it have you had?"

"Just a taste. Martha and I shared a glass before I came in here. Good stuff."

"Um…sure. Okay. Whatever," Riley muttered. "I guess we should go…mingle."

Ian didn't move.

"Dad? You coming?"

"No."

Riley rolled his eyes and went back to stand in front of his father. "What is going on? You just said I should go out there and then when I say I am, you won't go with me. Why not?"

"Because you don't really want to celebrate out there. I can see it in your eyes and I can hear it in your voice. You did a hell of a job out there on stage, Riley, and you did it for a lot of people. What is it that you want to do right now?"

He sighed. Honestly, he'd stick to his original thought—he wanted to be alone.

Liar.

No. He wanted to be with Savannah. He wanted to share this night with her and no one else.

"You do so much for everyone—your fans, your friends, your music people, and your family. Why not take right now and do something for you?" Ian asked softly.

It was on the tip of his tongue to say how he wanted to go to Savannah's, but he was afraid to say it out loud.

There was another knock on the door. Really, Riley was surprised there hadn't been more of them. People were probably beginning to wonder where he was and why he wasn't out there celebrating with the masses. He pulled the door open and found his brother Hugh standing there.

"Hey," Riley said. "Come on in."

Hugh looked around the dressing room and smiled. "That was a hell of a show, Riley."

"Thanks."

"You know, we were all blown away tonight," Hugh said, slowly walking around the room. "But the whole time I was listening to you I kept reminding myself that I had something important to ask you."

"Oh yeah?" Riley asked curiously. "What?"

A slow grin crossed Hugh's face. "What would happen if you just got in your limo, drove across town, walked up to Savannah's door, and knocked? What do you think could possibly go wrong if she opened the door and you took her in your arms and kissed her?"

It took Riley a full minute to realize what Hugh was doing. And then he started to grin. "I… I'm not sure…"

"She'd probably kiss you back. Then she'd probably invite you in. And then, if you're lucky, she'd ask you to stay." He threw out his hands. "Dude, what have you got to lose? Women love a man who can be spontaneous! Don't be the guy who celebrates alone because you're too scared to simply go with what you're feeling!"

"You know," Riley said, stripping off his shirt and going in search of a clean one, "I seem to recall having a very similar conversation with someone. Tell me… how did it work out?"

Hugh laughed out loud and grabbed Riley by the

shoulders. "It was the best damn advice I'd ever gotten, and it led to the most incredible night of my life. Don't let fear and uncertainty paralyze you. You wrote all that music for her. Doesn't she deserve to know that?"

"What if… What if she doesn't want to know that?"

"She does," Ian said. Both of his sons turned and looked at him. "Paul saw her earlier. She's as miserable as you are."

"But…earlier…you said… You said she was out on an assignment," Riley reminded him.

Ian shrugged. "I was trying to be nice."

"Oh, for crying out loud," Riley muttered and quickly shucked his jeans and changed into clean ones before looking around his dressing room in case he needed anything else. He turned to Hugh. "Don't let him have any more champagne. It's clearly too strong for him."

"No problem, bro. Limo's waiting for you and you've got your own bottle of champagne chilling back there for you and Savannah. I expect to hear some whistling tomorrow as a thank you."

Riley laughed, feeling lighter and happier than he had in a long time. "You hate whistling."

Hugh shrugged. "I used to. Someone helped me see the error of my ways."

At the door, Riley grabbed the knob and stopped. "What about all those people? I should at least put in an appearance out there."

Both Hugh and Ian shook their heads. "Everyone knows what's been going on. I told them we were encouraging you to go get the girl. There was a collective sigh of relief," Ian said with a wink. "Now, go on.

It's late and you're not getting any younger. And neither am I for that matter!"

Riley looked at Hugh as he opened the door. "Uh… yeah…definitely don't let him have any more champagne."

And then he was gone.

———w———

Sleep was eluding her, and rather than adding to her already sad and emotional state, it simply pissed her off. Kicking the blankets away, Savannah got up and decided to grab something to drink.

The sound of someone banging loudly on her front door made her scream.

Her immediate thought was that something had happened to her parents. No one else would be here at this hour unless it was bad news. Sprinting to the door, she yanked it open…and froze.

"Riley? What…?"

His arms were bracketing the doorway, his breathing almost as ragged as hers. He looked up and down at her body and smirked. "I've been looking for that shirt," he said, his arms dropping.

"You…you have?"

He nodded and advanced on her, forcing Savannah back into the house until he was inside and could close the door behind him. "I had a show tonight. That's my lucky shirt. I needed it."

Savannah's eyes went wide. "I…I'm sorry. I didn't know! It was here and I had forgotten that I had it…" Her back hit a wall.

"The entire show was shit because I didn't have my shirt," he said, stopping when they were toe to toe.

"No!" she cried. "That's not true! You were incredible! Every song sounded perfect and the crowd loved you and every minute of the show!"

His smirk turned into a full-blown smile. "How do you know?" he whispered.

She turned her head to try to hide her embarrassment. "I...I heard the reviews on the news. The radio." She shrugged. "You were big on the local news tonight."

With a shrug, Riley continued to watch her. "I don't care about being big on the news. I don't know what the big deal was. It was only a show."

With a gasp, Savannah turned back to him. "Only a show? Are you crazy? You sold out the Hollywood Bowl in twenty minutes! All those people wanted to come and hear you sing even though you refused to release any of the new music! They had no idea what they were coming to hear, but they wanted to be there! People love you! They love your music! You should be proud of that!"

Slowly, Riley lowered his head until his forehead rested against hers. "I think it's great how people love my music, but there's only one person's love that I want. That I need."

Savannah felt as if everything was happening in slow motion. Her eyes slowly lifted to meet his. They were still in the shadows, the only light in the house coming from the kitchen. "Oh?" she said quietly.

"Yeah. Only one."

She swallowed hard, her heart beating erratically in her chest. When Riley's hand came up and caressed her cheek, her knees weakened. Thankfully, his arm banded around her to catch her.

"Only you, Savannah," he said softly. "I could sing in front of millions of people who screamed they loved me, and it's not the same as hearing it from you."

She knew what he wanted. Knew what he was asking. "I do, you know. I do love you, Riley."

He sagged with relief and pulled her close. "I've missed hearing you say that."

"I'm so sorry," she said, her voice quivering as she felt her tears building again. "I…I can never make up for what I did to you…the time I cost you…"

"Hey, hey," he crooned. "Shh…it's all right." He instantly pulled back and began to wipe away her tears.

She shook her head. "It's not… It's not all right. You said—"

"I know what I said," he quickly interrupted, kissing her cheek. "And I was wrong. I was angry and I stupidly lashed out. I tried calling you to apologize, but you—" Then he stopped himself. "I was wrong, Savannah. I shouldn't have said the things I did, and I should have come here and forced you to listen to me. I took the coward's way out by calling." He shrugged. "Then I'd be able to stay in my own world and feel bad for myself because you wouldn't take my calls. I'm so sorry."

Looking up at him, she gave him a weak smile. "I've missed you."

Riley's thumbs continued to stroke her cheeks and wipe away any remaining tears. "Every day without you was hell," he said quietly.

"For me too."

Taking a step back, he held up his hand to her. "Wait there. I'll… I forgot something in the car." He opened the door and sprinted out into the darkness.

Savannah stepped into the doorway, curious to see what he was doing. Off in the distance, she heard a door close and then saw a car pull away. Her heart sank. Did he leave? What in the world? She was about to step out into the night when he was back in front of her.

"Sorry," he said. "I'm afraid you're stuck with me now. I sent my driver home."

She smiled, grabbed the front of his shirt, and pulled him back into the house, shutting and locking the front door behind her. "Good. Because right now, I really want to be stuck with you."

"Only right now?" he teased.

She shook her head. "For as long as you'll let me," she said honestly, waiting for him to haul her into his arms and kiss her.

But he didn't move toward her. Instead he held up a bottle of champagne. "I had to grab this." Then he moved by her and walked toward the kitchen. Behind him, Savannah growled with frustration and he chuckled. "Patience, my love. Patience."

Easy for him to say, she thought. He wasn't the one who'd been alone for over two months. At least he'd had his friends, family, and management team around him to keep him busy. She'd been doing nothing but writing about wood and cutting hair.

Leaning against her counter, Riley turned and faced her. "Do you have plans for tomorrow?"

She shook her head.

"And the day after?"

Again, she shook her head.

Riley stepped away and began to move toward her. "How about next week?"

She grinned. "Nothing I can't move around."

He stopped and studied her before nodding. "Okay then." He clapped his hands and rubbed them together. "Please tell me you have the makings for a sandwich or anything I can possibly have to eat. I'm starving!"

And just like that, Savannah felt like her world was going to finally start to right itself.

They worked together in the kitchen putting together plates of food—sandwiches, chips, drinks—before heading into her living room. She reached for the TV remote, but Riley stopped her. "No TV. I want to talk with you—hear what's been going on with you. Two months was a long time to be without you."

"There isn't much to tell. I was…surviving," she said, sitting down on the sofa.

He joined her. "Me too. Well…that and finishing the album. I think I slept about ten hours total in that entire time."

"You work too hard," she said sadly, finally allowing herself to reach out and touch his face. She saw the exhaustion etched on his beautiful face. "I hope you'll be able to take some time to relax now."

"I have exactly two days to myself before the media circus begins," he said, reaching for his sandwich and taking a huge bite.

"Can't it wait?"

He shook his head. "I was told that people waited long enough. The album came out at midnight, it will start getting radio play now, and your article hits the stands in the morning."

She looked at him oddly. "My…my article? But… Tommy said…"

"Yeah, I pulled rank," Riley admitted. "We told him our marketing plan and he agreed with it. The entire article is in this one special issue. And it's great." He winked. "Your name is almost as big as mine on the cover."

"No!" she cried but couldn't hide her smile.

He nodded. "It's true. We got advanced copies, and my family is thrilled with the way you incorporated them into the story. Darcy's a little upset because now she fears people will totally be stalking her on campus, but I think she'll survive."

"Oh my goodness…"

"They're all here, you know. They all flew in for the concert. Zoe really had to argue with her doctor to get clearance to fly because she's so far along in her pregnancy, but she finally got him to agree. Aidan's a nervous wreck."

"I'm sure!"

"They're not leaving until after lunch tomorrow and I know they'd love to see you."

She smiled. "I'd like that a lot."

He nodded. "Good. Then it's settled." He devoured the rest of his sandwich in a few bites and then leaned back against the couch and looked at Savannah's plate. "You're not going to eat?"

"I thought I was hungry," she said, "but it turns out it wasn't for food."

He grinned and sat up a little straighter. "Really?"

She nodded.

"I like the sound of that. A lot."

Standing, Savannah reached for his hand and pulled Riley to his feet. "I like the sound of your voice in my living room," she said, looking up at him. "A lot."

"Well, don't get used to it," he teased, sweeping her up into his arms. He started to walk toward the bedroom.

"Wait…what?"

"Oh, didn't I mention? You're coming on the media tour with me. Then you're moving in with me."

She laughed. "I am? When did I decide that?"

"Just now," he said seriously. "And you're doing it out of the kindness of your own heart. Plus, you feel bad because I haven't been able to sit out on my deck in my favorite spot in months."

"You haven't? Why not?"

He gently laid her down on the bed. "Because every time I look out there, all I see is you. And if I force myself to stand out there, I look out at the city and wonder where you are and what you're doing."

"Oh…Riley…"

"So you see why it's so important for you to be there with me."

Solemnly, she nodded. "If that's what I need to do…"

Kicking off his shoes, he grinned. "Well, there is one other thing."

Her surprised expression was her only response.

Pulling his shirt over his head, he said, "And really, I think it's something that needs to be dealt with immediately."

Savannah pushed up on her elbows.

His belt was the next thing to go. Then his socks.

She licked her lips, certain she knew where this was going, and her body was humming in anticipation.

"You look really good in my shirt," he said and began to crawl over her on the bed, but he never actually touched her.

She sighed his name, almost begging for his touch. And just when she thought he was finally going to kiss her, he rolled to her side facing her, the mattress bouncing beneath them. It was beyond frustrating. When he finally reached for her hand, she almost whimpered.

"Savannah, the night we almost shared a meal together—at the beach—changed everything for me. *You* changed everything for me. I loved the way you enjoyed a meal. I loved the way you talked to me like I was just an ordinary man." He squeezed her hand. "And from the moment you walked into my home, it was like you belonged there." Releasing her hand, he stroked her cheek. "My life is crazy and chaotic, but when you're with me, everything feels normal. Right. Marry me, Savannah. Marry me so we can live together and be together and give each other that feeling of rightness every day."

"Oh my gosh… I didn't… I thought…"

He gave her a crooked grin. "Yeah, you thought I was just bringing you in here for sex." He paused and then his expression was serious again. "Savannah, I love you. I don't want to live another day—another minute—without you. Say you'll be my wife, my lover, my friend…forever."

All she could do was nod as Riley finally wrapped her in his arms and pulled her close.

"Thank God," he sighed. "I was afraid you were going to toss me out of here!"

She pulled back and looked at him like he was crazy. "I would never do that. Ever. Now that I've had to live without you? I don't ever want to deal with that again."

"You never will."

And then he finally kissed her.

—〰—

"Any chance we can make this media tour a road trip?"

It was four in the morning and neither had slept, but Riley didn't mind. Savannah was naked in his arms—had been that way for hours—and it was perfect. Sleep was highly overrated. He chuckled at her question. "I don't know. Most of it's going to be done here in L.A. The press is coming to me for the next couple of weeks."

"Oh."

"Then we're going to finalize the tour dates."

"Uh-huh," she said and then yawned.

"But here's the thing," he began and rolled to his side to face her again. "I want to marry you."

She smiled broadly. "I know. And you already asked and I already said yes so we're good there."

He shook his head. "No, I mean I want to marry you, like, now. As soon as possible."

Savannah sat straight up. "Riley, we can't. I mean… When would we even…?"

Sitting up, he laughed at her shocked expression. "My family is really the sticking point here."

"What do you mean?"

"Well, Aidan and Zoe are going to have a baby like any minute."

"Right."

"Then Quinn and Anna's wedding will be here and we don't want to steal their thunder."

"Okay."

He reached for her hands. "So here's what I'm proposing: There's no waiting period to get married in California. I can pick up the phone right now and get things rolling. We could be married this afternoon. You know, while our families are still here."

"Riley!" she cried. "That's… It's so…"

"Yeah, I know." He grinned. "It won't be big or fancy or perfect, but…" He shrugged. "We don't need it to be. It's us. And it will be private with only our families there." He kissed her. "Say the word and I'll make the call."

"I…I don't know," she said nervously. "I don't see how we could pull it off."

"Mick has a house on the beach. It would be perfect. And he would love to host it. No one would know until after it was done, Savannah. No chance for the paparazzi to show up or the press. Just you and me."

"And about a dozen family members." She looked at him and saw the first traces of disappointment at her response. Before she could change her mind, she cupped his face and kissed him hard. "Go wake some people up!"

His eyes went wide. "Really? You really want to?"

"I want to be your wife more than anything, Riley Shaughnessy. Now go make the calls so we can sleep for an hour or two before we have to get up and shock our families."

Ten minutes later, she was back in his arms, but sleep wasn't anywhere in sight. "I love you, Riley."

"Mmm…I'll never get tired of hearing that."

"Good. Because I plan on saying it for at least another fifty to sixty years."

He hugged her close. "Say it forever and we have a deal."

She chuckled. "Done."

Epilogue

Two months later…

"OH LOOK, ANOTHER TUMBLEWEED," RILEY TEASED and then grimaced when Savannah elbowed him in the ribs.

"Knock it off. I think it's great." They were riding on his newly designed tour bus and driving across the state of Texas on their way to the next stop on Riley's tour, and Savannah was loving every minute of it.

He chuckled as he scanned through his emails on his tablet. "Hey, look! The wedding pictures are here!"

Savannah jumped up from her seat and practically fell into Riley's lap in her excitement. "Yeah! Oh, I can't wait to see them!"

Riley opened the link and together they sighed and smiled at the first pictures.

Two brides.

Two grooms.

Riley shook his head. "Didn't see that one coming at all."

"Me either but it was awesome." She turned and kissed his cheek. "I still can't believe we pulled it off without anyone knowing."

"Now that the pictures are here, I'll let my publicist know which ones we want released to the public and they'll make the announcement."

They scrolled through more pictures. "Have you talked to Quinn lately? Are things better with Anna and her family?"

On the morning of Riley and Savannah's wedding, when he had called his family and let them know what was going to happen, Riley had expected a lot of different responses. He'd never expected his older brother to ask if he could horn in on the ceremony!

"Yeah, they got over it pretty quick. Her folks were pretty disappointed they weren't there to see them finally get married, but they understood. They're still going to have a party like they'd planned."

"I think babies have a way of making that happen," Savannah said, scrolling through the pictures.

"Married and a baby on the way," Riley said with wonder. "My brother never does things quite like the rest of us."

"Nothing wrong with that. Look how happy they are." She pointed to a picture of Quinn spinning Anna around on the beach, her face looking up at the sky as she laughed. "I almost feel like we were the ones intruding."

"I'll admit, I kind of felt the same way, but I think it worked out exactly right. Anna wasn't big on having a traditional wedding, and Quinn wasn't big on waiting. I like how we were able to help them."

"Me too. Plus," she said with a grin, "we got to call dibs on godparents!"

Riley laughed as they high-fived each other. "I don't think Zoe's going to get over that one quite so quick. She wanted the honor."

"Oh, hush. She's Connor's godmother and she now has her own sweet baby to spoil."

"Lillian Grace," Riley said. "I must admit, I love Connor, but I think that little girl just about snagged my heart whole."

She hugged her husband. "I think the feeling was mutual. After all, you sang her her first song."

"When she wrapped her little hand around my finger, I was a goner."

Savannah rested her head on Riley's shoulder as they finished looking through the pictures. "Did they send the link to Quinn and Anna too or do we need to do that?"

Riley scrolled back and looked at the email. "They got it, too." When he went back to the pictures, he scrolled through the masses and then stopped at the one he'd been waiting for. The sun had been going down on the beach, and he and Savannah had been dancing out on Mick's deck while he sang to her. He stopped and pointed to it. "That's the one."

She nodded. "Definitely."

In a matter of minutes, Riley had the email and picture sent to his publicist for release. "Are you disappointed you didn't get a traditional wedding?"

"No," she said without hesitation. "Although I do wish I'd had more time to find a dress. Not that I didn't love mine—your people were amazing—but I do think I might have liked to have a little more time to decide."

"Are you kidding me? I'm still getting compliments on how great you and Anna were to shop for and how I should take a couple of lessons from the two of you. My stylist tells me I am way more of a diva than two brides on a timeline!"

"That's awesome! I love it!" She laughed. "And it's

totally true. You definitely have a bigger and better wardrobe than I do."

"Sweetheart, you look good in everything you own. I particularly like it when you're wearing something of mine, and I don't mind sharing."

"Mmm...that's nice," she purred. "Personally, I prefer you in nothing at all."

"Keep talking," he said, rising to his feet with her in his arms.

"I think that just about covered it," she replied, grinning when she saw they were walking back toward their mobile bedroom.

"I hope you don't mind if I slip into one of your favorite things then," he said softly, laying her down.

"Oh, I don't know," she said seriously, "what if we miss something exciting out on the road?"

"Baby, the tumbleweeds can wait." Swiftly shutting the door, Riley proceeded to ensure that his wife's mind was fully focused on what was happening inside the bus rather than outside.

A Sky Full of Stars

Book five in the beloved Shaughnessy Brothers series
by Samantha Chase

———

As the class came to a close, Brooke stayed in her seat and watched as the hall emptied out. Several students stayed behind to talk to Owen, giving her an opportunity to observe him as he interacted with them.

He seemed a little stiff—and he was oh-so-serious. Maybe astronomy questions required a serious response, but surely a little humor or a smile couldn't hurt. He had patience. The last student was the one who had asked the meteorite vs. meteor question and a long list of others. She began putting her notebook and pen away and organizing her purse while she waited for them to be done.

"Thanks, Dr. Shaughnessy," she heard the student say. "I appreciate the help. See you next week."

Brooke stood up, straightened her skirt, and made her way down the stairs toward Owen. He watched her warily as she descended. When she reached the bottom, she smiled. "Hi."

"Oh…um…hi. Brooke," he stammered.

She stepped closer to the podium and he took a small step back. "So I figured I'd come for an entire class today," she teased lightly and immediately realized he didn't quite get the joke. "You know…since I showed up late for the last one."

"Ah," he replied with a nod. "It wasn't necessary. It's not like I'm taking attendance on you."

Brooke relaxed. In his own way he was making a joke, so she chuckled. "It's a good thing; showing up late for my first class wouldn't look good on my record."

And this time, when she laughed, Owen laughed with her.

"I…I haven't come to a decision about the position yet," he said, his gaze focused on the floor and not directly at Brooke.

"Oh, that's okay," she said quickly, trying to put him at ease. "I just came to hear today's lecture. I felt awful about the other day and…well…I was kind of curious about those dust trails and tails."

His head snapped up and he looked at her with a hint of disbelief. "Really?"

Brooke nodded. "I have to admit, I had no idea what you were talking about half the time, so I was kind of happy that other guy asked so many questions. It made me feel a little less…stupid." She meant it as an off-hand comment, but the look on Owen's face was serious.

"Of course you don't understand what we're talking about. And Mr. Kelly may have been the one to ask the questions, but I can almost guarantee you that everyone in the room benefited from them." He shook his head and began stuffing his papers into his satchel. He was silent for a few moments before he stopped and looked at her. "You shouldn't put yourself down. There's nothing wrong with you and you most certainly aren't stupid." He shoved the last of his papers in the bag and then seemed at a loss for something to do with his hands.

They stood in awkward silence until Brooke figured she needed to be the one to break it. "I...I appreciate your saying that. I don't think I'm stupid most of the time. But the level of intelligence in this room was a little intimidating."

"If you're going to work with me, then you'll need to get used to it," Owen said and then looked surprised by his own statement—as if he hadn't thought it through.

Brooke went for calm and professional to be sure she didn't spook him—her uncle's words, not hers. She cleared her throat and said seriously, "I believe I'll have no problem adjusting. After all, if I'm going to be surrounded by scientists and students all day for several days, I'll be sure to do a little studying beforehand so I can better understand them."

"I...I still haven't decided—for sure—that this is going to be feasible. For either of us," he quickly added. "I don't think you fully understand what you'd be dealing with. They're all very smart and socially awkward. Like me."

Her smile was meant to reassure him, but she wasn't sure he got it. "Dr. Shaughnessy…Owen…do you want my honest opinion?"

Brooke saw him swallow hard before he nodded.

"I don't think you're as socially awkward as you think." When he started to correct her, she held up a hand to stop him. "It's true. I don't think you're comfortable in social settings but here you are, talking to me, defending me, and you're doing fine. I'm sorry if I make you nervous. I hope the more time we spend together, the more relaxed you'll become."

"Umm…maybe," he murmured.

Brooke looked over her shoulder at the clock on the wall and turned back toward Owen. "Would you like to grab a cup of coffee with me?" He looked like he was ready to bolt—or at least turn her down—so she added quickly, "We don't have to talk about the job. I just would like to get to know you."

He frowned. "Why?"

She laughed. An honest-to-goodness laugh. "Why? Because my uncle does nothing but sing your praises. Because I enjoyed listening to you teach. Because I think what you do is fascinating." She gave him her most confident look. "Are those good enough reasons?"

Owen looked at the clock and seemed to be weighing his options. "I need to go back to my office and make some notes and return a call first. Maybe I can meet you in an hour at the cafeteria?"

It wasn't hard to see what he was doing—he wanted to stay in a neutral zone and was giving himself a clear out if he needed it. Well, she'd just see about that.

"How about this—you take care of what you need

to and I'll get the coffee and bring it to your office. That way we can sit someplace a little quieter and less chaotic. What do you say?"

"Um…"

"I'm not a huge fan of the coffee in any cafeteria," she went on pleasantly. "There's a Starbucks up the block, so I can go there and grab us coffee and maybe a slice or two of cake, or some cookies. Although they do have some fabulous brownies. Do you have a preference? I'm a bit of a chocoholic, but I know it's not the case for everyone. The marble pound cake is a good choice too—it gives me the chocolate I crave while balancing it out with the yellow cake. Of course, there are scones if that's more your thing."

"You talk a lot," he stated very matter-of-factly.

And that had her laughing again. She liked his bluntness. "I know. Sometimes it works for me, sometimes it doesn't. I tend to chatter when I'm nervous. Most of the time I don't even realize I'm doing it. The words just keep coming with no end in sight."

"You mean like now?"

Brooke immediately stopped talking and considered him. "Oh. I guess I was kind of yammering on there."

"Why are you nervous?"

Was he kidding? She shrugged and twisted the shoulder strap of her purse. "You make me that way."

Owen's eyes went wide. "Me?" he asked incredulously. "I make you nervous?"

She nodded. "You're a little intimidating."

"Me?" his voice came out almost as a squeak.

Brooke nodded again. "You are a highly respected man, Owen. I'm sure you're used to sitting around and talking with people who are more on your level. I'm afraid of saying something ridiculous and putting my foot in my mouth."

"Brooke, I…I don't even know how to respond to that. I'm intimidated by *you*."

She already knew that because her uncle had prepared her, but she was curious. "Why?"

"I may be respected in my field of study, but…that's it. Outside of the lab and away from the telescope, I'm fairly invisible."

"I find that hard to believe."

He gave a mirthless laugh. "Trust me. As you learned the other day, my brother is a world-famous rock star. Do you think anyone sees me when he's around?"

In that instant, she wanted to reach out and hug him.

"I have five siblings including Riley—four brothers and one sister," he said, not meeting her gaze. "They all have impressive jobs and wonderful lives. All of my brothers are married and have kids. Well, Riley and Savannah just found out they're pregnant so…" He stopped abruptly and this time he looked directly at her. "Forget you heard that," he said quickly. "No one is supposed to know! Dang it."

And that was totally adorable—he didn't even curse.

Unable to help herself, Brooke reached out and placed a hand on his arm. They both seemed a little shocked by the contact. He was…muscular. Much more so than she would have imagined. Forcing herself not to focus on that, she gave him another reassuring smile. "You don't have to worry. Their secret is safe with me."

Owen nodded and shyly returned her smile. "Thank you."

She felt like they were having a moment. And she didn't really want it to end.

Patience…

"Okay," she finally said, taking a step back. "Tell me what I can get you from Starbucks and I'll meet you in your office in an hour."

———

It was quite possible that Owen would pass out before he made it back to his office.

Doing his best to recite the names of all the planets and constellations as he walked, he almost sagged with relief when his doorway came into view. He hurried in, pulled his phone out of his satchel, pulled up Riley's number, and hit Call.

It went to voice mail.

He put the phone down without leaving a message and tried to figure out what he was supposed to do. He didn't have any notes to make or papers to grade or any scheduled calls. No, he had said that to Brooke to buy himself a little time. Most things that came out of Owen's mouth were carefully considered, but in one conversation with her, he had managed to blurt out that he was probably going to hire her and then lied about his immediate plans.

Who the heck was he?

He sat down in his chair and tried to consider his options. By his own calculations, Brooke would be knocking on his door in about fifty-three minutes. He could probably come up with a reasonable excuse why he had to leave before she returned and just text her his apology.

But he didn't have her number and he didn't much care for lying. Again.

And just because Riley wasn't available didn't mean he couldn't call one of his other brothers. Owen knew if he picked up the phone and called any one of them, they'd be happy to help him. Okay, there was his solution.

He called Aidan first. But Aidan was in the middle of an inspection on one of the new homes he was building and after a quick apology and a promise to call later, he was gone.

No big deal, he was going to remain hopeful.

Next he called Hugh. Unfortunately, according to Hugh's wife Aubrey, his brother was getting ready to cut the ribbon on a new property. And with another quick apology and a promise to call, she was gone.

Great. That left Quinn. And although he knew Quinn would make the time to talk—if he could—Quinn was the most confident and cocky brother and somehow that wasn't what Owen needed right now. He needed a little…sympathy. It wasn't Quinn's strong suit.

But…desperate times called for desperate measures, so he called.

"What's up, bro?" Quinn asked as his way of greeting.

"Oh…um…I was wondering if you had a few minutes to talk. I need advice."

Silence.

"Um…Quinn?"

"Yeah, yeah…give me a minute. I'm trying to process that. You—the brainiac of the family—want advice from me—the guy who almost flunked out of school. Wow."

Owen sighed. Why did everything come back to IQ and academics? It was beyond frustrating!

"Okay, sorry, man, I'm ready," Quinn said, interrupting Owen's thoughts. "Lay it on me."

Taking a steadying breath, he quickly explained the situation with Brooke. "So what do I do?"

"You mean other than drink the coffee and talk to her?"

"Quinn…" he groaned, "there's more to it—at least there is for me—and you know it! She's different. She's not a colleague and she's not shy like me and I have a feeling that by having her come here to the office where there are no distractions, it's going to be like there's a spotlight on me or something and all of my… awkwardness is going to be on full display."

"And what if it is?" Quinn countered. "Dude, we've all been saying it for years—there is nothing wrong with you. Hell, there's nothing wrong with being smart or quiet or shy or even just different! And if anyone doesn't like it, then it's their problem, not yours. If this woman says anything to make you feel that way, then she can leave. Don't hire her. Don't talk to her and tell her uncle you don't appreciate his interference."

"Wait, wait, wait…" Owen said. "Brooke hasn't said or done anything to make me feel uncomfortable. This is about me. This is how I feel. All the time."

"Oh."

"Yeah…oh. So what do I do? How do I stop feeling like that? She's going to be here in…" He stopped and looked at his watch. "Thirty-seven minutes. How do I act, what do I say to guarantee I'm not going to have a panic attack?"

"Owen," Quinn began seriously, "there is nothing you can do in that amount of time."

"I wish Riley had answered the phone," Owen grumbled.

"Hey! I take exception to that!"

"Sorry."

"Look, I get it. You and Riley—the twin thing—I get it. But there isn't anything he was going to be able to do or say to transform you into a different person full of witty conversational skills and confidence in the next thirty minutes."

"Thirty-six…"

"Whatever!" Quinn snapped. "There's no quick fix here, Owen. You need to believe in yourself. You think you're the only one who gets nervous around a beautiful woman? Well…you're not."

"I bet you never were."

"Are you kidding me?" Quinn laughed. "Holy crap…I was always nervous, but I knew how to hide it. And even though Anna and I knew each other for practically our entire lives, she scared the hell out of me when we first started dating. My feelings for her terrified me. I suddenly felt insecure and clueless."

"I remember," Owen said, recalling a conversation the two of them had had when Quinn and Anna began dating.

"So you're not alone, Owen. It's not just you. And you know what? It's not a bad thing to be a little bit nervous around a woman." He paused. "I think the difference is…when it's the right woman, those nerves make you want to be a better person, a better man. And being that you've never freaked out over a woman before like this, I'm thinking this Brooke has to mean something to you."

"How is that possible? I just met her. I barely know her." But even as Owen was saying the words, he knew. He hadn't dated as much as his brothers—but he'd dated enough women to realize Brooke was different.

About the Author

New York Times and *USA Today* bestselling author Samantha Chase released her debut novel, *Jordan's Return*, in November 2011. Although she waited until she was in her forties to publish for the first time, writing has been a lifelong passion. Her motivation was her students: teaching creative writing to elementary age students all the way up through high school and encouraging those students to follow their writing dreams gave Samantha the confidence to take that step as well.

When she's not working on a new story, Samantha spends her time reading contemporary romances, blogging, playing way too many games of Scrabble or Solitaire on Facebook, and spending time with her husband of twenty-five years and their two sons in North Carolina.